A PLUME BOOK

HOW TO BUY A LOVE OF READING

TANYA EGAN GIBSON lives in Marin County, California. This is her first novel.

Praise for *How to Buy a Love of Reading*

"Brimming with literary allusions, commentary on the rich and famous, and the necessary ingredients for a successful novel, Gibson's ingenious debut succeeds on many levels." —*Booklist*

"From the opening sentence of this strongly sardonic satire, Gibson's debut, it is clear that nothing is sacred. Whether examining trendy charity functions or the muted morals of the so very rich, her acerbic, acidic book is right on the money. The major surprise is that the novel also has a heart, and Carley leaps off the page as the most real character. . . . Readers fond of Claire Messud and Marisha Pessl might want to try Gibson's bold outing." —*Library Journal*

"Ladies and gentlemen, please welcome to the stage Tanya Egan Gibson, a fresh and funny new voice in the world of fiction. *How to Buy a Love of Reading* is an original and highly readable novel with a most unusual premise that should captivate anyone who loves to read." —Mark Childress, author of *Crazy in Alabama* and *One Mississippi*

"In her lovely debut, Tanya Egan Gibson blends humor and sentiment in the most surprising of ways. The story she weaves is a joy from start to finish." —Laura Dave, author of *The Divorce Party* and *London Is the Best City in America*

"Carley Wells, the protagonist of Tanya Egan Gibson's *How to Buy a Love of Reading*, is at once a sympathetic antihero and a much-appreciated antidote to the cultural pretensions of Long Island's aristocracy. This is satire with heart." —Will Allison, author of *What You Have Left*

How to Buy
a Love
of Reading

A NOVEL BY

Tanya Egan Gibson

A PLUME BOOK

PLUME
Published by the Penguin Group
Penguin Group (USA) Inc., 375 Hudson Street, New York, New York 10014, U.S.A. • Penguin Group
(Canada), 90 Eglinton Avenue East, Suite 700, Toronto, Ontario, Canada M4P 2Y3 (a division of
Pearson Penguin Canada Inc.) • Penguin Books Ltd., 80 Strand, London WC2R 0RL, England •
Penguin Ireland, 25 St. Stephen's Green, Dublin 2, Ireland (a division of Penguin Books Ltd.) • Penguin
Group (Australia), 250 Camberwell Road, Camberwell, Victoria 3124, Australia (a division of Pearson
Australia Group Pty. Ltd.) • Penguin Books India Pvt. Ltd., 11 Community Centre, Panchsheel Park,
New Delhi – 110 017, India • Penguin Group (NZ), 67 Apollo Drive, Rosedale, North Shore 0632,
New Zealand (a division of Pearson New Zealand Ltd.) • Penguin Books (South Africa) (Pty.) Ltd.,
24 Sturdee Avenue, Rosebank, Johannesburg 2196, South Africa

Penguin Books Ltd., Registered Offices: 80 Strand, London WC2R 0RL, England

Published by Plume, a member of Penguin Group (USA) Inc. Previously published in a Dutton edition.

First Plume Printing, August 2010
10 9 8 7 6 5 4 3 2 1

℗ REGISTERED TRADEMARK—MARCA REGISTRADA

The Library of Congress has catalogued the Dutton edition as follows:

Gibson, Tanya Egan.
How to buy a love of reading: a novel / by Tanya Egan Gibson.
     p.   cm.
ISBN 978-0-525-95114-8 (hc.)
ISBN 978-0-452-29609-1 (pbk.)
1. Rich people—Fiction.   2. Teenage girls—Fiction.   3. Birthdays—Fiction.   4. Parties—Fiction.
5. North Shore (Long Island, N.Y.)—Fiction.   I. Title.
PS3607.I274H69 2009
813'.6—dc22   2008043005

Printed in the United States of America
Original hardcover design by Daniel Lagin

PUBLISHER'S NOTE
This is a work of fiction. Names, characters, places, and incidents are either the product of the author's
imagination or are used fictitiously, and any resemblance to actual persons, living or dead, business
establishments, events, or locales is entirely coincidental.

For Josh, Dylan, and Cole—
my everything

How to Buy a Love of Reading

PART I

Setting

All good writing is swimming under water and holding your breath.

> —F. Scott Fitzgerald, from an undated letter to his
> daughter, Frances Scott Fitzgerald

Greer and Cissy Gardner

Invite you to

An Homage to Sculpture

In celebration of

BUNNY'S SIXTEENTH BIRTHDAY

Saturday, the Twenty-sixth of September

At seven o'clock

The Glen Club

Fox Glen

Formal Attire

CHAPTER 1

The idea came to Carley's father amid the whir of a hundred handheld sanders at Bunny Gardner's Sweet Sixteen, an event that had burst into life with the birthday girl's parents whipping a satin drape off their pedestaled daughter at the center of the Glen Club ballroom, where she held a pose she would later tell her classmates was "Winged Victory, except not headless" through applause people would say she milked a bit too long before stepping down. Hours later, not long after the genesis of Francis Wells's idea, the party would meet a premature death with a cloud of plaster dust covering the Gardners' guests, as well as the dessert table graced with spun-sugar Giacomettis and the life-sized ice sculpture of Michelangelo's *David*, whose penis had all evening been dripping syphilitically.

The Thinker's meltdown was considerably less dramatic, his forehead slowly receding while his chin trickled down his arm. Unlike the *David*, he'd been placed far from the marble fireplaces. Like Francis Wells, he looked bored. By ten p.m. there had been three slideshows—one of which, "Hop Art: A Portfolio," projected photos of Bunny's own work onto the ballroom walls—interspersed with a series of dinner courses as carefully presented and unsatisfying as Francis's wife.

Four heirloom beet slices—one golden, two albino, one striped—next to a Cyrillic drizzle of dressing above a pinch of bitter greens had constituted the composed salad. The "tower" of veal medallions and foie gras had taken longer to deconstruct than to eat. And the flavor of Bunny's silver-iced cake in the shape of Koons's *Rabbit* sculpture remained a mystery, guests having been enjoined from approaching the dessert table until after the presentation of the party favors—bottles of 2005 Mouton-Rothschild Pauillac for the adults, and *heads* for Bunny's friends. Their own. Cast in plaster. Which were at this moment—to use Cissy Gardner's phrase—being *finished tableside.*

Across the table, one of Gardners' hireling artists used a sander to reduce the pudginess of Francis's daughter's plaster chin and eliminate acne bumps from her plaster cheeks while Carley looked on silently with an embarrassed half-smile. A month earlier, after she and her friends had been summoned to the Gardners' home for their castings, she'd returned home in a rare expansive mood, smears of alginate on her cheeks and flecks of plaster in her hair. At the dinner table she'd laughed about the solarium having been turned into a triage ward with kids lying faceup on portable massage tables while plaster was applied to their faces. About Bunny requiring the presence of her hypnotist to "talk her through" the same claustrophobic process to which she was subjecting one hundred of her friends. About how Hunter Cay's agreeing to hold Bunny's hand through "the ordeal" had inspired in so many of the other girls a similar swoon-worthy malady.

Francis had relished the stories for the way his daughter captured people without trapping them, laughing about how they acted without laughing *at* them. Though he knew most of those girls didn't invite his daughter to things—didn't *include* her, as his wife put it—there was still a lilt of affection in Carley's voice for them, as if to say, *It's funny, but I get it. It's funny, but we're all funny. It's funny, but I'm no better.* The richness of her stories, the detail in which she told them, had nearly compensated for the usual bland fatlessness of the dinner his wife had designed and had had the cook execute, everything poached or steamed or raw. He'd stood and gone over to Carley's chair to pat her on the back and say, "My funny, tough girl."

"The tender ones get picked," Gretchen had said, studying an asparagus tip poised on her fork. Carley had shrugged like a turtle desperate not to be seen, retreating into the humid silence she'd begun emitting at puberty. All it took to shut her down, shut her up, was a barb from his wife or a slight from the same classmates she knew were phony and insipid. For the first time Francis had formed in his head the words for what worried him: Carley was disappearing, letting insubstantial people chip off pieces of her self.

As the air thickened now at Bunny's party with the dust of everyone's children's effaced pimples and straightened noses and sharpened cheekbones, Francis was overcome by a lightheadedness another man might have attributed to the poor ventilation or his third after-dinner scotch. Francis, however, recognized it as the exact sensation he'd experienced the night he'd brainstormed the Marvel-Bra, the invention that had made his fortune. It was the promise of creation, the dawning of change.

He reexamined his newborn idea from every angle, counting its fingers and toes and falling in love. A birthday present for his daughter. A gift for a girl who sat still at the table while she watched her own erasure.

ONE TABLE AWAY, Hunter Cay coughed from other people's dust, the artist appointed to him having pronounced his face perfect without turning on the sander. Did he model? she asked. Or act? He looked like *someone*, she insisted before reluctantly moving on to assist with someone else's less-flawless head.

"The way you are with her isn't fair," Bunny Gardner said next to him, as Hunter yearned for fresh air. In the four-foot-high silver Koons *Rabbit* balloons anchored to every centerpiece, dust wrapped the party's distorted reflections in a layer of static.

"The dancing and whispering," Bunny continued. "The way you let her touch you. The way you touch her. It's cruel, really, how you give her hope."

For years, friends both male and female had insinuated that his friendship with Carley Wells was too impossible to exist. In Europe this summer, his cousin Ian had kept saying it was time Hunter *outgrew* her. But not until tonight had anyone suggested he was hurting her.

They danced close because it was comfortable and because he always felt balanced near her, even with the floor undulating as it had been doing tonight since he'd gone through his flask faster than he'd meant to. They whispered because he never ran out of things to tell her that only she would understand. He liked her touching him for how she never tousled his curls like he was a pet, or tickled or poked like he was a toy whose job it was to be played with—things girls he had sex with always ended up doing, things he let them do.

He touched *her* because it made her happy and because it didn't make him unhappy and because nobody else did. Not Carley's mother, Gretchen, who made ice sculptures look cuddly. Not Francis, who hadn't known how to hug Carley since she'd developed. Not people from school or the Club or even Carley's bunkmates this past summer at Camp Metamorphosis, girls who let their backs burn in the sun rather than lotion each other, as if each other's fat might carry yet another strain of the malady. When during a massage at a day spa visit at summer's end she'd begun sobbing, the panicked masseuse had called her parents, who'd called her shrink, Dr. Sinkman, who'd diagnosed her as being depressed about coming back from fat camp five pounds heavier.

She'd just felt so grateful to have hands on her, she'd explained to Hunter a week later when he'd returned from Europe. Even if the hands were just being paid. Even if she knew the body they were kneading was repulsive.

She'd said it dry-eyed. To keep himself from crying, he'd bitten the inside of his cheek until he tasted blood. They were selfish tears, inspired by her but not *about* her. They were about the world, and how sad it was, and how desperate he was not to have to see its sadness. Since spring he'd been feeling far too much, as if his skin had been pulled back to reveal raw flesh the slightest breeze could burn. It was the first secret he'd kept from Carley in years. To ward off further tears, he'd dry-swallowed secret number two, the pills he'd promised himself he'd leave behind by summer's end.

Lying with her in his bed, he'd rubbed her back for hours until she said to stop because he had to be tired and it wasn't his fault she was untouchable and he was the last person in the world who had to make anything up to her. They'd fallen asleep spooning the way they often did, sleeping together platonically with his arms wrapped around her, she at his core.

"It's a wonderful body," he'd whispered the next morning while she was still asleep. Not even the blue silk Loretta Caponi pajamas he'd brought back for her from Florence could disguise its lumpiness. But it was so gorgeously strong. She almost never got sick. She could outswim riptides and ski double diamonds. And even when a wave scraped her into the sand or a patch of ice threw her to the ground, she rarely bruised. He loved that body for taking care of her, for sheltering the one thing he couldn't live without.

He felt a hand on his shoulder and heard Bunny shut up. In a balloon reflection he saw Carley's father standing behind him, convexed. Francis opened his jacket to reveal cigars in the inside breast pocket. Hunter nodded. Like his daughter, Francis had a knack for offering people what they needed without their asking.

He braced his hand on the table when he stood, his legs threatening to fold. Fortunately, Francis was already halfway to the back doors that led from the Club ballroom out to the deck.

"Don't let my parents see you like—" Bunny whispered. Not that they hadn't served him at their house and on their yacht countless times when he and Bunny had dated. But Hunter appreciated the liability issues. Two years earlier, a guy who would have graduated with Hunter's cousin, Ian, had driven from the Glen Club's Snow Ball into a tree.

"Just pins and needles," Hunter said. "Lost the feeling in my—"

"Liver," she said.

He shook his head and blew her a kiss. Once outside, he gulped the salt air. A breeze rippled the Long Island Sound, the moon catching the movement and silvering it.

It would be the last memory he'd be able to summon tomorrow of the evening: the wind promising clarity and water tinseled with light.

"I suppose Carley told you about Gretchen's meeting with that teacher," Francis said, cutting a cigar. Its head disappeared over the railing of the deck into the darkness down to the beach below. Bradford Nagel, who taught junior-year English, was an institution at Montclair Academy. One most people agreed needed institutionalization. Despite his manifest insanity, getting a college recommendation letter from him was crucial—appealing instead to a sophomore-year teacher implied you'd started slacking off halfway through high school, while scraping one up from a senior-year teacher implied only someone who didn't know you well could have anything decent to say.

In thirty years I've never encountered a student less intellectually engaged, Nagel had told Gretchen earlier that week at Parent Educator Administrator Conferral Evening, or as it was better known at Montclair, PEACE.

Nagel was the kind of person who would only notice Carley's extremes, her gaudy laughter in the hallways and her silence during class suggesting a not-there-ness that was far from the truth. She was more *here* than anyone. She let herself *see*, never ignoring something just because she didn't know what to call it. Most people passed by the unnamable like a stray at the side of the road.

He thought about trying to tell Francis this, but the flask of scotch and the handful of Vicodins he'd taken over the course of the night had swaddled him beyond words.

"*She has the passion of a puddle*, the bastard said." Francis took a deep breath.

Hunter coughed, though not from the smoke. He was used to cigars, Francis having opened his humidor to Hunter years ago. His throat itched with dust he still couldn't seem to swallow. "Carley *has* passion. Not just intellectually, but—"

"The Gardner girl has herself an *interest*," Francis said. "That's what you're supposed to have these days, Gretchen says. Carley needs a passion; I'm gonna *get* her one."

It was the kind of statement that occasioned Francis being laughed at behind his back. A nouveau directness that for years had kept him and Gretchen out of the Club until Hunter's mother had sponsored them in.

That Francis had earned his money instead of inheriting it, that he'd made his millions by focusing on his own passion—breasts—was one of the many things Hunter admired about him. That vanity had no grip on him was another: at six-four, two inches taller than Hunter, he had the build of an ex-athlete who'd let his muscles go to fat because they no longer served him a use. No matter how well-tailored were his Armani suits, he always looked a little wrong in them, like a bear in a tuxedo. A dancing bear you thought was tame—until you turned your back and it decided it was hungry.

Glancing behind him toward the floor-to-ceiling windows, Hunter caught a glimpse of Carley and their friend Amber dancing with their plaster heads held out in front of them, trunkless partners. At the tables, guests rubbed their eyes and fanned the air. "Overwhelming, Bunny's *passion*," Hunter said. "Seems she wants us to breathe it."

Bunny's actual interest was, in fact, musical theater, though she wasn't a particularly good singer or dancer or actress. She performed in plays for the love of it. Or *had*, until last year when her private college counselor had insisted to Greer and Cissy that their daughter needed rebranding if she wanted any shot at the real Ivies or the "hidden Ivies" or even—given Bunny's inability to break the ninety-fifth percentile on her PSATs—the "public Ivies." If she couldn't be *good* at something, she ought to at least take up a unique activity. *Curling*, the counselor had suggested, archery having already been adopted several months earlier by another Montclair Academy student whose parents had taken their progeny's mediocrity more seriously. Luckily for Bunny, who'd been dreading spending the summer in remedial curling camp in Canada, her art teacher had mentioned Bunny's mixed-media sculpture project to the Gardners at that month's PEACE. Though she hadn't exactly said Bunny had talent, she'd called Bunny's choice to create a mobile out of old computer parts and raw vegetables *unusual*.

"One of a kind," Francis said now, as he described to Hunter his idea for a birthday gift to ignite in Carley an "intellectual passion." Not a car, like nearly everybody else received for turning sixteen. Not a trip to Europe under the supervision of a semi-famous sculptor, like Bunny's parents were giving her. "I want to buy Carley something to love."

"It's an . . . interesting concept," Hunter ventured. "Original," he added when his silence was compounded by the band cutting out mid-song. He turned toward the windows. On the other side of the glass, guests were evacuating the ballroom in a controlled stampede of stilettos and silk and bespoke. He waved at Carley, who looked around the room, cradling both their heads. They could leave down the back stairs to the beach, return tomorrow for her coat, and avoid tonight's crush at the cloakroom. He'd wrap his jacket around her shoulders; they'd meander down the sand and around to the parking lot, taking their time deciding what to do, every *next* an adventure.

She looked right through him, the party lit so brightly and the deck so dark that beyond the glass she could see only reflections of the ballroom within.

He lowered his hand. "But Francis, will she *love* this love?"

IN THE PARKING lot, guests heading for cars and limos glowed ghostly, lamplight clinging to the dust they'd missed brushing off. Given the Gardners' knocking off the exact color scheme planned for Carley's Sweet Sixteen, their party being shut down early by Club management for having covered the ballroom in a likely carcinogen was an anti-climax Gretchen Wells deemed well-deserved.

Pondering the idea her husband had proposed to her on the walk to the car, she stroked the velvet bag containing her daughter's favor, Carley having abandoned it to her in her rush to follow her classmates somewhere. She was a girl who would be forgotten otherwise, left behind. A girl whose college counselor had summed up her nearly sixteen years on earth as *undistinguished.* A girl whose less-euphemistic English teacher had several days ago at a mortifying parent conference called her *blank.* Had he children of his own, that teacher? Had he understood that being told such a thing was like learning of a stillbirth—the bundle of cells that were once your own cells and that were supposed to have multiplied into something greater than yourself instead adding up to nothing?

For years she'd been telling Francis something was missing in their only child, fears he'd dismissed as her being *critical* and *controlling.* Carley didn't want to *become* anything, Gretchen tried to tell him, but all Francis would say was, *She already is something.* It was the kind of thing Francis often said, perching himself on what sounded like high moral ground but was actually landfill. Nice words. Ad-slogan pithy. He spent his evenings upstairs in his office surrounded by mannequins and searching star charts for names— every Marvel-Bra style was named for a constellation—while leaving to her their earthbound daughter who couldn't wear the cute little fashions the other girls did, and didn't get asked to sleep over other girls' houses or go on dates with boys, and whose saving social grace was Hunter Cay's reflected glory. She'd been trying to tell Francis for months now that once Hunter left for college next fall, Carley would be faced with a dismal senior year—few college prospects and no social life—if something didn't change. But it had taken that horrible English teacher and the Gardners' pretentious fête to convince him something needed *doing*.

On the drive home, as Francis grumbled that his *meat coins*—as he'd called their entrées within earshot of everyone at their table despite Gretchen kicking his shin—hadn't been enough food to *fill a flea*, Gretchen untied the silk drawstring of the bag (Dew, that shade of blue was called, the exact hue Gretchen had chosen for Carley's table linens and favor bags, never mind Cissy Gardner's insistence that their bags were, in fact, Hummingbird) and removed her daughter's hollow plaster head. On the floor by her feet rolled the bottle of wine given to adult guests, its label a series of vine leaves evolving into a hand. A famous sculptor had designed it, Cissy had announced before dimming the lights for the final slideshow of the evening, "Giuseppe Penone: The Blurring of Nature and Art," which Bunny narrated dutifully at the microphone from index cards everyone knew Cissy had prepared despite Bunny's opening the presentation with "And now let me share with you my secret artistic obsession." As if Bunny—or for that matter, any successful junior at Montclair—had the *time* to acquire an interest in an obscure artist.

Gretchen herself had found the artist's work off-putting—giant glass fingernails, live trees imprinted with bodies, dead trunks carved back into saplings, vegetables grown into casts of the artist's own face. Yet it was still less disturbing than people's features being shaved tableside, as if one's nose were a truffle.

With her index fingers she traced the contours of the Carley head from brow bone to cheekbones to curve of nostrils, bringing them together on the Cupid's bow. She ran one up an earlobe and into the curve of cartilage that suggested a conch. The face was as gentle and guileless as a baby's. The face of a girl unable to fathom that the world was a thief who'd palm a dollar from a beggar's cup. A girl who despite her mother's warnings would divulge the Bottle Green/Dew/Silver color palette Gretchen had designed for Carley's upcoming Arthurian-legend-themed Sweet Sixteen.

Perhaps Bunny had oohed over Carley's Sweet Sixteen dress, then wondered aloud how it would look against the table linens as she sat at the dais. *Oh, Dew, of course. Accented with . . . Oh I love Bottle Green*. Perhaps while pretending to want Carley's opinion about how to dress her Sculptural Homage serving staff, she'd prompted the divulgence of the silver chain mail uniforms Gretchen had designed for the servers at Carley's (K)night of Medieval Merriment, and thus the matching centerpieces, chain-mail-covered vases displaying a combination of rare lavender live roses bred so light they appeared silver, mixed with preserved roses dipped in sterling.

All this evening Gretchen had had to stare at those exact flowers, holstered in asymmetrical silver-cast vases, the original of which the Gardners had bragged about Bunny-the-artiste having made herself, though Gretchen knew for certain—her personal assistant, Grace, being friends with Cissy Gardner's personal assistant, though not as good of a friend as Cissy's assistant believed she was—that Bunny was so clumsy a potter that after multiple attempts at the vase had produced nothing but deflated clay beach balls, the Gardners had paid an artist whose work they'd seen in a Hamptons gallery that summer to throw the vase while Bunny watched.

She ran her hand past the forehead to the plaster hair. Long after Carley's appointment at what Cissy had called "the cast party," Gretchen had learned the other girls had shown up with photos of themselves to be forwarded to the artists who would be turning the castings into busts. Photos with their hair pinned into updos, or styled into face-framing waves, or at least brushed. It had been raining that afternoon, and Gretchen could imagine Carley letting someone just snap a digital photo on the spot, her hair limp, her part crooked—now captured that way for eternity.

"You can still change," Gretchen whispered to the head, which unlike her daughter didn't roll its eyes when she said it.

The world was a body to which you only needed to tailor yourself to be accepted. And then, to make it love you, you customized just enough to be remembered.

The man Gretchen had married she'd built from scratch. He'd had been *Frankie* when she'd met him, selling plus-sized lingerie out of cartons and living in Astoria. Her own body had been a size eight when they'd met at age twenty-two, a six when they'd married within the year and her parents disowned her, and a double zero at age thirty-five, when she'd had their only child. But while the Wellses' friends' children became increasingly tailored with every passing year, her own daughter grew only more common and sloppy, as if she believed her destiny to be off-the-rack.

Her husband turned the car into their driveway.

"Custom," Gretchen said to him and to the bust and to the beautiful newborn Carley had once-upon-a-time been, with seashell ears and downy eyebrows and gray eyes so odd and intense that Gretchen had been almost as relieved as she'd been disappointed when they'd turned a conventional brown.

"A chance to *star in her own life*," Francis said, typing their gate code into the keypad. So enamored of his idea was Gretchen that she said nothing about his quoting one of his own brassiere advertisements.

As they drove into the arc of light emanating from the front portico, she noticed a smudge on the plaster forehead, a mark that rubbing with her thumb seemed only to compound. Inside, later, she would find treating it with water worsened it still.

Only when a piece of paper fell out of the velvet bag would she stop scrubbing at it. The card from the Gardners instructed the head's bearer to drop it off at Studio Bust for the application of a finish of choice—clear flat, clear glossy, colored, or metallic. Gretchen kissed the smudge gently, then checked the box next to Bronze, adding a Light Verdigris Patina to suggest subtle maturity.

CHAPTER 2

There are people who understand life the first time through. They grasp what someone's saying when it's said. Read stories into gestures and expressions. Draw out moments, slow down time. Shape what happens as it happens, sculptors of their lives.

Carley Wells was no sculptor. Only after a moment had already set—past changing, past *tense*—could she ever get her hands around it.

Only later when she revisits this *now*—her father announcing "We're making you a de' Medici!" over brunch at the Glen Club while her mother edged the pastry basket out of Carley's reach and told Francis to leave off the de'—will she think of everything she might have said if she were a person who knew what to say, every action she might have taken if she were a person who acted. In the present, it was just another untitled moment, part of an endless exhibit called Things Happen.

"It'll be *made* for you," said her father.

"It will *make* you love it," said her mother.

It was a book. One that hadn't been written yet. They would pay someone to write a book to Carley's specifications, someone they'd move into the mansion so Carley could direct every page of it—as if Carley were like Gretchen and *enjoyed* ordering other people around. Instead of getting her a Range Rover for her sixteenth birthday like Amber's parents had, or a Mercedes like Hunter's, her parents had decided to buy her an author to drive.

"We're buying you the love of reading," Francis said, reaching into the basket for a blueberry muffin, its crown browned and sugared and promising the satisfaction of something that resisted your teeth just enough before giving way to softness.

"A unique *commission*," her mother said, "Your own *Pietà*."

The *Pietà* had been featured in the first of last night's slideshows, "Patronage, Plaster, and Power," which Bunny's mother had put together in order to prime the audience for the unveiling of their heads. *Foreshadowing*, Bunny had said her mother had kept calling it when Bunny complained that between all of the presentations Cissy planned there'd be hardly time for dancing.

"Eye rolling is for horses, Carley. Uppity horses."

It wasn't hard to imagine her mother using her birthday present to out-custom the Gardners. But Francis? Inhaling the plaster dust had done something to his brain. What else could explain his plan to scope out an author at tomorrow's O'Neil Foundation for Adult Literacy dinner, settle it into a guest room in the Wells mansion, and pay it to write what Francis called *the book of your dreams*.

That Carley in fact had no dreams at all involving books went unmentioned. She tried to think about books as little as possible. Of course, if Carley had never mentioned her book-hate in the first place—to say, her English teacher, Mr. Nagel—she wouldn't be spending her Sunday morning at an Intellectual Intervention at the Club after already having sat through an eight-a.m. appointment at home with Gerry, an SAT tutor who was constantly stopping her mid-sentence when she spoke to make her define aloud any word she used "imprecisely." *Precision*, Gerry said something like ten times an hour, was the difference between the "right" multiple choice answer and the trick "almost-right" ones on the reading comp section.

She should have just lied on that homework handout Mr. Nagel had entitled "Getting to Know You," like everyone else had done. A *sculptor* could have predicted an assignment advertised as "confidential" would be shared with one's parents.

"*This*," Nagel had announced to Gretchen at PEACE, "explains *everything.*"

everything (ĕv´rē-thĭng´) *pron.*

1. Carley's tenth grade PSAT (practice for the practice SAT) score last year.
2. Her going to sleep during the PSAT.
3. The incident that got her thrown out of PSAT "enrichment"—a remedial after-school class that was supposed to raise her "PSAT self-esteem."
4. Her failing to contribute to English 11B class discussion.
5. Her failing to submit two *Great Gatsby* essays.
6. Her failing.

this (thĭs) *pron.*
See pink-inked responses on handout below:

Name: Carley Wells
September 7th
Mr. Nagel
English 11B: The Archetypal Journey and Its Insubvertibility

GETTING TO KNOW YOU

Feel free to answer the questions below however you see fit. Colloquialism and even incomplete sentences are okay!

1. **Outside of school, what is your favorite activity?**

   Watching __The Arion Annals__. Which was cancelled last year. You can buy the DVDs, though. Also __The Frog Princess__, __Bouncy House__, __Caveman Land__, and __Mr. Hotness__. Which I don't think you'd like.

2. Describe the best (most stimulating, rewarding, educational? YOU decide) academic experience you've ever had. (Don't feel like you *have* to write about English 11B! We've only just begun! ☺)

In sixth grade we rode floated went on a boat on the Long Island Sound and netted things and touched them and threw them back. It was cool. Except lunch sucked (soggy tuna sandwiches). I don't know why you'd give kids tuna on a field trip. Maybe to match the boat? Like a theme.

3. Whom do you consider a role model?

4. What are your (tentative) college aspirations? Name at least ten schools, and describe in detail why you are interested in three of them. Dad or Mom having attended the institution DOES NOT COUNT as a REASON. ☺

5. What career paths intrigue you?

6. What is the best book you've ever read? (It's okay if it wasn't assigned for school. ☺)

Never met one I liked.

7. What is the most important quality a person can possess?

Love.

"A cry for help," Nagel had called her responses. Carley could picture him sitting next to Gretchen on a mahogany Victorian settee in what Montclair called *the parlor*, blowing on his tea venomously, the way he did in class. "An SOS from a sea of intellectual impoverishment. Her fascination with television, her *dire* disenchantment with the written word indicates, as I've said—"

"You've *said*."

"Perhaps you and your husband"—he would have glanced meaningfully at the empty chair next to Gretchen—"might consider enrichment activities. Intellectual engagement. At home."

As if Carley hadn't been *exposed* to literature, Gretchen had whispered to Carley and Francis when she returned home—whispering being her version of screaming, the topic at hand undeserving even of breath—while air-quoting Nagel with piranha snaps of her fingers. As if she, the newly elected vice president of Montclair Academy's Board of Trustees, hadn't just last spring purchased one thousand hand-tooled, twenty-two-carat-gold-accented books bound in midnight blue leather to accent her refurbished library.

A *sculptor* might have thought to remind her parents that the nut responsible for Gretchen's humiliation was, in fact, the same person who'd been forced by the headmaster to apologize to Carley's whole class two weeks earlier after the ill-fated literary terminology lesson in which he'd asked for a definition of *Setting*.

"Time and place?" her friend Amber had volunteered.

Everyone had been already writing it down (it was the exact definition they'd been given at the beginning of every year since sixth grade) when Nagel's tirade began. "Time and place? Time. And. Place? Is Setting making an appointment, Miss Weiss? An assignation? Do you think Setting is a working girl? A lady of the night, a bawd, a cocotte?"

He stamped his foot. "Setting is, in fact, story's mother, Miss Weiss. A homemaker. A limit-setter. And most of all a nourisher, for story suckles at its tit. Setting, Miss Weiss, is nobody's slut."

As her father bit into a second muffin, Carley cast a look across the room at the buffet where white-hatted omelet chefs and crêpe makers kept up a crack-stir-flip rhythm. Her stomach growled. How much longer would her parents insist on waiting for Hunter?

"You are not *blank*," her father said, taking from his jacket pocket a veiny-looking copy of the too-familiar handout. A copy of a copy, Gretchen having torn up the original upon her return from PEACE and then reassembled it until dawn, aligning every edge as she pasted hundreds of scraps onto cardboard. "You are not *nothing*."

"And where did this outré practice of making hearts over your i's come from?" said her mother. "Did you get this from Amber?"

"This isn't about *hearts*, Gretchen! It's about *nothing*."

Nothing had been Francis's theme since the morning after PEACE, when he'd called Carley upstairs to his home office. "You don't go writing nothing because you're afraid of what some asshole thinks." He'd spread open a leather photo album on his desk. In a print on the wall behind him, a galaxy was born from the breast of Hera, stars pouring from her nipple as she pulled away from a suckling baby her husband had stuck there while she slept. "That girl knew she was something," he said, as if the pink-bibbed eight-year-old girl wearing a downhill ski medal and giving the camera a thumbs-up was an ancestor she'd never met. Francis jabbed at another picture—age six, touching the edge of the pool to win a Minnows Freestyle. "Didn't have the right build, didn't care. She knew conformity smothers."

Even Hunter, who adored her father, might have asked after a few inches of scotch if this speech weren't *ironic*—one of Nagel's favorite words—coming from the inventor of the Marvel-Bra, whose ad campaigns showed saggy mismatched breasts transformed into identically high, firm *Galaxies of Beauty.*

"You didn't like that asshole's questions? Could've made up your own instead of shutting up. Went outside the box. Written something smart-ass. Could have shut the fucker up."

When Hunter had had Nagel last year, Francis reminded her, he'd covered every inch of this very assignment with a short story—receiving extra credit for it despite his calling the protagonist *Mr. Bagel, the teacher with a hole in the middle.*

As Francis kept on talking through muffins about Carley's opportunity to *direct the creation of a world*, and Gretchen vowed to replace the party favor order for three hundred Bottle-Green-leather-bound copies of *Le Morte d'Arthur* with copies of the yet-to-be-written book bound in a new hue for which Gretchen would reengage the color consultant tomorrow,

Carley studied a constellation of dust the cleaners had missed on the nearest damask window treatment. On the herringbone walnut floor was another splotch. Even on the wave-patterned blue cornices far above were splatterings of white, as if a hundred years after being carved they'd finally crested. When someone had opened the back doors last night a breeze had carried dust all the way up past the crystal chandeliers, from which it had ridden a current to the sander-free end of the room where the band had been playing. When it descended upon them, the musicians had insisted on packing up, despite Bunny's sobbing that *no one's* Sweet Sixteen ever ended until the playing of "New York, New York," and Cissy's threatening to sue them for emotional damages.

Francis looked at his watch and left a second message on Hunter's voice mail.

"He's probably still sleeping," Carley said. "With college apps, he's exhausted." Both her parents nodded, smiling the way people did at the thought of babies or Gandhi. Hunter was allowed to still be in bed at ten a.m. Hunter was allowed to be late. Hunter. . . . They were thoughts she pushed away, rare jealousies about which she felt guilty. Her best friend was the golden child of Fox Glen because he worked hard at everything: at school and at sports, at being polite and kind, at even his body, which he forced through laps in his pool and reps in his gym even through its betrayals—the frequent illnesses large and small he endured with good humor.

At last, despite Hunter's absence, they began the long walk to the buffet from the back corner table, the most coveted seating at Club brunch being farthest from the food. The primary objective of brunch was, after all, this procession.

They stopped first at the Gardners' table, where her mother announced to Cissy their intentions. "A commission," Gretchen said, working the word into conversation three times, "in honor of Carley's passion for literature."

"We'll be book de' Medicis," Francis told Greer.

"Last night was cool," Carley said to Bunny, trying not to look at her plate of brandied orange crêpes.

"Cool? You guys didn't even *show up* to my After," Bunny said. Halfway to the afterparty at Bunny's house, Hunter had told their cab driver to turn around and take the Meadowbrook Parkway south to the Station, a bar where their fake IDs were always welcome. She'd thought he meant to make it an early night, one of those times they just drank and talked and went back to his house to talk more. And for a little while it was like that—Hunter telling her about how his private college counselor kept shooting down his application essays, Carley telling him about how two days after PEACE she'd come home from school to find Getting to Know You added to her bedroom mirror, so that between Nagel's two eight-and-a-half-by-eleven pages and the personal trainer's eleven-by-fourteen assessment that put Carley's body at forty-two percent fat and fifty-seven pounds over optimal weight, there was barely surface left for Carley to see herself.

There'd been something intimate about their being dressed up in the back booth of a dive bar. Hunter's bowtie tucked into his pocket and his wing collar open. Her legs folded under her and the Christian Lacroix T-straps that had bitten pink rings into her ankles abandoned to the beery floor. Their hands clasped across a wooden table carved with ballpoint pens and knives into a tangle of graffiti you could read with your fingers.

But then other people started showing up saying Bunny's afterparty was lame. One of whom, Lauren Vandergraf, Hunter had stumbled out with two hours later, his shirt untucked over his hard-on, his hand on her size-zero ass.

"You shouldn't go pretending to be where you weren't," Bunny said now. She glared at Carley.

"By *cool* I meant the *party*-party."

Bunny shrugged an *Oh, that.*

"I don't know anything about art, but I liked that guy in the last slideshow—the one on the wine label. I'd never seen anything like his stuff. It didn't feel like, dead?"

"He's *not* dead."

"Not him, the *art.*" In the Penone slides, a single bronze tree had stood outside among real ones instead of stuck in a stuffy room smelling of air-conditioning. Indoors, he'd sculpted a tree that dripped water from a long branch into a pool below, forming endless rings on its surface. He'd carved into real felled tree trunks to find baby trees, turning back time ring by ring, sculpting out saplings that looked alive. *Thus revealing memories,* Bunny had read aloud last night from index cards.

Bunny shrugged again. "Cissy Googled *wine* and *sculptor* together and found one who'd done a label. So the favors and the theme would, you know, *match.* Where's Hunter?"

Carley shrugged back and thought about Penone's series of tear-shaped clay figures imprinted with his body. They were supposed to be breaths, except solid.

She wasn't supposed to care who Hunter slept with. Except she did.

At the Weisses' table, her father pulled up a chair to tell Bernie, his business partner, "I had a shoulder-pad moment." It was an *allusion*—to use a word from one of Nagel's terminology lessons—to the story of the night Marvel-Bra was born. Francis and Bernie had gotten shitfaced on a bottle of bourbon Francis had unearthed from a desk drawer while they were packing up their desks, having just let go their employees at Poly-Pad, the polymicrofoam shoulder-pad business for which they'd taken out second mortgages on their homes in Queens and into which they'd sunk the small inheritance Gretchen's father had left her, the majority of his estate having been bequeathed to her sisters, who hadn't eloped with commoners.

It was supposed to be "the filling of the future," polymicrofoam. They'd believed its "natural" flexibility would revolutionize clothing. They'd kept believing even when the complaints had started coming in about the weight of a garment bag or even a heavy purse making someone's shoulders look like the armrests of a cheap sofa. They'd believed until the chemical that their supplier added as a remedy to firm up the material turned out to be flammable. It didn't matter that the supplier, not Poly-Pad, was liable for a commuter's shoulders having combusted in an unair-conditioned Long Island Rail Road car one August afternoon. Without the firming agent, polymicrofoam was useless.

Or so it had seemed until that night when Francis, half-drunk and emptying old stock from the storage room into a Dumpster behind the factory, came upon a carton of bras Gretchen had made him store at the factory because she didn't want them in the house. Remnants from his days of selling plus-sized lingerie out of his car.

Bernie had been playing against himself at shoulder-pad basketball and losing, sliding back and forth in a desk chair to garbage cans at either end of the concrete factory floor, when Francis walked back in wearing a size 48-F red lace bra stuffed with untreated back-stock pads, the ones with the firming agent having been confiscated that afternoon by the Consumer Product Safety Commission.

"Feel me up," Francis said. "Seriously! Do it! They feel *real!*" In those pre-anorexic days, when his double-A-cup wife still wished for curves, she wore padded bras that made her look like she had socks in her shirt. Copping a feel was like squeezing a Dr. Scholl's insole. But this. *This* was *tit.*

Francis spent the rest of the night, and then week, and then month in front of a desk covered with pads and bras of sizes double A through G that he cut up and resewed a hundred ways and weighted with everything from bean bags to buckshot. Polymicrofoam could be sliced into the thinnest layers to fill in gaps and reshape, and even plentifully endowed women could use *molding.* He read up on anatomy and architecture, corsets and cantilevering, teaching himself the physics of support. Two years later he and Bernie made their first million.

"May we *all* move beyond giving our children *things* to providing *experiences,*" Gretchen said now, standing over Edie instead of taking a seat. Later, Carley would come up with the words *literally talking down to her.* Now, while Amber commiserated into her ear about Hunter's having sex with every girl thin enough to see through, she could only think about how impossible it seemed that their mothers had once been best friends. Carley might have been young then, but she remembered. Sitting in each other's kitchens in Queens drinking box wine until their husbands came home, Gretchen and Edie had been like sisters, and not just because no one else in the neighborhood had known what to make of Gretchen's prep school accent and her not knowing what to do with herself at barbecues or ball games and her always returning favors with bigger favors, so that nobody ever wanted to give her an extra casserole lest she'd bring to their door a

five-course meal a week later. When Carley and Amber were supposed to
be upstairs playing, they'd sneak downstairs to eavesdrop, their mothers'
commingling reassurances—*you're not fat . . . he's just tired . . . they weren't
talking about you . . . you can borrow . . . there's always time . . .*—the sound
of comfort as they tried to make up the world to each other.

They'd cried on each other and trusted each other and shared their
secrets, and then six months after they all moved to Fox Glen, Gretchen
just *didn't* anymore, like love was something you could turn off.

"Lauren's a slut anyway," Amber whispered to Carley. "A *slut*-slut," she
clarified. Amber herself was only a flirt, an identity she'd forged this spring
while Hunter was out of school with mono and Carley was spending all her
free time at his house. Amber, whose mother was so hypochondriacal that
her visiting Hunter was out of the question even after he was no longer
contagious, had spent those two months changing. Until then, she and
Carley had just gone wherever Hunter went, hanging out with his friends—
people like his older cousin Ian, last year's student council president. But in
Hunter's absence Amber had gone back to spending time with people she
and Carley had hung out with in middle school before he'd moved to town,
people who mostly weren't invited to *the* parties but who *liked* her. "Why
do you want to hang out with people who act like they're doing Hunter a
favor by letting you come?" Amber had started saying. Though it was true
that people like Ian and his then-girlfriend Violet and Bunny Gardner *were*
elitist, Hunter wasn't like that at all. And when she was with Hunter, Carley
didn't care who else was around.

As for Amber, for the first time she felt like *someone*, she told Carley.
Someone who wanted to take herself seriously. Someone who had more
than two friends. She'd stopped wearing clothes that were silly and just *fun*,
the way she and Carley always had done—novelty T-shirts and black-and-
white fake cow skin fuzzy pants and geometric-patterned dresses they wore
over jeans and sneakers made out of unsneakerish materials like lace and/or
green patent leather, all of which they'd mix and match—and instead started
buying outfits *shown* together in the store, as if the fun hadn't been in
making it all up themselves. She got a nose job during the summer after
their sophomore year, the way most of the other bump-nosed girls at

Montclair had already done the year before. And instead of spending hours on the phone with Carley making up stories about what they would do with a fantasy guy (who was always Hunter, but who they'd stopped calling *Hunter* a couple of years earlier), she'd started fooling around with guys for real—though without going far because she liked the idea of someone wanting to fool around with her more than actually doing it. Thus, *flirt*, a word Amber liked to say aloud, letting her new identity tickle her tongue.

When Hunter was well again and she'd started bringing those friends along to the Station and to parties at Hunter's—events from which they'd never technically been excluded because Hunter didn't believe in exclusivity, but to which they'd never been invited, either—it felt to Carley like she wanted to be the old Amber and the new one, too. She knew she should be happy for Amber, but, as she'd admitted to Hunter one night this September, it seemed greedy, this straddling of worlds. He'd looked into her eyes a long time before saying, *She's trying things on, C. She's allowed.* And then, gently, *So are you, you know.*

But didn't people have to *choose* who they were? Unless you were bulimic—something else Amber had been trying on since the spring— weren't you not supposed to get to eat your cake and have it, too? Or, for that matter, Carley thought with a parting glance at Amber's plate as her father stood and told Bernie to come over later to watch the Knicks game, your scrambled eggs with truffles and ham, poached oysters, Hokkaido pancakes, and chocolate bread pudding.

At the buffet, omelet chefs cracked eggs one-handed and complimented members on their excellent choices—lobster, white asparagus, and morels for Francis—as they folded them in. At the custom egg station, chives rode foaming butter in one pan, the heat releasing their scent. In another, thyme awaited a scramble to be removed from the heat the moment soft curds formed. On the plate they would become a landscape, butter glistening in the valleys like painted-on light.

She could have ordered any of it—all of it—and piled her plate high, too, with bacon and compote-topped crêpes and crab cake Florentine without Gretchen chancing a word about it in public. But eventually she'd have to go home to Swann's Way, a mansion where Gretchen's disappointment could be heard from every room, a home where just *being* was like standing in front of a mirror naked.

She picked at a plate of berries when she returned to her seat, staring out the window at the Sound as her parents, who normally agreed upon little, pumped each other ever higher about The Book. All Carley had been missing was *this*, they told each other. All she needed was a story told by someone who would understand what she liked. Someone paid to understand her.

Later, in bed, Carley would wish she'd said, *But I don't know what I like, I don't know me.* Now, she just watched a cormorant stand on an algae-covered rock, hooked beak pointed at the sky and dark wings splayed to dry its feathers. It looked out of place in sunlight—like something that was supposed to be nocturnal but didn't know it.

"I'm so sorry," she heard from behind her, and then Francis was standing to shake Hunter's hand. "I overslept, and I had my phone turned off, and . . . well, there's no excuse . . ."

"None needed," said Francis.

"Of course you're tired," said Gretchen.

"Get yourself something to eat, son." Francis signaled the waiter to pour Hunter coffee and juice.

"Hey, C." He kissed her on the cheek and took the seat beside her. She watched people at nearby tables pretend not to stare. No matter how many times you saw Hunter walk into a room, he always glowed new. That he'd shown up with his shoulder-length blond hair still wet from the shower and his shirt cuffs unbuttoned only made him look more perfect. Like Hunter always said, Club Brunch was a *faux-casual faux-occasion.*

He sipped his juice, a wince passing through his eyes. No one else would notice, but she could tell: sore throat. First illness of fall. Under the table she squeezed his hand.

"Great scarf," she said. A blue and gray striped wool and silk blend he'd worried was over-the-top. She'd been with him when he'd picked it out at Gucci last week on the Gold Mile. *You'd tell me if it came off pretentious?* She would have, but it didn't.

He draped it around her neck, looking into her eyes with a we-have-secrets smile that Amber once said was the reason Carley had no other female friends. She pretended not to feel all eyes on her, pretended not to know that they all wondered how a creature as elegant as Hunter could want to decorate something like her, pretended not to know that even her own mother was thinking it. Pretended it didn't matter to her what her mother thought.

He cleared his throat softly before reassuring her parents he'd foray to the buffet momentarily. She could tell he was so hung over he feared food. She could tell conversation hurt his throat.

With her index finger she traced letters one by one on his wrist: I'LL TAKE CARE OF U.

Between an I and a U he traced back a heart.

THERE WAS A game Ian and his friends had taught Hunter when he'd first moved to Fox Glen. A variation on Spin the Bottle, with a person being spun. They'd play it drunk, out on the Sound, a group forming a circle around the "bottle," who was taken out over his head, blindfolded, and spun while he treaded. After the spinners retreated, he would swim with his arms outreached until he touched someone of the opposite sex who he'd eventually make out with. The several yards in complete darkness until his fingers connected with someone's skin would feel like miles, disorientation making him panicky inside and the thought of someone noticing his panic the most terrifying part of all.

Today felt like that. How long had he spoken to Francis last night? Long enough, apparently, to make brunch plans. Long enough to encourage a present Carley would hate.

"It's not just a book," Gretchen said to her daughter in a tone that suggested she'd been saying it all morning. "Or a favor. It's an internship in the art of story. Who else will have *that* on their college applications next year?"

"The *love of reading*," said Francis. "What greater gift?"

Y DIDN'T U WARN ME? Carley traced on his arm.

On a moonless night there were no edges, no horizon. You could swim forever without knowing it.

He furrowed his brow, pretending not to understand her question, and chased a bite of brioche French toast with a deep breath he prayed would keep it down.

Under the table, Carley pressed her thumb hard into a point between his thumb and index finger. The nausea backed off. He felt his breath catch as he inhaled again.

IT'S OKAY, she wrote. She applied pressure a couple of inches above his wrist.

He saw her glance at his plate and quickly away, hunger legible on her face. He didn't trust himself to look at Gretchen—he felt too prickly with sickness and sadness and truths he feared he'd yell out like a madman: *If you'd let her eat in public, she wouldn't gorge in private.* He whispered into Carley's ear. "*De trop* citrus in the batter. I'll make you some at home that doesn't evoke furniture polish."

"*Our* party favors will keep people up all night reading instead of coughing," Gretchen said, covering her mouth as if the cattiness had slipped out against her will. It was the kind of overt criticism she wouldn't risk in front of most people, much as she wouldn't mention Carley's shortcomings in public but discussed them freely with him. So many of his mother's friends "flattered" him with this kind of unwanted honesty, surrendering pretenses in his presence and making him privy to things he didn't want to know.

"Have you chosen a finish?"

"A finish?"

"There was a card," she said, detailing for him his options. Why, he could have his head dipped in sterling!

"The Help has enough to polish," he said evenly. Francis laughed. Gretchen didn't.

"The studio is halfway to the Hamptons. Inconvenient, truly. I'm having Grace bring in Carley's on Monday. We'll have her take yours in, too, if you'd like."

He thanked her. "I'll bring it over when I drive Carley home later."

He felt Carley kick him under the table. He met her eyes and couldn't understand why she looked upset.

WHAT? he spelled on her leg.

Carley wrote back too quickly, letters evaporating before he could process them.

"I'm thinking maybe gold for the head," he joked to Francis. "Diamonds in the pupils. Engagement present for Suzanne. Something subtle for the mantle."

"Engagement?" said Francis. "En*gage*ment."

"My God, she *did* it. Mrs. Lawrence. Talbright. The Fourth." Gretchen said it like a prayer.

Too late, Hunter remembered promising his mother he'd let her do the announcing herself upon her return from Newport. Her phone call had come right after dinner last night, just before the unveiling of the heads and a conversation with Bunny that all at once came back to him.

His head throbbed, his throat burned. Carley wrote on his leg faster, faster, and he understood none of it. He could finish whole books in hours, devouring language with his eyes. But to convert sensation to meaning took a different kind of mind.

"OVER THERE'S WHAT'S left of your head," Carley told him in the parking lot. She pointed at a small chunk of plaster that could have been a nose. The bigger pieces she'd thrown in a trash can last night so no one would know whose favor it was. They'd been arguing about her taking his car keys when he'd tripped over the curb and the bust had slipped from under his arm.

"Can't believe that happened," he hedged, not looking at her. The silence was thick as he waited for her to say enough for him to piggyback her words and pretend he remembered. She'd suspected for a while that he'd been losing time when he drank. He was good at piecing things together, taking in what everybody said. If you were a good listener, she'd realized, you could have blackouts for months before anyone caught on.

A cloud shifted over the sun. In its shadow, the piece became an ear, or a curl.

"Just one more reason your favor will trump Bunny's: non-breakability." He was growing hoarse, and his laugh was nervous. He rubbed his eyes the way he did when his contacts were killing him, and she knew all he wanted to do was go home and take them out and sleep the sleep of someone who'd done nothing wrong.

"I tripped," Carley lied. "Stupid shoes. I turned my ankle. If you hadn't dropped it to grab me, I would have splatted." He smiled and breathed deep, and already she could feel it becoming the truth. "You saved me from this puddle," she said, pointing. At its edge, she could see their real feet and reflected faces simultaneously, their heads and the clouds appearing equally distant. "You always save me."

PART II
Plot

What people are ashamed of usually makes a good story.

—F. Scott Fitzgerald, *The Last Tycoon*

MR. AND MRS. FRANCIS WELLS

Invite you to join them
For cocktails
In honor of writer

BREE McENROY

Friday, the thirtieth of October
Seven o'clock in the evening

Swann's Way
1 Stonebridge Drive
Fox Glen, New York

CHAPTER 3

Hunter read aloud on the marble pedestal at the edge of the pond, where the statue of the god with a fish tail and giant fork used to stand. ". . . And stripped though he was of armor, Lance evinced invincibility." He laughed. "Evinced . . . invincibility. *Mon dieu*, C!" He handed the joint down to Amber, then turned toward the water to muffle a cough into his coat sleeve. When he turned back, his eyes were moist. They were always most gorgeous when he was sick or sad.

In a poem Carley had written for English class she'd likened his eyes to *green sea glass before the sun opaques it*. She'd felt naked handing it in, afraid Mr. Nagel would recognize "Ocean" as a love poem to Hunter though she'd never used his name (Montclair was a small school and who else had such beautiful eyes?), but when she got it back he'd only circled the word *opaques*— *Not a verb, Miss Wells*—and written at the bottom *Review fundamentals of meter (pp. 32–34) and resubmit.*

"Perhaps her contract stipulated annoying assonance. Along with the ubiquitous unicorns, I mean." Hunter choked back another cough. "Gwen knew Lance could protect her from anything," he read, "except her . . . dum Dum DUM! . . . conscience."

He gave in finally to the round of the coughing he'd been trying to suppress. When Carley caught his eye, he disguised it as funny faux hacking, as if the pages in his hand had tear-gassed him.

Amber giggled, though there was no way it hadn't occurred to her, too, that Hunter was coming down with something. And that Amber had been sharing with him. And that with Amber's sister's birthday coming up, Amber's mother would freak out more than usual if Amber even sniffled.

A gust of wind spun dry leaves and a paper napkin past Hunter into the pond. Arching their backs, the leaves floated on the surface. The napkin in which Carley had wrapped some of the petite crab quiches the caterers were planning to serve in a few hours at her parents' Come Stare at the Author We Bought Our Daughter party bloated and sank.

Hunter got down on one knee. "On page twelve, dear maidens, the unicorn claims fluency in English, Horse, Dragon, and of course Uni. So, a *polyglot* unicorn."

He winked, brushing his hair off his face as if the breeze weren't already doing it for him. A chance to catch his breath. Insert a beat. Pose.

pose (pōz) *v.*

1. to model for artistic purposes
2. to put on affectations
3. to present a puzzle or mystery
4. to introduce

Pose was on SAT List Number Eighteen: Alternative Definitions of Elementary Words—along with *flag*-as-in-to-get-tired, *table*-as-in-to-put-off, *temper*-as-in-to-make-strong, and *temper*-as-in-to-make-soft, all printed in a bubbly font that was supposed to turn words friendly, like adults who squatted when they talked to little kids.

You'd think they'd at least make a rule against a word having two opposite definitions, Carley had told her SAT tutor, Gerry.

He'd raised an eyebrow—like anyone ever raised just one—and said, *And who might be "they"?*

"Returning from battle at Lathamshire, Arthur would be expecting of his new wife that which was his right. His due." Hunter laughed. "In other words, tonight the blood of maidenhood will spotteth the Pendragons' sheets. Do stop looking stricken, C. It's horrifically funny."

"Bored already," Carley said, trying to sound it, though she wanted to cry. "Enough reading." The pages in his hand were supposed to be *fixing* things, and instead they were making things worse. For the last month she'd felt Hunter drifting away, as if after four years of friendship he'd gotten tired of carrying her weight. Or disgusted by it.

Though a book had been the last thing she wanted for her birthday, because Hunter *loved* books she'd hoped his interest in her parents' commission for her would give them something to share—something to pull him back to her. He was the only person at Montclair who didn't regard books like fetal pigs, carving out little hearts to present to teachers like Nagel, or buying them, pre-butchered, in Apex Notes. He didn't just read to show off, either, like every adult she knew who skimmed jacket copy and Amazon reviews to make themselves sound smart at O'Neil Foundation for Adult Literacy dinners where everyone got tanked anyway. He wrote stories himself, too, and more than anything wanted to be a novelist some-day instead of growing up to live in a place like Fox Glen and spending weekends at boring parties with boring people you tried to impress with stories about your investments. He saw something in books she couldn't fathom—a whole other life.

All week she'd imagined sitting on Hunter's bed discussing author Bree McEnroy's manuscript-in-progress, the painted figures on his muraled walls listening in. He'd read aloud from it, complimenting Carley on the author's sophisticated choices, which, because she was Carley's author, were like *Carley's* choices. Carley would lay her head on his chest, her face rising as he breathed at each Carley-sanctioned comma. He'd give her his private smile, the left side of his mouth a bit higher than the right.

After hours of such imaginings every night, she'd gone to sleep without reading a word of the work-in-progress Bree McEnroy had been e-mailing in advance of her move into the mansion tonight. She'd *meant* to read it. But with Hunter and her parents saying how smart the author was supposed to be—she knew for a fact that neither Gretchen nor Francis had managed to get through even a chapter of the author's published novel, *Between Scylla and Alta Vista*, Gretchen's bookmark having been stuck on page fifteen of her copy for weeks and Francis's copy dog-eared on page twenty— she was too intimidated to even open the documents the writer had been e-mailing. By the time she'd finally printed the chapters tonight, she'd decided she'd understand them better, anyway, by just giving them to Hunter to read and listening to him talk about them.

The wind curled the pages he'd finished over his thumb and whipped the rest around his palm. Their edges met like the point of a heart.

He crooked his finger for the joint; Amber climbed onto the pedestal with it.

"You're shivering." She rubbed his shoulders. He didn't pull away. Mossy gray Neptune stared up at them from the mud, tail curling around over his penis and balls, fist clenching his fork. (*Trident*, Hunter would have called it. As would have List Number Twenty-two: Words of Weaponry.)

Carley stared from the back of a stone lion with a broken-off ear. It wasn't that Amber didn't usually touch him. Everyone touched Hunter. But there was something about the way her fingers lingered tonight. "Giving him back his coat would warm him faster."

"I'm fine," Hunter said. His breath and Amber's and the smoke tangled in the air.

That Amber would hike through the woods from Carley's house coatless on a cold night was the sort of thing Carley used to love about her. Not that she'd stopped loving Amber—Carley wasn't like Gretchen, who could unlove. But Amber didn't *used to* be wearing a silver silk halter dress under her un-coat. After making sense to Carley for so many years, Amber just *didn't* anymore, the way a word started to sound like Martian language if you said it a hundred times fast.

"'No,' Guinevere whispered as Lancelot tried clumsily to . . .'" Hunter crossed his hands over his chest, pantomiming Gwen's warding off advances on her maidenly bosom, although as it turned out, Lance was just reaching to unbraid her golden plait.

"Bor-ed," Carley repeated. She unstraddled the lion, her stockings catching as she slid down its side. Later, she'd rewrite this moment in her head, transforming herself into the kind of girl who'd shrug at the run, hold her leg in the air as if amused at her own clumsiness, then pirouette and bow.

Later in her head, she'd be a girl who wasn't embarrassed about having

told her über-intellectual best friend that the book was "impossibly sophisticated" (a phrase she'd heard her mother utter the morning after an O'Neil
dinner). "Oops," she'd say, giggling in the way only cute girls could get away
with. "Guess I was too busy watching *Bouncy House* to actually read it."

Later in her head she'd be a girl who'd announce, "I'm Gwen. Hunter's
the unicorn," cracking up as Hunter pawed the ground and lay his head in
her lap.

Later, she'd be a girl you'd want to hang out with for an entire story, a
girl you could love.

Love (lŭv) *n.*

  1. a deep feeling of affection or desire for another person
  2. the object of one's affection or desire
  3. a strong enthusiasm for something; a passionate interest
  4. nothing-to-nothing (*Tennis*)

Backward, Mr. Nagel would have called how Carley went about trying
to make sense of life. *Inside-out.* He expected people to figure out what they
wanted to say *before* they said it instead of after. (*Do not clutter my classroom
with* ums.) More into *precision*, even, than her SAT tutor, he made his
students look up every word in a poem before reciting it. (*You must know
what you're tasting before you swallow.*)

"Anyway, Lance vows to keep trying to touch Gwen's . . . hair, all the
while proclaiming the innocence of his intentions. And Gwen vows to
remain faithful to new husband Arthur, who hasn't been home since five
minutes after their wedding when he armored up to kill dragons and
Frenchmen. And . . ."

"Stop," Carley said as she walked up to the pedestal with the run spider-
tickling up her thigh. "We're all kinds of done."

She reached up for the pages. When he didn't hand them over, she
pretended to jump for them. Little hops, like something pathetic but cute
that could will itself into air. "Bored," she said once again, instead of
humiliated.

"Amusé," he said, instead of *feverish*. And stoned. And disgusted to find himself with his fingers wrapped around *merde* when he'd expected art. "Are you certain your parents didn't specify satire?" The pages fluttered.

She wanted to hit him. She wanted to hold him. She wanted to cry.

He turned into the wind to cough into the crook of his elbow. "Or more accurately, parody."

"Like Swift. With eating babies," said Amber.

Hunter smiled his yearbook photo smile, his soccer team smile, his Glen Club Young Philanthropists smile. Fold his face in half and everything would match up. "Parody," he said, bending to offer Carley the joint, "differs from satire in that—"

"Amber catches your cold, Edie's gonna drown her in Purell." Carley squinted at the joint like she could see the billion germs on it. The air cracked with change. Until she'd said it, she hadn't realized how much she'd wanted something to break.

"What *are* you talking about, C? I'm all kinds of fine." He squeezed Amber's shoulder. "Peachy. *Exactement comme une pêche.*" He jumped down from the pedestal, then lifted Amber down by her waist.

"If you're sick, you're sick." Amber's smile was stretched, gummy. She kept her hands on his arms as if they were dancing to a song she didn't want to end, yet you could see her trying not to breathe his air. "I'm not my mother."

Carley snatched the pages from where he'd laid them on the pedestal and shoved them into the canvas bag in which she'd brought out the napkin-wrapped food. "Let's go in," she said to Amber. "Get him something warm."

Hunter blushed and shook his head, staring at her like he did when people talked about what things cost. "You're out," he said, letting go of Amber and gesturing at the joint that had gone cold in Carley's hand. He sat on the pedestal and held out to Carley his palladium cigar lighter—a birthday gift last year from Francis. "So look, on *The Simpsons*, the embedded cartoon, *Itchy and Scratchy*, is parodic, as it plays off another text, *Tom and Jerry*."

Amber took a seat next to him, nodding like someone Hunter wouldn't have to resort to cartoons for. Like the three-point-eight student she was. Like someone who didn't Choose Her Own Adventures backward.

Carley's father had bought her Choose Your Own Adventures when she was a kid, mazelike books that begin with you waking up places like the planet Zantor and having to make choices like whether to trust a family of six-headed purple Zantorians who tell you to follow them home to safety before sundown when the planet's carnivorous plants will wake up. Only problem is that the Zantorians, with their six mouths of fangs, are a little vague about what they themselves eat. *If you take the Zantorians up on their offer to "have you over for dinner," turn to page four. If you decide to take your chances tiptoeing through the snapping tulips, turn to page ten.* The only thing Carley ever liked about them was working backward from the end, taking the forks in reverse to figure out how to end up on a spaceship bound for home.

"But *The Simpsons* as a whole is satire because—"

"Thanks, Nagel," Carley interrupted. She knew she was being mean. She knew he was just being Hunter, but all she wanted was for him to understand how un-*Carley* she felt. She couldn't *be* without him.

"—It pokes fun at, among other things, the values of suburban—"

Carley gripped the lighter hard, the diamond-headed texture biting into her hand. Like she was meat—stupid, fatty meat—and it was one of those tenderizing mallets Gretchen used to use before they had cooks, before Fox Glen, before Marvel-Bra, to pummel the chuck steaks they could afford into the filets Francis craved.

She heaved the lighter into the pond, rings making rings within rings on the water.

"C?" Hunter said. He stood and turned, staring at the epicenter.

"What's your problem?" Amber stood, too, downwind of his coughing.

"I know what satire is," Carley whispered. List Fourteen: Words About Literature. "I fucking know *satire*."

Amber came over to her. "You've been weird tonight," she whispered. "You've been weird for a while. Like you don't want to be happy. You need to call Sinkman?"

Dr. Sinkman, whose lips looked like drowned earthworms after a storm, was the last person Carley ever wanted to talk to. Her parents had started sending her to him last year after a getting-asked-to-leave-remedial-PSAT-class *debacle* (List Twenty-nine: Words of Disaster) in which her instructor had mistook the butt-squeezes *Vogue* recommended doing "at work, in the car, anytime you're sitting, for a tight behind" for public masturbation.

When she'd tried to explain it to her parents, they didn't exactly say her story was so far-fetched that she must be a lying desk-humper—Francis, embarrassed by the whole subject, spent weeks working late to develop Marvel-Bra's first exercise bra, the Virgo, rather than discuss it; Gretchen taped to Carley's mirror an article about how jogging flooded you with feel-good-all-over chemicals—but from the first time she saw Sinkman, it was clear they'd suggested she had a problem with truth.

"Did that really happen?" he would say, running his ring finger over the underside of his rimless glasses and scribbling without looking down.

Ordinarily she made a point of telling Sinkman nothing meaningful, but for weeks she'd felt so lonely—what with Hunter's being there yet not *there*, and Amber's being excited about things like Libertine jeans coming out with a line of Swarovski-crystal pocket designs, and her parents' having invented for her *a passion for reading* they'd seemed to have forgotten was an invention—that yesterday she'd confirmed his suspicions by divulging something she'd never told anyone. She'd found herself telling Sinkman about Aftermemory.

Aftermemory (ăf´t rǎměm- -rə) *n.*

1. a time when Carley has the right words to say
2. a present that doesn't move too fast for her to grasp
3. a dream of making things happen
4. what maybe might have been

Late at night, she'd explained, she'd rewatch her day in her head, slow it down, go frame-by-frame at the most confusing parts like her life was a DVD, and figure out the things she should have said. Like an *incantation*

(List Twenty-six: Words of Magic), those perfect words opened doors to secret passages, to all the paths she could have taken. Choices for adventure she hadn't even seen. Do-overs.

"The director's cut," she'd explained. "Like in the collector's edition of *The Arion Annals: Seasons 1-9*. Alternative endings. Deleted scenes."

Like: In Aftermemory, she writes *The Great Gatsby* under Favorite Book before it's even assigned for class. Thus Nagel knows she's the kind of girl who deserves his writing *good image* on her ocean poem instead of pulling it apart. Thus Gretchen returns from PEACE without ever hearing the words "Getting to Know You." Thus she doesn't whisper-scream at Francis about Carley's "anti-intellectualism" being something Carley inherited from *his* side of the family, like her chest or thighs. Thus he doesn't decide to turn her birthday into an excuse to become Fox Glen's first Patron of Literature.

"So you fantasize at bedtime."

"Yes. No. Not only at night. Sometimes I realize what I should have said right after it happens, sometimes I can't think of the words for a long time. And it's not *fantasizing*. It's almost real because it could have happened, if only . . . I mean . . ." She couldn't find the words.

He'd nodded and said truth was "a slippery slope," and five minutes later they were out of time.

She'd nodded back silently, feeling like she'd given away something huge for nothing. Like losing her virginity to someone who wouldn't remember. That night, in Aftermemory, she'd tell him "slippery slope" was a cliché and that one of Nagel's favorite expressions was *Cliché-mongers are the fungi of language*.

She stared at the bulls-eyes now, imagining the lighter settling into a blanket of leaves on the bed of the pond and clenching her fingers around its absence.

"We done with the literary terms?" she asked. "Or do you want to define *noun* for me?"

"*Noun*'s not a—," Amber said. "Let's just go inside." She swallowed hard, as if testing for spontaneous sore throat.

Carley shrugged.

"You *wanted* to get Hunter something warm a minute ago. And it's cold, like you said. And anyway, I have to pee." She slipped out of Hunter's coat and wrapped its gray cashmere around his shoulders.

Up at the house Amber would be sticking out her tongue in the bathroom mirror, searching her throat for spottiness, then gagging herself over the toilet with the handle of the toothbrush she kept in her purse. *Just don't anymore*, Carley wanted to yell to her as she walked away. She wanted to tell her she'd been beautiful even before the nose job and two dropped dress sizes and necklines so low you could see the Marvel-Bra star in her cleavage. She wanted to tell her she understood the ache of wanting to be desired, and how it went so much deeper than arousal that it made sense for Amber never to want to finish what she started with a guy.

"What are you doing, C?" Hunter said when Amber had disappeared up the path. He took a shuddery, fighting-not-to-cough breath and held his head in his hands.

She rubbed circles on his back.

He pushed her hand away. "What's wrong with you tonight? Why can't you let me be fine?"

He walked to the edge of the pond to blow his nose, his back to her.

"It's just me," she whispered, words that promised she'd never be grossed out by snot or phlegm, and would never mind taking care of him, and would never think he was weak for needing comfort. Words that summed up how they fit: Hunter was Greek-statue-hot and a virus magnet, and Carley was—to use Gretchen's word—*hardy*.

"I'm not stupid," she said when he turned back.

"Since when do I think you're stupid? C, what's this all—"

"You told me that writer wrote *smart* stuff, not crap about unicorns and—"

"Since when do you care about the *book*?" He shook his head. "How should I know why it's so . . . laughable? What I saw of her writing . . . her published work . . . was nothing like this. Serious literary fiction. *Too* serious for—"

"Me."

He coughed. "Don't put words into my mouth. It's not . . . fair." He reached into his coat pocket. "I'm going to bring Amber by Ian's for a while. We'll be back for the party, I promise. Go take a walk or something. Take a bath. Take a nip." He pressed his flask into her hand. "Macallan, fifty years. Ginger-citrus nose. Kiss of peat in the finish." He brushed his dry lips against her forehead. "We love you"—he stared past her, as if he could see all the way to Swann's Way through the trees—"but we're going."

TO BE HONEST with himself, Hunter had left the flask with Carley to keep from breaking one of his own commandments: Thou shalt not drive drunk with passengers.

He could have called a cab, but he enjoyed chauffeuring the girls. Being *useful* was one of the few things that distracted him from thinking too much, feeling too much. Though Carley and Amber were in the same grade behind him, Carley, who had a December birthday, was still too young for even a junior learner's permit. Amber, who'd been born in January and thus, like him, was nearly seventeen and had a junior license as he did, had parents who paid attention to the actual DMV rules about junior licensees only driving to and from school unaccompanied by an adult. Hunter's mother, like nearly everyone else's, figured a license was a license, depended on the local cops to interpret "school" loosely, and had been thrilled when her ex-husband's birthday gift to her son had relieved her of paying for a full-time driver for him, as keeping up an estate requiring twenty-five full-time employees had been eroding her prenuptial lump settlement. Eliminating Hunter's driver allowed her to hire a full-time professional *stager*—someone to walk through the main house daily behind the cleaning staff and move things around in rooms as if they'd been used by an entourage of people sophisticated enough to have played out a game of chess on Suzanne's once-owned-by-John-F.-Kennedy ebony and ivory set before taking leave of the solarium, accomplished enough to have played through the Chopin stacked on the bench of the Steinway grand piano in the salon, and au courant enough to have left out on a circa-1810 octagonal library table a spread-paged copy of the newest slim Darren Connelly novel about Manhattanites who bemoan their own solipsism for one-hundred-and-ninety-nine pages before embracing it on the two-hundredth. When actual guests did visit, they would thus wonder about who had proceeded them on her social schedule and feel fortunate to have been slotted in.

He emerged from an overgrown path onto a manicured one that demarcated the boundary between the acreage Gretchen cared about and the woods beyond it. She concentrated her gardeners on the parts of Swann's Way she'd created or tamed—the man-made koi pond and Japanese tea house and rock garden, the English maze, the scent gardens and flower gardens and statue gardens. He doubted she knew her daughter spent hours on the overgrown, unlit paths, feeling at home among the broken statuary and the dark water, sitting beside ruins. He turned and considered going back. It wasn't like Carley to destroy things. Nor was it like her to make him feel self-conscious.

But if he went back, he'd find himself hugging her, and then being consoled and stroked and tended to in a way he craved nearly as much as the pills in his pocket. Comfort so overwhelming that he'd give himself up to it, rest his head in her lap. He was weak, a person who would undo weeks of trying to redraw the boundaries between him and his best friend for just a few minutes of solace. What Bunny had implied at her party but was too kind to say was that he was selfish.

He pressed on to the koi pond, in the middle of which a fountain erupted twenty feet high, a titan's bidet. At its edge he tapped two Vicodins into his hand—only two, though he wanted four. He needed to tamp back, then give them up altogether once he'd set other things right. Once his applications were all done, once he'd caught up in math, once he and Carley were where they should be.

Painkillers, they were called, a misnomer. They were a wonderful, terrible paradox that neutered hurt rather than murdered it, putting pain at arm's length, like something he shouldn't be able to hold in his hand and look at but could: hot coals, rattlesnakes, his beating heart.

The electric numbness began as soon as he'd swallowed them, an anticipatory relief before they kicked in for real. He stroked the rest of the vial in his pocket to remind himself he had plenty, that when the time came he'd take withdrawal slowly, that he wouldn't have to endure what he'd gone through cold turkey after Bunny's Sweet Sixteen, when his dealer, Antoine, had gone out of town without notice before Hunter could be refilled.

He'd been on edge and shaky when Francis Wells had come by with a list of ten authors, nine of whose names were already crossed out. The only writer who hadn't summarily refused the Wellses' commission was Bree McEnroy, whose résumé boasted a Blaine University education, several short story credits, a novel called *Between Scylla and Alta Vista*, and most recently an award called the E.T. Wahlrod Fellowship.

Francis didn't have to ask Hunter to assess McEnroy's seven-hundred-page out-of-print book. Hunter volunteered. He needed a distraction from the strep throat that he'd woken up with the morning after Bunny's party, and he wanted Francis to leave before he noticed the trembling of withdrawal, and most of all he was curious. *The* Darren Connelly had recommended her at the O'Neil Foundation for Adult Literacy dinner, Francis had said, but Googling her mystified Hunter as to why Connelly would think her "perfect" to write a book for a book-hater. The reviews of her novel characterized it as abstruse, the magazines in which she'd published were obscure, and the criteria for the E.T. Wahlrod Fellowship—which, according to its Web site, was closed indefinitely to further applications—were nebulous.

Too feverish for school and too restless for sleep, Hunter had crawled between the book's covers. Though he was a fast reader, it was a slow read, laden with footnotes within footnotes within footnotes whose parasitism annoyed him—a feeling he pushed away because he feared it suggested intellectual immaturity, an inability to appreciate a book crafted to produce the effect of something being hollowed out from inside. (In a short Q & A on *The Simulacra Review* Web site, Bree McEnroy had cited emptiness as one of the book's controlling metaphors.)

Characters drowned in word-tsunamis of description, lying flat on fictional shores so laden with jagged rocks—the narrator reminded the reader with conspiratorial, intrusive winks—that the reader couldn't hope to save them without his own body being shredded. Rip currents dragged him into subplots of no consequence whose point, clearly, was to be of no consequence ("Another Instance of Nothingness Spun into Sugar," was one chapter heading, and "Bildungromanesque Babbling" another), the author unwavering in her quest to demonstrate pointlessness.

When *Scylla* had finally released him, he lay dazed and dizzy, stunned by its relentlessness. He wanted to hate it, but suspected he needed to push beyond feelings to assess it. Being so ill with withdrawal that by the end of the book he was dry-heaving, what faith anyway could he put in his gut?

"It blew me away," he'd told Francis when he called Hunter for his opinion. He'd been in a hurry to get off the phone, his body knotted, his brain cramped.

It would make a fine trophy he'd told himself later—the more intimidating to the Wellses' friends, the better. And given that Carley had expressed as little interest in the commission as she did in her own Sweet Sixteen, a several hundred thousand dollar affair with a theme staked out by her mother last year after the Oscar-winning film *Lancelot* had sparked nationwide interest in Arthurian legendry, he doubted she'd even read it. The book was not *about* her, he'd told himself, any more than the party would be.

"It's done, then," said Francis. "I'll sign her tomorrow."

HALFWAY THROUGH HUNTER'S flask, staring out at the pond, Carley knew exactly where the lighter had gone under. The rings were long gone, but she could see in her memory the shadow of an overhanging branch, now converted in the moonlight to reflection. The lighter had broken the surface right beneath the very end of it.

She thought about how all Hunter had wanted tonight was not to be sick. How he'd asked with his eyes for her to let him hang on to his last hours of wellness. How she'd tossed them away as if she didn't know how precious they were.

She stripped to her underwear so as not to ruin her party dress, then walked into the pond, up to her waist and then shoulders and neck, mud sucking at her toes. Her knee connected with movement, perhaps a descendant of the trout Francis had stocked when they'd first moved here before he'd realized he didn't like fishing. Her soles passed over fish skeletons scavenged clean by flatworms and turtles; and over the nubs of hundreds of joints smoked out here with Hunter, who called bongs or pipes *disaesthetic*; and over the stones she'd heaved in as a kid, taking Francis literally when he'd said you could turn a pond into an ocean if you only made waves.

She searched until she shook with cold, until the darkness was complete, until something tripped her—a fallen branch or tangle of pondweed or perhaps a statue that had drowned before the Wellses had ever come to Swann's Way. The pond forced its way into her mouth and nose, gagging her. She crawled out empty-handed, a taste left in her mouth that was vegetative, ancient, older than earth. It tasted like the opposite of water.

CHAPTER 4

In Aftermemory Carley breaks the surface, her fingers clutching the lighter like a shiny silver fish as a beam shines from shore.

"C, you'll catch your death!" It's a breathless shout, the voice of someone not yet used to his voice.

It's also a cliché and because Hunter never ever uses clichés, his saying it *means* something, like he's too worried to choose his words. His lighter feels cool and ripply. She holds it lit in front of her as she walks through the water.

It is as real, this moment, as if she were breathing it.

He snaps the lid closed when she reaches him and whispers that the lighter is just a *thing* and what did she think she was *doing* and did she want to worry him *sick*, and she says that's two clichés in one minute and anyway he's sick already, he's always sick, and he laughs and strokes her wet hair. He wraps his navy pea coat around her inside-out so its soft side can cocoon her. All his pockets are exposed, her body bulging the lining against everything he carries: handkerchiefs and pillbox, a leather journal and a pen.

"I'm stretching it," she says.

He quiets her with his lips and every goose bump sighs, the moment so strong it doesn't matter that she'd find herself alone, shivering on the pedestal, if she opened her eyes. It doesn't matter that Hunter hasn't fit into that coat or spoken in that breathy voice since eighth grade. It doesn't matter that she's messed with time. All that matters is that as he'd walked away, she'd said the perfect thing, words that grew in his head and made him turn around, change his mind, go back to her. What *were* those words? Always, after Aftermemory, she forgets.

"I don't want their stupid gift," she whispers to him. "I can't love *words*. The only thing I love is you."

He traces her face with his fingertips. "Maybe *I'll* write you a present, someday," he whispers back. "Something about us." He traces her body. He traces her chills. He picks her up and swings her in weightless circles, the pond and pedestal and stone lion there and not there, again and again. "Maybe I'll give you the story that changes your mind."

CHAPTER 5

Just east of Penn Station a gap brings on darkness. Minutes after *All Aboard*, its journey still in infancy, a train surrenders its grasp of the third rail as it leaves the central track for a line of its own. Lights extinguish, baring opportunity.

Ignored by commuters with the *Times* or *Journal* spread open in their laps, seized by lovers new to squeezing each other's hands, and squandered by children who miss their chance to squeal before it ends, the moment of darkness works its way down the train, running past and through and into people, and once in a great while—as it did on one particular Friday afternoon—lends a person respite from who she is. Bree McEnroy, duct-taped suitcases at her feet and three hours late for her future, dreamt, in that moment, of ponies.

Later, she'd come to call the moment *the beginning*, pinning it to past tense, telling it like truth, turning it once-upon-a-time. Now, exhausted from packing and insomnia, and lulled by darkness and movement, she'd lost her bearings. She might be crossing the Atlantic by ship, or passing over foggy moors. She might be an orphan, age eight, precocious, and not formally schooled, on her way to a foreign land where strangers have agreed to take her in. She might begin what is called—by people who believe in such tales—an adventure.

Compulsory to such a story would be trials. An imposing mansion. Taunts from to-the-manor-born brats. Condescension from their parents. Though she'd require pluck and humility—qualities concomitant, naturally, with penury—to melt her patrons' hearts, she'd have allies, as orphan-children always do: wise servants who offer warm milk and biscuits and nurture, socially awkward invalids who befriend them, animals with huge brown eyes who understand orphan-feelings and lick away tears with rough tongues.

Perhaps there'd be a pony to whom she'd feed carrots and apples and sugar cubes. Outgrown by the manor children, it would explore forgotten gardens with her and witness by the end of her adventure a life-changing discovery—a treasure, a birthright, a secret.

Lights come up throughout the train. People blink. The switch is over, past tense.

Bree shook off the daydream, its mawkishness making her head rush as if with recollected shame, and squinted at her cloudy Plexiglas reflection as the train tunneled beneath Manhattan, burrowing through the flaky schist of the island's foundation and beneath the East River's floor. By thirty, she'd lost faith in adventure, where things happened and happened and *happened*, all adding up at the end. It was not the kind of tale she believed in. Not the kind she told. Not the kind she'd read for years. And anyway, every good adventure had already been snatched up.

"Change at Jamaica," a disembodied voice commanded, a public address.

CARLEY STUMBLED OFF the path into overgrown boxwoods, crying out as branches stabbed her chest through her crushed velvet bodice. The path from the pond—which Gretchen called *the bog* to distinguish it from the man-made Serenity Koi Pond—was unlit, like all parts of the estate Gretchen wanted to keep from guests' eyes.

She'd left her bra to dry out on the lion's head with her panties, not wanting it to soak the party dress, which was the color of a cocker spaniel and the softest, plushest thing ever. In Barneys she'd stroked it like a pet, refusing to leave it behind in the fitting room despite Gretchen's trying to convince her to buy instead the kind of boring black dress you put on a person you're trying to hide.

At last, she stepped onto a groomed path and into the glow of faux gaslight streetlamps. She dug mud from beneath her chipped French manicure and pulled duckweed from her hair. The lighter lay underwater, forever lost.

At Serenity Pond she stared at Swann's Way across the endless lawn that attracted white-shitting Canada geese her mother paid a geese-shooing-dog-handling service to get rid of. Every room in the mansion blazed for the party, edges blurring to gas. She raised Hunter's flask as the timed fountain at the pond's center gave its once-a-minute burst, the last drops hanging in the air a long moment, suspended to nothing.

Two-foot-long fishes came to the surface of water the groundskeepers freshened monthly with blue dye. A black and orange one snouted the air. A flesh-colored koi pleaded with its eyes.

"Can't," Carley said, her breath turning to fog. When the groundskeepers had stopped feeding the fish that first autumn after the pond was built, she'd snuck them shrimp and crab from the kitchen, which at the time didn't have locks on the refrigerators. Being ten at the time, she'd thought Gretchen had ordered a diet to flatten their stomachs.

Turned out koi didn't *have* stomachs. Food went through them all summer—they could eat forever—but when it got cold, their systems slowed down. Food sat in their intestines and rotted. To live in winter, they needed to starve.

ON ANY FRIDAY at six p.m., on an elevated eastbound platform at the hub of the Long Island Rail Road, women clutch shopping bags abulge with promises while briefcased men try to read papers in the wind before giving up to read each other. Across the track, teenage girls their daughters' ages huddle with Kate Spade purses held tight against their bodies, planning a night in Manhattan a world away from their parents and checking out young men two platforms over who look like their parents' gardeners and pool boys. Caught ogling, they edge toward dark-skinned women who remind them of their once-upon-a-time nannies.

To change here, at Jamaica, is to never set foot on the ground. To never feel on one's neck the hot thick breath of Goat and Lamb Livestock Market or Human Hair Beauty Supplies. To never read the neon promises of Grace Iron Works and Do Rite Auto Glass and Robin Hood Chicken, places named for what's supposed to be. To change at Jamaica is to stay a story in the air.

With the screech of metal on metal, Bree's connection arrived. Doors opened on both sides of the train, bridging the gap between platforms. "People are trying to *get* places," snapped a woman, losing her grip on her purchases while trying to get around Bree. She snatched up her Saks bag with a red-creased palm. People rushed in and out and only Bree stood still. Jamaica: eleven routes converging, one hundred thousand people passing through.

Three steps forward and Bree would be on the eastbound train to Meridian, a leg closer to Fox Glen. Several more and she'd be through the railcar to the opposite platform, fleeing back to Manhattan, to Alphabet City, to her fish tank and books. Two tracks over, another train would chug south toward Vernal, where Bree had been born and her sisters had settled and their mother had died.

Twelve tracks, ten platforms, eleven routes. A place to change one's mind.

"Your funding's come true," Darren had told her on the phone. He always knew official things pre-officially.

"Is it the Chatterby?" After all the applications she'd filled out since the E.T. Wahlrod Fellowship had run out—grant money she'd managed to make last nearly three years instead of the two for which it had been intended, another foundation *finally* understood her work. "A full or a—"

"The Chat . . ." Her former professor sighed. "Dear. No. This is more of a . . . residency."

"Oh," she said. "*Oh.*" She hadn't expected him to petition Blaine University to reconsider her for Writer-in-Residence. He'd sounded outright annoyed, in fact, when she'd suggested it last month, saying, *Your references didn't help your application. Three dismissals in a year?* But of course she'd hoped, still. She could see it now: Bree McEnroy sitting at the head of an oak conference table, encouraging undergraduates to look beyond the approval of their peers and their families and the critics.

"There's a family," Darren said, "on Long Island."

Nurturing experimentation. Bolstering deconstruction. Fostering the anti- and the meta-.

"They need a book written. With . . . specific . . . stipulations. Call it a commission." Darren cleared his throat. "They say fate flings serendipity at artists with the whimsy of tourists tossing coins to natives."

"*They* don't say that. No one says that." She hated her heart for beating so fast. "It's not a *saying*. You made it up just now."

"It's lucrative." He went silent.

She'd maxed out her last credit card, her cokehead landlord was running short of patience for late rent, and she had thirty-five dollars to her name. As mercenary as *commission* sounded, there might be certain ideas—yet-unwritten stories—with which she could part. The one about the lawyer, for instance, whose right arm takes up a newspaper route without his consent and grows strong enough to drag his body behind. The arm has terrible aim, every paper landing in a puddle, newsprint smearing illegibly. It is also having an affair with the lawyer's wife. Frightened and jealous, the lawyer ultimately severs it, despite its attachment to his writing hand. A celebration—she intended it—of language's self-cannibalization.

She envisioned the final draft written in longhand on a roll of cream wallpaper—*an installation* the Wellses would give its own room. Pasted over the walls, ceiling, and floor, the work would deepen as visitors touched it, smudged it, scuffed it. A living monument to language's demise.

Warhol's socialite portraits. Picasso's *Guernica*. Calder's fountain, mercury flowing like melted mirrors. *Commission* need not be hollow.

Twenty-five thousand dollars upon her patron's approval of the final draft, plus a small living stipend to be paid immediately, enough to cover her rent until December. "There are," Darren continued, "a few unusual provisions. You need to create the work on-site, live there to assure you're *available* to them whenever they want. Very tight time frame. Social obligations written into the contract. A wrap-up at the project's end with what you might call an educational bent." He took a breath. "Also, dragons."

"*What?*"

"Knights. Maidens. Armor. Magic. And battles to the death."

Train doors closed and opened, blinking chances. Bree rubbed at a speck of grime in her eye. To the west, eviction. To the south, shame. To the east, dragons.

THE KOI'S SUCTION-CUP mouths begged the air with kisses.

"Food would kill you," Carley yelled. Her fingers connected with paper as she shoved the flask back into her purse. The pages fought back as she tried to crush them, the edges razoring her wet fingers with invisible cuts.

EASTBOUND, A TRAIN races through Queens toward Meridian, a rail yard, a graveyard, and buildings stained to nicotine, invisible to people who see them each day. Graffiti rushes by unread—words morphing into pictures, tangled like snakes, interwoven and impenetrable—a language of the dead.

Bree squinted through her tearful Plexiglas reflection. They said, *I was here.*

CARLEY SAT IN the Serenity Rock Garden across from the pond, tracing spirals with the fingers of one hand and holding the manuscript in the other. *Great*, she'd e-mailed back to Bree McEnroy every time she'd received one those attachments she hadn't been able to make herself read.

She licked a paper cut, tasted salt, read the first page. At page fifty, she clamped her hands over her mouth. Behind the Serenity Pagoda, she threw up.

HALFWAY BETWEEN THE North and South shores of Long Island is Meridian, a town more often referred to as Moreland—the mall that took it over. Like its courts and college, its breath-strips of lawn and the fifteen-hundred-square-foot split-levels they front, its train station stands in the shadow of the three-floor, four-hundred-store Galleria.

It had been a single story when Bree was a child, anchored by JCPenney—where her mother had taken her and her sisters to buy clothing for special occasions—and Macy's, where they'd ogled mannequins dressed in clothing their mother said was the province of "richies" and got their hands slapped for touching. Always during such trips there was one perfect moment: the first instant Bree's hand connected with the heavy brass door handle at the entrance. Anticipating the burnt-sugar-and-Freon smell, and the mannequins with their matching shoes and bags, and the neat piles of unaffordable Gap sweaters and jeans that promised an all-American someday, anything seemed possible.

The glow of Nordstrom and Bloomingdale's signs now muted the stars and illuminated the platform where Bree stood checking her watch, peering down the track for a headlight, and studying the transit map. To the east of the knobs of land Fitzgerald had dubbed East and West Egg was a quail ova Fitzgerald hadn't bothered to mention.

"Like a Fabergé," Francis Wells had said when she'd come out to Fox Glen to sign her contract. "A world to crack open."

"A custom-made world," said Gretchen Wells.

"The only one of its—"

The door to what Bree's mother would have called the *den* and Gretchen had referred to as the *drawing room* flew open to reveal a short, heavy girl in a denim miniskirt and patterned tights whose candy-stripes tumefied as they climbed her thighs.

"Huh," she said, looking Bree up and down. "So you're the love they're buying?"

CARLEY STOOD AT the edge of Serenity Pond, fistfuls of words awaiting drowning. Did the Author think she was ten years old or just moronic? Everything was so corny and obvious and you wouldn't ever want to be

friends with *anyone* in this book, so that even if you *did* like all that Arthurian crap you'd want to throw it across the room and concuss the characters.

The wind fluttered the pages, begging for her to release them to the
water. The koi stared up at them like food.

Taking her pink glitter-gel pen from her purse, she stabbed the paper
deeper and deeper. And then, beneath the faux gaslight, she began.

THE PENULTIMATE STOP on the Mallard Bay Line of the Long Island Rail
Road is a one-platform station with a lot overflowing with parked Beemers
and limos and wives.

"Fox Glen," called the conductor.

"I can't do it," she'd cried to Darren over the phone just hours before,
though she'd been sending pages for two weeks and had advanced her
landlord her entire stipend from the Wellses and hired a fish-sitter.

"Try not to get fired."

"The mother's mean. The way she looks at me—"

"*Mean?* How old are you?"

"One month to write a book—one shot, and no guarantee of payment
unless Birthday Girl likes it."

"Then write something one would *like*." Darren sighed. "Is that not the
point of what we do?"

Twenty-five thousand was enough to pay off the credit card debt she'd
acquired since the Wahlrod had run out. Enough to feed her fish, her
landlord's nose, herself. Enough to buy time after this was over to finally
write *Geppetto in Florence*, her tale of a time-traveler who redresses wrongs
wrought upon artists throughout history.

For three years she'd done research for the novel, collecting boxes of
notes about artists' humiliation and suffering in the hope of redeeming
herself in the eyes of the critics. A *writer's writer*, she dreamt of being called,
no longer remembered as the author of a *seven-hundred-page death sentence
in Cyberia* (thank you, *Washington Post*) or *postmodern death rattle* (fuck
you, too, *San Francisco Chronicle*).

No matter what you've heard, went the new novel's first—and thus far only—line, Geppetto sought not to vandalize time, but restore it.

"Fox Glen," repeated the conductor.

She stepped onto the platform, her fingers reading the grain of the linen invitation in her pocket: **In Honor of Bree McEnroy.** It felt like money.

In the parking lot, a limousine driver held up a sign: **Macintosh, Brie.**

She raised her hand slowly, as if unsure of an answer. Her fingers stroked the air.

CHAPTER 6

At every moment in Fox Glen, a party was in some stage of creation. Dubbed *galas* or *soirées* or *bashes*, they were conceived months before their births and remembered for years. Living fictions, they seized their first breaths long before mansion doors swung open and gasped their final ones long after the last slurry farewell.

It was at parties, after all, that Fox Glenites availed themselves of the most luscious bitters: a dearest friend's husband's erection; a third vodka tonic disguised as sparkling Ty Nant; a pyramid of potato cones filled with salmon tartar and beluga and crème fraîche, devoured in the bathroom where only mirrors stared. Tonight in the octagonal, ballroom-sized entrance hall of Swann's Way, two hundred people complimented their anorexic hostess's gastronomic refinement and obeyed their jug-wine-bodied host's commandment to try a glass of the Amnis Reserve Cabernet—*pressed*, he said repeatedly, *from the best grapes of eleven vineyards*—and feigned belief in the Wellses' assertions that their daughter couldn't wait to banter about Sartre with her very own Author. Beneath the grand chandelier igniting the stained glass of the dome above, people milled about tables shining with silver chafing dishes and bars proffering backlit liquors while trying not to bump into the five-foot-tall vases of callas blooming the colors of flame. (Though the party planner had assured Gretchen that such arrangements would *render the room warmer*, after a few glasses of the Amnis and in peripheral vision, they in fact evoked people caught on fire.)

Nearly two hours into the party, when the Wellses' Author still had not appeared, Swann's Way glowed with equal parts anxiety—it would be impossible to keep up with her in conversation, as she was acquainted with Darren Connelly, whose books everyone owned and nobody ever finished or understood—and anticipatory schadenfreude—perhaps she'd already thrown over her patrons.

Gretchen Wells, busy chiding her assistant, Grace, for not finding a way to hurry the author down after her late arrival at the servants' door an hour earlier, did not notice when the Author finally made her entrance. Nor did Francis Wells, engrossed in whispering to Suzanne Cay about the fingernail scratches she'd left on his stomach that afternoon. Nor did Suzanne's son, Hunter, preoccupied with fighting the symptoms of a cold to which he hadn't given in until his best friend had put words to it.

It was Carley Wells whose attention was caught by an odd sound coming from the balcony. She looked up. "Holy shit!"

The Author's vinyl pants squeaked as she took a second step down one of the symmetrical cantilever staircases. Amber Weiss clapped her hands over her mouth.

Conversations fell away. Fox Glenites prided themselves on collection—of shoes and statues, of trophies and friends—but not since Emily Leighton Logan had pedestaled a spiky orange sculpture in her Great Room had they been so flummoxed by a display. Below her dire, black skintight pants the Author sported platform boots; above them an unbuttoned men's tailcoat over a cinched men's vest over nothing.

Gretchen signaled with a finger curl. A server trailed her up the stairs with Dom Pérignon and two flutes.

She took the Author's arm, and walked her back up. "You were expected long ago," she said through a tight smile.

"Missed my train." The Author took some folded papers from her jacket pocket. "We need to talk. There's a . . . a . . . serious . . . problem."

"This isn't the time." She brought to mind a maid Gretchen had fired for trying to fix a jammed vacuum cleaner by dumping its contents on the sitting room carpet. *But I would've vacuumed it back up*, the girl had protested, as if you could toss dirt around without leaving traces.

"But there's something you need to—"

"It is my and Francis's honor," she announced to the crowd below as she pressed a glass into the Author's hand, "to renew the time-honored tradition of patronage."

"Like de' Medicis," Francis boomed from the floor. *Duh Medicis.*

"To art." Gretchen pretended to drink. Just *Medicis*, she'd begged him. No *De*, no *Duh*. Just once, couldn't he edit himself for her happiness? She couldn't make herself look down into any of her guests' faces, his gaffe doubtless reflected in them. She imagined two hundred glasses smashing to the marble floor, a collage of bubbles and shards.

"Totally bored," Carley told Hunter below. She tried to hand him her glass, the bartenders having been instructed by Francis to overlook Hunter's (and *only* Hunter's) minority to allow him the courtesy of "a civilized drink."

"Not up for holding you under the shower again." Though he meant it to sound playful, an edge crept into his voice.

It wasn't that he resented stripping out of his suit to his boxers and washing Carley's hair for her after he and Amber had discovered her passed out on her bed when they'd returned from Ian's. Or wrapping her in a towel and rocking her on the bathroom floor as she drunk-cried apologies. Nor was he squeamish about her nakedness—they'd seen each other's bodies before, they were just *bodies*. But remembering the way she'd pressed against him, the palpability of her want, made him angry at himself and angry at Bunny and angry at everything for not staying still.

"You went into the water," he snapped. "Drunk. Alone. And what if your parents had come upstairs and found you? You had *my* flask. They trust me."

"My drowning would've seriously fucked up your image."

"That's not . . . fair." His eyes teared as he sneezed into the crook of his elbow.

Amber sucked down her drink and smiled with forced casualness. It wasn't the shared joint she was so worried about. It was the exchange of saliva last night following what had happened that *shouldn't* have. He reached into his jacket pocket, came up empty, and sneezed again into his sleeve. Amber sidestepped out of his airspace but kept staring into his eyes.

Definitely a mistake, last night, though at the time he'd thought of it like helping a person carry packages or giving someone stranded a ride home.

"There's maybe cold medicine in my parents' bathroom," Carley said. She raised her hand to rub his back, then caught herself, combing her fingers through her own hair to hide her intent. He hated that what had been natural between them had become so loaded.

"I don't need anything," he whispered. He scrubbed at his cheekbone to ward off further sneezing until he could duck into a bathroom for tissues. Like his cold pills and his Vicodin, the handkerchiefs he routinely carried were at Ian's. Not until they'd returned to Swann's Way had he realized Amber, whom he'd again given his coat on the drive to Ian's, had forgotten it behind. There hadn't been time to go back for it.

"Thanks... thank you... for... welcoming... me?" Carley's Present said from the balcony.

He fought a wave of chills and tried to reconcile this collision of androgyny and stammer with the intellect that had produced *Scylla*. Where the unicorn fetishism fit in was beyond even fevered imagination.

GRETCHEN DESCENDED THE staircase with the Author. At the bottom, she crossed her arms over her chest, deepening her cleavage and making Gretchen's stomach clench the way it did when she tasted butter or overheard Francis's masturbatory bathroom groaning. "What an outfit," said Edie Weiss. "*Luuuve* it!" Last weekend, Suzanne Cay had overheard her call the Wellses' patronage *a stunt*.

Gretchen tolerated Bernie Weiss and his Brooklyn accent and giddy ties for the sake of Marvel-Bra and her noblesse oblige and her own identically accented husband, but for Bernie's wife she'd lost patience long ago. Eight years they'd lived here, but you'd think Edie had just gotten off the stoop.

"Adapt," Gretchen had begged her not long after their families had first moved to Fox Glen, when Edie had shown up for a prospective members' summer cocktail party at the Glen Club wearing an off-the-shoulder magenta blouse she'd bought on clearance several years earlier at Mandee, and matching cork-wedge sandals. For months Gretchen had been trying to convince her to donate her wardrobe to charity and engage a personal shopper on the Gold Mile.

"Like you know from adapting?" Edie had said, adjusting the elasticized neckline that climbed over her shoulders when her arms weren't flattened to her sides. As she'd gone to shake the president of the membership committee's hand, the ruffled overlay had sprung up around her neck like the collar of a clown. "Look, forget I said that, Gretch. I'm just saying you gotta be who you are." The final word of which she'd pronounced *awe*.

Twenty years it had taken Gretchen to get back to where she should be in life, a place she hadn't counted on missing when she'd married Francis. Edie *knew* how much this meant to her, to feel finally at home after being adrift. Just the night before, as they'd sat in the kitchen of Edie's new house, which Edie called *intimidating* for its "cold" marble countertops and glass-doored Sub-Zero refrigerator that made her feel "naked," Gretchen had read aloud to Edie from the Glen Club's materials for prospective members, giggling with anticipation like a twelve-year-old girl about to go to her first dance. "Invitation to the Club is based solely upon a family's character," she'd read from the charter, a clause that implied that the Club didn't exclude on the basis of race, but did on the basis of wearing rayon, and laughing bawdily, and retelling an anecdote from a sitcom about proctologists called *Bottoms Up*.

"You couldn't even *try* to blend?" Gretchen had said at the end of the party, after the head of the membership committee had pretended not to understand Gretchen's inquiry about future such events. "For me?"

Edie had stared at her a long time. "That's something you ask a friend?"

It would take four years and Suzanne Cay for Gretchen to receive her invitation. Suzanne, the godsend who herself had been accepted into the Club the day after she arrived in Fox Glen because her sister, Plum Buchanan, had married into *those* Buchanans. Suzanne turned out to know Francis, of all people, from her youth. Suzanne, who'd sponsored into the Club both the Wellses and the Weisses (Francis having insisted that he wouldn't join any club that wouldn't have Bernie). The best thing Francis had ever brought to their marriage, Suzanne was to replace Edie as Gretchen's closest friend.

Edie's shar-pei forehead creased now as she slapped the Author's leg. As it happened, Edie had not only owned pants like that two decades ago but had been wearing them the night she'd met Bernie at Our Lady of Something's Italian Feast in Astoria, where they'd reached for zeppolis at the same time. "Who would've thought it, two Jews falling in love in a church parking lot?"

Gretchen had nothing against Jews. She was friends with the Strausses and Goldmans and Fursts, all of whom knew how to be Jewish demurely. Why, the Rosenthals were even religious—Mimi turned off her cell Friday evenings—but you didn't hear *them* foisting their Judiosity into every conversation.

"I used to have *this*." Edie squeezed the Author's waist and shrugged extravagantly.

"Your daughter's vision for her book," the Author whispered to Gretchen, "is closer to Chaucer than Rowling." She shifted her hands to her hips, her breasts fondling each other like incestuous siblings. "*Wife-of-Bath* Chaucer."

Gretchen tried to recall who, exactly, Chaucer was, and wondered at the whereabouts of her daughter, who was supposed to be responsible for introducing her Author to the guests.

The Author peered at Gretchen. *Chaucer.* Had Carley read him in school this year? Or was he a contemporary of Darren Connelly? The Author was quizzing her, Gretchen was certain, sneering the way the authors assigned to each table at the O'Neil Foundation for Adult Literacy dinners always did at women like Suzanne, entertained by moneyed ignorance. She'd so hoped for a *friendly* writer when they'd started shopping for one, or at least one who wrote comprehensible books and didn't show up for her contract signing wearing a bowling shirt, gauchos, and fishnet stockings. But as Francis had pointed out after hiring the Author over Gretchen's objections, such disaffection and attire might well be construed by their daughter as *interesting*. That Carley had been insisting on keeping the Author's work-in-progress to herself thus far seemed to bear this out. "She's taking ownership," Francis had said, overriding Gretchen's concern about their not yet seeing a word of what they were paying for.

Hunter Cay cut through the crowd carrying three drinks, one of which Gretchen assumed destined for her daughter. "So you're not a *stranger* to the Island?" Edie said to the Author. "*Vernal!*" she said at the top of her lungs, announcing the woman's working-class origins to the room. "Of *course* I know Vernal."

"Tune her out by counting her pores," Gretchen said into the Author's ear, a tip bequeathed to her years ago by her own mother about how to pretend to listen when other women talked. She flashed her a half-smile with a hint of a nose wrinkle, a facial emoticon Gretchen had honed over the years in the mirror to mean *just between us girls*. The Author narrowed her eyes.

At the back of the room, between the staircases and blocking the double doors through which the catering staff needed to pass en route to the subterranean kitchen, Gretchen found Amber and Carley cooing at a Latin server whose hairy chest made his white shirt appear dingy. Carley took a lamb and zucchini tartlet and a mini venison potpie from his tray, crumbs clinging to her dress. Hunter handed the girls drinks.

On her BlackBerry, Gretchen typed a message to the party planner to either have an undershirt procured for meat pie boy or send him home. "*Habla inglés?*" Gretchen whispered into his ear. "No *más* for her."

She sniffed her daughter's drink. "It's virgin," Carley said. "*Diet.*"

"Just soda," said Edie's daughter.

"They're under control," said Hunter. "Trust me."

Despite whispers at the Club, Gretchen did indeed trust Hunter's judgment, supposing rumors about him to have been fomented by members with very unpopular children—girls who chewed on chapped lips and limp hair, ferrety boys who catalogued science fiction trivia. Such children's parents were liable to exaggerate Hunter's occasional misstep: his stumbling on deck at brunch on the Gardners' yacht this June, his whimsically driving with the top down during a thunderstorm in August, his forgetting by the end of the Club's Labor Day dance exactly whom he was supposed to be escorting (Bunny Gardner—infinitely forgettable).

"Why might your Author be complaining of a *problem?*" Gretchen asked her daughter.

Carley shrugged, the dress swallowing her neck like an animal intent on eating her. There had been two dresses with lovely lines last week when they'd shopped. The black one, a faux wrap, had given her daughter shape, suggesting angles where there weren't and revealing Carley's neck to be a good feature. But this one, Carley had insisted, was "fun."

"In the black dress you look like that actress," Gretchen had said as her daughter kept *touching* the brown one instead of looking at it in the mirror. "I don't remember her name, but the one who plays the makeup artist in that movie where she's in love with the actor but because she's . . . big he doesn't notice her."

"*Big.*"

"But he ends up falling in love with her. And she's thin in the end."

Carley made a sound like she was ridding herself of a hairball. "She's *the same* at the end. That's the *point* of the movie. He loves her for who she *is.*"

"I remember her looking considerably more . . . streamlined after—"

"That was the *actress. After* the movie. She was *paid* to gain forty pounds for the role, then crashed it off so she could play Squidgirl next."

"Let her wear what she wants," Francis had said later that night in bed.

"She wears ugly things to protect herself," she tried to tell him, "like something playing dead. You're not helping when you tell her strange outfits look *cute.* Neither, though he means well, is Hunter. She smiles for you in the moment to make *you* feel good, then spends God knows how much time afterward thinking about how you lied. How *cute* do you think that makes a person feel?"

Under the fuzz and the giggling, the fat and the crassness, there was a girl who had been born with gray eyes and who had skipped first grade because it was too easy for her and who, if she ever let her mother free her from her cocoon, could be *happy.*

From the center of the room, the party planner waved frantically.

"BlackBerry," Gretchen mouthed.

The party planner only waved harder and pointed at the floor.

Clean it up, she typed.

People knelt. Something rose unsteadily, a human spill.

Waving a broken Jimmy Choo, Cissy Gardner, known for guzzling attention at other people's social events, hobbled to a couch. Gretchen checked her watch. The Gold Mile was still open. If she sent Grace right away, Gretchen could have Cissy reshod within the hour. *A consummate hostess,* Cissy would have no choice but to call her. *The definition of graciousness.*

"Might I impose on you to help Carley show off her Author to her best advantage?" Gretchen asked Hunter. Innately—and often to her own detriment—her daughter was good at making other people look good. It was a skill worth honing—a powerful tool if the person you were promoting understood, albeit tacitly, that he or she owed you—but Gretchen was the last person Carley would allow to teach her anything.

"She can show herself off," Carley said. She grabbed Amber's hand. "We've gotta *pee.*"

"It's no imposition," Hunter said.

When Gretchen squeezed his hand in thanks, she found it unpleasantly moist.

She released it quickly. Color rose in his cheeks. She was immediately sorry, for what was a little perspiration? He was probably unwell, but he was *here* nonetheless, his presence beside her daughter suggesting to everyone that Carley had, indeed, angles.

"You're all right, Hunter?"

"Of course."

She lowered her voice. "Is Carley being . . . *taxing?*"

"Not at all."

The sounds of feigned enjoyment pitched higher and higher, Gretchen's party threatening to crack open. A shrill compliment behind her, a squealed greeting to the right. The squeak of the Author's pants.

"She's on drugs, I suspect."

Hunter coughed and shook his head. "No. *No.* She's just—"

"She's from *Vernal*," Gretchen whispered.

"Oh. Carley's Present. Well, I don't know about *drugs*, but there's something I don't quite understand. What she's writing . . . for Carley. . . . Have you *read*—"

"Cissy's walking about *barefoot*!" This inelegant did Cissy deem her party and the money that paid for it. *Mrs. Marvel-Bra*, she called Gretchen behind her back, despite Gretchen's always supporting Cissy's ideas in Club committee meetings and at Montclair board meetings and spending weeks looking for the perfect hostess gift on each of the rare occasions the Gardners had had them to dinner.

As she tapped a message to Grace to play farrier, something landed on her head. From her hair she pulled a dried leaf, painted ochre and calligraphed in black: *Indigestion is charged by God with enforcing morality on the stomach (Hugo)*.

"Oh," gasped Constance Vandergraf as a second leaf came down upon the tray of antelope carpaccio.

To match her harvest theme, Gretchen had commissioned *delicate* hand-painted leaves, which at intervals were to flutter from above gracefully, bearing quotations about the *joy* of parties.

A vermillion leaf inscribed with *What is food to some, is to others bitter poison (Lucretius)* caught on Hunter's blond waves. "Go decapitate the planner," he said, disentangling it. "I'll take care of the Present."

HUNTER WILLED HIMSELF to breathe shallowly as he watched guests wander the octagon, their faces flushed with the heat of so many bodies and the steam of chafing dishes and the fumes of liquor, a pinkening of flesh that extended even to the walls, the entire room tinted the hue of an infant WASP. They were its organs and blood. It neutralized and naturalized everything that entered it. A starving body could digest nearly anything. Even the Present.

Dolce&Gabbana, he imagined his mother thinking as she stared at the Present from across the room. She'd presume designer because she couldn't fathom Wal-Mart. *That retro-androgyny suggested last year on the runway.*

She has a bite to her like tonic water, he imagined Francis thinking. *Or licorice. The black and ropey kind.*

Hunter wished he had his journal so he could write it all down, the projections of other people's thoughts that came to him unwanted and overbusied his head.

"But your family can't possibly live in Vernal still? What with"—Edie stage-whispered—"the *element.*"

"They do," said the Present, turning. Her boot skidded on a crimson leaf as she walked away: *Unbidden guests are often welcomest when they are gone (Shakespeare).*

He caught up to her where she stood facing one of the giant vases, her back to him. When he grew closer he realized she was blowing her nose.

He waited until she'd balled the cocktail napkin. "May I get you a drink?" She shook her head without turning. "Hot water and lemon, a little bourbon? A toddy's just the thing if you're not feeling up to par."

When she turned to face him, he understood his mistake. She dabbed at tears still rolling down her cheeks. "How old are you supposed to be?"

"Older than the Cabernet. Younger than the scotch."

She shrugged and blew her nose again.

People nearby attributed the Author's tears to Edie Weiss, who'd doubtless said something that reflected badly on everyone. Suzanne Cay, standing by a bar with Francis and worrying about having forgotten to ask her son to tell her about the Author's published novel, mistook the shine on the Author's cheeks as a cosmetic that drew light to one's face. Francis missed Bree's face altogether as he stared at her chest: low thirties below the bust, three inches more across the fullest point. About a 34-C.

An indigo leaf the size of Hunter's hand fell between him and the Present: *Work is the curse of the drinking classes (Wilde).*

"I want to go home," she said, her voice raw with *home*'s impossibility. She covered her face but made no move to leave.

He cupped her elbow. "Breathe deep. I can help."

She said something into her hands. When he whispered for her to repeat it, she snapped, "Help *how?*"

"I can't *know* until you tell me what's wrong." He held his glass to his cheek, cut crystal limning cold angles on his skin.

"Who *are* you?"

"A friend of the family. A friend of Carley's."

"Wonderful taste you have in friends." She took from her pocket several mangled pages and thrust them into his hand.

One page in, he flagged a cocktail server.

How much longer—said a note in Carley's handwriting next to the paragraph in which Lancelot unpins Guinevere's hair—*til he pulls out his dick?*

Scrawled over a scene where Guinevere's pet unicorn lays its head in her lap was: *When Uni goes down, does the horn . . .*

Ménage à trois suggestions for Arthur, Guinevere, and Lancelot. S&M with chain mail. Foreplay on the round table. Carley had doodled frowny faces inside every O.

"Fuck," he said under his breath. "Excuse my language." He rubbed away the tickle of a sneeze before it could take hold. "Gretchen hasn't seen—?"

"I found them waiting in my room. The *mother* refused to even *look*—"

He tucked them into his own pocket and sighed. "Then we're fine."

"We?"

"*Oui.* Carley will apologize. You'll write something that doesn't involve unicorns. And everybody will live happily ever after." He turned away to cough deeply as her wine and his Glenlivet arrived. His eyes teared. His palms sweated. Just one—no, two more pills—would have taken the edge off his worrying about people resenting his sharing their air. Chronically healthy people, he imagined, enjoyed the moral superiority of conscientious gardeners: a neighbor's coughing signified bad caretaking, weeds, and a lawn pitted by rodents.

"Are you all right?"

No, he nearly said, though he was usually loathe to mention feeling ill. Later, he would come to understand that something about Bree brought forth truths. Tonight, he thought it to be fever and craving.

"Your parents know you drink like that?"

"Strictly medicinal. Numbs a sore throat." The words came without his permission. "God, I apologize. People who discuss their health are ever dreary."

"You're not dreary. Just loaded."

She said it matter-of-factly, as one might say *It's about to rain*, or *That's a minor Kandinsky*. He laughed for the first time in hours, despite knowing it would ignite another round of coughing.

"I don't usually sob on strangers' shoulders," she said. "Or strange kids' shoulders."

"I'm not a kid. Though about *strange* I'll let you decide. But I'd think to a person adrift in a wine-dark sea of ones and zeros, anything non-binary might seem terra firma." The line had appeared in a footnote where Odysseus had, for a short time, jumped out of cyberspace into an ever-revolving Aeron desk chair that sat before a stranger's monitor. But then a footnote to the footnote informed the reader that the scene, in fact, had been only a dream.

"Am I supposed to be flattered at being quoted?"

"Just enjoy yourself—let me introduce you around. Tomorrow you'll sit down with Carley, whom I promise you'll find to be nothing like the brat she's made herself out to be, and come up with an idea for a book you both can live with." He tapped the stem of her wineglass. "Sip. I'll cut you off before you belt out something from *Rent* or try to make out with a Doric column, both of which happened at the Club's Roaring Twenties Gala this spring. And so Odysseus, spurned by Athena, took for his guide the only god who would have him: Dionysus."

"You try very hard."

"Thank you. For noticing." His breath snagged as he inhaled. He tried not to wince as the cough ripped though him.

She looked around the room. "Do you even *have* parents? Someone to recover your body?"

"It sounds worse than it feels." He lowered his voice. "But if you're worried about catching . . . I'm sorry I'm so *symptomatic* . . . I couldn't blame you for limiting your exposure."

She shook her head. "Just wondering who's supposed to be watching out for *you*."

"*Supposed to.*" He laughed. "Like a field trip buddy. *We can't leave yet, Mister Bus Driver. Someone's still in the . . .*" He barely caught himself before *restroom*, Carley's supposed whereabouts in the forefront of his mind. He needed to lie down for just a few minutes, needed a break, needed her to return. She was the only person in the world to whom he could make himself whisper that he *needed* anything. ". . . *gift shop.*"

"Take a breather from the scotch, Dionysus," she said gently as Connor and Carolyn Dalton caught his eye. For the first time he heard a trace of Vernal in her voice, an accent she'd doubtless worked hard to efface. *Breath-a.*

"My buddy?" he whispered as the Daltons approached, their hands extended. "That would be Carley."

CHAPTER 7

On the highest stone terrace behind Swann's Way, a pair of stone panthers crouched at the balustrade in the scent garden, searching the lawn below for prey. On the lowest, a nude Aphrodite reclined in a deflowered rose garden among heaps of mulch lain at the base of each plant for the winter (unsightly, complained Gretchen; necessary, claimed her gardening staff). And on the terrace between them, a bench with legs carved into flute-playing satyrs bore a greasy paper bag of hors d'oeuvres, a bottle of Amnis Cabernet, and two girls telling lies.

Amber said she'd slipped the hot Cuban waiter a hundred dollars to raid trays before they made it out of the kitchen and gave a weak-chinned bartender some tongue for the wine. But the truth was probably that she'd just asked them nicely. It wasn't like Amber to dash cash, Edie being the only mother in Fox Glen to heed the admonitions of PAP (Parents Against Pot), PAX (Parents Against Ecstasy), and PAO (Parents Against Opiates—pronounced as in Kung Pao Chicken) about controlling one's child's spending money. And she wasn't the kind of girl who'd make out with someone to get anything but attention.

"You only had a few puffs of his joint. You won't get sick," Carley assured her, though with Amber's luck she would just in time for her sister's twelfth birthday party at Disney World next weekend. Edie acted like Amber was sororicidal if she as much as sniffled around Jazzy, who as a little kid had had the kind of scary asthma that required emergency room visits. Edie checked used tissues for "color of discharge." She quarantined. Never mind that Jazzy had outgrown the attacks eight years ago.

The wine made them squeeze each other's hands as the air heavied with mist and the cold seeped through their dresses. The hors d'oeuvres hugged them from inside, their lips and tongues caressing brioche-swaddled pears and seafood-stuffed dumplings and a mound of beluga and countless tiny meat pies and a silky wedge of Fromage d'Affinois with peppery crackers and slices of duckling nested on sweet potato pancakes with candied quince and prosciutto-wrapped figs on lollipop sticks and bread sticks dyed to harvest colors.

Carley's pantyhose bit into her stomach. She drank from the bottle, then offered it to Amber. Amber covered her mouth. She'd developed a hair-trigger gag reflex. "Breathe deep," Carley said. "You can control it. Just breathe."

She walked to the other side of the bench and twisted sections of Amber's hair to distract her, making soft knots and little braids. In middle school they'd had sleepovers where they'd brush each other's hair while they told stories about Hunter until they tingled. *Did you see his cool loafers?* (After Hunter had come to Fox Glen, every guy at school had copied his footwear, foregoing tennis shoes for anything but tennis.) *Did you watch him dancing with Marcia Braden at Winterfest?* (Nobody should be ignored, Hunter thought, even people who smelled weird and talked to themselves.) *Did you hear he told Langston "Bullying is the produce of cowards"? That's province, Carley. Same difference.* (The bully in question had been his ninth grade social studies teacher. The victim had been a kid Mr. Langston gave a nickname after every failed quiz—*Mercator* for misidentifying North America, *Ickaroy* for misnaming the native American tribes of New York. During his two-day suspension, Hunter had drafted a twenty-page, seventy-five citation paper on the negative effects of shame in the classroom, which he'd left on the headmaster's desk with a one-line note: *I am not sorry.*)

For years they'd told these stories. He was so different and special and brave that it didn't matter that they would never be his girlfriend because he was too beautiful and they were too ordinary. Their love for him had only made them love each other more.

Amber turned to face Carley, mid-braid. She took a deep breath. "Something happened."

IT HAS THE *tannic sweetness of green tea ice cream,* Hunter told Carolyn Dalton.

A *bouillabaisse of mythology and technology,* he told the Vandergrafs.

Like drinking absinthe while wandering Disneyland, he proclaimed, and for a moment the author of *Between Scylla and Alta Vista* was so intrigued that she forgot he was describing her own out-of-print novel.

Imagine going on the Net to check one small thing—Cissy Gardner wiggled her toes in anticipation when he paused—*and finding yourself lost there forever.*

Scylla, people said to each other, a truncation that suggested familiarity. Despite her appearance, clearly the Author was someone of whom they ought to have heard. The room itched with sibilance, the word flowing over tongues, tapping front teeth, forcing lips open like a sigh. Perhaps they'd read her book and forgotten. Yes, that *must* be it.

"I've read all your work!" Suzanne Cay cooed. Why, even Suzanne—who'd been heard complaining poolside that *W* contained entirely too many articles and recently had introduced underwear-model-turned-author Clive Close as "a fictional novelist" at an O'Neil Foundation fundraiser—had heard of her.

"All," she repeated. Beaming, Francis and Gretchen joined the throng around their Author.

"There's only the one novel," Bree said and waited for Hunter to spin her recent lack of publications into something like *a period of artistic germination.* "Also a few short stories," she added, when she realized he was staring up into the cupola, lost in his head. "But that was a long...long time ago."

"In *The New Yorker?*" said Suzanne.

"No."

"You're sure?"

"Um, yes," said Bree.

"Wonderful!" Suzanne nodded at her hosts.

"Better than Grisham," said Francis. "And much higher brow!"

"I wouldn't say anything if you *had* been in *The New Yorker*, but now—since you haven't—I can say Tina Brown ruined—"

Hunter sneezed twice into the crook of his elbow. "That was a long time ago, Mother. A century, practically."

"Grace," Gretchen said. "She's returned, with shoes." She pointed Francis toward the door. "And the Laphams have arrived."

"Now the book for Carley—" Suzanne said when she'd run out of epithets for Tina.

Hunter ran an index finger under his collar.

"Your son is impressively stoic."

"Stoic?"

"He manages to be so *on*, despite his feeling wretched."

"Wretched?"

Hunter shot Bree a look. "A mere *soupçon* of a cold," he told his mother. "Nothing to get in the way of Monday's postmark. The essay needs only one more proofreading anyway."

"Why, I have the most inspired idea! Perhaps Bree could take a look at your application and suggest—"

"Mother, no. It's . . . done." He bit his lip as he watched something over Bree's shoulder. "Excuse me," he said. "Please." She turned to see a beefy man with thinning red hair pumping people's hands.

"Larry must have come right from the airport," Suzanne said, fluttering her hand in the air. "He so wanted to meet you. We so loved your book. The main character—remind me of his name, I'm so poor with—"

"Odysseus."

"Odysseus! Of course. We both adored how *Odysseus* . . ." She looked around quizzically, as if just now noticing her son was gone. "The way Odysseus was—"

"Trying to get home?"

"Exactly." Suzanne waved frantically.

"To Ithaca."

"Ithaca!" Suzanne squealed. "Larry, we're discussing Ithaca." She squeezed Bree's arm. "Larry studied in Ithaca."

"Lawrence Talbright. Call me Larry." He squashed Bree's hand. "Gorgeous place, Ithaca. Cornell, sixty-nine."

"Different Ithaca, different story. We were talking about a hero—"

"Oh, *The Odyssey*." Larry patted Suzanne's hand like a teacup dog. "Remember Hunter's essay about it last—"

"Your book is being read in schools?" Suzanne signaled the champagne server with her index finger. "How wonderful!"

"Not . . . no. *Between Scylla and Alta Vista* is about a modern-day Odysseus, an anti-hero, who searches for the other Ithaca. The Greek one. In the World Wide Web."

Suzanne's forehead creased, her eyes remaining open unnaturally wide.

How could Bree have thought she'd been *talking*? Hunter had been charming people; she'd just been nodding. "*Scylla* is a commentary on the electronic age." She heard herself speak of it in present tense, like a phantom limb. "He begins by Googling Homer and gets hits for a thousand *Simpsons* Web sites instead of *The Odyssey*. Thus, he begins to doubt his own existence. For how can he *be* without a creator?"

"Indeed," said Larry. "Indeed."

Suzanne drained her champagne. Larry's smile snapped. They didn't want to *keep her all to themselves*, they assured her. Neither did the Bellmores, to whom they handed her off, or the Stillmans, or the Whitings, to whom Bree found herself explaining the difference between a novel's Subject (Man Gets Lost in the Internet) and Theme (Questing for One's Self Is Futile). Soon she was among people without being *with* them, attempting to untangle her hair from a branch of an ornamental tree bearing cornucopian vegetables while staring up into the gold dome above the octagon—whose center, she just realized, looked exactly like an inverted nipple—and shifting from leg to leg, her pants making that awful noise, as if just tonight they'd learned to speak.

CHAPTER 8

Everyone a protagonist and one hundred plotlines at once, a party is a tangle of want and fear and need. "Jackie Kennedy used vegetables that way," Suzanne said, pointing at orange and yellow chiles arranged with tea roses the color of dawn. "Yes," said Gretchen, "yes," counting it as the twenty-seventh floral compliment she'd received. Twenty-eight if one counted Edie Weiss crowing *it looks like you spent a fortune.* But really one couldn't. "De' Medici," Bree heard Francis tell Perry Vandergraf, and imagined Michelangelo loitering in Florence the day after a snowstorm, his commissions having evaporated after the death of his patron, Lorenzo. Into the courtyard of the Medici palazzo he is summoned by Lorenzo's son, Piero, who cares little for art and less for its creators. *I have a job for you,* Piero says with a smirk. He points to a drift. *From snow, sculpt me a man.*

"Slut," Carley said to Amber. A worm twisted on the ground, its insides moving ahead of its skin. Francis rested his hand on Suzanne's back, his thumb feeling for the star-embossed back closure of the Marvel-Bra Carina that held her breasts as high as they'd been when she was eighteen and he was poor and they'd dated in secret, before she'd chosen a silly college-that-was-not-college—a finishing school—over him and married a man twice her age from six generations of money. Bree imagined time-traveling Geppetto propping Piero's lifeless body up in the courtyard, molded with snow. Hunter tried to fight the room's spinning by concentrating on a calla arrangement, hundreds of blooms arranged into the shape of a single lily, while the pills he'd filched from Gretchen's medicine chest kicked in too fast and hard. *The part is the whole*, he told himself as he stared at the vase, *the whole is the part*.

And standing beneath the pediment of Swann's Way, flanked by Corinthian columns, an uninvited guest convinced himself to walk in if it killed him.

"In honor," he whispered, "of Bree McEnroy."

CHAPTER 9

Scylla, Larry Talbright said to Cissy Gardner, wondering where Suzanne's no-doubt-drunk son was hiding. *Scylla*, Cissy repeated to her husband, falling in love with her new shoes and hating Gretchen Wells for having purchased them. *Scylla*, said Greer Gardner to Connor Dalton, both wishing for sons like Hunter Cay, who'd surely explained the book to his stunning, insipid mother.

Sil-́uh. Even as they relished its taste on their tongues, people worried. Perhaps it had been misspoken to them or they'd misheard. Perhaps it was *skil-́uh* or *sil-́ee-uh.* Perhaps repeating such an error was a faux pas as indecorous as Edie Weiss's demanding of Hunter Cay—as he weaved charmingly toward the back of the room, his severely tailored black-on-black striped Versace accessorized with a pocket square of roguery—"What *genre* is it?"

"*Recherché Pomo,*" he'd answered, a phrase evoking something tomato-based. A stew made with rabbit or brains.

A new wave of whispers came at cross-currents to *Scylla*, a swell that began at the front door and worked its way back as the crowd parted for a cane and the man behind it. *Justin Leighton.*

"Forgive the pop-by," Justin told Gretchen. "Happened upon my parents' invitation . . . they're still in Portofino, yes. We were college compadres, Bree and I, and when I saw her name . . ." He relished Gretchen Wells's stunnedness even as his chin began numbing, the first sign of one of his panic attacks. "To lay eyes again on Bree would be delightastic."

People he didn't know hugged him and patted his back as Gretchen led him through the party. He couldn't believe he'd ever borne all this touching. *Was* that numbness in his chin, or perhaps just the fear of numbness? Just the fear of an attack could bring one on, the snake eating its tail.

"She said she needed air." Edie Weiss pointed at the doors at the back of the room. "I told her how to get to the backyard."

"*Terrace gardens*," Gretchen corrected stiffly.

Edie shrugged and rolled her eyes. "The problem with vinyl? The shvitzing."

"HAD TO PHONE up Darren," a voice called behind Bree, "and confirm this was verily genuine." Bree knew the voice before she turned. Justin, who *phoned up* people. Who wore silk velvet overcoats—tonight's was midnight blue—or leather blazers. Who tied back his long black hair at the nape with black ribbons and wore eyeliner. Who spoke with a British-cum-southern accent cobbled together during adolescence at the four boarding schools from which he'd been expelled, wielding vulgarity and neologism as punctuation. Who'd been dubbed "The Rock Star of Literature" by the host of *Shine On, America*, Gia Pepper, after women had camped out three days on the sidewalk for a chance to be in the studio audience for the taping of a book club episode featuring his second novel.

That Justin was here made sense like a three-a.m. nightmare.

He pressed his cheek to hers. He smelled of smoke and peppermint. Still. Leaning back against the railing, he propped his ebony cane beside him. She tried not to stare at it. It was like he'd sprung a tail.

"Might you?" He handed Bree his lighter, then took a cigarette from his coat with his left hand. His right hand, the ruined one, he kept in his pocket.

She cupped the flame. In the distance, a fountain ejaculated into a pond that glowed with submersed light.

" 'Now why would Bree McEnroy,' I asked Darren, 'literary elitist, be sucking Francis Marvel-Bra Wells's proverbial dick?' "

"To which dick-proverb are you alluding?" She took a step back. Her pants squeaked.

FROM A BENCH in the shadow of the evergreen garden on the east end of the terrace, Hunter watched Justin Leighton chain-smoke while Bree ground out his dropped cigarettes with the toe of a four-inch-high, Lucite-soled boot. He'd been cursing himself for mixing pills (he'd thought Gretchen less likely to notice the absence of one from each of several bottles) when Bree had first come outside to the terrace, crying and pacing, and though he'd felt terrible for her he hadn't felt secure enough of his footing to go over.

He told himself he wouldn't have left her inside to be devoured by guests if it weren't for Larry's arrival. He told himself it wasn't his craving for pills that had driven his exit. He told himself he deserved a little pharmaceutical help with dealing with Larry, and with Suzanne's trying to coerce Bree to review his Princeton application, and, most of all, with the obviousness (to everyone but Suzanne, who wouldn't notice if he were covered with buboes) of his illness. Since he was a kid doctors had been reassuring him his poor resistance was something he'd grow out of like acne or baby fat, promising it wasn't a *symptom* of anything. But it was the symptoms *of* the colds after streps after flus that killed him with self-consciousness.

His cough won a round against the stolen codeine.

"Hunter?" Bree called out.

He got up slowly, the stars above him winking, and attempted a straight line toward the center of the balustrade. "Hey, Rock Star," he said, extending his hand. Justin nodded at it and smiled, his right hand—the damaged one—sequestered in a pocket. Stupid of Hunter. Thoughtless.

"I prefer *Justin* these days."

"Can *I* call you Rock Star?" Bree said.

Justin raised an eyebrow. "Between the sheets, perhaps."

She laughed, giving his sleeve the slightest brush of her fingers as she shook her head. "Are they velvet, too?"

This, from a woman who all night had stammered every time Hunter had let her speak for herself. Talking now to the one person at this party who awed all of Fox Glen, she sounded for the first time relaxed. Flirting with him, she moved like she was made for her odd clothes. Touching him, she looked at home.

Hunter squinted. "Wait. You *know* each other?"

"University," said Justin. "Practically dormies, us two."

"That's right, *Blaine*," Hunter said. Her résumé. He should have remembered. "So you're friends? You're friends ... with ... Rock Star." The ground swayed. He held the railing to steady himself.

"Shouldn't quaff what you can't hold," Justin said.

Hunter's face burned. "I'm simply floored by the coincidence. Bree's here. You're here. Though the tabloids and gossip blogs still have you in Tibet ... or was that last month? Is it now the Caymans? Or that castle in England that Madonna—"

"Just arrived stateside, still jet-lagged," Justin said to Bree, who nodded, straight-faced. So, she didn't *know.* "Ticklish business matters needing caretaking. Staying at my parents' place."

Hunter strangled a cough.

Justin slapped him on the back. "Get thee someplace warm." When Hunter didn't move, he added, coolly, "See you."

Since seventh grade, Justin had been Hunter's idol, the author he himself one day wanted to be. He felt tears threaten now at being dismissed like a child. Like the pesky son of Justin's parents' neighbor. Like a kid Justin hadn't seen in years, instead of someone he waved to silently nearly every week on the wooded trails between their estates when the rest of the world thought him in Paris or Japan or Rome.

Three years ago, after Justin was shot and nearly killed by a fan, those worldwide "sightings" of him had begun, a flurry of dead-Elvis contradictions that had him everywhere glamorous at once, his unwillingness to be interviewed or photographed only heightening his post-injury mystique. Hunter, who lived not in the main house of the Cay estate with his mother, but rather in the Play Palace, a building abutting the woods that separated their property from that of the Leighton Logans, frequently walked the trails to clear his head. It had been during one of these sojourns two months after the shooting that he'd come upon Justin on the ground, beating his new cane against a tree root with his good arm, kicking at the dirt and leaves with his good leg, and growling, *Fuck, fuck, fuck.*

Hunter had sat beside him and thought about asking if he was hurt, then didn't. He thought next about patting Justin's arm, but as he was still trying to figure out the physical boundaries between men—before he'd moved to Fox Glen he hadn't had male friends, or for that matter *any* friends—he just waited until Justin finished cursing and extended a hand. "If you ever need help"—he wrote down his cell number and pointed to the Play Palace—"I'm right there."

"*I'm* not *here,*" Justin mumbled, as Hunter helped him back to what had once been the gardener's cottage at the back of the Leighton Logan estate.

Hunter just nodded silently, as he did every time they passed each other thereafter, for three years respecting the paradox of Justin's not-there-ness when in fact Hunter could see from the Play Palace the lights of Justin's cottage.

"You're inside-out, kid," Justin said now, and dropped his cigarette. "I'll have my car take you home." That he'd slipped out of his Rock Star patois to sound parental stung worst of all.

"The night's gotten away from you," Bree said. "Sleeping it off would do you good."

Her sincerity curdled Hunter. He patted her hand. "I must tell you Gretchen was quite beside herself about your hailing from Wal-Martland." The cruelness rose in his throat like something he couldn't keep down. "But now, with your turning out to be college chums with Rock Star. . . . Well, *quel* redemption!" He couldn't meet her eyes or make himself stop. "It's nearly enough to make up for those pants."

"THE CABBIE'S PROBABLY the only reason Hunter kissed you afterward, you know," Carley said on the bench on the terrace below. "I'm sure he wanted you to look like a *girlfriend* in case the driver saw you being fingered in the rearview mirror."

Earlier last night Amber had been flirting at the Station with this guy Tad who'd accompanied Ian back from Princeton for the weekend and who Hunter would later call, on the cab ride to Carley's house, M&M—Moldy Money—the kind of person who thought his family's fortune going back nearly as many generations as he had fingers gave him the right to arrogance. Amber ought to have known better than to start anything with him—even if she hadn't noticed his rolling his eyes at everything she said and asking if she was "Amber-dextrous," no friend of Ian's was ever going to think she was special. Tad, whose name she thought was *Todd*, wasn't like the guys on the lacrosse and ice hockey teams at Montclair, who liked Amber because she was funny and sweet and considerate enough to use her hands or mouth if she'd gotten them harder than she'd meant to when she was ready to stop.

Which is why five minutes after they'd disappeared together, Hunter had tracked them down to a locked bathroom, demanded the key from the bartender, and broken in on them. He and Ian had gotten into a shouting match at the bar afterward, with both Tad and Ian's new girlfriend from college claiming Hunter's friends were "too immature" to be borne. That on the cab ride home Amber was still telling him how wrong he'd been about Tad/Todd said less about how much she'd had to drink than about how badly she wanted to believe in the same fantasy that Carley's own mother did: you could *make* people like you.

It was hard to imagine what was going through Hunter's head after they'd dropped Carley off. Probably he'd wanted to do something to make Tad up to Amber. After ten or so drinks, laying his jacket over her lap with his hand beneath it might have seemed to him like chivalry, laying a cloak over a puddle so a lady could cross.

According to Amber, when she'd offered to do something back, he just shook his head with a smile and whispered, *I'm fine.*

"Like saying no to food when you're hungry but you're being polite," she told Carley.

"Disgusting food," Carley said. "Food other people spit out." She wanted to see Amber's tears like she'd wanted to see Hunter's lighter drown like she'd wanted to see Getting to Know You remain in a thousand pieces instead of being resurrected on her mirror. She wanted to see something get broken and stay that way, and she knew it made her a monster because good people were supposed to want to *fix* things the way Hunter always fixed things, but she couldn't stop herself from wanting to crack the world open.

Amber pressed her hands to her stomach. "At least it wasn't pretend. He was hard. I could see." She wrapped her arms around her knees. "You guys *sleep* in the same bed and do *nothing*. With you, he just plays house."

There was a perfect retort to this somewhere in Aftermemory. Words short and sharp, like what she'd five minutes ago heard Bree tell Justin on the terrace above them after Hunter had retreated down the stone stairway to the back lawn.

"Don't mind Alchy-Cay," Justin had said. "He knows not his rudeness."

"Don't apologize for other people," Bree had answered after a long while. "You haven't got the right."

"DO ME A great favor, Ian?" Hunter pressed the phone to his ear and kept close to the house's foundation. "Don't have it in me to wait an hour for a cab. Yes, Swann's Way's that tedious. Well, it's not like *you* never end up places out of obligation. Bunny's *chatte*, for instance?" He sighed. "Can *anyone* there drive? I need to not be here. No, it's fine, then. I won't. I'll be by soon. Don't worry, I'll find another way. Yes, I heard you. Did you not just hear me say *I won't*."

After he'd returned with Amber earlier that evening he'd parked on the side of the house, bypassing the valet service hired for the party—a habit he'd taken up since an evening at the end of summer when the head valet at the Glen Club refused to return his car keys on the grounds that Hunter was slurring. It was barely ten minutes from Swann's Way to his home, all side streets. Few cars. No cops. No problem.

He waved to the guard at his gate and parked at the Play Palace—a Tudor building across from the main house that had been designed for entertaining when the estate was built in the early twentieth century. Contained within were an indoor tennis court, pool and atrium, sauna, steam room, dressing rooms, bar and gaming area, kitchen and formal dining room, and a second floor made up entirely of guest bedrooms—one of which Hunter had moved into at age twelve so Suzanne could pretend to her boyfriends and herself that she was not a mother.

From the carved art nouveau coat rack in his entranceway, he took an umbrella. From the ebony medicine chest in the bathroom of his twelve-hundred-square-foot bedroom suite, two cold pills. From the hidden safe in the deco-tiled poolside dressing room, a handful of Vicodins. He walked the half-mile down the road to Ian's in the rain so he could look his cousin in the eye when he said, "Didn't drive here. Kept my word."

BREE WATCHED JUSTIN straighten out of his lean on the balustrade, readying himself for the approach of Gretchen's guests, who all at once emerged from the glassed-in porch resembling a giant contact lens at the back of the house. That Gretchen had given him even these twenty minutes of privacy said much, Bree imagined, about her esteem for him. After three years of itinerant reclusion, tonight's return would make him not only the hottest attraction in Fox Glen but in the entirety of New York.

He brushed ashes off his lapels, stretched his neck and back, then took a stiff step forward. His cane slipped on a dead leaf. Bree caught him by his bad arm. He winced, his hand coming free of his pocket. His fingers hung like the branches of a weeping willow, as if they'd surrendered to gravity.

"Did I hurt—"

"My feelings?" He returned the hand to its grotto. "Quite. Three years, and not a call or e-mail—"

"I sent a card."

"A Get Well. It rhymed. Might have scrawled *Sorry You're Not Dead* on ass paper."

"That's not—" The choke of people descended in a fog of perfume and well wishes and handshaking and back-patting and stroking. Since the day she'd first met him, people had been mad to touch him. She'd always hated him in a group as much as she'd adored him one-on-one.

Justin kissed Gretchen's hand. "Thank you again for letting me get away with crashing."

As if Justin hadn't always *gotten away with* doing what other people couldn't: donning white aviator scarves in college without undermining his masculinity, bringing to creative writing classes stories in which way, way too much happened, and getting offered a six-figure advance for his senior thesis, a novel entitled *Crawling*, which chronicled a year in the life of the Spindles, a lower-middle-class family whose humor and graciousness in the face of bankruptcy and cancer made poverty and illness seem downright exhilarating. Critic Lex Pritchett, infamous for having once-upon-a-time skewered a Pulitzer Prize winner—"a pithily tedious fairytale"—and a National Book Award nominee—"a seductively repulsive yodel"—deemed *Crawling* "a nostalgically fresh masterwork." Three years later, the sequel, *Clinging*, was book-club heralded by *Shine On, America.*

That he was an impossible contraction, this slight, fey man in makeup and leather whose books flew off the pallets at warehouse clubs in middle America, made the world somehow love him more. Everyone believed he was *theirs*: the working-class moms who found themselves in his pages; the literati who claimed *Crawling*'s and *Clinging*'s "illusion of accessibility" masked a vein of reconditeness to which they alone were privy; the front-row fangirls who screamed as he strutted into readings to the beat of bass-heavy music. They shared him.

Until Tori Wilson, who wanted him all to herself. Who opened fire on the podium where he read from *Clinging* at a Books for Children benefit before putting the gun to her head to join him in the Afterlife. He'd survived the five bullets. A mother and child in the front row had been killed.

Six operations. Three years of absence. Rumors that *Climbing*, the gerund that was supposed to complete the Spindles trilogy, would never be. A RealLife Channel Docudrama: *Lit Star: The Rise and Fall of Justin Leighton.*

And finally, his reduction to a metaphor for Icarian plunge:

Twenty-year-old author Whitney Cantrell, this year's Justin Leighton, saw her novel hit number one on The New York Times *Bestseller list after . . .*

Responding to accusations that he'd Leightoned *the radical procedure into public acceptance, the plastic surgeon contended* . . .

The season before he tore his ACL, the Leightonian pinnacle of his career, point guard Nick Walker had averaged . . .

"You haven't changed a whit!" shrieked Cissy Gardner. A wrinkled hand adorned with a nickel-sized ruby grabbed at his lapel. A man reeking of gin reached over Bree's shoulder to pound him between the shoulder blades. The air blurred with breath.

"Bree!" she heard him call as guests poured themselves into the space where she'd been. Standing room only. Front row to a myth.

THE BROKEN LOCK to the library door had only increased Francis's arousal, the risk of discovery bringing to the act an exquisite pressure. He was almost there when the muted party exploded into distinct voices.

Footsteps approached. Suzanne pulled her head back, her lips sliding over the head of his penis as she released him to the air. He thumbed through a mental catalogue of the unarousing to keep himself from slipping over the edge. Hemorrhoids. Ebola. His wife.

The footsteps stopped, then backtracked. Someone who didn't know the house was stuck in Biography, the southeast corner of the library.

He and Suzanne crawled behind the leather sofa.

"Shit!" he heard from another dead end. History. And then again from Poetry, though the library maze was, in fact, simple, Swann's Way's original owner having been obsessed with symmetry. All one had to do was take the single path unlike the others.

Another curse. A squeak. Suzanne's breath tickled his neck as she dug her nails into his arm.

"She thinks I'm garbage," the Author shouted not two yards from where they hid. Twenty phones in this house, and she'd come in here for one. "He stares at my chest like he *wants* something." Francis shook his head at Suzanne. He'd done away with affairs when they'd begun sleeping together. "Believe me, they're *not* missing me. Not with everyone gawking at Justin Leighton. That's what I said. *Justin*."

"Justin Leighton?" Suzanne said, slipping back into her Marvel-Bra after the Author cursed her way out of the maze. He fastened it for her, kissing her back. Her skin was as soft as when she was eighteen. The Carina—went his marketing campaign—turned back time. "Justin is *here*?"

"I NEED . . ." Justin repeated, only his eye sockets and forehead still spared from numbness, his face nearly completely given over to the attack. "To go. I need." Gasping, he pushed through the crowd determined to absorb his breath.

"BEST GRAPES FROM, like, ten, um, places," one of the bartenders told Perry Vandergraf, one of the few people besides Francis not mobbing Leighton outside.

Francis strode to the bar. "Eleven." Until he'd studied the label of this particular Cabernet, he'd never considered the allure of *eleven*, but the more he contemplated it, the finer number it became.

Eleven points of support—a quiet, perfect prime for the Vela, a seamless cotton push-up bra he would target to women who couldn't admit to themselves that they pushed up. Twelve evoked cartons of eggs. Ten connoted false perfection. Eleven effaced itself into truth.

"Eleven vineyards," Francis repeated. "Write it down."

He shrugged. "Ten, eleven, same diff—"

"It's the difference"—Francis leaned across the bar, barely resisting grabbing him by the collar—"between the schmuck who earns two hundred bucks for a night's work and the man who pays it for a bottle."

He walked around the near-empty room. Why neither his wife nor lover hadn't redirected Leighton inside, he couldn't fathom. Pivoting to avoid a decorative tree whose branches were arrayed with miniature fruits and vegetables, he collided with a floor vase shaped like the newspaper cones from which he'd eaten fries from Nathan's as a kid. The callas at the lowest point of the V brushed his crotch, feathery, like the top of Suzanne's head when she was on her knees. Their yellow centers ripened mid-petal into nectarine and blushed red at the edges.

He tried to free a bloom, the stem refusing to break. Finally, he slipped the whole stalk under his jacket, water soaking his shirt as he pressed his arm tight to his side.

In the bathroom, it glistened. Against him it felt like Suzanne's tongue.

THREE APRICOT SCONES split open, spread with ginger chutney and topped with roast duck; two blood orange soufflés, served in the fruit's own hollowed-out skin; five deviled quail eggs, garnished with osetra.

"We *shared* him," Carley had claimed outside. "We used to share him and you're selfish and you ruined it."

"*I'm* selfish? You have ninety percent of him to yourself, and then you're greedy about what's left. Bunny Gardner used to say dating him was like eating your leftovers."

"Whore."

"Pig."

The moment the word had left her mouth she'd wanted to swallow it. She'd meant *pig* as in not-sharing, not *pig* as in fat. But she couldn't take it back, you couldn't purge words.

Seared foie gras with a fig balsamic reduction; black truffle ice cream; venison tartlets; chèvre grapes; Gruyère puffs; crudités; shrimp.

Amber thrust her finger down her throat. All gone now.

SIXTEEN BLUE VALIUMS, V's cut into their cores to form hearts. Twenty-two round OxyContins—eight green, fourteen yellow. Two orange eggs of Xanax. Twenty-six capsuled candy corn Dexedrines. Seventeen, eighteen, nineteen ... there had been twenty. And twenty Percocets. Gretchen never misremembered. And never, *ever* kept odd numbers. *Ten* white-as-nurses Vicodins should be there, not nine. *Fourteen* codeine tablets. Who would keep *thirteen* of anything? She nudged them one at a time across the counter-top of the bathroom sink.

Justin Leighton had left as abruptly as he'd appeared, the Author had gone to bed without a goodnight, and Carley had run upstairs in tears, refusing, as always, to explain herself to her mother.

Gretchen's party had whimpered to an end.

And now something was missing.

CHAPTER 10

I n the winter of her seventeenth year, Glory Masters lost her parents and
her memory to what locals called a "pea souper."

"It sounded like a kitchen appliance, *pea souper*," she said in voiceover
in Season One, Episode One of *The Arion Annals*. "As if these people I
couldn't remember but who hugged me in a hundred photos had been
victims of a Cuisinart." Carley loved that you could hear Glory's thoughts.
She'd told Hunter once that she wished you could hear everybody's.

"Scary idea," he'd said, and then, "Little enough is private. One's head is
the last safe place left to keep things."

As Glory walked through her house after being released from the
hospital, every room of it felt foreign ("It looks like a gift shop," she told the
viewers, "nautical motif in every room, and cute little whales on every
linen"), even her attic bedroom with its widow's watch that looked out at
the ocean. ("I seriously collect *scrimshaw*?") But everybody—her soon-to-be-
former best friend, soon-to-be-former boyfriend, and even the town sheriff
who'd pulled her from the wreckage of the accident—swore she'd lived here
in this house on this beach on the island of Arion forever with those parents
in the pictures, people who'd died when their car skidded off the road in
the fog.

At the closing credits, Carley pressed Skip on the DVD remote and
restarted the episode for the third time. The beginning of the series was the
best part, every revelation still ahead: who Glory really was, how she'd really
lost her memory, and why she walked around Arion feeling constantly

misplaced. This last, Carley understood even without the "why." There was a broken feeling she felt herself sometimes, a misfire that told her she was supposed to be doing something different somewhere else, though not what or where. She'd tried telling Sinkman about it once, but "I'm just not supposed to be here" got heard as "I don't want to live," and the next thing she knew, he was asking if she had *a defined suicide plan* and pressing into her hand a magnet shaped like an ear:

Teen
Listen
555-TEEN
Day or Night
Always
Hear

The punning, Hunter said when he picked Carley up from her appointment, *is enough to make one slit one's wrists.*

Hunter used to know what she meant about being in the wrong place; he used to understand how you just needed to be held until the feeling passed. He didn't have the right words for it any more than she did, but sometimes he called himself *misshelved.* Other times he said he felt *homesick.*

Glory used to be popular, her former best friend kept telling her, but now people couldn't handle her "morbidullness": her hanging out with Tern, the new kid and only Goth Girl; her endless questions about the car crash; her not giving parties at her beach house even though she was an emancipated minor with no one to stop her. Her talking about a hot, shirtless guy who kept showing up at night on the bluffs below her window. A *delusion,* people said, for on an island less than ten miles long and three miles wide, nobody else had ever seen him.

Glory had just broken into the sheriff's office to get a look at the accident file when the knock came at Carley's door. Three sharp raps—the way Hunter always announced himself when Grace waved him upstairs. Though Grace was supposed to formally announce visitors, Swann's Way being the only home in Fox Glen without intercoms because Gretchen thought them déclassé, she only did so when Gretchen was around. Given Gretchen's foul-moodedness every time she undertook a search for a new personal assistant—four in the last two years—neither Carley nor Francis ever let Gretchen know.

Hunter came in and sat down on her bed, his hair smelling like citrus and mint. She wanted to bury her nose in it. Lick it. Tangle her fingers in it. Yank it out.

"What was going on last night? What you did to Bree? What you wrote? Your dumping her on me and never returning when you knew I felt awful? That's not *you*, C."

"How would you know?"

"C . . ." He sighed. Taking off the glasses he rarely wore outside of the Palace, he rubbed his bloodshot eyes. "*Talk* to me. It's just us. Just me."

"And I just hate you, okay? And Amber. And Bree. And everyone. You all think I'm stupid."

For years they'd held each other tightly to comfort each other, no air between them. When he hugged her now, he held her a little to the side so her chest didn't touch him. "I don't ever think you're stupid. But sometimes you do things . . . impetuously . . ." She felt his body tense. He released her before he lost the fight to coughing.

She pressed her lips to his forehead, the way people learn from their mothers and she'd learned from Hunter. "One-oh-one."

He shook his head. "Low-grade, if anything."

She got a thermometer from her bathroom.

"Unnecessary," he said, rubbing his cheekbone.

She stuck it under his tongue. "One-oh-one-point-three," she read when it beeped.

"Miscalibrated."

"Nothing's broken," she said. She folded back her quilt and fluffed her pillows, an invitation. "You're just sick."

He didn't take off his jacket and shoes and let her tuck him in like a letter the way he usually did when he was ill. He just sat there and patted her leg. "Bree's not going to tell Gretchen what you did, C. She'll work with you. Beneath the pleather, she's absurdly kind."

"You basically called her trash. To her face."

He squinted.

"Amber and I were outside in our spot, we could hear. When you said that stuff when she was with Justin? Shit, do you even remember *talking* to Justin?" She got up to get him Tylenol. "You know," she called from her bathroom because she couldn't look at him when she said it, "Sinkman says blacking out is . . ."

"I did not *black out*. And since when are you talking to Sinkman about me?"

"I said it was *a friend*. He probably thinks it's me." When your shrink thought you were a liar, your being a lush wasn't a leap.

He dry-swallowed the pills, waving away the bottle of cold water she brought back from what he called the *negative-calorie closet*, a storage room down the hall that Gretchen had retrofitted with a microwave and refrigerator and stocked with fat-free popcorn, rice cakes, and mineral water so Carley could have no excuse for wandering near the kitchen.

"It's just water. You know, *water*? Good for a cold. And a hangover." He set his lips, shook his head. She lowered her voice. "H?"

"What did I say to Bree? Please." He covered his eyes.

He let her hug him for real, then, his breath shuddering through them both. Hunter needed to be touched when he was sick. When you thought no one wanted you close, to be held was the world.

GLORY AWOKE AT the beginning of Episode Two to discover a scar-faced intruder about to plunge a stiletto into her heart. Rolling out of bed, she karate-kicked him using martial arts training she didn't know she possessed, then chased him over the dunes into the ocean. As a wave broke over them and his hands went to her throat, she saw on his wrist a seven-sided tattoo. *The Order of Lethe*, she thought without knowing how she knew.

"From the sea you were born," the man said, as the world went dark, "to the sea you will return."

She revived to the mysterious-shirtless delusion giving her mouth-to-mouth. "Are you real?" she asked when she could breathe.

Hunter's cell rang. He broke off a low snore and patted himself down for it, the SAT cards on Carley's lap (List Twenty-six: Words of Heroism) falling to the floor as he flung back the quilt he'd finally gotten under with her.

She leaned over the side of the bed to retrieve *Palladian* and *Valor* from the floor. "They can call back."

"Suzanne's flying." While it didn't interfere with her getting to important destinations like spas or adult tennis camp, Suzanne's airplane phobia required Hunter to be available when she was in the air in case she *needed to say good-bye*.

"The wheels are *supposed* to start engaging," he said into the phone when he found it. "It's not too early, Mother.... Listen to the flight attendant, please." He mimed tossing the phone out the window. "You can't stay on the line while you're landing. Larry? Larry, hold her hand, be patient. I didn't *say* you weren't. I didn't... Mother... you've got to hang up. Give the attendant... because it's a rule. I love you. We'll talk when you've landed."

But they wouldn't. On the runway, she'd be too busy calling Newport about tonight's parties and Fox Glen about yesterday's. She was always closest to Hunter at thirty thousand feet.

He stretched slowly, carefully, as if testing the weight of his head. "After you meet with your tutor and have a conciliatory chat with Bree, might we take a field trip? Talk over lunch in the Hamptons. Ocean should be gorgeously fierce. A treasure on shore awaiting your collection." He was the only person in the world who'd spend a whole day helping her fill her pockets with shells, or petting starfish at the aquarium touch tank, or feeding animals at the petting zoo—stuff she was supposed to be too old for.

"You feel shitty, and we don't have to go all the way to the Hamptons to talk. I mean, we always talk." Or used to.

He smothered a cough. "Let's get out and play. Sojourn to the East

Hampton Saks, post-repast, to conduct a survey: 'Might you help us out for a sociology project, Ma'am? Would that La Perla Black Label you're purchasing be *affair underwear*?' "

His face slackened. A sneeze overtook him before he could rub it away. She walked over to her desk to get her SAT workbook while he blew his nose because even after years of friendship he'd never shaken his self-consciousness. As she passed her dressing table and the six square inches of mirror not taped over with papers—Gretchen's latest addition being Carley's mid-semester report in which Nagel informed her parents of her two missing essays and failed *Great Gatsby* test—she caught a glimpse of herself, T-shirt riding up to reveal a pale roll of fat above the waistband of jeans she hadn't buttoned because she couldn't. Her hand hovered at the hem of her shirt, desperate to pull it down at the same time as she didn't want Hunter to see she cared.

"Let's just *play* in the Palace," she said, giving it a quick tug and turning, "and you can rest up for tonight." With it being both Halloween and the last night of Ian's and the rest of last years' seniors' four-day fall break from college, there was no way he'd stay in. "We'll plan costumes. Eat pancakes. Lie around and watch *Arion*."

It was the best thing in the world, lying around in Hunter's bedroom, a place that was completely *him* because Suzanne let him do whatever he wanted with it. She hadn't protested when he'd refurnished it with pieces that, to use his words, *skewed toward whimsy*: the king-sized bed with its mahogany headboard and footboard out of which pieces of wood had been carved, sanded, and replaced, making the bed a puzzle where you could slide out squares and cylinders and arches if you were bored; the twenty different sets of linens he changed daily, remaking the bed himself every morning before he left so his craving for variety wouldn't create extra work for the Help; the pine cabinet with a hundred compartments of odd sizes and shapes in which he tucked away souvenirs of the everyday like they'd never come again—movie ticket stubs and theater programs nestled in a trapezoidal drawer, fortune cookie slips fed into a little piggy-bank-like slot from which they tumbled down to a hollow at the cabinet's base accessible only by a two-inch-high hinged door shaped like a cartoon mouse hole, shells and

stones Carley pressed into his hand on their outings that he arranged
carefully in the long, flat top drawer like an exhibit in a secret museum
devoted to their friendship.

Suzanne didn't care, either, about Hunter having piles of books around
his room or about the heavy scent of burning wood that settled into it from
September until April from his keeping a fire going whenever he was home.
She rarely came inside the Palace, let alone up to his bedroom, calling him
over to the main house when she needed him.

His room was as familiar to Carley as her own was forever foreign,
everything in it having been chosen by Gretchen—the silk-covered quilt
(Alabaster) with coordinating cushion covers (Pebble) that were so easily
stained that Carley would sit on the edge of her bathtub and rinse off her
feet before she felt safe putting them on her own bed; the tasteful clusters
of black and white photos taken by strangers of clouds and gardens and
trees; the compartmentalized drawers in her dresser and desk that both
Gretchen and Grace (on Gretchen's orders) rifled through for telltale candy
wrappers and purged of memorabilia that Gretchen considered "clutter."
Nearly everything personal Carley kept at the Play Palace in the guest room
where her parents and his mother thought she slept when she stayed over.

"Carley!" Grace yelled, slamming the first syllable of her name as in
damn it or *tampon*, like Gretchen did. "Tutor!"

She tried to hug Hunter close, the way he'd let her earlier. He pulled
away, her mountain of flesh ruining everything. "Don't you ever tire of TV,
of watching that *merde*?" He dabbed at his nose with his handkerchief. "And
you know, a normal person would be disgusted by the idea of lying around
with someone who's *dripping*."

She wanted to apologize for being abnormal and disgusting. For not
being disgust*ed*. For wanting him to feel completely loved and beautiful
every minute of his life. For wanting him so much that when she thought
about him, there was nothing else in the world left to want.

She snatched up her cards, slammed her door, and left him sitting on
her bed, rubbing his eyes.

IN AFTERMEMORY SHE says, "You can't help being a sniffle with legs, H. But you could *do* something about being an asshole."

He laughs, and then the tears he's been keeping in since she told him what he'd said to Bree start down his cheeks. "Légged sniffle." He folds his handkerchief into his jeans pocket and takes his journal from his jacket, half smiling and half crying. "May I write it down? It's so exactly something you'd say."

He pulls her into a half-sitting, half-lying-down hug so tight it feels like the world is becoming whole, the continents fitting together like puzzle pieces the way her ninth grade geology teacher had said they'd done hundreds of millions of years ago. Her body is hot and light, like something rising. She aches between her legs.

He lays his head on her chest. "Don't know why you put up with me, but I so love you. *Légged sniffle.* It's so *you*, the synesthesia." Word List Fourteen: Words About Literature. "No boundaries between things."

She doesn't need to understand him or the word or the world to know she wants to keep this moment inside a glass ball with glitter or fake snow: her body tingling with what hasn't happened yet, drunk on what might.

CHAPTER 11

Bree swung open her door to muffled sneezing and an ocean of flora. A crystal vase of crimson tulips, straining to hold their weighty heads upright. A bronze urn containing three dozen peach roses, tight-budded like virgins and destined to die splay-petaled slatterns. A potted, four-foot tree of silver-white orchids that made Bree think of Mother's Day in Vernal, where women once a year came to mass wearing proof of their families' love—orchid corsages, usually purple, pearl-top-pinned to them like butterflies to boards.

"Good morning." Hunter thrust a dark green paisley handkerchief into the back pocket of his jeans, then picked up the tree and walked it past her into her room. He evaluated its placement next to her desk and by the window seat before settling it next to her bed. The air was thick with the rootless smell of cut flowers.

"What *is* all this?"

"Read," he said, returning to the hallway. He sneezed into his sleeve and handed her a little card from the arrangement of tulips: *Congratulations on your Fox Glen debut. —Bernie and Edie Weiss.*

On the card accompanying the roses: *Might you grace our engagement dinner with a literary reading? —Suzanne Stanton Cay and Lawrence Talbright IV.*

On the card that came with the orchid: *Bree McEnroy, Finlandesque. So beautiful and cold.* Unsigned.

"I'd say Rock Star has a crush." Hunter winked.

She followed him down the staircase and through the octagon to the foyer, where dozens more arrangements awaited. "Moonlighting as the Wellses' butler?"

"I like to pretend to be useful. Also, delivery is Grace's job, and you don't want to piss her off with twenty trips upstairs. Take my word."

"Unreal." She took a silk-covered box from his hands that contained what looked like an orange sea urchin. She poked it.

"Pincushion." He turned away to sneeze. "A type of . . . I think, Protea. Suzanne took a flower-arranging class last year," he said, in answer to Bree's unspoken question. "There was actual homework. She needed support."

He rubbed his face, then sneezed yet again.

"Brutal cold, kid."

He shook his head. "Already ebbing, doubtless gone tomorrow." He cleared his throat. "Though I do appreciate *brutal*. Makes me sound brave."

Upstairs, after centering a basket of purple flowers on her desk, he took off his glasses and rubbed his eyes with the back of his hand. "Please accept my apology for last night. What I said . . . before I left . . . I didn't mean. I was trying to be . . . I don't know what I was trying to be."

"How's your head?"

"Embarrassed. It has an immature streak that bares itself to the people it most wants to impress."

"Don't worry yourself on that account. You're impressive. But one thing, Hunter? You drink dangerously."

"Interesting word choice. You might have said *copiously*."

"You know the distance between a story's mood and tone?"

"The former changes scene to scene. The latter tends toward consistency."

She nodded. "I don't think last night was a mood. Which makes me worry for you."

"Worry. That's . . . quaint." He ran his fingers over the flowers in the basket, the vines of which were wrapped around its handle. "*Passiflora*. A seventeenth-century monk saw the crucifixion in them. Crown of thorns. Nails. Blood. Prosecutors in the leaves, apostles in the petals. I can lose myself in symbolism as deeply as the next lit-geek, but at least I know what's real." He crossed his arms. "That's what you were getting at in *Between Scylla and Alta Vista*, right? Lose yourself in metaphor, and you'll never get home."

His cell phone rang. He glanced at the Caller ID. "Excuse me," he said. *"Bonjour, mon père,"* she heard before he walked down the hallway.

He returned fifteen minutes later, his eyes red-rimmed. "So what's the plan for Carley's book?" He wiped his eyes with a fresh handkerchief. Solid navy.

She shrugged. "Shoot myself."

"Gretchen will go apoplectic. Blood stains." He pointed. "Persian rug." He took a shuddery breath.

"Do you need to talk—"

"Please, no. Don't. Don't . . . worry. I'm just tired. Look, you know you need to start over. To throw away everything you . . ." When his voice broke, she turned away and busied herself rearranging the flower arrangements on her desk—the basket and the silk box and a vase of lilies a Three-card Monte of flora. She could hear him sniffling.

"Take a look at these for me?" she said, turning back when it sounded like he'd gotten control of his tears. "I'll be back soon. Maybe you can tell me what I'm missing."

She handed him a copy of her contract and three file folders: Research—Medieval Romance and Legendry, an inch thick; Teenagers—Mind-set and Culture, another inch; and, finally, Discussions and Correspondence, a few pages of notes from a conversation with Gretchen about Carley's enthusiasm for her upcoming Medieval-themed Sweet Sixteen and printouts of the e-mails Carley and Bree had exchanged over the week regarding the direction of work Bree had sent, about which Carley repeatedly had typed the word Great.

When Bree returned a half hour later with a cook's assistant who'd refused to allow her to carry up the tray, Hunter was sitting in the middle of the floor and scribbling in his journal, her notes spread around him.

"Good morning, Claudia," he said to the young woman, who blushed before leaving. He smiled at the baskets of muffins and hot bread, the tea and juice.

"When the cook heard your name," Bree said when the servant had gone, "she insisted I wait for fresh bread."

"Patrice knows my tastes run . . . simple." He took a careful bite. "Thank you. As I told Carley, you're kind."

"I didn't do anything. They wouldn't let me boil water. Said they'd get fired."

"I wasn't thanking you for the attempt to nourish me. I was acknowledging your allowing me to recoup my dignity." He checked his watch. "In answer to your request," he said, handing her something entitled Getting to Know You, "here's what you're missing. I'm not sure Carley would appreciate my sharing it, but I can't stay for her permission. That phone call earlier? It was a summons."

She looked over the pages. "This is supposed to help me understand *what*?"

He sighed. "What do you *see*?"

"Nothing."

"*Nothing*."

"She watches television."

"That's like walking through someone's private library sans a glance at the spines and opining *He has books*." He took a ragged breath.

"And that's the exact look you gave me last night when I told your mother you felt miserable."

"I'm sorry. I get impatient when I'm not feeling. . . . No, to be honest, that's not it. I get impatient with smart people who don't think beyond words. Suzanne's obliviousness to my health should tell you something neither of us should have to say aloud. And the empty spaces on these pages—they not only tell you what *isn't* important, but also what *is*."

"TV."

"Yes. And no. For someone who overuses symbolism in her writing, you're being ridiculously literal."

"I *overuse* . . ."

"Let's try another angle. You like research, right? I mean, you have twenty pages of notes from a book called *Understanding Your Teenager*. So, research your patron's interests and try *talking* to her about them. You'll find she gets irony. And humor. And likes things for reasons that aren't that straightforward. In any case, she owns *The Arion Annals*, all nine seasons, and, my guess is, would gladly make them available to you as *reference*. On my way out, I'll ask Grace to venture to the video store for the reality shows. Oh, and not *Mr. Hotness*, which you can inform Carley I told you was a joke. Now *Caveman Land*—that's hysterical after a couple of drinks: twenty people living in the jungle, competing in fire making, spear throwing, and mastodon hunting 'challenges'—animatronic, obviously. Contestants spend the rest of the day carrying around foam clubs that ensure invulnerability to being 'clubbed off' the show by the other contestants. You're safe with club in hand, but say you let go of it in your sleep, or feel the urge to take a dip in the prehistoric river and your weapon floats away on a current—"

"You can't be serious."

"Serious as a club-wielding, faux-animal-skin-wearing management consultant desperate to win the Stone Tool Making Challenge. I'll have a bottle of Glenfiddich sent over." He tore a page from his journal, folding it before he handed it to her. "Here's all you need—"

Grace rapped twice and opened Bree's door. "A car is waiting." The only words she'd spoken to Bree since she arrived had been *You're late* and *Vehicle use and reimbursements go through me*, uttered in the lockjaw of people not born to it.

"I adore your earrings," Hunter said to Grace. "Tell the driver I'll be down shortly? I need to retrieve a few things from down the hall."

"Hunter?" Grace's face softened. "You should know—it's Griffin's driver, not the service. I believe your father's in the car."

"Thank you." He bit his lip.

WHEN CARLEY RETURNED to her room after tutoring, she found her bed empty, the sheets tight. Hunter had remade the bed with fresh linens so as not to leave his germs behind. As if he and Carley hadn't hundreds of times hung out together all day and night when he was sick, whole heady weekends of shutting out the rest of the world, squeezing fun out of every moment when he felt well enough, settling into companionable distance when he felt overwhelmed by discomfort and just wanted to read in quiet. When he awoke with coughing or fever, she'd wake with him and distract him from worrying about it being four a.m. *It's just time*, she'd say, and get him something cool to drink, and they'd put the TV on and pretend it was the middle of the afternoon until finally he began the drift back to sleep.

That was his favorite time, what he called *the insomniac's dream*, those moments when you could feel yourself sinking into the arms of sleep. He'd had a nanny when he was young who sent her salary back to her children in Central America and who understood how sad he'd get when he fell sick right before things to which he'd been looking forward. No matter how ill he was, no matter how unlikely it was that he'd be well in time for holidays or vacations or field trips, she'd always promise at bedtime the possibility that he'd feel better tomorrow. Years later, he'd told Carley, he still clung in those magic pre-sleep moments to the idea of waking up new.

She took a folded note from her pillowcase and lay down to read it, trying to imagine Hunter's cologne next to her cheek, though all she could smell was the lavender water the maids ironed into the linens.

C,

Have been summoned to the city for excoriation regarding financial discrepancies (brought to Griffin's accountant's attention in a phone call by, of all people, Larry). Truly wishing we could have whiled the afternoon away in the Hamptons, but given its now-impossibility, might you spend the time with Bree? (Try not to be scared—it's the only time you're ever mean.) Watch <u>The Arion Annals</u> together, perhaps. (I'm sorry I put it down before. And I'm sorry I've said things that made you think I think you're stupid. God, I really don't.)

About my recent snappishness and flippancy I do owe you an explanation. Reserve tomorrow for me, please, and I'll make good our lunch at the beach.

See you tonight at the Station, but I must admit an intrusion first.
Two, actually. The first I committed unthinkingly, the second out of
expedience.

One: I read your mirror. I hope you know I never have before. But while
talking to Griffin and trying to distance myself from his name calling
(Do you really think "spoiled dandy" is a fair characterization? For me,
it evokes a pesty flower gone to seed), I found my eyes taking in the
print Gretchen taped there. And now, because I've looked, I can't help
but to "worry," for lack of a better term, about what's going on for you in
school. (Bree manages to intone the word "worry" with sincerity rather
than condescension, by the way; please know this is how I, too, intend
it.) You just can't afford to fail English, C. It's not an elective.

Two: I liberated Nagel's handout from the mirror and gave it to Bree.
Don't hate me.

Je suis désolé.

Yours always,

H

To Discussions and Correspondence, Bree added the page Hunter had
torn from his journal.

What You're Missing:
Carley.

The rest of the page he'd left blank.

CHAPTER 12

What is plot?

It was a question Nagel would have asked, though not one he'd have wanted an honest answer to. And he'd be a total dick if you dangled a preposition while giving the opinion he didn't want, like *what you said—Plot's more important than pretty words and symbols because everyone's life has a plot but not everyone has big words or tons of meaning so it's something we can all relate to. And how come in class we don't ever just talk about what happens in a book (and what we wish had happened) instead of all the symbolism?—*wasn't as important as *how* you said it.

What he'd want to hear when you raised your hand—what he'd expect you to say if you were a hand-raiser—was a definition: *plot is stuff that happens that leads to other stuff that all adds up to a big climax followed by a little death.*

Except using better words for *stuff*, and without *little death*, the correct term for when-there-are-no-more-surprises-left being *dénouement*.

"That's the worst part of a book," Carley said to Bree, who sat in Carley's room wearing a red satin men's smoking jacket over what looked like pajamas at three in the afternoon, only half-watching the TV from where she'd set herself up at Carley's desk where Carley herself never ever sat, "when you know nothing new can happen."

A flurry of clicking. Like Sinkman, Bree was taking notes. Then a sigh.

"Try not to think about *dénouement*. By the time we get to that point, we can figure out one that doesn't . . . depress you. Let's just focus on my original question: Plot. If we're throwing out the old book completely, we have to start *somewhere*. So what do you want?"

"To get back to the show already." They'd paused Season One, Episode Three right where Glory and Tern try to spy on one of the Town Council meetings that take place in a creepy storm shelter you wouldn't think would exist underground in a place prone to flooding. "And I can't . . . *someone* can't . . . just not *think* about the *dénouement*. From page one, you know the book's going to end. And that everything will be stuck wherever it is, no chance for change. I mean, if you have *eyes*, if you have *fingers*, you can tell there's only a certain number of pages—"

"Your TV shows have *endings*. The series we're watching right now has an ending, however many tedious episodes from now, and—"

"But because you can't feel it coming with your fingers, time is . . . I don't know what the right word for it is—*elastic*? Because it's not written down, I mean. When you're watching something, even if you know you're already halfway through season nine of a series that never made it to season ten, you can still *pretend* it's going to go on, daydream about everything that might still happen."

"So you suspend disbelief," Bree said, typing what sounded like paragraphs. *Suspend* sounded dangly in a way Carley was sure didn't match what she'd meant.

"You know you're going die someday, right? But you don't have a calendar showing how many years or months or days you have left. So you can pretend you'll have episodes until you're, like, a hundred. Daydream about all the *nexts* you're going to have . . ." Click, click, click, went Bree's fingers, every thought Carley was trying to get out being Superglued to words that weren't exactly what she meant, Bree choosing among them the way Sinkman did to end up with something Carley really *really* wouldn't mean and leaving out words Bree probably didn't think were important— little words like *chance* and *could* and *might* that meant everything.

There was more, too, to why she hated books. But to explain it to Bree would doubtless turn out as badly as telling Sinkman about Aftermemory had. Carley wanted to *feel* a story, be *in* it the way TV let you—laugh and cry and not analyze—instead of *think* it the way Nagel and every English teacher she'd ever had said you had to do with books.

"Could you stop *doing* that already?"

"What?"

"Typing." She got up from the bed where she'd been sitting cross-legged and walked over to her desk. "Roll back a little?" Carley pulled open the top drawer and took out a microrecorder Gretchen had bought her. "I'm supposed to say my SAT words into it. I don't. Just record everything, okay? Instead of typing?"

Bree sighed, closed her laptop, and turned on the recorder. "It would help if you could think about what you want to *happen*."

"Jules. I want the main char … *protagonist—*" from List Fourteen: Words About Literature and also from Nagel's class, and maybe the right word would show Bree she wasn't stupid?—"to be called Jules."

"That's … not plot. Not *even* character. It's only a name."

"And the boy is Buck."

"So there's a boy."

This was also something Sinkman did, repeated what she said as if she couldn't hear her own voice. Carley pushed Play on the DVD remote rather than answer, a line from Hunter's note stuck in her head: *Try not to be scared—it's the only time you're ever mean.* Glory ducked behind a half-closed door as the possibly-evil mayor walked by. Bree's tone echoed in Carley's head, Sinkman-esque, Nagel-esque. Carley hit Pause.

"Um, Bree? There's always a boy."

CHAPTER 13

"To be good at darts," Hunter told Carley, watching Amber in the bar mirror that twinned every bottle, "requires more than just a steady hand." Amber missed the entire board, hitting a paper skeleton; the guy she was letting buy her Goldschläger shots traded her a drink for the rest of her weapons. "One needs to *believe* things"—Hunter tapped his empty glass—"will go where one wishes." The new bartender, an old guy with skin so potholed even Hunter's dermatologist-to-the-stars stepmother couldn't have fixed it, ignored him. Hunter coughed hard, laying his head in his crossed arms while he caught his breath. Carley put her palm to his forehead before he could protest and took it away before anyone could notice. In the mirror they sat reversed—Hunter beautifully wrecked, the subject of art photographs; Carley a passerby destined for cropping.

His cell phone rang with the sound a video game made when you got an extra life. "My pleasure," he said into it. He raised his empty glass to Violet Burroughs across the crowd, then poured himself off the barstool, catching his balance like he'd pulled off a trick. Heavy-lidded and loose-smiled, he moved through the room with a silken languor in which everyone wanted to be wrapped: his cousin Ian Buchanan, who used to rule the Station before he left for Princeton two months and twenty pounds ago; Ian's ex-girlfriend Violet, in from Dartmouth and having lost more weight than Ian had gained; Jake Dalton, who believed next September he'd become Hunter like Hunter had become Ian (but wouldn't, because he'd only become one of the Station crowd last spring when he and his girlfriend Olivia started hanging out with Amber and because his father's money was from a string of car dealerships and because Jake was a guy who used the word *posse*); and Olivia, who was forever trying remedies for her acne that turned her skin peely or swollen or angry, and who always laughed at jokes too late. But not tonight. Tonight, out of nowhere, Violet had chosen Olivia as her porta-buddy, whispering into her ear what was funny: Ian's new girlfriend from college, Ian's girlfriend's pink skirt, Ian's girlfriend's pronouncing *really* like *rolly*.

Hunter brought Violet a mineral water. Hunter's own drink, poured by the manager, Reggie, after the new bartender had continued to ignore him, was golden and neat.

Carley pulled Amber away from the shot-buying guy in the bad jacket, who was nobody anybody knew. "Hunter should be in bed."

Amber shrugged, as if hanging out with Bad Jacket wasn't all *about* Hunter, to show him she didn't care about what had happened the other night and didn't care about *his* not caring about it, then faux-flashed Ian, pulling up her orange T-shirt with *Treat* across the chest. Underneath was a black layer: *Trick*. Ian laughed; his girlfriend stared like she'd thought he was someone else before she'd met his friends this weekend, like she wished she'd gone back to Princeton early with Tad/Todd.

Carley's own costume was a combination of toilet paper and Hermès scarves. Above her left breast she wore an official Montclair Academy Board of Trustees nametag, the word *Mummy* taped over Gretchen's name and title.

"He's slurring," Carley said.

Amber took gum from the plastic jack-o'-lantern she carried as a purse. "Where've you been for, like, ever?"

It wasn't like this before. The words formed in Carley's head and got stuck there, voice-over-less. But before when? Change was like drunkenness, snakelike and difficult to hold unless you grabbed it right behind its scary head.

Violet trailed her fingers under the neck of Hunter's crisp collarless shirt and up to his gold earring, a tiny hoop she teased with her pinky. "*Really* cute," she said to Ian's girlfriend about her skirt, shaking her head the way people said *no*. Instead of a costume, like most of the returning alums Violet wore a single item that suggested a costume she would have worn if she weren't too cool for one. Violet's *synecdoche*—Word List Thirty-six: More Words About Literature—was a cowboy hat. Over a white French-cuffed shirt buttoned halfway over a black cami, she wore a black bolo tie fastened by a silver bull that swung back and forth where her breasts used to be. In high school she'd been the kind of bumpy you studied. A topographical map. But everyone said this new look suited her even better—it was a memorable flatness, like the edge of the world.

"That *fringe!*" Violet said to Ian's girlfriend. "Fringe is the *thing*, is it not? Tell me where you got it? Imitation, you know, is the most sincere flattery. Don't you *want* to be flattered?"

She'd grow up to be more beautiful and cruel. She'd get bored of anorexia before it turned her ugly and starve other people instead. Carley knew this as strongly and suddenly as she knew that last night, after he'd left Swann's Way, Hunter had slept with Violet—and that her tracing his earlobe was them *doing it* again, only this time in public.

Amber's iPhone alarm chimed midnight with the chorus of "Party Puker," from the new Whiplash Bouffant album. Autodialing Hunter from five feet away, she yelled, "High Dive Time!"

He raised a finger to ask her to wait, and returned to Violet's tracings.

Amber's finger hovered above the redial button. "Don't," Carley told her.

He'd been edgy since he'd walked into the Station with his eyes glassy from spent tears, shaken about Griffin's finally having caught on to Hunter's inventing expenses and double-billing for real ones. Most of the money Hunter had been pilfering from his father he gave away to people he thought needed it. Some he used to fund parties, the liquor store willing to accept his money despite his age as long as he paid in cash. The rest he kept in a hidden safe in the Play Palace, a remnant from the building's Prohibition days.

He liked clothing and entertaining and was generous to a flaw, but for all Hunter spent, money seemed less important to him than to anyone else Carley knew. During the fifteen minutes she'd been able to talk to him tonight in the back booth before everyone else had arrived, he hadn't bemoaned Griffin's saying Hunter would need to call him to approve bank withdrawals over a hundred dollars from now on or that he was considering cutting up Hunter's credit cards. All he'd whispered, as he pounded two scotches and refused to let her hug him and wouldn't let himself cry in public, was the list of names Griffin had called him—liar, thief, bastard—every word a slash too jagged to heal.

"*Don't,*" Carley repeated now as Amber walked over to Hunter anyway, putting herself between him and Violet and announcing High Dives into his ear and voice mail simultaneously.

Hunter took Amber's elbow as he walked her to the booths at the back. Carley followed. "Go back to your gold shots," he snapped. He'd once confessed to Carley a cache of secret snobberies, among them his disgust at Amber's love of Goldschläger, cinnamon schnapps flecked with twenty-four-karat gold. *Is there anything more nouveau,* he'd asked Carley, *than wanting to swallow something because it's precious?*

"But High Dives! It's *time.*"

"Grow up, first. Children don't get to play with fire."

"Oh, Toilet," Amber called over her shoulder. "I mean *Violet* . . . just wanted to let you know you're doing a crap job of making Ian jealous." Amber giggled. "*Crap job.*" She pulled up *Treat* for no one in particular. Bad Jacket oozed over to her like a slug.

"He's creepy," Carley whispered to Hunter as he led her to where people were waiting for him. "He's old. Like *Old*-old, not college."

Jake, dressed as a caterpillar to coordinate with Olivia's butterfly costume, and Ian, in a Rastafarian wig, long-sleeved polo shirt, and khakis, sat at the bar with Olivia and Violet standing behind them. Ian's girlfriend talked to someone on her cell, pacing the sidewalk on the other side of the plate glass. She'd already taken off her synecdochal headpiece: pink cat ears on a band.

Hunter gave Carley the stool that had been saved for him, holding her hand as she bent her leg to step up to the rung. One of Gretchen's scarves ripped with a sound like a fart.

Violet leaned to Olivia. "She makes you want to burn Halloween."

"Dark or light?" Reggie asked at the taps.

"Dark," Hunter said.

Reggie took out the shot list from under the bar. "You're at K. Kahlúa."

"Amber was the only one to do the Jägermeister on Thursday," said Carley. "We owe her for getting us over the J-hump."

"We'll give her a medal." Hunter patted his nose with a handkerchief. Carley looked away into the mirror. Bad Jacket's hair was too short across his forehead. His eyes were black-button rejects from the Stuff-Your-Own-Bear store at Moreland Galleria. His hand was layered between *Treat* and *Trick*.

Next to glasses of porter, Reggie placed shots of Kahlúa topped with Bacardi 151.

"One…," said Hunter as Reggie began igniting the shots with a barbecue lighter.

"Two…" The glass danced with flame as Carley picked it up with three fingers, holding it above the beer.

"Three."

She dropped it in. Clink. Splash. Chug.

Ian came in first, barely beating out Hunter. Then Jake. Carley was last, but with High Dives everyone won.

Violet kissed Hunter on the mouth, long and deep—"Love the end of a High Dive." She pressed something into his hand. "Hold this? For later."

Catching Carley staring, he shoved it into the pocket of the calfskin jacket he'd taken off and hung over his arm.

By the time they'd gotten up to Midori, Reggie was on break, Ian had gone outside to find his girlfriend, Violet was shaming Olivia into taking off her wings and antennae ("and tell your boyfriend to ditch his penis costume"), Jake was in the bathroom puking from having primed himself for High Dives by drinking six Red Bull and vodkas, and in the mirror Bad Jacket had his keys in hand. "Amber needs rescuing," Carley told Hunter. She'd decided this between Kirsch and Limoncello.

Hunter raised an index finger at the new bartender.

The man came back with coffee. "On the house."

"Not my order." Hunter dropped a fistful of crumpled bills on the bar. They opened like tiny breaths.

"I'll call you a cab," said the bartender.

"Amber's *leaving*," Carley told Hunter, sliding off the stool and grabbing his arm to pull him toward the door. "You *know* it's about you, H, the way she's being tonight, and no one knows who that guy is or where they're going or—"

He shook his hand free and handed Carley his jacket. "I'll take care of it."

"I'm *coming*, she's my friend, too—"

"For godsake, C, if you *know* why she's upset with me, then you should know there's not room for three in this discussion. Just keep the bar warm."

He pushed through the crowd. A minute later, she watched him take Amber's hand from the guy on the other side of the picture window. She watched Ian, already out on the sidewalk with his girlfriend, join Hunter in getting into Bad Jacket's face. She watched Hunter sit down with Amber on the curb, holding her forehead and rubbing her back while she threw up gold.

Carley stroked the jacket in her lap and tried to tell herself that she *wanted* Amber to feel comforted, and that she didn't want to be the kind of person who didn't want someone she loved to be taken care of, and that she wasn't the kind of person who would ever unlove.

The jacket slipped in her lap, a tube falling from the pocket. She got off the stool to retrieve what Violet had handed Hunter. It was pink and squeezable, the kind of container that lip gloss for twelve-year-olds came in. Except it wasn't for twelve-year-olds. The label read XXX *Hot Cherry Pie* XXX.

Girls offered Hunter sex so often and easily that he'd had to make rules for himself, rules Carley had watched him write in his journal years earlier: no virgins, no freshwomen, no crushy types. Carley would hear girls talk about him at parties through noise that made them think they weren't shouting. So *considerate*, they'd say he was as a lover. So *creative*. So *patient*.

He used to be like that *out* of bed all the time, too. Not just sometimes. Not just when he remembered. But maybe it had just gotten to be too much. *She* had gotten to be too much—all her neediness, all the times she embarrassed him and he pretended she hadn't. Had he stopped loving her a little at a time or all at once? If only she'd known it would happen, she would have hung on to her last moments of feeling safe in the world.

When he'd put Amber into a taxi, he came inside and flagged Reggie, looking toward the new bartender and shaking his head. Reggie nodded and grasped Hunter's hand in a gesture halfway between a handshake and high five. Hunter got what he wanted here. When he and Ian had created the midnight High Dive three years earlier, turning the Station into their clubhouse, they'd filled a once-moribund three-dollar-Budweiser bar with a ten-dollar-drink demographic. Reggie would serve a ten-year-old with a decent ID if he came in with Hunter.

As soon as Hunter went to the restroom to blow his nose and double up on cold pills, the new bartender came over to Carley.

"Don't get into a car with him," he said, despite her just having heard Reggie lecture him about *attending to the needs of certain customers.*

She smoothed the bills one by one without looking at him. "No one's driving."

When Hunter returned, Reggie came over with a bottle of Midori.

Carley shook her head. "I'm done."

"I'm not." Hunter signaled Reggie to pour for both of them.

"You should take a break," she said. "Violet's not drinking, and what if you want to, you know, hang out with her later?" Though it gagged her to say it, she was desperate to slow him down. He was at the point of drunkenness when his personality could seriously change, turning him warm in fake ways, cold in real ones. A point when he'd piss people off without caring, and feel deathly ashamed in the morning. "I mean, what if you're too messed up, H, to ..."

"What are you doing?" he whispered as Reggie took out the lighter.

"One," said Reggie.

"Being your friend."

"Two."

"You've got to leave my private life pri—"

"I'm seriously worried about you—"

"Three!"

Hunter slammed his empty glass on the bar and shook his head at her full glass. "You're making me drink *alone*? You want to turn me into an alcoholic?"

Skating on a slick of beer, his glass collided with Carley's still-burning shot and overturned it. The shot glass rolled over the back edge of the bar and smashed. A tongue of flame shot down the bar. "I used to think if you hammered glass," Hunter said, putting it out with Carley's beer, "you could turn it back to sand."

The new bartender argued with Reggie as the barback swept up. *Fucked up*, Carley heard. *Minor. Liquor license.*

"Hunter, my man," Reggie finally said, "time to pack it in."

Hunter raised his chin in the mirror to Ian, who'd managed to get his girlfriend back inside. "He's under control." Ian put a hundred on the bar.

"He's welcome tomorrow. But tonight? Tonight's over."

Carley stood. "Let's go to the Palace, H."

Ian took Carley's stool and put a second hundred on top of the first. "He just needs to relax," he told Reggie. "Princeton app's due Monday. She's a serious bitch, I should know."

People behind them shoved for drinks, their money the level of Carley's face. She squeezed between Hunter and the bar, putting a heel onto the lowest rung of his stool so she was half sitting on his knee, half standing. Ian put down a third hundred.

Reggie shrugged and took out Ouzo—Ian and Hunter having decided long ago to forego the letters N, U, and Z when the liqueurs beginning with them proved undrinkable. Carley whispered into Hunter's ear that she knew how tired he was and how sick and how sad. If they went back to the Palace, he could lie down in bed, where she'd lay a cool compress over his eyes and not turn on the TV at all and read him to sleep from anything he wanted, no matter how long it took, no matter how thick the book or small the print. She wouldn't expect anything of him, she tried to say without saying it, though how did you say *You can close your eyes and pretend I'm someone else?* He tried to turn away as he coughed, but there was nowhere to turn. "Please let's go home," she said, rubbing his neck instinctively before realizing she was *touching* him again. "I'll take care of you."

In the mirror, she saw in Ian's eyes that he'd heard her. She saw Hunter see it, too.

He stood, spilling her off his lap. "My God, C. Are you trying to fuck or nurse me?"

Later, she'd realize she'd never slapped anyone before. Later, she'd feel how solid his cheekbone was against her fingers and hear how sharp the sound of her palm on his skin was. Later, remembering how his head turned with her blow, she'd realize that to protect itself a body sometimes gives in to force instead of resisting it.

Now, she only felt the burning on her hand and in her eyes.

Hunter's hand went to his cheek slowly. Ian placed his hands on her shoulders and walked her three steps back. His girlfriend and Violet shared a look, like strangers in a restaurant when someone's kid won't stop bawling.

Carley ran out the door.

At the curb a cab was disgorging Bunny Gardner and Lauren Vandergraf.

"We too late for Diving?" Bunny wore a corset and garters with long ears and cotton-ball tail, her costume a departure from the ones her mother used to make her wear for Halloween all through elementary and middle school—Easter Bunny, Peter Rabbit, the Velveteen Rabbit, Bugs Bunny, the White Rabbit, the March Hare. She waved at the front window of the Station and took off without waiting for Carley's answer.

Carley slid into the taxi, willing herself home faster than the cabbie could drive.

IN AFTERMEMORY, SHE calls out to Bunny, "Don't drown," as if she doesn't know we all ache to go under and have someone follow after us, tunneling through the water to pull us up before our last breath.

The street-side door to the cab swings open before the driver pulls away.

"You wore irony tonight," Hunter says, getting in, "and spoke truth." He shivers in the heat of the car. When they pull up to the Play Palace, he looks her costume up and down. "Layered, *dark* irony. Very Glory."

As in Season Two, Episode Eight, when Glory attends a Halloween dance because Tern has received a note signed "Secret Admirer" asking her to the dance and Glory's worried it might actually be one of the popular kids setting up Tern for a joke or a member of the Order of Lethe trying to lure Tern to her death. As a costume, Glory pastes a hundred labels from split pea soup cans over her clothing and wears a name tag that says Pea Souper—which of course gets her referred to the school shrink. Again.

"Why didn't you dress up?" Carley says in his room as he unfastens her scarves.

They sit close on his bed. He strokes the back of her hand, making figure eights around her knuckles. "Thought I'd go *sans* disguise. For a change. But I got scared. Hid in a bottle. Treaded booze." He clears his throat. "I know *wanting* doesn't mean much, but I wanted to do it for you."

In Aftermemory, she's a girl who gets things. A girl who knows when to just say "Oh," and nothing else. A girl whose hand you cradle to your lips. The girl you want to be brave for.

CHAPTER 14

My Manifesto

- No characters going around learning things.
- No long descriptions of rooms or food or flowers.
- No allusions. We learned about allusions in English—you need to know a shitload of old stuff to understand the new stuff you're reading. Which means the new stuff isn't new.
- No ending like on the very last episode of *The Arion Annals*, with everything starting all over again.
- No one dies.

Bree sighed.

"Did I use *manifesto* right?"

"I suppose." She abandoned the suitcases she'd been unpacking—*finally*—when Carley had burst in and thrust the paper in her face.

"SAT word. You said to write down what I wanted." She reached into a suitcase and held up a gauzy white shirt. "Guys love you in this, right? It's totally sexy. Diaphragm-less."

"*Diaphanous*," Bree said, turning on the recorder and glancing longingly at her laptop. She found her fingers typing words in the air: Purposeful Malapropisms? (Interesting passive-aggressive character trait for use in future story?)

"Has Justin seen you in it?"

"No."

"Has Justin seen you *out* of it?"

"We're not talking about Justin."

"Everyone else is. He hasn't been in Fox Glen since the accident, you know."

"I didn't. Know. I barely know him at all. And *accident* isn't the right word."

"I heard you guys at the party, you know. Outside. He was like, *Even though you didn't call after I almost died, I wanted to be around you so bad that I crashed the most boring party in the universe instead of going to the city to hang out with models.* And you were like, *Even though I'm acting bitchy, I want to cry with how happy I am to see you.*" She picked up one of Bree's bras between her thumb and index finger. "The elastics are seriously shot. Francis can give you, like, a carton of new ones."

"Do you see me going through *your* underwear?"

"Was Justin's book as romantic as the movie they made of it?"

"I wouldn't call *Crawling* romantic, unless you really believe a married couple trying to fix a leaky toilet themselves because they couldn't afford a plumber would end up having sex on the bathroom floor. Moral of the story: poor people know how to make our own fun, and you can *see* why we have so many babies!"

He'd turned a family's eviction and the repossession of their property into a story about—as he put it time and again in interviews—*needing people, not things.* "As if Justin would ever understand about not needing *things,*" she said to Carley. And then there was the "uplifting" end of *Clinging,* when a mother dying of cancer turns her hospital room into a jungle gym for her kids because, as she says in the last line, she wants to *die watching them climb.* Subtle transition into the still-unwritten *Climbing.* "Dying's not a fucking playground. Can we get back to talking about *your* book?"

Carley sighed. "*Fine.* So how's it gonna make people feel?"

"By *people,* do you mean a certain high-cheekboned acquaintance of yours who spends hours in front of the mirror tousling his overlong hair before donning a social persona so stunning it distracts people from his unquenchable thirst?"

"You don't want your boobs to get floppy." She pulled out a pair of striped velvet pants, Bree's Christmas present to herself last year, and measured them against herself. Bree saw her bite her lip. "You have really small hips."

"For the record, I didn't know Justin was *from* here. I didn't even know *here* existed. You grow up in Vernal, towns like Fox Glen are all just *The North Shore* or *The Gold Coast*, places you go for a field trip to an old mansion turned into a museum, then read about in *Gatsby* years later. You don't know them by name."

"I hate *Gatsby*."

"Then we have exactly one thing in common."

"So listen, I was thinking I want you to throw in some of the weird smart stuff you did in your long-ass novel."

There was a crisp knock just as Bree was about to suggest Carley read a few pages of *Scylla,* if only to be able to differentiate between *good* weird "smart" stuff and *bad* weird stuff—à la whatever happened in the last season of *The Arion Annals,* which Carley had complained had included *a weird-ass episode where the camera was, like, upside-down.*

"Mister Hunter Cay," Grace announced when Bree opened the door, then turned back for the stairs. Voices resonated from below.

"We're *more* than happy to lend Bree to Suzanne for her party, of course," said Gretchen. "We're *flattered.*"

"Still, I'm certain she intended to ask you before she issued Bree the invitation to do a reading there. An oversight. With her leaving for Newport—"

"And the excitement of the engagement."

"There's that."

When he came up, he leaned against the wall. His cheeks were flushed, his nose chapped. Coughing softly, he wrapped his arms around his stomach as if to protect it.

"Come sit," Bree said. "Before you fall."

He shook his head. "Field trip when you're done, C?" He spoke carefully, slowly, taking shallow breaths. "Not the Hamptons, if that's all right, but something closer to home? I'll be outside, taking air. No rush." He took a dog-eared paperback copy of *The Great Gatsby* from inside his jacket. "My notes are in it. For those essays you owe."

"Stay and help? Bree wants to know what I want. And I don't know. What I want, I mean. But you would."

"Sounds like something you're supposed to figure out yourself." From someone else it might have sounded unkind, but he said it without sarcasm. He took a deep breath that reignited the cough. "I need to be outside. Take your time."

"Take care of yourself," Bree told him.

He gave her a smile that was a breath away from tears.

"You going to get him help?" Bree asked when the door had closed.

"Help? He doesn't. . . . He just gets these awful colds. They wear him out. And he's . . . you're giving me that look like you think you know something about Hunter. People always think they know him."

"He's self-invented. Thinks he's self-contained. Drinks to ignore his seepage. I feel truly sorry for him. He's very young to be so lonely."

"*Lonely?* You know *nothing*. He's—"

"People who make fiction of themselves can't be otherwise."

The recorder caught the sound of the door slamming. Lonely, Bree typed into the air before she turned it off.

CHAPTER 15

Hunter slouched in the driver's seat, *Tales of the Jazz Age* in his lap and a handkerchief in his fist.

"You so need to be in bed."

"Been there all morning."

He put the car into reverse, made a cautious three-point turn, then slammed on the brakes and swung open his door. He barely got the seatbelt off before he started retching.

She looked away, out the passenger window, until she could no longer hear him turning himself inside out.

"It's going to rain tonight," she said when she turned back. He kicked fallen leaves over the vomit. "It'll wash away."

"I'm so sorry," he whispered as he got back into the car. "For last—"

"Your hands are shaking. Want me to drive?"

He'd begun teaching her right after he'd finished driver's ed himself last year, and though she was too young to have a piece of paper saying she *could* drive, she was still far more comfortable behind the wheel than he was. "It's exactly something you'll love," he'd told her, never resenting how hard he had to concentrate to do something that indeed felt so natural to her. They used to practice together on nights when he suffered from insomnia, at first winding around and around on the circular drive that connected the several buildings of the Cay estate, and later moving on to the sleepy town roads, empty at three a.m. of even the Fox Glen police.

He shook his head at her offer, looking left, right, left before pulling out. He looked gorgeous in his car when it was parked, or when he was idling at a light, but as he'd said himself once on a fevered night: *I drive like I learned from a book.*

"I wanted to come by this morning," she said. "I knew you'd be feeling really bad. Sick and hungover and ... I wanted to make you feel better, but ... I know you were trashed last night, H, but—"

"I had to call Ian to find out why you wouldn't pick up my calls. I didn't ... know ... remember. I've been trying to convince myself I'm still asleep, having a nightmare, about to wake up sweating and tangled in my sheets. It's impossible I could have been so cruel."

He pulled over to the side of the road (side view mirror check, rearview, blind spot) and cupped her hand. "It should have been a conversation just between us. I should have brought it up a month ago. I should have brought it up sober."

"It."

He flicked on his signal though the road was empty. Looked in every direction but hers.

HE SETTLED THEM onto a rock near the tide line, setting out cheese and a loaf of bread on a checkered napkin though they both knew he wouldn't be able to eat anything. He took from his leather backpack a thermos that was sleek and silver, like a slow-motion bullet. The steam smelled like Carley's grade-school trips to Hudson Valley orchards, where the crispness of fall and possibility of hay rides and novelty of picking food from trees turned fruit into something exotic. She and Amber would sit on hay bales, their hands wrapped around Styrofoam cups of cider and their mouths filling with a tangy sweetness that made Carley's head rush. She'd imagined alcohol would make her feel like that. Or blood. At the time she'd been into this show, *Undead High*, about vampire kids who wore Gothic clothes and didn't have curfews, and had thought about becoming a vampire at least as often as becoming an adult. Inhaling the scents of burning wood and fallen apples, she was sure that getting bitten or growing up meant living forever in a feeling you chose.

Hunter raised a cup to her lips. She sipped as he tilted it, moving together like they used to. In the moment she formed the words *used to* in her head, he angled it too steeply. Cider dribbled down her chin.

As she rubbed at her coat and he patted her face with a handkerchief, she longed for him to lick the juice from her neck, an ache mixed up with knowing she'd never go apple picking again because she was too old for it the way she was too old for touch tanks or petting zoos or choosing a pumpkin from a bunch laid out in tall grass to make kids think they've chosen something when they really haven't—and all of this, everything, made her desperate to cry and desperate to kiss him and desperate.

She stared out at where the sand met the Sound, waiting for something to break their sticky silence. *This is where you live,* her teachers used to say when they took her class for field trips not a mile from this stretch of private beach on the Cay estate. As if they could ever forget they were on an island, a place with edges. As if they might wake one day and walk right past the shore.

In second grade she'd sat cross-legged, drawing pictures of what she saw—gulls, ducks, and sandpipers; a confetti of shells; broken pilings covered with algae and barnacles, rising from the water like crooked teeth. In fourth grade she'd written reports on ghost crabs and moon snails and egrets and ospreys. In sixth—the year before Hunter moved to Fox Glen and the last time kids could move around and touch things on field trips instead of being told to "act their age"—she'd gone out on a boat and netted bluefish and blackfish and baby flounders whose eyes hadn't yet joined each other on the same side of their bodies.

Something blue-black dropped from the sky. The gull shrieked as it dove for its mussel. She'd worn a puffy orange life vest. She'd run her fingers over clams and eelgrass. She'd watched the guide hold up a live horseshoe crab—which wasn't a crab at all, but a marine spider whose not-shell was just a skin it left on the shore when it outgrew it. *Behold,* the guide had said before tossing it back, *the oldest living fossil.*

She'd had a teacher that fall who didn't last through winter, a teary woman who was always cleaning her glasses with the hem of her skirt and who'd made kids say the things that used to live in shells had *passed away* instead of *died.*

Carley handed the cup to Hunter. He shook his head and took out a second one.

"We always share, H."

"We need to talk about your feelings." He scraped the toe of his loafer into the sand.

"My *feelings.*"

"About sex. About . . . me."

"You finger-fucked Amber one night, and made love to someone I hate the next." She took XXX *Hot Cherry Pie* XXX from her pocket and dropped it into his hand. "What do you think I *feel* about your sex life?"

"What I meant . . . mean . . . is I understand you're *having* them. Feelings. *Sexual* feelings. Which are normal. Very normal." He stared at the tube. "But which to talk about are rather . . . awkward."

Awkward was Gretchen laying out tampons and pads on Carley's bed and arranging them into rows and columns, a Bingo board of feminine protection, while she explained in monotone Carley's womanly options without looking at her. Carley had been ten and already school-informed. Gretchen had been ashen and double-dosing Percocet and whispering, *There can be a smell.*

Discussing Carley's *sexual* feelings for Hunter *with* Hunter was an undiscovered continent past awkward. A place overrun by flesh-eating monkeys who sucked on your intestines while you were still alive.

"What Ian told me this morning—what he said I said—made it clear we *need* to discuss this more directly than I'd—"

"You needed to be *told* what you said. *That's* not something to discuss?"

"For a long time people have been trying to get through to me about how we act—the way I *let* us act. The back rubs, the lying around together, the co-sleeping. It's selfish of me. It's not fair to you."

"Fair. Don't *I* get to decide what's fair to me?"

"What you want ... what you're hoping for ... it's not right to give you that hope. We go around acting like we're married, but C, we're not a couple. And we won't be."

In her head she formed gorgeous, long paragraphs of breathtaking sentences that explained exactly how wrong he was about her feelings for him, which were *nuanced* and not at all needy or clingy or an urge away from humping his leg.

"I'm losing weight. Two pounds last week." Only after the words left her mouth did she remember he'd read what Gretchen had taped to her mirror. "You *should* be with pretty girls. It would be a ... a waste. But maybe someday it'll turn out underneath ... this ... me ..." She couldn't stop saying things she didn't exactly mean, none of the words matching what was in her head. "We don't know, you know. Underneath, I could maybe be beautiful."

The wind blew his hair into his eyes. In the seconds before he raked it away, he could maybe want her. Sometimes in bed she ran her fingers over her stomach, pretending her hand was someone else's hand, trying to separate the feeling of stomach-on-fingers from fingers-on-stomach and telling herself they were the fingers of a blind person, the kind who's been blind since birth and couldn't match the shape of a person to a picture in his head. She told herself blind fingertips could think her belly was velvet and fur, textures that let you in.

Hunter took her hand in his but didn't squeeze it, his loose grip like a blank piece of paper you'd expected to be a note. "Why we can't work, C? It's not what you're thinking. To feel ... turned on ..." He breathed deep. "Let's take Violet."

"You already have."

"You know who Violet thinks she's sleeping with? The guy I see in the mirror. The not-me guy with the face and the charm and the confidence. And when I sleep with girls like her—people who believe I'm him—I lose myself in *being* him. To be blunt, it turns me on." He blushed, shrugged, looked away from her at the water. "But you know me, C. And you can't unknow me. My ugly truths, my pettiness, my cowardice." He turned back to her and kissed her forehead. "I'm not turned on by being me. And I can't be anyone *but* me with you."

In his eyes she saw how badly he wanted to believe the lie. He wanted to be someone out of a book, a self-hating prince who didn't notice the fat chick was fat. A prince in Prada shoes and a Patek Philippe watch and a five-hundred-dollar haircut who didn't care that she had the shape of a profiterole and the muscle tone of pâté. You needed to be able to live with the you-in-your-head.

They sat still as shells. The air was salty with the ocean she couldn't see beyond the Sound. The wind was louder than their breath. She stared at the runnels in the sand, paths water had taken back to its body as the tide pulled away.

CHAPTER 16

"Action is character," wrote F. Scott Fitzgerald. Reflect upon a choice you have made that defines your character. Your essay should be approximately five hundred words.

Hunter had answered this question no fewer than a dozen times, not one of his responses having satisfied his private college counselor. His first attempt had been written in the spring while he was home sick and exhausted to the point of truth:

Among the friends my mother has made since moving to the town of Fox Glen four years ago, there is a curious phenomenon that occurs when their eyes fall upon photos of me in my youth: they claim I was a beautiful child in whom they can see the future handsome man. Herein lies the seductive power of regression, the reasoning backward from conclusion to evidence: I was a fat, pimply kid, blind without my thumb-smudged glasses.

They bring to those photos my nowness: cheekbones they imagine beneath the avoirdupois; highlights they believe have been forever in my hair, though such subtlety has been rendered bimonthly only since the summer before eighth grade when my mother first ushered me to the colorist; and, of course, that distant gaze they imagine as my young self looking out at my Golden Boy future. In fact, because I refused contact lenses out of bookish obstinacy and my mother refused to let me wear my glasses in photos out of aesthetic fascism, I was staring at a blur.

A month before that summer, just as my family was about to move from Manhattan to the Long Island estate my father had purchased for the same reason he buys companies, art, and people—_investment_—and in which my mother had invested two years of renovation and redecoration, my parents discovered each other's affairs. Hers with my pediatrician; his with my au pair. (My mother was the more aggrieved party, her catching Griffin in the act—marble foyer, desperate sex, the Help—having not at all mitigated the clause in their prenuptial agreement that capped her alimony were _she_ unfaithful.)

To distance me from the vortex of bitterness and communal property that our penthouse became, I was sent to a place my classmates relished and I regarded as horrible urban myth. Camp. Given the five-hundred-word limit, I'll skip the specifics. Suffice it to say it was the first domino in a series that overturned who I was: deprived of books in the three months in which I grew four inches, I had nothing better to do than learn soccer and lose thirty pounds.

When at summer's end I began school in a new town with new clothing as the new-kid cousin of Ian Buchanan, teen WASP god, I hoped for little more than to avoid harassment. I didn't understand the power of beauty. I didn't know I had it. I couldn't properly decode the _me_ in the mirror.

I knew only that I was still eccentric. In that, if only that, I haven't changed. Understand, I never meant to construct a persona. I am not self-created. They made me.

If I were not already somewhere past word four-hundred-and-fifty with my conclusion not yet in sight, I would tell you creation stories. About how my saying _films_ turned my peers squinting at anyone who dared speak of _movies_. About how my complying with my mother's overzealousness to correct twelve years of unkempt-ness led to a sea change in the attire of every other boy in the eighth grade. About how when my first cold of the school year hit, my punkness was mistaken as hangover—a misapprehension I kindled that day to avoid being cast as the sick kid I'd always been, and encouraged so frequently afterward that long before I drank much, I'd displaced Ian as the reputed partier.

And, if you had the time, I'd summon the courage to tell you about the moment I looked into a mirror and realized there was little I could do that my face wouldn't excuse.

I'd tell you everything they built me up to be began with something real. I'd tell you I didn't expect the facade to grow so quickly, nor did I expect to grow into it. I'd tell you removing it would have been like peeling off my skin. I'd tell you that when I'm ill, I sometimes think my body is trying to expel me from it.

I'd tell you I know nothing above qualifies as a "decision."

I don't expect admiration for my non-choices, my allowing the world to define me. I merely ask you to consider this: I am signing my name right now to this truth, in all its ugliness. It is this decision, this day, which defines my character.

Indulgent, the counselor had called it. *Arrogant.* And, finally, *Suicidal.*

Each successive attempt to get to what she called "the heart" of his character brought him further from it. The community service essay about spending a month in South America building huts for poor people through a program designed to plump up the community service sections of rich kids' college applications she called *Overdone.* The rebounding-from-adversity essay about losing a bid at student council vice-presidency his junior year to win the presidency as a senior she called *Pseudo-hardship.* Scoring the winning goal in the championship soccer game his sophomore year despite an injury that turned out to be a fractured collarbone she called *Thinly veiled braggadocio.*

He did not write about gifting his drug dealer, Antoine, thousands of dollars toward his daughter's cancer treatments. He did not write that at times he became so depressed over his own insignificant illnesses—*death by paper cuts*—that he secretly wished for some "real" disease. He did not write that his guilt over such thoughts was only heightened by Antoine's gratitude and only alleviated by Antoine's pills.

He did not write about how the act of writing that very first essay, putting truth into words, had left him raw and irretrievably sad.

Last week, in desperation, he'd brought the counselor a short story he'd written years before. "This is it," he'd told her. "My most important truth."

Fiction is unacceptable, she'd said, shaking her head three paragraphs in. *Might have anyone close to you died?* It was an overdone topic, she admitted. But handled creatively, death always left an impression.

Now, hunched over his laptop in bed, he gave it one last shot:

Derived from a Greek word meaning to inscribe and a Middle English word meaning imprint on the soul, **character** is defined not by words, but by actions. Not a single action, but an entire lifetime—which makes answering your question nigh impossible. (Does my using "nigh" lead you to think "Pretentious kid," or are you willing to ride out this essay on the off chance I've saved an orphanage or returned from the dead?)

He deleted the last line, then lay back on the pillows. He didn't dare close his eyes. For weeks he'd been getting into trouble for oversleeping, missing classes and tests and last Saturday's soccer game. The application had to be postmarked tomorrow, and he couldn't skip anything—make-up math test first period, Student Council meeting at lunch, bus to an away game after school. (As his coach kept reminding him, he was lucky to still be *on* the team.)

He shouldn't have taken more pills, but his stomach had ached from the coughing, and his throat felt torn up, and he hadn't been able to get Carley's tears out of his mind.

He'd wanted to tell her the truth. First yesterday, and then again today. He'd planned to explain it hadn't been *him* snapping at her for weeks now, but rather withdrawal or fear of it. It hadn't been *him* saying that hurtful thing last night, but rather an amalgam of synthetic opiates and booze and feverishness. But as she'd sat beside him in his car, he'd realized what telling her would really mean. Not just telling the story of how the Vicodin prescribed by his doctor for throat pain when he'd had mono had so dependably comforted him and eased his insomnia that giving it up at the end of the prescription had been as unthinkable as giving up his best friend. Not just letting Carley ease his fear and shame. Not just bathing in the love she'd never withhold.

It would mean breaking up with the pills. Saying good-bye forever.

And still he'd be left with an unfinished application, Griffin's anger, failed math tests, his mother's dumb and mean-spirited fiancé, insomnia, a runny nose two-hundred-dollar handkerchiefs didn't render any less disgusting, and a best friend he'd always disappoint. This last—he'd convinced himself this afternoon when he again couldn't bring himself to speak the truth—was in fact the root of his problem. He hadn't just been hurting her, he'd told himself—she'd been hurting *him* with the pressure of her expectations. Without having to carry the weight of her unspoken hope, surely he could wean himself from his crutch.

Now, lying alone, remembering how little her hope had weighed, he knew he'd lied to himself. Her hope had always been there, a tiny thing she'd held close since the night they'd first become friends. So many times they'd cuddled it between them in his bed. It had asked nothing of him and had made her happy. He could have been patient about weaning Carley from it. He hadn't had to rip it away.

He picked up the phone. He put it down. What could he say? And why, really, would he be calling? Not to comfort her, but to be comforted.

What **is** an action, really?

No matter how hurt she was, no matter how he'd embarrassed her, she'd help him if he asked. If her parents let her, she'd come over to stay up with him. If not, she'd tell them Hunter was sick and alone—as she'd done before when Suzanne was out of town—and Francis would have Hunter ensconced in a guest room at Swann's Way within the hour.

Is it the time it takes to do something?

He could sleep a little if he went there—an hour, just to take the edge off the exhaustion. Carley would bring him coffee afterward. Francis would stay up with him, saying ridiculous, well-meaning things like *All-nighter, everyone!*

Is it the time it takes to decide to do it?

And in the morning Carley would feel confused. And used. And . . .

In a minute he would just get *himself* up. Brew espresso. Open the windows. Walk himself awake. He could do this. Vanquish sleep today, pills tomorrow. Be better. Be brave. Be a man.

CHAPTER 17

Bree McEnroy <btmcenroy@yahoo.com> November 1 10:07 PM
to: Carley Wells <seawells@gmail.com>
cc:
re: Respond ASAP or I'll forward to your parents

Despite your terminating our meeting, I managed to use my newfound understanding of television (I'm up to season two of *Arion Annals* and have reviewed representative episodes of three different reality shows) to cobble together an idea I believe you'll like.

I have attached my plan. With only a month for its execution, I require your immediate feedback.

NOVEL FOR CARLEY WELLS, V.2

Notes—November 1st

Setting:

Medieval-themed Reality Television Show in which ten families compete in a series of Challenges and Votes to become the ultimate

Lords of the Manor—winners of the million-dollar prize. (Satisfies
Client's interest in TV; satisfies Client's mother's stipulations
re: book "matching" Medieval party theme.)

Characters:

Jules, a sixteen-year-old contestant who, per Client's request,
must "dress cool." (Given the Medieval Reality TV Show premise for
the book—see above—and the clothing participants would be
obligated to wear, e.g., kirtles, tunics, surcoats, and wimples,
satisfying such a request might prove difficult.)

Buck, a seventeen-year-old contestant. Among Buck's talents is his
ability to "figure out things about a person without them [sic]
telling him."

Plot:

Forced to spend their summer vacations on an embarrassing
reality program where their families' every move is evaluated by
a voting television audience, Buck and Jules fall in love on the
set of _____ (show yet untitled, see below). But with cameras
and microphones planted in every daub and wattle hut, can they
ever have a private moment?

Each section of the book will begin with a "Challenge" in which
the families compete to become that week's "Lords of the Manor"—
the players who get to live in the luxurious castle instead of in
huts and who nominate two other families for "Banishment," one of
which will be voted out of the kingdom by the television
audience.

Possible challenges include:

> Making almond milk
> Weaving cloth
> Plowing fields with oxen
> Shearing sheep

Style:

Client has requested author incorporate some of the "cool weird things" author did in her published novel, by which Author believes Client means the work's metafictional elements. Author would appreciate Client reading a few pages of published novel to make sure this is really what she wants, as very occasionally people find themselves put off by such devices.

For the purpose of clarification, examples of metafictional devices include the following:

- Characters who are aware that they're characters.
- Embedded fictions that comment upon their hosts (like that TV show Glory watches in <u>The Arion Annals,</u> in which an entire town of displaced-feeling teenagers discover they're in fact descendents of Atlantis).
- Calling attention to literary conventions that are supposed to be transparent. For example, my Odysseus announcing, "Enough for my point of view," before the narrator switches to Dionysus's POV. Or footnotes footnoted with footnotes that call attention to themselves instead of to what they are ostensibly footnoting.

Title:

I suggest having the "real" book and the "reality" TV show within
it identically titled, thus reinforcing the "unreality" of both.
Some possibilities I've considered are:

- Forty Days and Forty Knights (10 families of 4, in a 40-day
  competition.)
- Storming the Castle
- Family Fray
- Dark Ages (Unfortunately, it's intrinsically anachronistic—The
  Dark Ages predated the feudalistic system loosely used in the
  show.)

Carley Wells <seawells@gmail.com>   November 1 10:42 PM
to: Bree McEnroy <btmcenroy@yahoo.com>
cc:
re: ALMOND MILK CHALLENGE?

if u had a sense of humor id think ur kidding about people watching
other people crush up nuts or however u make almond milk and also
the weaving cloth and pretty much all the challenges suck.

i like dark ages its a good title and it turns out anachronism is one of
my SAT words for my tutor for next week what are the odds, right?
anyway i dont get why ur worried about things being misplaced in
time on TV or maybe you didn't see the episode of *Caveman Land*
when they were hunting for dinosaur eggs?

what else? that footnote thing you talked about sounds like something
hunter would like so yes on that.

and im sorry i slammed the door on u like that. hunter always says storming out is more cowardly than just running away because at least if ur running ur being honest about being scared instead of pretending to be something else like mad.

Bree McEnroy <btmcenroy@yahoo.com>   November 1 11:25 PM
to: Carley Wells <seawells@gmail.com>
cc:
re: New challenges

Jousting
Wresting a sword from a stone
Unicorn hunting
Dragon slaying

CHAPTER 18

Hunter tossed in his king-sized bed, searching his pillows for cool spots in his sleep. Amber requizzed herself for tomorrow's final *Great Gatsby* exam and tested swallows for soreness. Olivia ignored Amber's IM question about the meaning of Dr. T. J. Eckleburg's spectacles and IM'd another Hi! to Violet, who still didn't Hi! back. Justin wrote and erased three e-mails to Bree. Bree closed her eyes and tried to remember being a teenager and thought *Justin, Justin,* her mouth filling with the aftertaste of something sticky-sweet. Gretchen lay wondering if Suzanne would have been so gracious about *her* borrowing something like an author without asking. Francis stroked the drying lily hidden in his pillowcase. Carley stood in her bathroom, swirling her father's Bengay into flavored lip gloss to try to comprehend *Hot Cherry Pie.* She sniffed it, tasted it, gagged. Washed her hands until they pruned, until she cried herself sick. Until she turned back time.

IN AFTERMEMORY, SHE takes a cab back to the Palace after dinner, armed with Bree's words.

"You have to stop making yourself up, H. It's making you lonely. It's making you drink."

"I can't." He pulls the covers up to his waist to cover his boxers, though he's sweating.

"Who you are, he's not all noble and heroic all the time, but so what?

You like hotties and sex gel and sleeping late. You have a snobbish streak. You cry easily. You're afraid of open water. You like being babied as long as you can pretend not to. And you can't stand anyone doing more for you than you do for them. But none of that takes away from your being an amazing person. I *know* you, H, and that guy you were talking about before in the mirror? He's not *better* than you."

On a current of tears, he says tell that to Griffin and Suzanne and Larry and Ian and the college admissions committee for whom he lacks a *character-defining* action.

"Let's leave," she tells him. Go someplace far away and quiet where he could write, like he's always saying he wants to do. She could work anywhere there's skiing or swimming and little kids who need lessons. She hates sitting in school and likes *doing*. Though she's not very smart, she's good at showing people things. They'd eat pancakes because they cost almost nothing. They'd watch TV without cable. They'd learn how to take the bus. At night he'd read aloud to her from his book, which would be the most amazing book in the whole world that no one couldn't love. They'd hold hands and talk about their old selves like they were still suffocating in Fox Glen.

"*Old Carley* is crying in a fitting room again," she'd say.

"*Old Hunter* is kissing the headmaster's ass for a recommendation."

They lie in Hunter's bed listening to the whispers of their future selves until they're trembling to make a plan. Right after her Sweet Sixteen, when she'll get hundreds of envelopes of money, they'll pretend they're taking a day trip to the city. They'll dress in layers, stuff money belts with her birthday money and the cash in Hunter's safe. They'll buy Amtrak tickets to Boston with their credit cards to throw people off their trail. They'll dye and cut their hair. By the time their parents call the police, they'll be halfway to Montana or Idaho on a bus.

"It'll be a forever field trip," she promises as she hugs him. He sighs into her neck, his breath warm and sweet. "One that never ends."

CHAPTER 19

Hunter awoke to daylight and his soccer co-captains yelling over the phone that he'd better get to Montclair by noon to meet the requirement of being at school at least half the day in order to participate in extracurriculars. What was *wrong* with him for cutting it so close when they needed to win today's game to qualify for next weekend's tournament?

He hung up and squinted at the last line on his computer screen:

Or just the time it takes to type the worrrrrrrrrrrrrrrrrrrrrrrrrrr
rrrrrrrrrrrrrrrrrrrrrrrrrrrrrrrrrrrrrrrrrrrrrrrrrrrrrrrrrrrrrrrrrr

He'd lose his co-captainship and probably get thrown off the team if he didn't make it to school in a half hour. He'd already missed his last chance for the make-up math test he'd rescheduled three times already for a class he was close to failing. The FedEx envelope with the rest of his application lay at the foot of the bed, waiting for him to feed it one more thing.

He printed out the first essay the counselor had rejected, then the next and the next, staring at all of them and knowing none of them could make up for who he was.

He shut his eyes and pulled his knees to his chest, rocking as he sobbed, his hands balled. "Please," he said, over and over to no one without knowing what he was asking for. "Please."

The prompt baited him even with his eyes closed, the words burned into his memory: *"Action is character,"* wrote F. Scott Fitzgerald. *Reflect upon a choice you have made that defines your character.*

When he finally opened his eyes, he unclenched his fists and stared at his fingers. Swallowing back another wave of tears, he typed:

```
My father, Griffin Cay, could buy you.
```

PART III

Devices

Writers aren't people exactly. Or, if they're any good, they're a whole lot of people trying so hard to be one person.

—F. Scott Fitzgerald, *The Last Tycoon*

The pleasure of your company is requested
at a dinner party celebrating
the engagement of

SUZANNE STANTON CAY

and

LAWRENCE TALBRIGHT IV

Saturday, the seventh of November
at eight o'clock
20 Brookside Road
Fox Glen, New York

CHAPTER 20

Later, Suzanne Cay would retell that evening as her greatest social coup, the story of a party for which not one invitation had been declined and to which the most sought-after man in Fox Glen had called to beg room at her table. She would forget having invited Justin's mother and stepfather, away in Italy and inclined to invent previous commitments in response to her invitations when they were in town. She would forget "inviting" the Weisses, whose declination had been rigged, the date of the party having been chosen to coincide with Jazzy's Disney World party, which her son had mentioned in passing. She would forget finding the beef overcooked and the Pinot reedy. She would forget her fiancé's being too busy glad-handing to notice her lover tickling the back of her neck with an anthurium petal. She would forget her son getting combatively drunk before the first course.

"I don't know which is more bewildering," Hunter said to her as Justin Leighton cut through the salon, his cane parting guests like the sea. "People treating Rock Star like the guest of honor at someone else's engagement dinner, or your having betrothed yourself to a man with the IQ of sweetbreads."

"Do stop," she whispered. Larry strode past without taking her arm. With mermaid steps she followed behind, the way she inevitably did after a man netted her. Her Grecian-style gown, a celadon that muddied her blondness, was a replica of the Oleg Cassini that Jackie Kennedy had worn to a White House dinner honoring Nobel Peace Prize winners. *Robert Frost* had been at that dinner, she'd told Hunter when he'd shaken his head and urged her to stick to the red Dior. *Pearl Buck*. Three years ago, while dating the heir to the Swiggfield candy fortune—a man renowned for his deep faith in both reincarnation and polo—Suzanne had decided her November 22nd birthday bonded her spiritually to the Kennedys.

"I was born the day Jack died," she liked to tell people. When Hunter had once pointed out that such a statement could be construed as deceptive—the actual *year* of her birth having predated 1963 considerably— she'd accused him of calling her *old* and reclused herself in her bedroom with her *A Tour of the White House with Mrs. John F. Kennedy* DVD on auto-repeat for an entire weekend.

Hunter sidestepped a knot of guests to cut in front of Larry. "Forget something? Perhaps Suzanne?" He bumped into a floor vase of gymnastically tortured willows.

Larry took Hunter's glass. "Careful where you're going, Prince." It was a pet name Hunter allowed only Suzanne, who needed fairy tales, Camelots.

Larry handed Suzanne the glass with a quick hard blink, then thrust his palm at Justin Leighton. Justin nodded at the hand and smiled without extending his own.

"The president was always rushing past Jackie," Suzanne whispered, returning Hunter his drink.

Larry squinted expectantly at the jacket pocket containing Justin's right hand, as if candy or a magic trick might emerge.

"Jack couldn't help it," she told Hunter as he offered her his arm. "So many important people coming to the White House. So much to keep straight. Jackie would hold her head high and laugh as he took off like a hound after foxes."

"*The unspeakable in full pursuit of the uneatable*, Wilde called hunting."

"When you love someone you let things go."

"Foxes. Hounds. Such pursuits are unsporting."

Making no effort to conceal his eavesdropping, Justin smiled and leaned back against the piano that was Suzanne's newest commission in her quest to turn her home into the Jackie-era White House, the salon being Suzanne's East-Room-in-progress. The piano's legs were gold eagles. Its bench was upholstered in gold fabric to match the furniture and window treatments. Above all this gilded horror loomed a decidedly un-Jackie-ish ceiling mural depicting the myth of Orpheus that Suzanne could not renovate away despite its gruesome depiction of the demigod being torn apart—literally— by women. When she'd first begged Griffin to purchase the estate, she'd been entranced by the idea of moving into a designated historical landmark with wall and ceiling murals from the nineteen twenties—*We'll live in history*, Hunter remembered her saying to justify the fortune she put into restoring the house, grounds, and Play Palace, the property having lain fallow for years due to the previous owner's inability to afford its upkeep.

Once the Kennedy obsession had taken hold after the divorce, Suzanne decided she in fact hated the murals. But when she mentioned to a local decorator her plan to have them painted over in both the main house and the Palace, the woman asked if Suzanne *meant* to offend the Gold Coast Preservation Society *and* the Fox Glen Preservation Society, of which Emily Leighton Logan was president. Did she want people to think she was a woman who'd cover up history?

Hunter looked away from Justin now and drank deeply, sips warming into waves. It wasn't just last weekend's exchange with Justin that made it hard for Hunter to meet his eyes. At the heart of Hunter's unease was a folder of his short stories that Suzanne had forwarded in the spring to Justin through his mother in the hope that the decade's most famous writer would pen a recommendation for Hunter's college applications.

Hunter had worried Justin would interpret such a request as a demand: *Read these or I tell the world you're hiding out in the gardener's cottage.* But not even to get into Princeton and satisfy Griffin would Hunter have ever blackmailed the man.

Since he was six years old, Hunter had been coming down with writer-crushes, longings that hit like fever and were symptomized by book-binges and daydreaming. During stiff dinners with his parents, later supplanted by stiffer dinners with his mother and her boyfriends, he'd fantasize about the subjects of his literary affections, imagining them milling about wine bars and bookstores and cafés in wait for someone like Hunter to engage them in witty banter that would tumble into bittersweet profundity by the end of the evening, by which time his crushes would be revealed to be exactly who their books had told him they would be—generous, brooding, wounded, kind. His favorites broke his heart with kindness.

He didn't often think about God, but certain lines of certain books ("And so we beat on, boats against the current," and "All moments, past, present, and future, always have existed, always will exist," and "I could hear my heart beating. I could hear everyone's heart") he reread like prayers. In Fitzgerald and Vonnegut and Carver was assurance of one's not-aloneness. To be a devout reader was to be an acolyte of solace.

By the time Hunter had borrowed *Crawling* from his mother halfway through eighth grade, he'd experienced dozens of such literary pinings, and had also fooled around with girls, one of whom—a sophomore—had relieved him of his virginity in the coat closet of the Glen Club. Thus he knew many varieties of longing coexisted. He regarded his preoccupation with Justin Leighton with no more trepidation than he'd felt several months earlier during a short-lived Edith Wharton obsession: crushing on the former no more made him gay than crushing on the latter made him a necrophiliac. Many of Hunter's best crushes had, in fact, been dead.

Crawling had been on *The New York Times* paperback bestseller list for forty weeks and *Clinging* was number one on hardback when Justin had taken the podium at the fundraiser for Books for Children at which Tori Wilson waited with a thirty-eight special. They were still on the lists two months later when Hunter first saw Justin through the woods. Two years after that, with *Clinging* still maintaining a foothold on the paperback list, Suzanne had come up with the idea.

No, Hunter insisted, as his private college counselor jumped on it. No, even if a personal recommendation from a famous author was his best chance of being taken seriously by the Ivy League. No, even if a testament of literary precocity was his only chance of redeeming his B's in math and the courses he had to drop when he'd had mono. No, even if, as the counselor kept reminding him, *many* above-average, soccer-playing, well-liked, well-rounded wannabe writers from Long Island with wealthy alumni fathers had better chances of getting into Princeton than he did.

A week later Griffin showed up at the Play Palace unannounced with the folder of Hunter's stories in his hand and suggested Hunter was reluctant to share his work with a real author because he feared a genuine assessment of his talent. Perhaps Hunter should concentrate on some other hobby. Perhaps at writing he was average.

I am terribly sorry, Hunter wrote in the cover letter that Suzanne would imagine being forwarded by Emily Leighton Logan to some other continent, to presume upon your time. Any recommendation you could afford me would mean the world.

His junior year ended. He left for Europe. He returned. He began his senior year. And then finally, a month ago, his stories lay in front of his front door when he returned from school.

His hands shook as he opened the package. Typed on a single sheet of unsigned notepaper were only two words:

Live First.

"I lost my size zero when I had Carley," Hunter heard Gretchen tell his Aunt Plum now, and turned toward them to break Justin's gaze. "Were there a God, he'd have made pregnancy shrink the attractive as incentive." Hunter knew she meant it, just as he knew Carley, standing next to her mother and practicing the look-slimmer-in-minutes posture tips from last week's episode of *The Frog Princess*, was imagining Gretchen halved and rehalved in a Zeno's Paradox of pregnancy.

He knew Greer and Cissy Gardner were coke-wired, as always at parties, and that while Violet's father was boasting about the success of his investments, Violet's mother—who used to co-chair Parents Against Narcotics with Cissy—was daydreaming about the masseur she employed when he was away on business. He knew Amber's father was the only faithful man in Fox Glen, and Carley's mother was the only faithful woman, though only because she was frigid. Some of this Suzanne had told Hunter herself, but he also had figured out truths she didn't suspect: that Greer had slipped into doing lines at work; that Violet's mother would one day leave video evidence of tongue massages out on the dining room table on purpose; that having affairs left Amber's mother loving Amber's father more and that Carley's father's philandering would not be what did the Wellses in. That fidelity was not synonymous with loyalty, and faithlessness was less trait than condition.

When Hunter turned back, Justin had found himself a diversion more interesting than eavesdropping: studying Bree McEnroy as she fumbled her way through reintroductions. He made no effort to conceal his staring, a soft smile playing over his face as he drank her in. It was the same look Hunter sometimes saw on himself in the mirror when he'd gone too long without pills. Bree, it seemed, was Justin's sigh.

CARLEY WRIGGLED HER thumb beneath the shell, shrimp flesh wedging itself under her fingernail. Gretchen turned toward her just as she pulled out the tail, her smile tightening as she looked away from Carley's hands with a see-no-evil expression.

At least she wasn't *wasting*, Carley wanted to tell her. There were people in the world, she wanted to say, who thought not-wasting was important. People who relished. Who kept. Who saved. Who didn't want to starve.

It had more than one meaning, *wasting*—you could use the word as a double-something-or-other, like Nagel was going on about with *Hamlet* at the beginning of the year instead of calling it a *dirty pun*. Except, in this case, not dirty.

Such wordplay, Nagel said, was what was called a "device"—a tool. There were tons of devices—similes and metaphors and alliteration and the seventeen other terms on SAT List Number Fourteen: Words About Literature. Also, irony and allusion and imagery and symbolism and foreshadowing and backstory. Not to mention point of view and theme and tense, which got their own headings on the blackboard like they were different categories but which, Nagel said, were devices as well.

It turned out nearly everything in a story was some kind of trick, the point of every device being to get across an idea without coming right out and saying it.

Carley cleaned under her nails with a napkin as Gretchen slit her eyes. She dug deep and wiped hard, but still her fingers smelled like something washed up on shore.

Lawrence Talbright IV intercepted Hunter at the bar where he was getting a scotch, making a ratty face so people would understand he was *taking care of this*. According to Francis, if Larry hadn't been born a Talbright, he'd be lucky to be an assistant manager at a fast-food place. When Larry was in charge of the Talbright Foundation for the Arts, his employees had swindled twenty million charitable dollars without his noticing. Being cleared of involvement, Francis had told Carley, had only made Larry look dupable, which was way worse than being crooked.

"There's a very nice man here," Carley heard Hunter tell Larry as she and Suzanne arrived between them at the same time, "who'd be happy to pour you one of your own. Say *please* and he might just give you a cherry."

Larry turned a shade of red that clashed with his rusty combover. Suzanne looked around as if someone had called her name from far away. A few months ago, Carley couldn't have imagined Hunter like this. *Disrespect*, he used to say, *is the inability to imagine someone else's centrality to his universe.*

She put an arm around Hunter's back, the first time she'd dared touch him since Sunday. He had on a cologne she didn't recognize. He usually chose light scents of clean places—the woods or beach or country. Tonight, what he wore took her someplace smoky and leathery and complicated.

Both Hunter and Larry gave her a *what?* look. As Suzanne, too, turned to her, she realized she was supposed to have a reason for having interrupted. "Um, I totally forgot to tell you about what happened yesterday in math?" She shouldn't have said *math*, in case it prompted Larry ask about Hunter's most recent pre-calc test. "I mean, *afterward*, in the hallway? Someone took, like, a frog from the Bio lab, not like a live one but the kind you cut open? And they"—it was the lamest story and she had no idea where it was going—"like put it into someone's locker? And it was like—"

"Excuse me," Hunter said, shaking his head. "All the upnotes giving me a cavity." He strode toward the door that led from the salon toward the back of the house, probably heading for the Palace to fill his flask.

"He just needs settling," Suzanne told Larry, like Hunter was a new house or a lawsuit. She smiled at Carley for agreement. "He'll find her at Princeton. The right girl."

CHAPTER 21

To look down into crowds is to see bald spots and slipped bra straps before faces and gowns. It is the viewpoint of spiders and kings, of cheap sports seats and God. From the second floor of the salon, a balcony where Hunter had ensconced her when she'd requested a place to decide what to read from *Dark Ages*, Bree stared down at Suzanne's guests and hated her patrons for having loaned her out to read—as if Francis were handing over Botticelli to the pope for a bit of Sistine Chapel work. (She had a special affinity for Botticelli, having taken countless hours of notes on every slight he'd suffered that might need avenging in *Geppetto in Florence*.)

"If you want to practice," Hunter said, lounging on the floor in a suit she supposed cost more than her last year's rent, "I'm a willing audience." He swigged from a silver flask.

She turned away from the rail and sat beside him carefully, the black silk dress Gretchen had purchased and insisted she wear for the occasion making her feel like a stranger to herself. She took the flask from him.

"Feel free," he said. "There's always more."

She shook her head, screwed it closed, returned it. "This isn't how to fix what's hurting."

He smiled. "No hurt, I assure you. Just ennui from being surrounded by Philistines. Carley says every time she mentions hating books you wince, the notion as aberrant to you as cannibalism. But just so you know, *nobody* around here reads for what you and I would call pleasure. Students at our school get assigned four hundred pages of reading a week, half of it for English, where text is dissected like a lab animal—that's *Carley's* metaphor, by the way, and I think an apt one. At home our parents skim whatever everyone else at the Club is skimming for reasons as cosmetic as Botox. So excuse my indulging in melancholy over your talent being wasted tonight." He shrugged. "Rock Star's inviting himself to tonight's gathering probably raised the mean IQ thirty points."

"*Inviting* himself?"

"He called Suzanne. Two days ago. He can't stay away from you."

"That's not—"

"That *is*."

Justin. The last time he'd attended one of her readings, at a bookstore years ago, there had been few listeners. One customer stood in the back, carrying what appeared to be all his earthly possessions in two plastic grocery bags and muttering the word *abaci.* Two others stood in the Reference section debating which same-sex wedding guide to purchase. And a handful were scattered among the rows of folding chairs like movie patrons at a last-run theater.

Bree was reading from a section of *Scylla* in which Telemachus, Odysseus's son, tries to track down his father via People Search and finds himself lured by a pop-up ad into the abyss of online poker, when the shriek came from the stacks behind the rows.

"Oh my God, it's *him!*" People turned. Craned their necks. Stood to see for themselves. Justin stepped out of stacks, looking sheepish. He'd been standing in the A-through-F Literature aisle—directly in front of the face-out display of *Clinging.*

A customer seated in the front row got up and walked over to him with an exaggerated tiptoe, as if miming stealth would excuse its lack. Others followed.

"Please," Justin said as they shoved his books at him. "Not now. Please."

Bree leaned into the microphone. "For godsake, just sign them."

Hunter interrupted her story. "He hid next to his own books?"

"Behind a full-length cardboard cutout of himself."

"An interesting . . . interpretation . . . of *anonymity*." He studied his fingers as they tapped against the flask.

"Do you need water?" Bree said, after they'd passed several minutes in silence. "Or coffee?"

"What? No, I'm not . . . unwell. Just thinking . . ." He shook his head as if to cut himself off. "I'm sure you're tired of talking about Rock Star. So tell me about *you*—what you've been working on since *Scylla*. Francis mentioned something about time travel and artists and . . . a prestigious fellowship. What was the name of it? Something German-sounding?"

"Wahlrod," she said. "The E.T. Wahlrod Fellowship."

He nodded to himself, mouthing the words, then went silent again. She followed his gaze to the ceiling to a mural that dizzied her with its detail.

"Are you *sure* you're all right, Hunter?"

"Just thinking about language. *Languages*. German's such a harsh tongue. And then there's French—pretty sure I failed a test on it yesterday. The subjunctive. Do *you* speak French?"

"Not at all."

He nodded to himself, his smile ever more distant. Under his breath he said something that sounded like *toile*, that fabric imprinted with pictures of animals or milkmaids or windmills.

CHAPTER 22

With its thirty-foot-high marble columns and yaw of red drapery, the yet-to-be-Jackie-fied dining room was what Suzanne thought *grand* (the decorator she'd employed during her historic-landmark phase having called it Vanderbiltian) and her guests thought *grandiose* and her son thought *cetaceous*. The room swallowed people, a sensation they tried to counter with congratulations and raised glasses, words cushioning the space around them and champagne settling into the spaces within. When the engagement toasts were exhausted, aromas of the past swept into the void: first seafood mousse molded into tiny crowns, then beef Wellington and paper-thin fried potatoes and artichokes with truffles and cream sauce, the dinner served to Nobel Laureates by Jackie Kennedy. That what was before them was simply rich and filling—no fusion of cuisines, no alimentary tongue-in-cheek, no less-is-more—only added to most guests' unease. There was nothing to do with this food but eat it.

But Bree—who was used to feeling dwarfed by her surroundings and had grown up on food you could feel going down—was not *most* guests. Nor was Hunter, who ate little and for whom food signified nothing. Nor was Carley, whose joy at being seated far from Gretchen where she could relish every last crumb of puff pastry didn't quite balance out her fear that Hunter, seated across from her, would pass out in a pool of Madeira sauce. Nor was Justin, who at five-foot-seven had long ago learned to make himself huge when he was bored or threatened or—as he was tonight—nervous. Two hours was the longest he'd ever ventured outside the cottage without having a panic attack. He kept expecting his body to beg for flight, his stomach turning inside-out and fear eclipsing his face one feature at a time.

Dipping one tine into the sauce on his plate, he drew three stick figures on the tablecloth to distract himself from the certainty that the tip of his chin was, indeed, growing numb. It was delightfully frightening how long people would act as if nothing was amiss about a wounded eccentric defacing the linens. When he gave the stick family a house, the roof of which he cross-thatched using multiple tines, even Bree feigned interest in Suzanne's story of acquiring a replica of Jackie Kennedy's sterling silver tape measure from Tiffany's. The stick family adopted a stick animal, the genus of which was unclear—unlike the blind person who develops the olfaction of a bloodhound or the paraplegic who pumps his arms into steel, his body hadn't compensated for injury. He'd been right handed; his left hand wielded a pen like a six-year-old, still.

"Did you know," Hunter said to Justin as the stick family purchased a blob of a car, "that table manners originated to ward off violence at mealtimes?" He mimed throwing his steak knife in Larry Talbright's direction.

Before last weekend, he wouldn't have supposed young Cay a drunk, and certainly not a sloppy one.

The nausea began to kick in, as it always did by the time his cheeks lost feeling. Could people see the sweat on his face? At what point did a droplet become visible?

"An announcement," Larry said. He lifted his chin at Suzanne, who stood at the other end of the table like he was raising her up. "As of the new year, I'll be taking a hiatus from managing family business investments to follow in the tradition of my grandfather, father, and brother." People looked to each other. A smatter of clapping. "I shall toss my château into the political arena as candidate for the office of state senator of Rhode Island." The dining room erupted with too-hardy applause, like at a school play when it was curtain-call time for the kid who'd dropped his lines.

"Hear, hear," said Hunter, standing. "I, for one, cannot wait to see you throw your house." He pretended to reach for the wineglass his stepfather-to-be had been indiscreet about having the server remove and feigned surprise at his fingers wrapping around air.

Justin felt for his lips with his fingers to assure himself that they were indeed parted. Though he could feel the air dragging past them, he was suffocating.

"Now the prohibition against using knives on salad," Hunter slurred, returning to his monologue about the origins of etiquette, "arose in response to the corrosive properties of vinegar—"

Justin bolted from the table.

LARRY WENT ON and on about *giving back to the public*, Hunter explained to no one and everyone at the table that the Tudors shared plates, Bree added that during Medieval times people just heaped their food onto pieces of stale bread like it was dinnerware, and no one went after Justin Leighton—as if there were nothing strange about someone leaving so abruptly that his chair had tipped backward. *Discretion*, Gretchen would have offered up as a reason for twenty-five people to ignore such a thing. Or *delicacy*.

"Let's go find Justin," Carley whispered to Hunter, following him into the hallway when he stepped out to hit his flask. *Someone* should make sure Justin was okay, and even though Bree, who didn't seem like the type to care about either *discretion* or *delicacy*, had been staring at Justin all night when he wasn't looking—which was what you did in middle school when you liked someone, when you didn't know how to be with a crush and just *be*—she wasn't getting up.

It would be good for Hunter, anyway, to have something to concentrate on besides hating Larry and keeping his flask full. No matter how upset he'd been by what Justin had written—or didn't—about his stories in September, taking care of people was what Hunter *did*.

"He can find himself," Hunter said, shaking the flask to weigh how much was left.

"I think he's sick or something, H. Like, he might need help." Everything she knew about how to treat people decently she'd learned from him. To respect. To apologize. To forgive.

"Then why don't *you* help him?" Hunter said, walking back into the dining room, where Suzanne was announcing that dessert would, regrettably, diverge from Jackie's original Laureates menu because Larry, who was *sensitive* to coconuts, would not have been able to partake in the Bombe Caribienne.

From the doorway Carley watched a server place a crème brûlée in front of her empty seat. She turned away, feeling like she *had* to find Justin now that Hunter had said it, though she'd never spoken a word to Justin, and she didn't know about anything literary to talk to him about, and she knew it was weird for a stranger to follow someone around saying, *Are you okay?*

After checking most of the rooms on the ground floor, she found him outside, smoking by the rectangular reflecting pool that was halfway between the main house and the Play Palace.

"Can I bum one?" she called over to him as she walked over. She tried to look bored.

"Settle for a peppermint, Minor Wells?" He rested his cigarette on the low marble wall surrounding the water and reached into the pocket of his chalk-striped gray velvet jacket.

"I'm not that minor."

"True." With his left hand he dropped the wrapped candy into the palm of his right, which he offered to her like a platter, the fingers flat and not at all gnarled or spastic, the way she'd expected them to be.

She untwisted the cellophane. "So your hand works? I mean it looks … normal."

"More exists than *works*." When he turned it over, his wrist hung limp, like in a cheesy caricature of a gay man. "Strange thing, the body. Scar's here," he said, pointing to the middle of his arm. He patted his hand before replacing it in his pocket. "Damage is there." He reached to retrieve his half-smoked cigarette and drew hard on it as if it were medicine—one of those inhalers Edie Weiss wouldn't let Jazzy out the door without. "Nerves. It's all about the nerves."

"Does it bother you I asked?"

"Nary." He grabbed for the wall. For a moment she thought he'd lost his balance. Then his chin dropped to his chest.

"Put your head between your legs." She helped him to the ground. She'd passed first aid and CPR tests for the last three years in order to teach children to swim at a community center near Moreland. Though Francis usually left school-related matters to Gretchen, he'd insisted Carley do something "real" to fulfill Montclair's community service requirement instead of having one of his wife's friends on the Fox Glen Preservation Society just sign off on a time card. Hunter, who drove her, helped at the tutoring center in the same building, never flinching at little kids' germiness as they coughed on him all winter. He adored being there, and unlike a lot of the awkward volunteers from schools like theirs, he didn't have to *work* at not talking down to kids or their parents.

"I shouldn't have asked you about—"

"No. *No*, you didn't do this, Minor Wells. It's a . . . condition."

"Is it why you disappeared? Not just from dinner, but from, like, life?" Justin's breath slowed from panting to something like sighs. He lit another cigarette and brought the drooping fingers of his bad hand to his cheeks and chin. "Is it that syndrome? Post-dramatic . . ."

"Post-dramatic. Exactly." He shooed her with the cigarette hand. "Go rejoin the feast."

"It's fucked up, you know, how everyone in there is so excited to be in the same room with you, all talking *about* you like you're special, but then they just make the same small talk with you that they could make with anyone."

He picked up his cane and began his way toward the woods.

"Bree's gonna think you don't care enough to hear her read."

He kept walking.

She shouted, "Can I tell her you're sick? After the reading, Hunter and I could walk her to your place. She could take care of you."

He turned, laughing. "Take *care* of me?"

Her cheeks grew hot. "I don't know how to say it sophisticatedly. I just know everyone wants to be able to close their eyes sometimes and know someone's there."

"You're truly charming, Minor Wells. Doubtless sprung from Zeus's head." He came back to the reflecting pool and sat on the wall, one leg bent, one straight. "What *should* they talk to me about?" he asked as he lit another cigarette. He said it like he cared.

She thought for a moment as she sat down a few feet from him. "You're a writer. And you're famous for making people cry. And well, not just cry, but *feel*. That's what Hunter says, at least. No offense, but I haven't read your books because I don't—"

"Read. I've heard."

"Anyway, you use words to make things happen, to *move* people. Which is cool. But you know what's more interesting than hearing about what someone's done *right*?"

He smirked. "Are you suggesting the well-bred citizens of Fox Glen ask me to regale them with my fuck-ups?"

"Me, I'd ask if you ever couldn't find the right words to say. I'd ask if you ever wanted a do-over. I'd ask, *If you could go back and change something you said—something that would make everything different afterward—what would it be?*"

FRANCIS WAS FULL. Of beef Wellington. Of pinot noir. Of brûléed tapioca pudding. Of 1963 Fonseca vintage port.

Of temptation to strangle the bastard Suzanne would marry.

"Jackie contributed *her* crème brûlée recipe to the Congressional Club cookbook," Suzanne said to Plum Buchanan, and he wanted to tell his lover that vermeil flower containers and French-country-estate decorating and a Talbright husband would turn her into mockery, not Kennedy. *Francis* was her true future, if only she could wait until Carley was away at college, far from what would be a scandal and an ugly divorce. He could smell destiny like he could still smell those pink, freckled flowers in the salon six rooms away, a scent like toffee and sex that wrung his salivary glands dry.

Larry rose and walked to where his fiancée sat at the opposite end of the table to announce the wedding would take place at Larry's family's Newport home. When they kissed it was long and deep, a very un-Kennedyesque embrace that came from Suzanne's heart and soul because nothing made her quite as hot as a politician.

Francis excused himself and strode to the empty salon. Journey's End, Francis would later learn the pink flowers were called. Tonight, with their fur-tipped stamens reaching for him, he didn't want to know their names.

In the bathroom, their pollen stained him an orange-red that would not wash off.

"ONE FRIDAY AFTERNOON," Justin said to Carley, "not two weeks into her freshman year, Bridget Theresa McEnroy was sitting on the steps of Reynolds Hall, eavesdropping on her classmates' conversations and staring at people's shoes and thinking about language. While critiquing a story written by Bridget's roommate, Professor Connelly had suggested a single word could *wake the reader from the dream*. The word in Marguerite's story, the necessity of which she'd argued until period's end, had been *chanteuse*."

"Wait," Carley told him. "Is this Bree's story or yours?"

"It's the answer to your question: What I'd change if—"

"You don't know what she was thinking, so is it fair to tell it that way? I mean, *she* could tell it that way because she knows for sure what she was thinking, but—"

"*Fair?*" Justin dragged on his cigarette, blew a smoke ring. "Were Bree telling this story herself, she'd neglect her own point of view entirely, leaving the story to be narrated by a nameless, faceless, proclamatory god who says things like, *Story begets story, recreating, revivifying, reincarnating while it kills.*"

"What's that mean?"

"You decide, Minor Wells. You're the reader. Next, she'd issue parenthetical commentary on what she'd just written: (*With the above statement, the narrator declares, This is how to think about what comes next.*)"

"Seriously? I mean, is that really, like, what Bree *writes*? Is that what she means by *meta*?"

Justin nodded.

On *The Arion Annals*, this was where Glory would break in with a voice-over: *Uh-Oh.* Carley had only seen an outline of what Bree was going to read tonight—Jules and Buck compete in a jousting challenge and realize they're into each other. She hadn't seen any of the actual writing, but this time it wasn't her fault—Bree kept saying she needed another hour and then another day, making sure it "resonated"—whatever that meant. Probably it meant something weird.

"What's a chanteuse?" Carley said to get off the subject. Weird or not, *meta* still sounded better than that Lancelot and Gwen crap.

"What?"

"*Chanteuse* was the last word. Before I interrupted and you got all puffed up—"

"I'm puffed *up*?"

"Just saying you sounded like Hunter when he's on a roll about something like the history of table manners. Full of yourself. Like a peacock."

Justin laughed. "Not sure they puff. And *chanteuse*? It means *singer*." He lit another cigarette. "Anyway, Bridget looked out at the quad and practiced *chanteuse* under her breath. In her mouth it felt like no word ever uttered in Vernal. She wished she'd taken high school French instead of Spanish, which her mother had insisted was *practical*. She wished she'd been educated where you learned to toss back terms like *bathos* and *pathetic fallacy* and shots of imported liquors with casual pride. She wished she had an exotic name instead of having been baptized a saint—a vision-having, meek-and-kind-to-every-living-creature saint. No Joan of Arc.

"She looked around her and tried to imagine the limitlessness of Manhattan, the landscape of which she still couldn't grasp beyond the quad and classrooms and dorms. She tried to read it in her classmates' faces. She tried to read it in their shoes. She'd left Vernal understanding nothing about the rich, her mother's only advice on the subject being a phrase she'd picked up from a fashion magazine decades earlier: *Shoes and handbag tell the wallet.*

"Three of her female classmates wore combat boots the color black turned when it got tired. Four wore strappy platforms. Marguerite wore stilettos that in Vernal would have signaled *slut* but in Manhattan translated entirely differently, perhaps because they were designed by someone French whose name she mispronounced every time. (Her attempts, Marguerite had informed her, were *très hilaramment.*) Bridget's male classmates wore low boots or scuffed loafers or white sneakers just dirty enough. And every shoe, no matter how worn it was meant to appear, had a thick, shiny sole. Every shoe but Justin's.

"A bit of black sock peeked through the ball of his left saddle shoe as he lay back on the steps of Reynolds Hall, face turned up to the fickle September sun, head resting on his folded blazer. His shoes were like the two-tone frosted cookies she and her sisters would buy at the bakery after Sunday masses. They looked solid. They looked sweet. The hole did nothing to detract from them. It made her ache inside.

"'Hemingway!' Marguerite called to him.

"He stretched, wrinkled shirt riding up on his stomach, wide orange tie flopping over his shoulder. He looked underfed. He stood and shrugged on his jacket, nubby and worn at the elbows. He seemed a person who had to try hard and didn't mind.

"'Careful,' said Harry, one of Marguerite's hangers-on, who was partial to the prepositional phrase *At Andover* . . . 'You don't want *the author* to blackball you at Scribners.'

"Marguerite shook Bridget's shoulder the way she often did, as if she didn't quite believe Bridget was awake. 'Last night at the bar, Justin was telling us about his intentions of fame. Turns out all you need to become a famous writer is *to want it enough.* I've a vision of him living on bread and water and writing on used newspaper, don't you? With blood.' She wrinkled her nose. 'After all, you need only . . . what did Justin call it? Ah yes, *The delight of the craft!*'

"Instead of accompanying her classmates to the basement bar where she imagined Justin nursed a single ill-afforded domestic beer, Bridget had been rushing to the library after class to study literary terminology. Instead of chatting with him when he showed up with the entourage who came to their room each evening to curry Marguerite's favor, she'd slunk off to the library. Instead of sitting close enough to Justin to smell peppermint on his breath and smoke in his hair, she'd been writing him in her head.

" 'They're wrong. And they're horrible.' She forced herself to speak loudly, the way she never could manage in class. She looked at Justin. 'A dream is enough. Being poor doesn't mean you have to take rich people's shit.'

"People whispered. Someone made a choking sound. And finally, came the laughter. Harry clapped Justin on the shoulder. 'I've been *telling* you to quit those *awful* ties.'

" 'Absolutely *precious*,' Marguerite tittered.

"And Bree? She was already on her feet and running, not knowing why they were laughing at her and dreading Marguerite's explaining it.

"And now, Minor Wells," Justin said, tapping his cane against the marble, "for the answer to your question about changing the past: 'Alas,' Justin would have called after her if he could relive that moment, 'you've leapt to the defense of a boor who is beneath your kindness. For in a moment of non-sobriety last night I compared my napkin-scrawled flash fiction to "Hills Like White Elephants"—' "

"You'd have said it straightforward like that? I mean, straightforward for *you*. Normal, except for *alas*. Normal-*ish*. I mean, is this *true*?"

"Is it *true* that I *wished* it happened, you mean?"

"I mean, have you thought about it before? Before I asked?"

He smiled. "Later, Justin came to believe those words might have changed the course of who he and Bridget McEnroy would have become. He might not have started sleeping with Marguerite out of boredom and continued doing so out of laziness. Bridget might have told him it was obnoxious to buy thrift shop clothing with his titanium Amex. He might have told her the manuscript she'd passed out to the class for next week's critique—the story he'd been reading while soaking up the last rays of the sun—had been such relief after their classmates' pseudo-intellectual crap. Her writing had been nakedly emotional, gorgeously pure. He'd wanted to get in bed with it."

He dropped his cigarette on the walkway that surrounded the reflecting pool. Carley ground it out with the toe of her pump, wondering if it would leave a mark.

"So now it's *your* flashback. I mean, it was Bree's before. Not *Bree*-Bree's but you-as-Bree's and now it's you-as-you's. If this was a story—like, a *story-story?*—would you be allowed to do that?"

"It's up to the reader to decide if the point-of-view-switch short-cutlery is justified. If I were *really* doing this Bree-style, by the way, I might also include a character *named* Justin Leighton in my book who was neither narrator-me nor author-me."

"Isn't that, like, memoir?"

"Sometimes." He laughed. Later, she still wouldn't be able to figure out why what she'd said was funny.

He lit another cigarette.

"Aren't you worried about dying?" She clapped her hand over her mouth. He'd already come as close to dying as you got. "God, I'm...I shouldn't be allowed to talk."

"Don't be quiet," he said. "Ever." He inhaled deeply and blew smoke rings. "As to your question on point of view, Bree might have handled it thusly, in parenthesis: *(Warning: below, the narrator will take the liberty of slipping out of one character's head mid-flashback and passing into another's. Some readers might deem this slippage disconcerting. A few might cry foul.)*"

Bree's "handling" sounded to Carley like your mother screaming for you to wake up when you were deep into a good dream. "So it's like she's using literary devices, but, like, *the opposite* of them. Because they *say* what they're doing instead of hiding—"

"Their point is *lack* of transparency. Exactly."

"Like they're being honest instead of tricky." Except they didn't feel honest. They felt annoying.

The satin ribbon was slipping from Justin's ponytail. He put down his cigarette to sweep his hair back and retie it.

"The following Monday, when Professor Connelly addressed her, she asked to be known henceforth as *Bree.* 'It's what my friends call me,' she said. It was the kind of clumsy, gratuitous lie that drove her classmates to inspect their fingernails and smooth out unwrinkled papers, anything not to look at her."

"So you think you, like, *changed* her?" As soon as Carley said it, she knew she'd made a mistake. He looked annoyed about being interrupted again. And anyway the point of a good story, according to Nagel, would be more complicated than *I changed her*, good stories having countless meanings and contradictory themes that couldn't be summed up in only three words. "Sorry, that was stupid. I mean, unsophisticated. I mean . . ."

He stood. "Among the meanings of *sophisticate* are *to trick with words* and *to make unnatural*." He looked at his watch. "I believe a demonstration of just that is about to commence inside."

The hand with the cane trembled between steps as they approached the house.

"It's brave, your coming back," she told him.

"You grade on a precipice, Minor Wells. And by the way, what you said before about someone being there while one sleeps"—he wiped his face with his palm—"that was something Bridget would have written."

CHAPTER 23

<u>"Dark Ages,"</u> Bree read aloud from pages propped up on a mahogany music stand in front of the fireplace. Wood popped and crackled behind her. Backlit, she glowed. "Footnote Number 1: About the Title. Best to get that problem out of the way." *What* problem? wondered her listeners. Had she officially started, or was this one of the parts you skipped when you read a book, an introduction? "Let us address both the anachronism and inaccuracy of <u>Dark Ages</u> . . ."

Throughout the fuchsia-walled library they nodded emptily, like passengers when the flight attendant demonstrates the oxygen mask nobody wants to ever have to remember how to use. "The word <u>dark</u> with its implications of ignorance and barbarism . . ."

"It's the self-consciousness of the narrator," Hunter whispered to Carley as they stood against the back wall, "and the awareness that she is *within* something entitled that lends the piece humor."

Carley caught panic on her mother's face. "Um, H? No one's laughing."

"They're Philistines." His breath was pure scotch.

"Though horses abounded on the set"—positions were shifted, legs crossed, drinks sucked down—"and were ridden by stuntmen in the background for 'authenticity,' the contestants weren't allowed within ten feet of one, the show's insurer recently having paid a considerable settlement to the family of a man trampled to death on the now-defunct, prince-switches-with-pauper reality show, <u>Park Avenue Farmer.</u>

"Footnote Number Two: <u>Park Avenue Farmer,</u> PETA, and Karma. Best remembered for the animal-rights protests that ensued after an episode in which 'farmers' hand-slaughtered chickens on screen, Park Avenue..."

As Bree detailed the death-throes of fowl, a server who had been offering guests truffles dropped her tray on Suzanne's Sotheby's-authenticated, from-the-estate-of-Jackie, nineteenth-century rosewood games table, fleeing the room.

Cissy Gardner nodded her familiarity with the fictional controversy about the fictional show, as did Carson Buchanan. The room wore toothless smiles and cocked heads, as if witnessing an outré art exhibition or a subtitled film about poor people.

"All of which explains why Jules and Buck, outfitted in full armor, jousted not on true steeds, but rather on mechanical bulls retrofitted with horses' heads with manes that felt like Barbie hair.

"Sometimes when she was alone at home, Jules recovered her Barbies from the back of the closet, though at sixteen she was too old for them, and dressed them in sherbet-hued outfits with matching purses and shoes despite her draping her own body in clothes that made her parents think she was depressed—black velvet and lace and veils. As he had for all of the challenges, the stunt coordinator had made her remove the rings from her chin and left eyebrow and the stud in her right nostril. Under the thirty pounds of metal and padding, he'd also forced her to wear wool long johns that made her itch and sweat in the L.A. summer. She was less worried about losing the Challenge than about stinking when it was over."

Despite that weird beginning, Jules sounded at least interesting, and who couldn't relate to being afraid of B.O.?

When Bree came up from the pages to look out at her audience, Hunter raised his flask to her, his shoulder bumping against Larry's engagement gift to Suzanne, a painting Hunter called *Russian neo-impressionistic Kool-Aid*.

"Buck knew for sure he stank. Unlike Jules's family, who by winning the Milwaukee's Best Bratwurst Catapulting Challenge several days earlier had become Lords of the Manor and earned the right to live in the castle with a cook and real food and baths, Buck's family had been sleeping in the hovel they'd built during the Pancho Sanza Tortilla Chips

Hut Challenge out of twigs, mud, straw, and dung harvested from guaranteed-disease-free livestock, a condition that assuaged the show's insurer's fears about dung-borne-illness but sadly rendered the dung to smell no less like shit. They relieved themselves outdoors (though due to the insurer's concerns about unhygienic conditions breeding lawsuits, they used porta-potties, dutifully following up with liquid hand sanitizer in view of a production assistant) and bathed in the river. A vegetarian, Buck refused the soap they'd rendered from animal fat during the Sharp's Cheeze-Food Soapmaking Challenge."

Hunter laughed. No one else did.

Carley searched Word Lists Number Fourteen and Thirty-six in her head for a term that would show Hunter she appreciated this. "Totally *surreal*," she finally said.

"Footnote Number Three: On the Production of Soap . . ."

"DEFINITOMENTE," JUSTIN FORCED himself to whisper to Helen Neulander when she petted his shoulder and asked if this was what they called *hypermodern*. There was much touching from Suzanne's female guests, and some from the men—Carson Buchanan, who'd gotten up to ask Justin what *he'd* thought about *Park Avenue Farmer*, continually squeezed Justin's shoulder for emphasis as Justin forced himself to breathe slowly and refused to allow himself to again run from a room. Once upon a time, other people's hands had been why Justin had loved wearing velvet. He hadn't been able to get enough of people wanting to touch him. There hadn't been enough strokes in the world.

"JULES KEPT HER lance aimed at the crest at the center of Buck's shield as her steed bucked forward. Buck's spring-loaded shield burst apart. 'Halfway there,' her father yelled. Now she just needed to pierce Buck's circular heart target before he pierced hers.

"Footnote Number Four: The Definition of 'Pierce.' Per the official, legal, and binding Dark Ages Rulebook: a valid 'pierce' with a lance requires the button on the end of the lance to be depressed with at least 4.9 newtons of force against a valid target. It will be confirmed by at least one of the following: a) buzzing sound; b) flashing of an (off-camera) sign bearing the word PIERCE.

"Footnote to Footnote Number Four (Footnote Number Four-A): Diameter of 'Heart' . . ."

"SCINTILLATING," CISSY GARDNER said to Francis, in line in front of him at the bar. Francis did not recall having commissioned an instruction manual. The line for drinks was long. His hands burned from his scrubbing them with Clorox—the kitchen Help's suggestion to remove pollen stains. He had no idea how long it might take for such stains to fade from what couldn't possibly be bleached.

Cissy turned to order her drink. It was impossible to miss the pachydermity of her bra band, which rolled and rode up to her shoulder blades. Her breasts were like a disaster in the news: a roof falling in under the weight of heavy rain, a double-decker freeway collapsing in an earthquake, a bridge undulating in high winds until its cables snapped.

Francis loved designing bras for the same reasons he'd loved spider webs and suspension bridges as a boy—to defy gravity was to be a god—but most of all because he'd never met a pair of breasts he didn't want to save. With cotton, with spandex, with Lycra, with lace, with double-D's in demi-cups, with double A's underwired, with plunge-front B's in racerbacks, with perfect C's black-satin wrapped, he raised women to the height of constellations, every Marvel-Bra named for the stars.

"What an *evening*," Cissy said, turning to him with a glass of port. "So *intellectual*." He yearned to widen the lower edge of the band of Cissy's bra. He wanted to sew casing strips on the sides. He needed to stop it from lynching her misfit D's. Breasts deserved *structure*. They deserved *boning*.

"This needs fixing," he said, cupping and lifting her left breast. In the moment before the slap, he felt like Atlas.

"**JULES TUMBLED OVER** her mount's head. Shield in front of her, she struggled to get to her feet from the mat. Buck's steed rocked forward. Her shield exploded at his lance's touch. They were both now unprotected."

Bree looked up. "The narrator feels it necessary to interject here upon several points. One: the heavy-handedness of metaphors such as thrusting-at-hearts (while-riding-bucking-pseudo-horses) is not the narrator's fault. Hold accountable the producers of <u>Dark Ages</u> for designing The Life-Fizz Lite Sports Drink Challenge, which is so obviously, symbolically sexual, and blame not the teller for the tale. Two: such interjections are therefore not the fault of the narrator, who greatly values unobtrusiveness and wishes circumstances did not dictate her repeated interruptions. Three: something important is about to happen. Pay attention. Yes, you."

SUZANNE CAY LOOKED up guiltily, for she had been admiring her own bookshelves—specifically the previously-Jackie-owned volumes she'd rearranged by color just that afternoon—and thus had *not* been paying attention. Then she remembered it was her party and this was not school and she was a grown-up. A grown-up about to marry a Talbright and who owned Jackie's personal copies of *Pageantry of Brazilian Birds*; *A New Treatise on Flower Painting, or, Every Lady Her Own Drawing Master*; *Greece: Gods and Art*; *The Common Sense of Baby and Child Care*; *Homosexuals in History*; and *The Military Costume of Turkey*.

And anyway, the entertainment hadn't been talking to *her*. Entertainment *didn't* speak to the audience so personally. Did it?

Speak to the audience. Why, it was a pun! And *speaking* to them the Author was clearly doing, if the impassioned whispering among Cissy and Greer Gardner and Francis Wells was any indication. How *delightful* that her guests were so engrossed in literary debate!

" '**FINISH IT!**' yelled Buck's family as Jules remounted. He had a good look at her heart while she was pulling herself up. 'Do it!'

"He hesitated, impressed. In the entire day of competition, she'd been the only female contestant able to bear the weight of the armor well enough to get back on after being thrown.

" 'Lance,' she called. Her father, her chosen Squire for this round, put the weapon in her right hand and then—in accordance with the rules read to them during the thirty-minute stop-down by doublet-clad host Cliff Daniels at the beginning of the challenge—backed off the mat.

" 'What the fuck's wrong, Choker?' Buck's brother yelled, which would be bleeped out in editing and was the same thing he used to yell at Buck's basketball games in the 'real' world, if you could call <u>real</u> a place where the bouncing of a sphere was important. With every day Buck spent on the set, it seemed more normal to live in the hut and more difficult to believe that other world existed."

"WAS THAT THE important part?" Carley squeezed Hunter's hand. Her fingers were sticky. "That was it, right?"

"What?" Words slid past Hunter like seasons. Or like molecules that bounced up against each other—or were atoms the bouncy things? Bree had been reading something about *worlds*, how none of them were real, and how true was *that*?

"I get why it's funny now? Because the weird stuff isn't any weirder than stuff we think is normal?"

"*What*?" Perhaps he was an ion. "Are you *talking* about something?"

"The weird..."

"Everything's *weird* to you, C, except that shit on TV that *tells* you what you're *supposed* to think about it. *Bouncy House*, where you know you're supposed to feel superior to that geek with the glasses because they edit in shots of him losing his balance in the house in *every* episode. *Arion Annals*, where foreboding background music warns you Glory's new friends are probably her enemies. No ambiguity. Fucking Philistinian."

" 'YOU GONNA let yourself get beaten by Elvira?' Jules hated Dale, Buck's brother, far more than all the other contestants. Not just because he was mean—the world abounded with mean people—but because he was way hairy, like he'd shed on you. It was hard to believe he was related to Buck, with his white-mouse coloring and spiky, short haircut and library voice.

"Footnote Number Twenty-Seven: The Once and Future Dale. <u>Dark Ages</u> would lead to myriad opportunities for the aspiring actor, including guest spots on <u>Reality All-Stars XII</u>, <u>Reality Stars Caught on Tape</u>, <u>Cops: Los Angeles</u>, and a starring role in the straight-to-video, XXX-rated, <u>Serf's Up</u> . . ."

GRETCHEN COULD IMAGINE no proper expression, nowhere safe to look. To leave the room would be to admit shame. To stay was to condone. *Cissy Gardner?* What had Francis been thinking? The woman was a pig.

"SADDLE-SORE AND BRUISED beneath the armor, they lunged and fell and got up again. Jules's horse's head fell off and had to be reattached. The medical team was called in to examine Buck and clear him for continuing after he was kicked in the head by his own steed. Editing the challenge to two minutes would prove almost as excruciating for the post-production team as it is unbearable for your narrator to keep, well, <u>narrating</u>. I'm bored. Closure, anyone?

"Hours will pass, the sun setting and artificial lights replacing it, and still, Jules and Buck will be trying for each other's heart."

"Thank you," said Bree. She folded the pages in half as she walked away from the fireplace.

That was *it*? Who'd won? Jules and Buck hadn't even *talked* to each other and wasn't the whole point how they fell in love? And what was the point of all those footnotes?

What *else* had she missed? Carley wanted to ask Hunter but the clapping would have drowned her out, and anyway her throat was still thick with the tears she'd held back when he'd yelled at her. She'd *tried* to understand, she'd *wanted* to.

All those years of his watching TV in the bed with her in the Palace, she'd thought he'd kind of liked it for how easy it was. He'd cuddled and laughed with her in front of those shows. She'd thought they'd been having fun by *feeling* together. They used to guess at what would happen next week on *Arion*. They used to make up stories together about what the reality shows didn't show. Wasn't that embracing *ambiguity*?

She looked over to where Justin had been sitting; the chair was vacant. The whole room began standing, people calling out *Brava*. As people rushed forward to hug Bree and ask where they could buy copies of her published novel, tripping over each other to tell her how *stimulated* they were, it occurred to Carley for the first time that just maybe it was like that story about the king with the see-through PVC clothing. He had all these butt-zits, but everyone kept saying, *What flattering pants! Gaultier, yes?*

CHAPTER 24

I ons. Hunter was still trying to remember chemistry as he walked up
behind Justin, but last year seemed so far away. Ions were *sticky*, he
recalled, sticky the way Carley's hand had been during the reading when
she'd taken his, because they either had too much of something or too little,
and other atoms were always trying to rush in and either grab the extra or
fill the void. *Electrons*—that was the word for the *something*.

To become a positive ion, all you had to do was give away an electron.
The atoms would flock to you then. *Electrically charged*, you'd be
über-attractive.

"I've been thinking about why you did it," Hunter said. Justin stood
staring at the two rows of paintings on the back wall of the library. Portraits
of strangers, a couple of generic landscapes.

"Did what?" Justin said. "Missed your referent, kid."

"Just trying to be *subtle*." He lowered his voice. "*It*, meaning *inventing a
fellowship to fund Bree.*"

Justin feigned interest in the paintings that nobody *possibly* could have
found interesting. It was an uncomfortable display, Hunter had tried to tell
Suzanne, too *literal* an interpretation of a wall from the Jackie-era Red
Room, where portraits of dead presidents and their kin shared space with
paintings of places like Niagara Falls. Suzanne had chosen an array of faces
and places simply for their colors and sizes. *It's like a Chanel knockoff*, he'd
tried warning her during the redecoration, putting it into terms she'd

understand. She'd shaken her head and asked why he didn't want her to be happy.

"Do I think it's a little stalker-esque what you've done, what you're *doing*?" Hunter continued. "Well, maybe. But love's a funny thing I figure, and who am I to judge?"

"There are people who make drunkenness look enviable," Justin said, finally looking at him. "You, young Cay, are not among them."

He hadn't meant to get so drunk, but he'd needed *something* to soften the blow of trying to taper down on the pills, like an ion in search of something to fill up its space.

"*E.T. Wahlrod*," Hunter said, speaking quickly because as long as he was talking things made sense. With all the noise in the library and in his head, it was *listening* that was so much harder. "Bet you've been doing a lot of word puzzles while you've been hiding out in that cottage, Rock Star. Tricky, clever little games where the meaning of something changes if you just pronounce it differently." He thought about his conversation with Bree on the balcony earlier that evening. "Take, for instance, the E.T. Wahlrod Fellowship. Instead of saying *Ee-tee-wall*, one might ignore the periods and pronounce it *Et-wahl. Etoile*." He pronounced it with a perfect accent, the failed French test about which he'd told Bree a complete invention, one of the self-effacing fabrications he considered social lubricant rather than a lie. " 'Etoile,' meaning *Star*. And, of course the word 'rod' is synonymous with *Spindle*. Starr Spindle, your protagonist. Your invention.

"You wanted to help Bree anonymously, yet there was a part of you that had to sign your name to your good deed. The kind of thing you'd expect from a man who hides at a reading behind a picture of himself.

"Easy to imagine you setting up the Foundation and having your friend Darren Connelly suggest to Bree that she apply. A decent sleight of hand, but not *magic*. What I'm *still* wondering about, though, is how you managed the *big* trick, the show-stopper, the encore. Getting Bree *here*, to Fox Glen, without her having *any* idea you've engineered it. Without *anyone* knowing you had a hand in it. I know Francis wasn't in on it. Or Gretchen. So it must have taken some subtle manipulation and a whole lot of luck. I'm thinking—"

"There you are, Justin!" he heard from behind him. "Wasn't our dear *minstrel* just arresting!" He turned toward his mother's voice, the room swiveling in the other direction and nearly knocking him off his feet.

"MINSTRELS *SING*," HUNTER said as he stumbled, the contents of his flask splashing onto the cerise, silk-upholstered wall. He grabbed a bookcase for support. Bree saw the frown cross Suzanne's face. She glanced over her shoulder at her fiancé, who was looking her way after breaking off a discussion with Francis Wells.

"It wasn't *groping*," she heard Francis tell his wife. "I was *mending*."

Suzanne gave her son another glance, shaking her head as if to mentally erase his condition, then slipped away to head off Larry's approach.

"You're a sloppy drunk," Bree told him.

"Hunter and I already covered this territory," Justin said.

"Fitzgerald couldn't hold his liquor," Hunter said. "Got trashed after even a couple of drinks. You'd think he'd have acquired a tolerance. Know what Zelda's father said when she tried to tell him Scott was a great guy when he was sober? *He's never sober.*" He shifted his weight from one foot to another in a precarious rhythm. "Which I think says something about destiny: a person *is* what he *is*, and just changes forms like ice to water to gas but he's still the same one H and two Os. Did you know that water, that tamest-seeming of stuff, can break down serious bonds, dissociating compounds into ions and—"

Bree took his arm and led him to an armchair upholstered the same color as the walls and patterned with large gold medallions. During her reading she'd kept wondering why anyone would decorate a room the color of fresh blood.

"It makes me sick to see this," Bree said as Carley came over holding a cup of coffee for him.

"You don't have to be mean," Carley said. "You don't *know* how good he's been to you because he's not the kind of person who'd go around *telling* you."

"I'm being frank, Carley. Which is the biggest favor anyone could—"

"Who do you figure thought of having Francis set up an expense account for you to buy research books so you didn't have to lay out money and get reimbursed? You think it would *occur* to anyone in my house that someone might not have a hundred bucks for something? And I *know* he bribed Grace not to tattle to Gretchen every time she puts through a call to you from Justin or lets you borrow the errand car or—"

Hunter banged down his cup, sloshing half the coffee into the saucer. "Stop."

Justin knelt awkwardly, propping his cane against the chair back and leaning his good arm against the seat. "You're a smart kid," Bree heard him say before Carley drowned him out.

"If it weren't for *him* liking your book," she yelled at Bree, "you wouldn't even be here. Do you think my parents read any of it? Here's the difference between Hunter and everyone else: other people will tell themselves they liked what you read tonight—was that supposed to be a *love scene*, by the way, and are you *frigate?*—because they don't think they're smart enough to understand it. But Hunter? He's smart enough to *get* it, but he's too *nice* to want to admit to himself that it sucks."

"Enough," Hunter said, grabbing Carley's wrist.

Justin reached up and grabbed Hunter by the collar. "Let go of her. Let *go*," he repeated, though Hunter had already done it.

"Justin," Bree said. "*Justin.*"

Carley rubbed her wrist. "Hate to break it to you, Bree, but in love scenes people are supposed to, like, touch. Not have *allegorical* sex with *metaphorical* cunts."

Justin released Hunter and rose shaking. "I'm sorry. I didn't—"

"It's okay, Rock Star," Hunter said softly. "Don't worry... 'bout anything. You know I can keep a secret."

"Walk with me?" Justin said to Bree. Standing with her a few minutes later in front of the reflecting pool he said, "You deserved what the girl said, you know. Someone should have said it years ago. Maybe it would have saved you."

"From what?"

He shook his head. He was sweating. His pupils were dilated. "You."

"Are you *taking* something, Justin? You're not . . . You haven't been . . ."

"What do you think you're doing, Bree? What you read tonight? Are you *never* going to outgrow writing that self-aggrandizing, indulgent shit? You're supposed to be writing for someone else for once in your life. For *her.* Don't think you won't lose this commission. That girl's tougher than she seems."

HE TURNED TOWARD the woods, his heart slamming so hard in his chest he was afraid to look down and see it rubber-banding in and out, a throbbing cartoon heart.

Someone should have said it to you, he'd told Bree. Someone like him.

When *Between Scylla and Alta Vista* was first released, Justin had sat with it for days. He wrote in it and on it and threw it against a wall. It felt like six a.m. after a long night spent in not-completely-sober philosophical conversation with a close, if thorny, friend, sunrise revealing that what you'd thought depth was merely a rut. She'd killed off causality and climax, torn symbols from their referents, stripped out love and hate until the only thing left was disappointment. Lex Pritchett called it *the cloyingly bitter language of suicide* in *The New York Times.* It felt like Bree.

He'd written out card after card to go with white roses and had torn them up. Finally, he'd settled on You Are Brave.

It was not what he meant. Nor was it the truth. Once upon a time, when they were young, she'd brought to class work that was truly courageous. This, before she began writing stories populated by characters who were all *commas,* or characters-who-knew-they-were-characters, or characters who were anthropomorphic words at a costume party disguised as people (*I itch under the latex of Homemaker* began her story "Masquerade of Nouns," published in *The Simulacra Review*).

Bree had been a year younger than the rest of them, a girl from a limited universe Marguerite couldn't understand her not wanting to disclaim. Her "good" shirt was a pique knit polo, pink with a green lizard appliquéd above her left breast. With jeans she ironed and Payless shoes she touched up with black marker, she wore the Izod knockoff on the rare occasions she applied makeup—when her stories were up in workshop, when she went to church on Sundays, and when Justin and Marguerite brought her shopping because taking her out, they thought, was so *funny*. Marguerite called it *the iguana top*, or sometimes just *guano*.

Once Marguerite had spelled out to Bree at the dorm who, exactly, Justin *was*—the boy whose grandfather had left to him billions in a bequest that had skipped over his father—they'd made a pet of her, the kind that tripped over its own ears with eagerness. They called her *sweet* behind her back and *sweet* to her face, and their lack of duplicity had made them think themselves honest.

In class she mumbled answers and phrased questions as apologies and wrote stories with happy endings. Whether deus ex machina or plucky ingenuity or dogged devotion, something inevitably delivered her protagonist from lovelessness or death.

Marguerite would underline phrases in Bree's work she thought most working-class precious—*dilly-dally* and *ants-in-the-pants, dolled up* and *smacked upside the head*—and make smiley-faces next to them.

In architect-neat print Justin would write witticisms like *Why not termites in the trousers?* in the margins. *Does one's head have a downside?*

Bree didn't argue, instead taking pages of notes and whispering the same words every time the class excoriated her for not writing the kind of fiction they called *true*.

"You have added," she would say, "to my education."

He reached his front door with his heart beating furiously from panic and from frustration with Bree and from anger at himself for having engineered what was turning out to be an atrocity instead of her salvation. A *transparent* atrocity, according to Alchy-Cay. He wished his heart would burst and just be done with him. The feeling of being about to die wasn't real, doctors told him again and again. His condition couldn't kill him. But what was the difference between dying all the time and thinking you were?

CHAPTER 25

Hunter had been absent from the party a half hour when Carley walked across the front lawn to the Play Palace. Her first thought, upon finding him passed out naked on his bed, was how embarrassed he'd be for her to see the vomit on his balled-up shirt and the bathroom floor.

Her second was to clean it up before anyone else saw. Larry would for sure be up here after the guests had all left, lecturing Hunter on how it looked for the prospective stepson of a prospective state senator to stand upon his mother's Sotheby's-authenticated, from-the-estate-of-Jackie-Kennedy-Onassis, Louis-XVI-style upholstered taboret and recite from memory the first page of *Between Scylla and Alta Vista*—in which the phrase *shit-dark sea* apparently appeared—and proclaim its author *the greatest fucking meta-ist alive.*

Her third was she didn't know how to clean.

Her fourth was that not knowing how to clean was the sort of thing that made Nagel call her class *Hothouse Pansies*, which he'd gotten in trouble for saying when her class was reading a poem called "On the Subway," and Bunny Gardner had asked *Wait, so is that where those weird steps on the sidewalk in front of Barneys in the city go to?*

She should be able to figure it out. She'd *seen* cleaning performed, after all. And not just by the Help. That Hunter did much of his own cleaning was something a person wouldn't guess about him. It was like an *ambiguity*. Something that deserved describing in an interesting way—maybe even weird-à-la-Bree kind of interesting. It was only one of the special things he did that were special because he didn't *tell* people he did them. Like a footnote that only someone who really knew a subject—the way she did Hunter—would understand *was* the main point. Even if footnotes weren't supposed to be emotional.

Footnote Number One: Four Interesting Things About Hunter Cay's Knowing How to Clean That Demonstrate to the Reader He's Really Not Just a Drunk Asshole but Is In Fact a Really Nice and Special Person Who's Just Going Through Something.

1. Hunter was too private to allow the Cays' sixty-year-old Mexican laundress to wash his underwear and handkerchiefs.
2. Hunter didn't think it was *right* for a sixty-year-old woman to have to touch his dirty underwear and handkerchiefs just because she happened to be poor.
3. Hunter had been home sick so much as a kid that he'd followed the Help around and begged them to teach him things he promised not to tell his parents about; thus, he knew how to do laundry and feel for fever with his lips and make soup from real chickens that came with the bones still in them and from vegetables still in their skins.
4. Hunter used to be happiest when he was just ill enough to beg off going out with Ian, so he and Carley could stay in the whole weekend. At night he would cook elaborate dinners for two that only the Help knew about—and only then because he'd occasionally ring the kitchen with a question about how to cook something like a duck. That he cleaned up himself after these culinary adventures made him happy, the way taking care of people made him happy (see Footnote Number Four: On Hunter Cay's Taking Care of People in General and Carley Wells in Particular), and the way nothing he was *supposed to* do ever did.

Carley brought his shirt downstairs to the room behind the kitchen where the laundry machines and cleaning supplies lived. Peering into the washing machine, she assessed the small drainage holes and decided you weren't supposed to put a totally vomity shirt into it unless you wanted there to be cleaned-off throw-up chunks left in the machine afterward. She discovered a deep sink in the corner of the room that had a vomit-appropriate drain circumference and held the shirt under the faucet, stretching the material taut from placket to placket between her hands as the water carried away everything of Hunter he hadn't been able to keep in.

Stitched to a seam she found a label with hieroglyphic washing symbols and instructions she found she could follow, though they were entirely in French. There was a little drawer in the machine with a compartment marked Detergent. On the dashboard of the machine were buttons labeled with temperatures. Carley chose Cold. A second set of buttons offered options similar to those of a masseuse. Carley chose Gentle.

The machine's door locked with a satisfying snap. Sheets of water poured down the porthole like rain.

The hard thing about cleaning, Carley decided as she stared at the bathroom floor, is that what you're getting rid of has to *go* somewhere. And you need to pick up what you're trying to get rid of—in this case, puke—*with* something—and then that *something*—in this case, a mop—would have something—again, puke—on it and you need to take it off *that*, and when did it end?

Footnote Number Two: About an Episode of Puking (and Worse) of Carley's That Hunter Handled with Total Class—One of Many Reasons She Owes Him This. During a school field trip to see a matinee of that new *Hamlet* where all the actors wear antlers, Carley had gotten food poisoning, probably from the street-vendor kebab she'd bought when their bus had dropped them off that morning in front of the Museum of Modern Art. During the third act, Mrs. Tinsley, one of the teacher-chaperones, kept asking through the bathroom stall door, *Are you sure it isn't a bad monthly?* By Act IV she'd moved on to suggesting an ambulance would have to be called, as none of Carley's emergency contacts could be reached. (Gretchen was at a spa in Massachusetts, unavailable during her Rain Forest Facial; Grace was on vacation; Francis was "unreachable" according to his secretary; and Suzanne Cay, the Welles' backup emergency contact who *lived* for her cell phone, oddly enough wasn't answering.)

Loose bowels, Carley imagined a white-clad attendant shouting to his partner as they loaded her onto a stretcher in front of the theater while the entire junior and senior classes of Montclair Academy looked on. *She needs tightening—STAT!*

"I've a cab waiting," Hunter called into the bathroom when Tinsley finally left. "Can you walk?" In the taxi he pressed his hand against the pain in her stomach and told the driver to take them to the Plaza. She cried into his shoulder, terrified she'd go in her pants or throw up in the cab. He whispered that he would take care of her no matter what happened, and let her squeeze his hand until his knuckles were white.

"Stomachs are the great equalizer," he told her through the door of their bathroom once they'd gotten a room. "On the toilet the sexiest people are reduced to shit."

Francis met them at the Plaza when his secretary finally reached him, spending the night in side-by-side armchairs with Hunter, the two of them drinking scotch with their shirtsleeves rolled up while Carley drank ginger ale and ate saltines Hunter ordered for her and watched pieces of movies in between journeys to the bathroom in pink cotton pajamas Hunter had bought her downstairs in the hotel boutique so she could put on something comfortable and pretty over her shame.

They were suspended for three days for *leaving a school-sponsored activity without permission,* despite Francis's lodging a formal protest with the headmaster suggesting the chaperones' poor handling of the situation had forced Hunter to "be the only adult." On his return, Hunter had deposited an unsolicited essay on the headmaster's desk entitled "On the Absence of Empathy."

Carley looked at the mop. And the bucket and sponges. She looked away from the mirror so she didn't have to see herself in her bra and panties, to which she'd stripped down so the cycle of cleaning-puke-off-things didn't include her dress. The bucket was empty, but she couldn't get it to the tub to fill it without stepping through vomit and she couldn't mop the vomit from the floor in the first place without having water in the bucket and it turned out a bucketful of water was heavy to lug even a little way.

"Verbally tone deaf, poor Carley is," she'd heard Hunter tell Bree as

Gretchen reeled Carley over to a corner with a crooked finger to ask what Carley had done to so upset Hunter. "She wrote this poem once that rhymed *fish* with *wash*."

The disinfectant she mixed into the water smelled not like *lemon*-lemons, but like fruit turned angry that wanted to sear her lungs.

Une belle lettre, Hunter had said about the ocean poem when he'd read it in September. He'd looked her right in the eyes.

Later, she'd realize she'd been off on how much a gallon was—the bucket had felt so heavy she'd figured twenty-five capfuls of disinfectant would be about right for the suggested gallon-to-capful ratio.

Footnote Number Three: About Lemon-Things That Aren't Really Lemons. *(Narrator's note: The narrator hates interrupting, but she wants to be honest about this footnote not being really about lemons—though Hunter does wear a lemon-colored tie in it. It's just that there's this story she wants to tell that's the kind of story that when she remembers the good part of it makes her feel like she's in a middle of hug. And when you're cleaning a whole bunch of puke off the floor and then cleaning the wastepaper basket and everything still smells bad and the stuff that's supposed to make the smell go away is making you dizzy, you need a hug.)*

On her third day of diet camp, Carley dropped her bath towel into poison ivy on the way back from the showers without knowing it *was* poison ivy and kept using it. By Friday, when she had special permission to come home for the weekend for the Glen Club's Twenties Gala and say good-bye to Hunter before he and Ian left for their summer in Europe, bumps covered her chest and stomach. She scratched the whole four-hour limo ride home from upstate, going at the itch like she could dig it out.

"If you just *try* to think of something else," Gretchen said, suggesting they cover up all the blisters with Band-Aids. They were just on her chest and torso, under wraps. As long as they didn't weep into the light pink silk dress her mother kept saying would make Carley look *timeless* and that Carley thought looked like washed-out cotton candy, it would be as though they didn't exist. "Don't *touch*," her mother kept saying until Carley had scratched her chest into buttons of blood and tried and failed three times to put on a bra over the welts without screaming, and finally lay crying on her bed telling her parents to go without her.

An hour after her parents had left, Hunter showed up in his cream linen suit and lemon tie.

"Don't touch me," she said.

He sat next to her and took from a paper bag antihistamines and calamine lotion. "It's not contagious."

She pointed to the spots of red on her sheets. She reminded him what he'd paid to have that suit made. Everything he wore after having mono was newly purchased—nothing old fit.

He laid his jacket on a chair and unbuttoned his shirt, blushing as if she hadn't seen him shirtless hundreds of times in his pool. She suspected it was out of self-consciousness over his thinness. Before the mono had destroyed his appetite, he'd been lean with a body defined by a regime of swimming laps. Now, he was thin in a way that made certain European clothing look fabulous on him, but which undressed made him seem a bit fragile, more naked than naked.

She could feel his ribs through the sheets when he hugged her.

She washed down the pills with sips from his flask. He dabbed pink liquid on her back with his handkerchief. She tried to do her front herself, but when she couldn't resist pressing her nails through the cotton balls, he took them from her and did that, too, gently pink-chalking her breasts and covering them lightly with the sheet.

An hour after she'd begun cleaning, having put away everything and washed her pruny fingers again and again, she finally ran warm water and soap over a washcloth and brought it to Hunter's bed. She took in his nakedness, the sprawl of his legs and the soft thready tangle of his blond chest hair. She looked away from his balls. She wiped his face clean and combed her fingers through matted spots in his hair.

Footnote Number Four: About Hunter Cay's Taking Care of People in General and Carley Wells in Particular. Hunter was as genuinely undisgusted by other people's illnesses and unconcerned about the probability of catching them as he was worried about disgusting people with his own. He loved making people feel better far more than he worried about germs. He made care exciting. He made helping seem like a privilege. He made you *want* to be kind.

On the rare occasions when Carley got *sick*-sick, as in fever-having, he drove her delirious with attention. He chilled a stack of pillowcases in the freezer to give her a night's worth of newness against her cheek. He tucked blankets around her and whispered blessings when she sneezed and wouldn't think of letting her stay in the room next door to his when she could fall asleep in his arms in his bed. People were most contagious before their symptoms, he'd tell her. They were together all the time, so anything he was going to catch he'd already caught. Why worry about what was a fait accompli? He piled DVDs on his bed for her. He squeezed fresh oranges and brought her honeyed tea in delicate cups. He always came down with whatever she had a few days later and always tried to hide it and never complained.

She'd cleaned up vomit from everywhere it could be, but still the room smelled like sickness. It was an odor no one would mistake for anything else and which would bring last night into the next morning like it had never ended, always present, the way Nagel says you were supposed to talk about events in books—like they're going on right now, never over, never ending.

She stood before the array of bottles on Hunter's bureau and caressed a cologne she'd bought him last year that used to be his favorite, an essence of cedar and rain.

Footnote Number Five: About Smells, *The Arion Annals*, and Dead Things in the Present Tense. During Season Four, Episode Eleven of *The Arion Annals*, Glory and Liam have to hide evidence of having killed a member of the Order of Lethe until the sheriff stops nosing around and the Order stops surveilling them and they can throw a dead body into the sea. Because everything's taking place during a heat wave ("Boiling Sea" is the episode's name) they keep squirting air freshener at the cedar chest where they've stuffed it. On TV, it worked.

In the mirror above Hunter's bureau, in a beige lace bra and control-top panties with a dune of flesh rising between them, Carley's reflection aimed an atomizer (List Sixty: "Cosmotological Words") of cedar and rain at the room in reverse, her thumb paused over the trigger she wasn't sure she should depress.

Narrator's note: The narrator did not forget to finish the above scene. That was the end. It's très sophisticated to leave people hanging mid-air.

CHAPTER 26

Dearest Bree, the Talk of Fox Glen,

Please judge not Carley by her poor choice of friends. Her rudeness to you last night was catalyzed by my own terrible behavior, which to use your word, dearly "worried" her. Loyal to a flaw, she only wanted to protect me from censure I deserved. I am terribly sorry about having been an intoxicated boor on whom you wasted time trying to protect from embarrassment and from himself.

Though I understand you're largely unfamiliar with the culture of television, might have you by chance some years ago seen those commercials in which "Beep" was superimposed upon an image of a car? "Beep," said the car in earnest, a printed word without an actual sound. "Beep."

"Beep," Carley would say to the screen in return. "Beep." Like she didn't want the car to think it had gone unheard.

You cannot harbor anger for a girl who beeps at cars. Reserve your wrath, please, for the man (dare I call myself a man?) who last night you termed "a sloppy drunk."

I am, alas, too much of a coward this morning (afternoon, to be fair, for even Carley seems to have already gone out to engage the day) to face you. I do apologize for slipping this beneath your door and slipping away.

Yours in ignominy,

Dionysus

CHAPTER 27

YOU ARE NOT HERE.

Carley blinked at the red dot on the map of Moreland Galleria until the text corrected itself. It was one of those games your mind played when you looked at something too quickly to see it. *That's right,* she told it. *I am.*

"What are you looking for?" Amber said from behind her. "It's not like anything's changed."

Carley shrugged and turned, offering Amber the paper sack of sugar-and-cinnamon pretzel bites they always shared at Moreland. They'd bought them for as long as they'd been coming to the mall, since before their families' move to Fox Glen, when a parent would drive them in and get them Johnny Rockets chili cheese fries and follow them as they darted in and out of novelty stores doomed to be priced out rentwise a few years later when the mall would undergo renovation—stores they wouldn't learn to call "low rent" or "tacky" until they moved from Queens. Giddy with everything that hadn't happened but could, they'd stuck their fingers through the bars for puppies to lick in the Pet Palace, and threw pennies carrying wishes into the fountains, and pooled their allowances at the kiosk that silk-screened people onto clothing, buying a T-shirt of them hugging each other. When Francis was the designated parent, he'd take them for drives afterward to the North Shore, where they'd stare through iron gates at the huge houses and shiny cars of strangers and he'd say, *Anything can be bought, the whole trick is paying.*

They took the glass elevator up to the third floor to Amber's favorite store, *chaton*, whose lowercase name Hunter liked to call *Teen Penthouse meets e.e. cummings.*

Carley took out her cell phone as Amber gathered up two short black dresses, a purple cashmere tube top, and suede fringed miniskirts in mauve, white, and gold, heading for the handicapped dressing room, which had the most mirrors and best couch.

"He's still not answering," Carley said, her call going through to Hunter's voice mail. She hung up, having run out things to say five messages ago.

"Hunter's not here. Let's keep it that way." All of the hooks were filled with other people's castoffs. Amber took an abandoned pair of jeans and a wool halter dress from a hook by the mirror and moved them to an already-crowded one by the slatted door.

"I wasn't going to ask him to come. I just want to make sure he's—"

"What I meant was, I don't want to talk about him." The dress, brown and orange chevron-striped and something only a beautiful or popular girl could get away with wearing, slipped off its hanger. As Amber leaned down to pick it up, she squinted at the tag.

"Are you pissed off at him for not asking you to come to dinner?" Amber wasn't in Florida with the rest of her family because after she'd ended up catching the slightest version of Hunter's cold, Edie had made her stay behind rather than risk infecting her sister. "You know what Suzanne is like—a last-minute invite would have had her freaking out over seating. I *know* he felt bad about your being home alone."

"I *said* I don't want to *talk* about him." She held the dress up in front of her, stretching the material across her hips with her hands. Amber was a size six; the dress—Carley could see from the tag—was a double zero.

"Are you still mad about last weekend? About his blowing you off at the Station? Because, you know, he was totally concerned about you and made sure you didn't go home with that guy and—"

Amber pulled off her pants and ventured a leg into the jeans that had been hanging with the dress. "The way you're being right now, Carley? *That's* why I don't want to talk about him. I'm sick of hearing you say why I shouldn't be mad at him. What pisses me off isn't the things Hunter does.

It's how he always gets to pretend he hasn't done them. He likes to think he's not a snob like his mother, but no one's forcing him to hang out with Ian and to sleep with bitch-WASPS who at least *admit* to themselves what they are."

"Like *you* know who you are? You hate them for not letting you be one of them. You hate Ian for liking preppy girls instead of girls who'd wear *this*." She held up the tube top. "And you hate Hunter for—"

"I don't hate him. I could never hate him." She sighed and gave up trying to tug the one jean leg higher, the top of the inseam stuck at her thigh. "But we spend time around people who hate us just to be with him. We go places we don't like where we're not wanted. We had a *place* before Hunter, we had friends. And he took us from them."

"No one *took* me. I *went*." She grabbed the tiny jeans from Amber's hands and threw them against the mirror.

Amber stood in her shirt and panties, staring at the jeans that lay splayed on the floor like half a body. Carley picked up the double-zero dress by its padded hanger. "You don't want to be her," Carley said. "The girl who fits this."

They left without Amber trying on anything she'd chosen, making their way in silence to the fountain where people threw pennies and made wishes, a silver-gray pyramid that spewed water and money, like a change return for dreams.

"Someone wanted something big," Amber finally said, watching a quarter slide down the side of the pyramid and into the marble pool below. Soon it would be sucked back up and spit out. *Coingasm*, Hunter always called it.

Not that Hunter liked Moreland. But ever since he and Carley had become the most unlikely of friends four years ago, he'd been going with her and Amber to places like the mall because *they* liked them. Back then, there'd still been a few stores in the fingerlings off the main concourses that didn't fit its newly upgraded image—places like the lava lamp store, the poster store that sold framed pictures of kittens playing in sewing baskets (like anyone owned a *sewing basket*), and—in the space now occupied by an Armani A/X—The Christian Supply Store.

Wanting to entertain Hunter on his first-ever trip to a suburban shopping mall, she and Amber and the people they'd hung out with thought it would be hysterical to make what they called *The Bible Store* a stop on his tour. They wanted to show him that even if Moreland was beneath his mother and aunt and cousin—who shopped at the Gold Mile, where Gucci and Cartier and Prada clustered like champagne grapes but were not considered a *mall*, Moreland was *fun*.

"Welcome to Crosses-R-Us," Jake had said to Hunter. Amber and Carley had cackled like Robin Quivers. Olivia stopped at a mirrored plaque engraved with the Footprints poem, fixing her lip gloss in the reflection.

"Sir," Jake addressed the clerk, a man with wire-frame glasses and dark hair down to his waist, "we're looking for a Bible made from human skin."

Hunter grabbed Jake by the shoulder. "He's sorry," Hunter said. He stared at Carley. "They're all sorry."

He stayed in the store a long time talking to the Bible Hippy while Carley watched through the window and everyone else left to buy Orange Juliuses. Hunter picked out a blank journal from a long shelf of them. After he paid, he and the hippy shook hands.

"I didn't know that's who you were," Hunter told Carley when he came out. He wrapped his arms around himself, the journal pressed to his chest. She wanted to cry, but he looked even sadder.

"It's not," she said, even though she wasn't sure it was true. Not until she'd met Hunter had she even given any thought to what kind of person she wanted to be. Before Hunter it had never occurred to her that you could choose.

The quarter fought the tide of the fountain. She and Amber squeezed each other's hands. "George Washington has a ribbon in his hair," Carley said. "Like Justin wears."

"You and Hunter hang out with him last night?" She said it like she wanted to know. Like she wasn't mad anymore. Like they were still friends. That they weren't fighting filled Carley with such relief that she almost told her everything—about Justin and his panic attacks and about Bree and her love/hate crush on Justin and about cleaning up Hunter's vomit—until she realized just about everything she wanted to share was someone else's secret, stories that weren't hers to tell. She felt the way she had when she'd returned from the party four years ago where she and Hunter had first forged their unlikely friendship, a story Carley hadn't felt right telling even Amber, a story she'd never told anyone.

Carley shrugged. "Not really. Want to eat?" They headed for the food court because what else was left to share?

Too early for dinner, too late for lunch, everyone at the food court was leftover. Middle school kids dropped off hours ago without a *next* in mind. Old women with lipstick-stained coffee cups and shopping bags kept close. South-shore girls who took the bus and wore black liquid eyeliner and ate chili-cheese fries with their fingers. Fat woman picking onions off her Double Whopper, the metal latticework of the tabletop imprinting her elbow through her shirt. Skate-rat poking his skate-rat friend. Half-wrappers of straws swept up by a retarded guy with rubber-soled shoes and an is-it-Christmas-yet smile. Everyone chewing and going nowhere.

They bought two face-sized slices each of Sbarro pizza and extra-large frozen yogurts with hot fudge that would coat Carley's thighs and Amber's favorite toilet, the stall at the end. They ate too fast to speak, every bite a sigh.

Amber scraped the last thread of fudge out of the seam of her frozen yogurt cup and tucked the plastic spoon into her purse. Ever since "Calluses on Knuckles" showed up on a PFED (Parents Fighting Eating Disorders) warning-signs pamphlet distributed last month at PEACE, she'd been trying out finger substitutes.

She started toward the bathroom.

"Don't," Carley said, coming with her. "Let it stay down. To make sure you still can."

She followed Amber into the stall. "Don't."

Amber locked the stall door behind them. "It gets easy, you know. It would get Gretchen off your back. You could wear clothes from *chaton*. You're so pretty already and—"

"I don't want to. I can't."

"We could do it like a race. Like High Dives. A game."

Later Carley would understand why she finally leaned forward and let

Amber put a finger down her throat. Later she'd know Amber really had wanted to give her a gift and that she'd really wanted to accept it. Later she'd realize a secret had seemed the only thing strong enough to keep them together.

Later she'd wish she had a weaker stomach, a stronger gag reflex, a less powerful jaw. "Ow!" Amber screamed. "What's *wrong* with you?" She massaged her hand where Carley's teeth had left marks.

"I couldn't help it. It was like . . . I don't know," Carley said, "like being raped."

"*Raped?* You opened your mouth. You said yes. You *decided.*" Amber waved her out of the stall. "I'd never hurt you. *I'm* not the one who's mean to you in public and who doesn't care if everyone's laughing at you and who only comes to you when he feels sick or sorry for himself. I'm not the one who's filled you up with himself and left you a shell. If anyone's *raping* you, it's—"

"Don't say it. Don't *ever* say that about him. Or you and me, we can't be—"

Amber closed the door. "We haven't *been* for a long time," she said from the other side of it.

They passed the photo kiosk again on their way out of the mall. Big-nosed twin boys on a baseball cap. A baby with arms like bread dough on an I ♥ Mom T-shirt. Fat people kissing on a sweatshirt like they didn't know they were fat.

The whole silent cab ride home Carley kept thinking about those shirts, about what it would feel like to know someone wanted to wear you.

CHAPTER 28

"The company you keep defines you." Larry put the Hangar One and Tanqueray Ten into a box. "Do. You. Understand?"

Hunter refilled his glass with club soda from the bar gun. "Je. Parle. Anglais." His mouth was still dry after a morning of gulping water.

Suzanne didn't look up from the French *Elle* she read in front of the fireplace while her fiancé was busy pillaging Hunter's bar. "What Larry means—"

"What *you* do reflects on *me*." He looked over at Suzanne. "And what *our friends* do reflects upon *us*. Which is why we're *all* going to be putting some distance between ourselves and people who don't reflect appropriately."

"Inappropriate reflections? Ah, vampires! I *knew* there was something about Greer and Cissy. Silly me, I thought it was just the blow."

"Larry's being serious." Suzanne closed her magazine.

"By *distance*, do you mean uninviting Francis and Gretchen to Newport?" Larry's family was throwing an engagement celebration next weekend to which a month ago Suzanne had been excited to invite the Wellses. Back then, she'd still thought of them like *family*, but it seemed Larry was helping her redefine the word.

"Those, too," Larry said primly, grabbing the handle of the bar refrigerator before the door could swing closed.

"One doesn't get drunk on *olives*. Or is it the pimientos that intimidate you?"

"The things you *do* come up with," Suzanne tittered. "I don't *uninvite*, Hunter. We're talking about *future* invitations. We all just have to . . . rethink . . . our social circle. We won't be here much longer anyway. You'll be at Princeton soon enough, and Larry will, after all, need to live where he works. Really, Fox Glen hasn't been what Plum always made it out to be. For every Burroughs or Leighton, there's a—"

"Wells. Your *friends*." Hunter dangled the bottle of maraschinos in front of Larry. "Francis Wells is a very good man."

Larry smirked. "When he's not molesting our guests."

"Haven't you ever found yourself doing something without *deciding* to? Francis explained this a thousand times last night. He was thinking about bras—it's his *business*, the way it's your business to sit in your corner office and wait for Daddy's money to make more money—and looking at Cissy gave him an idea, and before he realized it—"

"Keep your nose clean." Larry packed up the last of the scotch from the bar—though not the last in the Play Palace. In the poolside dressing room safe, along with the pills (without which he'd never have been able to face today's hangover and haranguing), and some cash no one knew about but Carley, were five bottles of the caliber of liquor you didn't leave out for your trashed friends to chug at four a.m. Because the safe was so well concealed in the mosaic tiles, it didn't matter that the eighty-year-old lock no longer worked. Hunter himself had only learned about the safe four years earlier because the dressing rooms were still being restored when he'd moved in. When the mosaicists who discovered it asked Hunter if his mother wanted the compartment sealed, he gave them five hundred each not to mention its existence.

"My *nose*? Again, I believe you should be conferring with the *Gardners*."

"It's an expression." Larry folded one set of parallel box flaps and then the other without crossing them; he squinted when they didn't stay closed. "It means—"

"God, you're stupid."

"Hunter!" Suzanne waved her hand like something smelled bad.

"What I'm referring to—*besides* your public drunkenness, which *we will no longer tolerate*—is that tank of a girl you drag behind like an anchor."

"Your mixed metaphor is as tasty as a tugboat."

"She makes you look like something's wrong with you." Larry left off packing Hunter's martini glasses and looked Hunter in the eye. "If you don't *like* girls . . . well, the Talbrights are *Democrats*, for godsake. Discretion's all I ask. Just get yourself a better-groomed beard."

Hunter didn't bother to remind Larry that he wasn't gay. "You know, Larry, you're *exactly* the kind of man who wins elections."

Suzanne came over to the bar, leaning into it like a customer at the Station. "The company a person keeps buoys or drowns him. Remember when we moved here, how you changed because of Ian? He *made you* somebody. That, Hunter, is buoying. But with Ian and his girlfriend gone off this fall, you've—"

"Violet's no longer his girlfriend."

"I fear that without the Buchanans and Burroughses, you're sinking—"

"I get the point, Mother." They never talked about who he'd been before Fox Glen, and now she wanted to discuss it in front of *Larry*?

"The *point*," Larry said, underhand-tossing Hunter's monogrammed Tiffany cocktail shaker into a box like a barbarian, "is that cow is a problem."

"A *problem* would be running for public office with no credentials but one's surname."

"You'd better not think she's coming to Newport with you next weekend."

"*I'm* not coming to Newport. Soccer championship?"

"I've already told you I'll speak to the coach," said Larry. "You're not so valuable to the team."

"You *must* come," Suzanne said. "Hunter . . . Prince, I . . ."

"I'm not your *prince*."

"Do you ever think of anyone but yourself?" Larry shook his head. "Would it kill you to let her have her pet names?"

"I suppose you let her call you *Jack* in the bedroom."

Suzanne couldn't get around the bar before Larry had him by the collar.

Club soda spewed onto the walnut floor as Larry punched him in the stomach again and again.

He was a picker, Larry. Of scabs he flicked onto the floor, of nasal detritus he mined when he thought no one was looking, of arguments he pinched like lint. Hunter had known it from their first dinner together, when Larry had scratched open a pimple on the back of his neck. As innocuous as Larry may have initially seemed compared to Griffin (a man who several days prior to Hunter's revealing his au pair affair had accused Suzanne of having raised *socially maladjusted milquetoast* directly in front of the milquetoast), Hunter had known a man who couldn't keep his finger in check would soon enough lose control of his fist.

"Stand behind your actions, *Senator* Talbright." Hunter gagged and doubled over. "Go for the face."

CHAPTER 29

There's this hero, Theseus, whose father is a king who owes money to another king and can't pay it back, so he has to send seven virgins and seven young men every year to the other king, who we'll call King Number Two to feed to King Number Two's pet, this humongous half-bull-half-man thing that lives in a maze so complicated you can never get unlost. One day Theseus tells his father, *Send me as one of the seven guys and I'll kill the Minotaur so we can stop feeding it,* and probably because it doesn't look good politically to keep feeding the voters' kids to a monster, the king says, *Sure, son. Good plan.*

Truth is, Theseus doesn't *have* a plan, but that's what heroes are like—so gung-ho about the saving that they don't always think about what it might take.

Anyway, Theseus lucks out because King Number Two's daughter, Ariadne, falls totally in love with him and says, *Tie one end of this ball of string to the entrance and unravel it as you go, so after you kill the Minotaur you can just rewind your way back.*

Theseus is like, *Duh! Why didn't I think of that,* but mostly he's just pumped up, since not only will he get to save all those people, but after killing the monster he'll also get to hang out with Ariadne, who's smart in a common-sense way that princess-types usually aren't. When Theseus finally emerges from the maze, covered with blood and leading a parade of teenagers grateful about not having been eaten, Ariadne is so glad to see him that she jumps into his arms even though he's all sticky and gross, and everyone lives happily ever after, the end."

"That's *not* the end," Bree said, and then, "Which way now?" At first the path through the boxwood hedges of the English maze had been unicursal, corners prompting two left turns and then a right, but now she and Carley had reached a T.

"Up to you."

"Which is the *right* way?"

Carley shrugged.

"You don't know or you don't want to tell me?"

"Do you skip to the end of a book to see what happens?"

"I don't *read* books that are *about* what happens. And I don't like games. And it's cold." All week Carley had complained that Bree's room and her own were too "boring" for her to "feel creative in." So every day they'd discussed the book in some outdoor location until the tape ran out on the microrecorder Carley continued to insist Bree use. So far they'd been to an overgrown pond, some gardens, and a gazebo. Tonight, in forty-five-degree weather, it was the English maze.

"Fine," said Carley. "Left."

Bree pressed Rewind. *The end*, she heard Carley repeat seconds later.

"How many times are you going to check the thing? It's worked every time. Left again."

"Theseus tells Ariadne he'll marry her," Bree said, "but when they make a pit stop on the way home, he abandons her on an island while she's sleeping. Some versions have her killing herself afterward. Others have her marrying Dionysus, the god of drunks. *That's* the end."

"Well, it was, like, a long time ago when we did the myth stuff. Ninth grade. And I might've gotten bored and stopped reading."

"A shock."

"Right, and another right, and don't go asking people if they know a story if you're gonna be picky about how they tell it."

"I said nothing when you referred to a mythological beast as *Manimal*.

A malaprop rivaled only by last night's *frigate*—which, by the way, means war ship."

Carley picked a leaf off the hedge. She tore it in half, then in half again and again. "Sorry again about what I said last night. About your writing about people with metaphorical c—"

"We've been through the apologies. But that's not the point. *I'm* not the point. The point is how you change when you're around Hunter like you did last night. You're so busy propping him up that everything sensitive and smart about *you* goes into hiding."

"There's a kind of curlicue thing coming up." She rubbed her eyes with her gloved hand. "The trick is to go all the way around instead of getting caught in it, which means taking a double left, even though we'll be walking away from the center of the maze in order to eventually go toward it. And about Hunter? You just don't understand. I wouldn't even know how to *be* sensitive if I hadn't met him. He's made me *better*. He always makes me better."

"Better than what?"

"What?"

"I'm not seeing the happening of *better*."

"You know"—Carley shook her head—"you sounded like Justin, the way you just said that. The weird order of the words. Except bitchy. *Justin* is nice."

"Justin is nice?" Bree stopped walking. "Justin's *image* is nice. *Justin* is a love-leeching—"

"Until last night I thought you had a serious crush on him, but this morning I was thinking about it and realized it's not exactly that. He's into *you* for real, like a normal person. But it's different for you. You say his books suck, but you're jealous of how popular they are. You dress all weird in clothing that looks more like Justin than *you*, then write stuff that's the exact *opposite* of what people who read his stuff would like. You want to *be* him, but you hate yourself for it."

It wasn't Bree's intention to lose herself as she stalked away through the maze. She just wanted to get away because cursing at or slapping her little patron was the kind of deal breaker alluded to in Roman Numeral Eight,

Capital Letter D, Arabic Numeral Three—Conduct and Ethics—of the contract she'd signed with the Wellses.

She'd gone back in the direction from which they'd come—at least she thought she had, memory being a tricky thing that sometimes filled in gaps with exactly what you needed and sometimes what you feared—but every juncture seemed foreign. Initially she debated at intersections, but as the time lengthened and the quiet weighed upon her she began choosing randomly, fighting panic and then panicking further at the idea of either Carley coming upon her running directionless or Carley having already gone back to the house and leaving her alone in hedge world. The longer she walked, the more it all looked the same. Soon she was blind with hedges.

The in-ground path lights went out at all once. Midstep, she lowered herself slowly to the ground. Freezing to the spot—was that fight or flight? She waited for her eyes to adjust to the dark—any minute now she should be able to count the stars as companions and see by the light of the moon.

She waited. The darkness didn't fade. She got up and walked a few steps with her arms out in front of her. She screamed as something tugged at her sweater. Just hedge, she realized too late. A tiny branch that had escaped shaping.

"Bree!" Carley's voice sounded far away.

"Why is it so dark?"

"They're on a timer."

"The stars?"

"The lights. I have a flashlight on my keychain, and . . . I can't follow your voice, you know, if I'm doing the talking."

"Come. Please?"

After what seemed like forever, a penlight beam came around the corner. "You do know there's like *no* crime here?"

"Carley?"

"No, it's the maze murderer who . . . Shit, are you *crying?*" She sat down beside her. "I'd tell you *it's okay*—but you'd probably say the *comfort* is *unrealistic* and *boring* like in a Justin Leighton novel and it would have been a way better story if I'd left you to find your own way out, because that's the kind of fucked-up, mean, *complicated* thing you like to read. Bree hears a noise that's really just an owl but she thinks it's a maze monster coming to get her so she starts running and the narrator writes a footnote about the Minotaur myth and another about monster movies and another *on* the one about monster movies about watching them *ironically* or whatever and the more lost Bree gets the more footnoted the footnotes—"

"*Embedded*," Bree corrected.

"Like those Russian dolls people get you as a kid that you always lose the top or the bottom of at least one of because it's hard enough to keep track of the pieces of one two-piece doll, let alone seven. And by the end of Bree's story she'll have found the exit to the maze but be stuck so deep in the center of a hundred footnotes that she's lost forever."

"That's a pretty decent Fuck You." Bree wiped away tears with her scarf. "Very meta."

Carley handed her a crumpled tissue. "It's clean. You know, you almost made it to the center. By accident, but still. Want to see it?"

"See what?"

"You'll have to *see*."

To appreciate it, Carley insisted as they entered the bestiary by penlight, you needed to feel the tiger's carved marble fur with your fingers. You needed to climb up onto the back of the elephant, shimmying forward on his neck and chancing falling just to run your fingers over his upraised marble trunk. You needed to put your head inside the mouth of a crocodile and feel his marble teeth on your neck. Bree obliged.

Carley settled onto the ground with her head back against a springing cheetah, staring at the moonless, starless sky.

"Why don't you like your room?" Bree asked.

"Why don't you like people?"

"I *like* people."

"You only see their backsides, so you think people are ugly. Of course you're gonna be a misantwerp if all you see is ass."

"Misanthrope. And I *do* like people."

"Who?"

"Well, I don't entirely dislike you."

"Only because you're being paid not to. I've had nannies and au pairs. I have tutors and a trainer and a shrink. I know paid-nice. It comes with gritted teeth."

"I'm not gritting. And I don't lie. If I say I sort of like you when you're not butchering the English language, then I genuinely sort of like you."

"Everyone lies when the truth's hard."

"I'm not afraid of hard truth." Bree ran her hand down the cheetah's tail. "Here's one: if it happens, Carley, what you want with Hunter, it'll be like fucking a ghost."

Carley held the cheetah's front paw. Minutes passed. "Gretchen goes through your things when you're not home," she said, finally. "You really should tape over that."

CHAPTER 30

In Aftermemory, Hunter steps into the center of the maze, to which he's found his way because he knows the path by heart. "Tape over what? What's being unsaid?"

"She thinks you'll hurt me," Carley says, the words slipping out like silk, like a trick, like a magician's red handkerchief that seems to emerge from his mouth holding a dove. "Amber thinks you already are."

"What do *you* think?" He shifts his weight from foot to foot, a habit he put behind him years ago when he'd learned to stand still against nervousness.

"I think . . . I'm afraid . . . you wouldn't notice if you were."

He stares at her like he's seeing the impossible, shaking his head.

And then, what? She squeezed her eyes tighter closed in her bedroom, trying and failing to imagine him admitting it, trying and failing to imagine a *next*.

CHAPTER 31

Darren Connelly <d.connelly@blaine.edu>   November 08 9:31 PM
to: Justin Leighton <litrockstar@gmail.com>
cc:
re: Unacknowledged invitation

Because you have yet to respond to the invitation to the book-launch fete I'm hosting for Marguerite's novel, and because EVERYONE has missed you so acutely, I decided extraordinary measures were warranted to coax you out.

I just issued an invitation to Bree, baited with the suggestion that there might be book-folk in attendance interested in acquiring an overwritten novel about time travel and vengeance. (Didn't actually put that fine a point on it; didn't have to.)

Time to return to the living, Justin. Looking forward to seeing you.

Justin Leighton <litrockstar@gmail.com>   November 08 9:46 PM
to: Darren Connelly <d.connelly@blaine.edu>
cc:
re: re: Unacknowledged invitation

do not use her. Please.

Darren Connelly <d.connelly@blaine.edu>   November 08 10:20 PM
to: Justin Leighton <litrockstar@gmail.com>
cc:
re: re: re: Unacknowledged invitation

What might you call withholding failure from a person who clearly
WANTS to fail, in order to quench your own thirst for heroism?

Justin Leighton <litrockstar@gmail.com>   November 08 10:35 PM
to: Darren Connelly <d.connelly@blaine.edu>
cc:
re: re: re: re: Unacknowledged invitation

love not yet unwrapped
brown papered sans return address
underworld yearning

Darren Connelly <d.connelly@blaine.edu>   November 08 10:55 PM
to: Justin Leighton <litrockstar@gmail.com>
cc:
re: re: re: re: re: Unacknowledged invitation

You can't bad-haiku
Away the truth of your deeds.
It will boomerang.

CHAPTER 32

Sound lied in Swann's Way. From the entrance, voices floated to the second floor. In a third-story hallway that wound around the servants' quarters and terminated at Francis's office, voices were snatched up. And from certain spots on the second floor, one's words pinballed around the balcony. Such a spot existed in the doorway of Gretchen Wells's bedroom, and like a pool player who knew her angles, she often conducted conversations from exactly there—her husband unaware of what she was doing—to broadcast to her daughter what she couldn't bear to look at her to say.

"Her stomach was rolling over the top of her hose. You could see it through that knit."

Carley bit into *rolling*. She felt the word's doughiness as it slipped over the ledge of her underwear and down to the floor.

Gretchen had heard Larry Talbright tell Suzanne last night that it was high time Hunter got himself "a real date" for such events, a comment no doubt triggered by Carley's tugging a wedgie through her dress seconds before. *Creeping undergarment*, Gretchen called it. As always, it was like listening to a one-sided conversation, Francis's responses inaudible because sound traveled differently—normally—on the other side of Gretchen's threshold.

As the silences between Gretchen's complaints about Carley's weight and mannerisms multiplied, Carley stuffed them with Francis's disappointment and then resignation. In a place like Swann's Way, you filled up quiet with the worst you could think of.

She stared at the phone. By the time she'd finally reached Hunter earlier in the evening he'd been drunk enough for her to hear it in his voice. She hadn't meant to start a fight, but the way he kept denying he was drinking, even as he spaced out his words the way he always did to try to sound sober, scared her so much that she heard herself saying, *I had to wade through your puke last night* and heard him saying back, *You don't know where you begin and I end.*

"It hurts me to look at her," Gretchen said to Carley's inaudible father. "It *has* to hurt her." The words seeped into the rugs and beneath Carley's door, and then the phone was in Carley's hand.

When Hunter picked up, thick-tongued and slurring, she pretended not to notice. She wanted him to come rescue her, but she didn't want him to drive. She wanted to flee to him in a cab, but didn't want him to know she knew he couldn't get behind the wheel.

"Your mother's the bitch that makes every other bitch-mommy in Fox Glen feel better about herself," he said. "Why do think Suzanne likes her?" She heard the tinkle of ice cubes. "You looked so pretty last night in that dress. So soft. Like a teddy bear."

She didn't tell him he was thinking of the dress from last weekend.

"People were talking about it," he said, "how elegant you looked."

She wanted to believe she'd worn something he remembered. She wanted to believe she'd been the most elegant stuffed animal on earth. She wanted to believe he knew what he was saying. She wanted to believe.

She let herself slip into the plushness of his voice, and they talked about things that didn't make sense until the pauses between his words settled into a blanket of quiet. She stayed on the phone another five minutes, just to hear him breathe.

CHAPTER 33

Carley Wells <seawells@gmail.com>   November 8 11:55 PM
to: Bree McEnroy <btmcenroy@yahoo.com>
cc:
re: devices

i know you put in the footnotes and annoying narrator because i told you to but i made a mistake. maybe some people like that meta stuff because it seems more honest like the tricks a writer uses arent being tricky because they r out in the open. and so a story isnt lying about being just a story. i think i get that.

but I don't like it.

i dont want you to feel like you have to go back and take out the weird stuff right now right after we ended up talking on the way out of the maze about whats going to happen next in the book. i like ur idea of bucks family being nominated for banishment but the tv audience not voting them off because everyone loves watching buck and jules sneak off together. thats something that would probably really happen. also having millions of viewers knowing they r dating when their parents have no clue because theyd be afraid of b & j not trying their best to win makes it smart because of the irony, right? anyway, my point is that if ur already on a roll with all that you can just write it (but without meta-ing it) and un-meta the beginning later.

my english teacher who i dont think youd like is always making us analyze stories to figure out all the devices a writer used to make the reader feel or think certain things. b4 it seemed to me like cheating that the writers tricks looked like magic but now i think id rather have a story lie to me without my knowing it than have to keep sitting through explanations of how the tricks r done.

sometimes you just dont want to know ur being tricked.

Carley Wells <seawells@gmail.com>   November 9 2:15 AM
to: Bree McEnroy <btmcenroy@yahoo.com>
cc:
re: buck

i was just thinking—you know that part you read the other night where buck thinks its hard to believe that the real world still exists? maybe this is a stupid idea but what if he starts losing his grip on life and starts believing he lives in medieval-world for real? could it happen before anyone notices?

PART IV

Backstory

The drink made past happy things contemporary with the present, as if they were still going on, contemporary even with the future as if they were about to happen again.

—F. Scott Fitzgerald, *Tender Is the Night*

Hunter Cay <huntercay@gmail.com>   November 13 3:30 PM
to: Carley Wells <seawells@gmail.com>, Amber Weiss <sexyyellow
stone@hotmail.com>, Bunny Gardner <caratlover@gmail.com>,
Bryant Gabel <bjg420@yahoo.com>, Colin Bradley <mrbradley2u
@ . . .
cc:
re: Party—tomorrow

In honor of Suzanne's entrusting to me chez Cay while she makes the
Newport rounds with the ass to whom she has been betrothed, I hereby
request your presence tomorrow evening, poolside, after day one of
the championship soccer tournament.

Libations will be provided. BYO other forms of entertainment, within
reason. Please, no substances with which you lack extensive personal
familiarity. (I'd prefer not to spend my night disabusing anyone of the
notion that his hand is an alien-grafted appendage in need of chewing
off—as I did with Brent Maddox last winter.)

On second thought, no hallucinogens whatsoever.

CHAPTER 34

Gretchen spoke to clothing in a private, wordless language—twitches and sniffs and blinks that commended lines for their smoothness or chided fabrics for their texture or heft. She assessed the hem and bateau neckline of a silk chiffon shift as she held it up against Carley, patting the dress for knowing how to flirt without giving anything away. Carley stood mannequin-still in front of the column-mirror, watching Gretchen compare the dress's bust to Carley's. It was a bad store for breasts.

"You wouldn't need a slip," Gretchen said. Cream with light orange roses, it was tiered at the hem. She turned the dress inside out to reveal its dark orange lining and discreet tags. Size ten. Always, Gretchen picked out clothing several sizes too small.

"It's not . . . me," Carley said, elliptic speech being Gretchen's preferred means of communication when there were no euphemisms left.

Later, she'd wish she'd said, *I'm too fat for this* at the top of her lungs. Later, she'd wish she'd said, *Stop telling me who I could be in the right clothing, in the right body, in the right skin—and just say to my face you don't like who I am.*

Later she'd wish she'd said she knew that today's frenzy to find the "perfect" replacement Sweet Sixteen dress on the Gold Mile was just Gretchen's way of distracting herself from memories of last night. She'd wish she'd said, *I know what you did.* She'd wish she'd said, *Last night wouldn't have happened if we ever said what we meant.*

Last night, again, was PEACE.

At the beginning of every Parent-Educator-Administrator-Conferral-Evening, before the "conferrals" in the parlor over tea and petits fours, parents filed into classrooms and sat through mini-classes the Montclair Academy Handbook claimed *fostered familiarity with Montclair's challenging curriculum.* Francis, who hadn't attended PEACE since the spring, when Carley's drama teacher had shoved a wig on him and forced him to do a Juliet-as-tranny Shakespearean interpretation, claimed they *allowed Ivy-League snots to treat the people who pay their salaries like ignorant fucks.*

His opinion was only solidified by the events recounted to him by Bernie after a PEACE where Carley's and Amber's history teacher had pinned flashcards with historical events onto parents and challenged them to line up at the front of the room in chronological order. Thinking the Restoration must have had something to do with getting rid of the Watergate tapes, Edie had wedged herself between Bay of Pigs (Connie Vandergraf) and Death of Elvis (Greer Gardner). Ms. Armstrong, with her inch-long bangs and I-don't-wear-animals-plastic-shoes, drove Edie to tears as she prodded her back century-by-century, smirking as she professed, *No cause for embarrassment, the Human Timeline is about connection, not perfection.* Even Spanish Inquisition (Cissy Gardner) had felt sorry for Edie.

But what had happened to Gretchen last night had set a new benchmark for humiliation.

Metal ran across Carley's neck like a razor. Dove-gray taffeta. The hanger was cold. "Jacqueline Minet's daughter," Gretchen said, giving the dress a shake and a wink, "the one who got fat and stopped shaving? She got a worm, nearly died."

She held the dress to Carley's hips. "Africa. That's what happens when girls let themselves go. Peace Corps. Worms."

Like so much of life, Carley had figured out last night backward, unraveling it from end to beginning. It had started for her when she watched Francis help Gretchen out of the cab she'd been poured into and ended when she found her mother's blouse tossed inside-out on her dressing room floor, strange markings on the sleeves. For Gretchen, it had begun with not going to dinner with Suzanne Cay, who traditionally calmed her before PEACE over uneaten entrées. Had Suzanne not left for Newport earlier that day to prepare for this weekend's festivities, she might have told Gretchen not to fixate on impressing Nagel. She might have warned her against doubling her pills. She might have dissuaded her from cramming for her daughter's English teacher's mini-class by writing notes all over her arms in a Percocet-induced brainstorm until she was late. But as it was, Gretchen had been left alone with her nerves.

Carley could picture her mother scurrying past the Corinthian columns and through the empty reception hall of the building that ninety years earlier had been the home of Walter Montclair, who'd made a fortune from inventing a bug-killing chemical that after he died was discovered to slowly kill people who spent too much time around it. At the end of the hallway, she'd have reached *The Archetypal Journey and Its Insubvertibility*, where Nagel was halfway through leading a mini-class mini-discussion on *Waiting for Godot*, a play Gretchen had no idea Carley's class was reading and which Carley, in fact, was not.

Gretchen thought they were still studying *Gatsby*, most likely because anytime she asked Carley how English class was coming along, Carley had said, "Great," relieving them both of further discussion. On Gretchen's arms, beneath her French-cuffed sleeves, she'd written down everything Apex Notes claimed to be important about *The Great Gatsby*. Characters, themes, symbols, allusions. So focused was she on proving to Nagel her love of literature that she didn't pay attention to what was being said.

Standing at the whiteboard, Nagel asked, "Why does Vladimir say, 'The essential doesn't change'?" and Gretchen, legs crossed at the ankles under her desk, went off about how Gatsby can't change his past and about boats that can't fight currents. Nagel tried interrupting. Edie Weiss tried passing a note. But Gretchen was in a rhythm about the symbolism of eyes and eyeglasses and the Valley of Ashes and then *waste as leitmotif*, an idea she was certain—given the number of pages Apex devoted to it—would bring Nagel to intellectual climax.

"The green light!" she shouted. "The green light!"

Nagel cleared his throat. People turned in their desks. Gretchen sweated with knowing *something* was wrong, but what? She wasn't used to things not fitting.

In *Godot* the green light was meaningless. In *Godot* it didn't exist.

Nagel wrote the name of the play in all caps on the board. He underlined it, then slowly read it aloud. Gretchen rolled up her sleeves and squinted at her arms.

"So sophisticated," said a saleswoman as Carley walked out of the fitting room cubicle wearing an ice-blue gown, the size of which she'd tactfully switched, though Carley still had had to hold her breath to get it zipped. "Such a complex hue."

Behind her, Gretchen wore the look of Tern's mother in Season Six, Episode Eleven, when Tern was written off the show and her mother had to identify her body at the morgue. Under the fitting room lights, the dress turned Carley the color of dead.

"A clash with the new color scheme," Gretchen said to Carley, "don't you think?" The New Color Scheme was turning out to be useful for eliding truths, one of which was that Carley's original Sweet Sixteen dress, commissioned during the summer, was now fifteen pounds too small. Upon realizing this several days earlier, Gretchen had pronounced it "redundant" with the newly chosen dais linens.

Perhaps because the lights also served to highlight Carley's pimples, the saleswoman asked Gretchen, faux-conversationally, if she'd happened to see Camilla Campden-Cay, the miracle worker of skin, offer those skin tips for teens last week on *Wake Up America!* Gretchen tripped over herself explaining that the Dermatologist-to-the-Stars' stepson, Hunter, was Carley's close friend, patting Carley's shoulder as if to say, *yes, really.* Why perhaps Camilla—whom in fact Gretchen had only met several times at school events—could squeeze Carley in before the big day.

"I have one that age," whispered the saleswoman as Carley changed into the cream dress, upgraded to a sixteen. "Did you plan the event around that-time-of-month?"

"Oh," said Gretchen, "*Oh*," at the thought of Carley bleeding on her parade. "Might you . . ." she called through the cubicle slats, "Might *it* be—"

"No."

"I mention it only because if a young lady is right at the edge of a size," said the saleswoman, "and she's a bit . . . *bloated* . . ." She whispered it like *fuck*.

"Again, *no*," Carley said.

"The edge," Gretchen whispered. "Perhaps we should try the next—"

"Oh," said the saleswoman, as if just now realizing a death. Of a sale. "It doesn't come in eighteen . . . most of those dresses don't run past . . . I'm sorry. Little does."

The dress was too tight to pull up the side zipper that ran from hip to chest. "The worm grew two feet in the Minet girl's intestine," Gretchen said as Carley emerged from the fitting room looking gutted, the orange lining flapping. "Took the whole thing over."

After watching her father put her mother to bed, after calling Amber to find out from Edie what happened in mini-class, after discovering her mother's sleeves covered with strange markings that looked familiar yet foreign, Carley had thought to hold up the blouse to a mirror.

She'd held it up the way right now Gretchen held between Carley and a fitting room mirror a cranberry colored size-eight gown saying, "You'd look like that spunky brunette in *Crawling*," then adding, "That Minet girl lost fifty pounds, you know. Because of the worm. But she needs a bag now—for her *functions*."

She held the blouse up to the mirror and read the world Gretchen had sweated onto it. Characters. Symbols. Settings. Themes. All stamped there in fear.

And then, at last, it was a story she could read.

CHAPTER 35

The first time Buck said something like, <u>I beseech thee, goodly maiden, to bare thy comely bosom</u>, Jules thought he was just <u>into</u> the game—the way people got into mandatory pep rallies at school even though they were lame. They were making out behind the water mill when Buck said it, his hands under her tunic and kirtle, and it felt so good when he ran his thumbs around her nipples that she didn't give it another thought.

Later, after the Common Grounds Coffee Purveyors Grain Grinding Challenge, which Buck's family had nearly won because Dale had turned out to be good with a quern stone, she heard Buck whisper, <u>Though soft repose I do so crave, I am bound and beholden to keep on.</u>

"What?" He looked glazed. "Buck?"

He shook his head. Laughed. "This sucks."

They saw each other next after dark. Not having clocks made planning trysts difficult, but they could always pinpoint midnight, a shift change for the crew.

A boom microphone hung above them like a sleeping bat as they caressed words off each other's tongues, words that filled them and buzzed through them and made them dizzy with needing to be closer. The audio assistant holding the boom pole yawned noiselessly, then winked at Jules as if to say, <u>no offense.</u>

"I beseech you, tarry longer," Buck said when Jules finally said it was getting late.

The only people who spoke like that were the actors who milled around the background when the contestants walked through "town" or the manor. The Miller. The Court Jester. The Servants. The Interchangeable Guys on Horseback.

"You've been spending too much time around the extras." She said it with fake coolness she suspected viewers would like, feeling guilty as she did it. Her parents and brother had had to drag her onto the show, her main points of resistance having been that she hated both TV and games for their unrealness. And now she was talking like not-her to make people who liked what she hated <u>like her.</u>

Buck shook his head with the rhythm of disappointment. "Why, good lady, no man in God's grace 'twas e'er <u>extra.</u>"

The producers were going to start freaking out because by talking Medievalese, Buck was making fun of their show. Though there weren't any explicit rules against what he was doing, the way there were against her modifying her surcoat into a two-piece bathing suit and wearing it to the RayGone Skin Protection Water Jousting Challenge, an infraction that the producers had called <u>against verisimilitude</u> and that had led to her family's disqualification from a competition where people standing on the prows of small boats tried to push each other off with those foam noodles kids played with in swimming pools. Except painted to look heavy and wooden, instead of neon.

"Thy piety verily gets me off, my lord."

She waited for him to laugh. He didn't. Which of course made the whole thing so much funnier. Buck was being hyper-verisimilitudinous.

"Nothing fits her." Gretchen's voice landed three feet away from where Bree and Carley sat in Carley's bedroom discussing *Dark Ages*.

Bree looked around and behind her. "What was—"

"It's the agnostics," Carley said. "Sound does weird things."

"Acoustics," whispered Bree.

"She plods into the fitting room like something headed to the slaughterhouse," said the disembodied Gretchen. "Like she's *given up*. Like she's *meat*."

Bree stood. "She needs to know you can hear—"

"She knows." Carley breathed shallowly.

"There's a place that can help her," Gretchen said. "I've looked into it.... No, this is different. That *camp* was far too unstructured."

"She knows you're with me, too," said Carley. "I guess you're like family now, like Hunter. Either that or like, um, the Help."

"There was this painter, Francis Bacon," Bree said, sitting back on the window seat next to Carley, "who wanted to paint the best human scream." At least now she understood Carley's reluctance to be here without the TV blaring—to live in this room was like not having a door. She looked out at the falling rain.

"Let's go to my room."

"There's a spot for that, too. Just so you know. In the doorway to that little kitchen down the hall."

"That *closet*?"

"Closet. Kitchen. Whatever. I know because your room is where they usually put Hunter when he stays over. She'll get Grace to come up and have a 'conversation' in there about how I don't need to be going to a diner for fries after Hunter picks me up from Sinkman."

"Sinkman?"

"My shrink. You don't want to know why."

Gretchen's voice raised in pitch. "You could at least *look* at the Web site: www.youbeneathyou.com."

"You think I think you'd need a *why*?"

"Look, Francis doesn't know about the sound bouncing around. Half the time he's lost in his head thinking about bras. Anyway, right now he thinks she's having a private conversation with him." Carley shrugged. "I just don't want you to think he's, you know, in on it. And please don't tell him. If she had to talk *to* me, it would be.... She doesn't *want* to be a person who'd say those things to her kid. And I don't want a mother who would say them. Sometimes pretending is better."

Bree shook her head. "I don't like pretending."

Carley shrugged again. "Ever occur to you that making stuff up for a living wasn't your optical career choice?"

"*Optimal.*"

Carley got up from the window seat and picked up the pages. "Yeah, I know." She took Bree's hand and led her to the back staircase and up to the third floor. It felt like the sweaty grip of one of Bree's nieces, who during her occasional visits to her sisters' houses tugged her by the hand to see snails or pebbles or a favorite toy.

"Francis calls it his home office, Gretchen likes to pretend it doesn't exist." Carley toggled a row of switches, illuminating a white-walled, marble-floored room connected on either side to other such rooms through arches. Everywhere Bree looked were bras—on wooden torsos, in glass cases, and mounted in wall displays. "You can't hear anything up here."

The bra museum took most of the third floor, Carley explained.

"I suppose it's better than finding Mad Bertha in the attic," Bree said.

"What?" Carley toggled a second row of switches.

"Nothing."

The display cases glowed with buttery light. The torsos posed sempiternally at attention—shoulders back, chests forward—bearing navel-less stomachs below bras made of everything from brocaded silk to marabou feathers to ocelot fur.

Carley ran her fingers over a deep orange corset laced up in gold. "Thanks for making Jules and Buck finally kiss." She walked Bree down an aisle of torsos clad in stiffly boned lace corsets.

"Just did what you asked."

"I know. I just didn't expect it to be so . . . hot?"

"I'm dead, true. And sexless."

"That was almost funny."

"Not to mention humorless."

"I figure if you're going on a date with *Justin* you can't be unfunny. Or frigate."

"*Frigid*. The word is . . ."

"I know. You told me. *Joke?*"

"It's not a date." She wasn't even driving in to Darren's party with him tomorrow, though he'd asked every time he'd called this week. Not that she would have minded going in a limo instead of taking the train, but she wanted to stop first at her apartment to check on her fish and she'd have rather died than have Justin see the tiny illegal apartment where she lived. With the sitter not responding to Bree's calls—she was an art student with a part-time job at a gallery in the better part of the neighborhood, and Bree wasn't paying much, but would it have killed her to call back about the pH?—she wanted to check her tank. Gouramis still nipping at each other's flukes? Enough brine shrimp left in the freezer? Algae growing too fast for the catfish to keep it in check? People didn't realize how many ways a man-made environment could go wrong.

"So not a *date*-date, but you're hanging out."

Justin would probably be "hanging out" with guest-of-honor Marguerite, author of the just-released *Annie Gone*, a retelling of *Antigone* through the eyes of a twelve-year-old trailer park denizen. There was no trusting Justin's attention. He was the kind of rich person who collected people.

Carley walked her over to one of the glass cases. "Want to feel something weird?" She took out a white cotton bra.

"I have my own, thanks."

"Come *on*." She poked the cup as demonstration.

Bree extended her index finger. "Feels more like the idea of a breast."

"It's air." She took what looked like a pink cocktail stirrer from the case, inserted it into one of the cups, and puffed. "From B to C in thirty seconds."

Pneumatic Bra, said the placard, *circa nineteen fifty*.

"So, you gonna kiss Justin like Jules goes at Buck? They caressed words off each other's tongues—"

"According to you, that would be like wanting to kiss *myself*. Or who I want to be. And just so you know, it feels weird to be quoted. When Hunter did it at his mother's party—quite a memorizer, that one, even when he can barely stand—"

"He doesn't forget *anything*." She crooked her finger. *Breast Enhancement Products*, *1800s*, said the placard on the next case. "Didn't," she said softly, as if pretending Bree couldn't hear so she didn't have to admit to herself that she'd said it. "Do you think if someone was, like, forgetting things when he drank, it would help him to read a book about it? Like, not a judgy book, but one that makes him think, *Hey, that's me.* Hunter gets everything from books. He even learned to . . ." Carley blushed.

"Last time we tried to talk about Hunter, it didn't go well."

She took out for Bree's inspection a jar labeled "Bust Food," a kit called "The Bust Developer," which included a metal tool that evoked a toilet plunger, and an array of falsies. "I was just wondering if you thought—since you like books and Hunter likes books and you'd know how book-people think, that if he like, *sees himself* in one, he might slow down or . . . stop looking at me like that . . . so it was a stupid question, fine."

"He's past *slowing down.* Which I tried telling his mother at her party before she cut me off with a story about John-John's teenage years. He's drowning. Don't let him pull you under with—"

"That's how you think, isn't it?" She slammed closed the case. "Save yourself. What about saving someone else?"

"A fairy tale. People *don't* save other people. At best, they survive them."

Carley opened a case of silicon inserts and juggled three, then four, then five. "Why do you hate it here so much?"

"I hate me here."

"What's that mean?" She lost her rhythm; the inserts hit the ground, where they lay like jellyfish.

"It's complicated."

"The part about everyone being rich, or the part about Justin? Do you feel bad about liking him because he's hot and loaded? Do you think it makes you superficial or something?"

"We should get back to your book."

Carley ran her fingers over a white satin corset, hand-embroidered with butterflies. "This is over a hundred years old, but Francis still let me play with it when I was a kid. He never worried about it getting ruined. I used to hang out up here all the time until Gretchen decided wearing bras made me too old to play with them." She looked up. "So why is Buck losing it?"

"The rest of the serfs have been supplementing their families' weekly loaf of bread and ration of porridge with eels and fish caught from the river, but because Buck is a strict vegetarian and his family has never won a challenge that would have earned him bread and vegetables in the manor, he's experiencing starvation-induced delusions."

Carley opened a case of bras that had zippered compartments and pouches sewn into them. "In the old days, people used to smell more, you know. Girls would put, like, perfume or something in here." She wiggled a finger into the little pocket between the cups of an ecru lace-trimmed bra. "Or money, if they wanted to hide it."

"About Buck.... Is changing the subject your way of disagreeing?"

Carley shrugged.

"His growing delusional was an idea you *wanted*," Bree reminded her. "You *agreed* to the starvation, and—"

"I know. When I asked why he's losing it, I didn't mean, *Remind me of what we've already talked about because I'm not smart enough to remember.* I meant, not everyone would go crazoid over lack of food, right? So why Buck?"

"You're worried about verisimilitude?"

"I don't give a shit about whether it's *real*. I just want to know *about* Buck. And Jules, too. I mean, you throw around these hints about what their lives were like before they got on the show, but you never get *into* it."

"The book's not about their lives before the show."

"It's about *them*, though. What happened to you before—your past—*is* you. *Tell* me their pasts."

Bree sighed. "Justin, the king of the backstory dump, should be writing this for you, then. Backstory is lazy, Carley, it—"

"My English teacher, Mr. Nagel, calls it *Afterbirth*."

"What?"

"*As you doubtless learned in biology*, he said, *what followed you from the birth canal wasn't a neat volume of Apex Notes. It nourished you and gave you breath underwater, but it's messy, clotty stuff.*"

"Clotty. You're fucking kidding."

"Nope. Bunny Gardner's mother complained to the headmaster and got Bunny excused from gym for extra therapy to scrub the image from her brain or something."

"And your parents *pay* for you to go to this school—"

"We're leaving in a few minutes." Bree flinched at the sound of Francis's voice. She turned. For a big man, he moved quietly. "Your mother wants to speak to you about not being late for the tutor."

Carley gave her father a quick kiss on the cheek, then handed Bree *Prototype Jog-Bra, circa nineteen seventy.* "It's made from two jockstraps," she said with a smile. "Ask him. He loves giving the tour."

Bree offered the bra to Francis, holding it between her thumb and forefinger.

"Got it on eBay for a steal," he said, refitting it on a torso. "You like history?"

"When it has a purpose. For research."

"So history you can *use.* You'll appreciate this, then." He led her through five interconnected rooms to a series of floor-to-ceiling dioramas. "Like those habitats in the Museum of Natural History. Except without the taxidermy. Made 'em myself."

Minoan Crete, said the placard on the first. A life-sized mannequin disrobed from her drapey garment, beneath which she wore a breast-baring corset. Outside the window of her chamber, in front of a backdrop of the sea, Ken-doll-sized men sailed two-inch boats and picked Tic-Tac-sized olives. Perspective wasn't Francis's strength.

Ancient Greece, said the next. The mannequin revealed a band across her breasts as she undressed. Outside her window, toga-clad Kens wrestled in the senate.

"Apodesme," Francis said, pointing at her chest. And that one"—he pointed at the next case, *Rome*—"is called a fascia. Don't know if you can tell, but it's tighter. Romans bound their women's breasts to stop them from growing. They were afraid they'd distract men from more important things. As if there *are.*" Francis chuckled. "I wanted to thank you for being patient with Carley. If she takes up too much of your time, don't be shy about letting me know. Carley doesn't have a lot of friends—she and my partner's daughter seem to be drifting apart, and Hunter ... well, just because she's in the habit of inviting herself over doesn't mean she's always wanted. Been catching hints from his mother. Sweet kid just doesn't know how to tell Carley to go home."

"I like Carley." She didn't realize it was true until she said it. "She's brave."

Francis smiled. He stepped into the diorama and freed the mannequin's plastic breasts, each one of which was larger than the coliseum outside her window. "Nero's concubine strangled herself with one of these," he said, holding up the fascia, "rather than give up his secrets to his enemies. Suicide-by-bra. I used to tell Carley that story and ask, *What's the moral?* You know what she'd say? *Keep your bra on.*"

"Francis? *About* Hunter—"

"Remarkable kid. Said he'd never read anything like *Killa Vista*, you know. High praise." Francis looked at his watch. "I've got a flight out of JFK at ten-thirty to Newport. Suzanne's engagement, part *deux.*" He winked. "Have a good time with Leighton tomorrow."

"Justin's slumming making headlines?"

Francis guided her to the door with an arm around her shoulder—a gesture she expected to feel predatory and didn't. He turned off the two banks of light switches with a single stroke of his paw. "Fascia," he said, "came back in nineteen-twenties America. Different name, same thing. That was the time of flappers and big parties. Musicians and hooch and chi-chi dresses. All these huge estates. Very classy. And you know what the ladies did at the end of the night as they pulled away in their fancy cars? Flung their underwear out the windows."

He walked her downstairs in silence. "Don't say *slumming,*" he said at her door. "The only difference between Fox Glen and Vernal is here servants pick up the panties left behind."

CHAPTER 36

Tomorrow, awakening with his face sticking to a floor sour with spills, Hunter would remember this moment when every bottle of liquor was still capped and standing at attention, every tray of hors d'oeuvres still garnished, every crease in his clothing still crisp. He poured himself the drink he'd held off having while he'd set up bars around the pool in the atrium and received deliveries from the caterers and liquor store. It had been a day deserving of scotch, and to have triumphed so many hours over the urge for it while going without a single pill made him feel crisp, and queasy, and very nearly brave.

He'd failed to quit the pills last weekend and the one before that, but this time he'd hold his mind as far away as possible from his body, allowing himself just a few drinks to pad him against the aches and fatigue of withdrawal and cravings so intense that the word *want* echoed in his head and interrupted every thought.

The doorbell rang. First guests. Everything about to happen, and nothing out of place.

JUSTIN STRAINED TO recognize himself in the mirror. Shirt the color of the Caribbean. Jacket, pants, silver-buckled ankle boots and cashmere duster, all black. Stagy, the mirror sneered, and he hadn't even gotten to the makeup. A man trying to be who he'd been.

He opened the coat closet to trade out his cane for something unscarred.

There were forty-seven like the one he'd used all day, all hand-carved with illegible verses of Donne and Keats and deeply stabbed *Fucks*.

He swallowed hard against the acid in his throat and gripped the knob of his front door like a handshake. Sweat soaked his underarms and collar; he felt himself melting. Lot's wife, after rain.

SQUINTING AGAINST THE busyness in his head, Hunter greeted and slapped backs and poured drinks, pretending not to notice being snubbed by his soccer teammates, who angry as they might be at him after today's tournament had still showed up because his parties were *the* parties. People bobbed and splashed in the pool, most in swimsuits, some naked. They floated on their backs, looking up through the glass ceiling on which rain pattered at a sky too dark to see. Is this fun? This is fun. Is this cool? This *is* cool. Drunk or pretending to be, trying out jadedness and ending up honest by accident. Saying, I can see the stars—though they were hidden by the clouds. Saying, look how bright. Saying, they could fall right on us.

Hunter rubbed his eyes and tried to concentrate on what people said and felt deafened by sound. There was too much talking, too much everything. It was like driving toward the falling sun in late afternoon, the windshield turning white as every speck of dirt on the glass glowed, gnat wings and fingerprints and road ash all crying *look at me*. There was no seeing past all of it, no making out a cat in the road or a bump or a child; always he wanted to pull over and always he went on.

He downed a double Glenmorangie, but without the pills the grit wouldn't wipe off. Grit like the way Jake had complimented Hunter on his fuchsia Ozwald Boateng shirt with the hint of a grin, as if he knew Hunter had unbuttoned and rebuttoned the neck and cuffs trying to make its wearing look casual, committing countless permutations to achieve an exact nonchalance. Or the way people to whom Hunter had never been formally introduced stumbled into the great room despite his repeated requests that the party be confined to the atrium. The way they peered to see if he noticed that a screwdriver had been spilled on the carpet in front of the fireplace. The way he didn't want anyone to know he cared about what happened to the place where he lived. The way after he'd cleaned it up and sat alone with his journal and flask, he could only write a few words at a time before his thoughts returned to how people who'd attended the soccer tournament—*everyone*—had paused after greeting him, their silence filling in for what they couldn't bring themselves to ask or say about what he'd done at the game.

SHE FOUND IT lying open on the stone hearth of the fireplace in the great room. All the years she'd known Hunter, all the times he'd left his journal out, she'd never once looked in it. She'd imagined it his safe place, like her pond with the broken statues and overgrown vegetation, somewhere dark and wild and fecund. As she picked it up now to protect it from other people's intrusion, her own name caught her eye. She couldn't look away. It was like staring into flesh.

Jake reaches into the crate of fruit next to the juicer set up for people who aren't drinking, groping two oranges while making sounds he apparently thinks a girl makes when satisfied.

Amber's breath smells like an attic closed up for years.

Carley wears black denim hip-huggers the size of wishful thinking and embossed with yellow happy faces, with dangling plastic earrings to match. Gretchen being out of town, she's dressed like her idea of sexy, a child dressed up as a fat prostitute's idea of innocent.

The worst thing in the world, she'd think later, was having to unlearn the lies you'd believed in. A tiny part of her had clung to his saying at the Sound that his lack of attraction to her had nothing to do with her unattractiveness. And now all the times he'd told her she looked "cute" unraveled like a hundred stitches with the pull of one loose thread. She was the kind of girl who couldn't wait for scissors when something dangled, the kind of girl who yanked at a string and then cried at the hole she'd made. She'd *done* this to herself by not just closing the book.

Alone in the great room, she sat on the hearth and sobbed for everything she'd never again believe. The rest of the pages begged her to read them. The flames in the fireplace begged her to feed them.

BREE'S KEY FIT into the lock, but the door wouldn't budge. She rang her apartment on the off chance that the fish-sitter was there performing her duties. When that failed, she gave in to disturbing her landlord. Eight p.m.— he should be about waking up.

Sliding sound. A deadbolt that hadn't been there when she'd left. Her landlord stared at her with sand-grain pupils. He edged up his T-shirt to reveal the gun in his waistband. "You don't live here anymore."

HUNTER SAT IN the grotto at the far end of the pool, looking out at his guests through the waterfall that spilled from the top of the ten-foot-high rock formation. Watching his friends watch him through the curtain of water, he and Amber and Olivia and Bunny all leaning on each other, he couldn't stop thinking, *Here I am casually lying around with three girls, the kind of person who is casual about multiple girls touching me.* Other people— normal people—acted casual about being leaned on because they *were* casual. Other people didn't narrate their lives.

Carley walked by with a distant look. Was she gathering the courage to put on a bathing suit? All around him girls wore colorful paradoxes, suits meant to reveal the hidden while pretending to cover it, while Carley was supposed to pretend the fat-girl skirts attached to her suits weren't hiding anything. He loved when it was just the two of them here at the Palace and she didn't feel forced to wear anything with underwire or skirts or "minimizing panels." She would put on a tank top with a pair of extra-large men's trunks from the selection stocked for guests in the dressing room and they'd talk and swim and lie on floats for hours.

"Hey, C," he said, climbing out. He bent to retrieve his flask from atop one of the rocks, his head rushing. He closed his eyes to clear the dizziness, but bathing-suit-bright flecks moved kaleidoscopically, still, behind his lids.

He shook them off and grabbed a towel. When he caught up with her, he took her hand. "On your way to change?"

She pulled her fingers away. Stared at him. Held something up. His journal.

She didn't say another word until they were alone. There were people in the great room and the game room and the formal dining room and the kitchen—everywhere he'd asked them not to be. When they reached the sidelines of the indoor tennis court, in front of the wall crawling with ivy that was supposedly there to exhale oxygen onto players but which, really, just existed for show, she read,

"**Carley wears black denim hip-huggers the size of wishful thinking . . .**"

He reached for the journal. "You're misinterpreting. Decontextualizing. Hyperbol. . . . That's not what—"

"It's what you *wrote*."

He stared at the page. "It's not what was in *my head*. Believe me."

"I *can't*."

He walked onto the court and sliced the air with an invisible racket.

"For once, can't you be scared instead of cool?" she yelled from behind him. She walked through his racket. "You have about a million reasons to let yourself be afraid right now, starting with the fact that you don't *remember* writing something you just wrote and ending with the fact that there's no way Suzanne and Larry and Griffin won't hear about what you did at the game. For godsake, our *servants* have already heard about it from other people's Help. Grace came up to my bedroom to ask what happened!"

Five minutes into the soccer game he'd gotten red-carded for calling a ref a *myopic fuckwad*, leaving Montclair to play the rest of the game a man short. His team had won despite it, advancing to the final game to be played tomorrow; he'd been stripped of his co-captainship and kicked off.

He wished he could end the party right now and go up to his room with Carley and cry. Maybe the fuzz would recede and he could understand how a simple bad out-of-bounds call could have made him so angry. He'd felt like he was watching another person lose it, a guy who'd refused to leave the field and swung at his teammates as they'd walked him off.

He touched one of her earrings. "I need to get myself a pair of these." Just another couple of days and the Vicodin would be out of his system. He could do this. He tugged softly at her lobe. "What you read, C? It isn't how I usually write. When I write about you—and I do all the time—it's like . . . praying."

He unscrewed the top of his flask, its tooled striations as familiar and comforting beneath his fingers as a bedtime story.

"You need to stop," she said. That she couldn't make herself say *drinking* touched him to tears. As if forgetting and stumbling were the worst things in the world. As if she couldn't imagine anything more frightening. He wished *he* couldn't. "It needs to stop, H."

"Ever want it all to stop?" he whispered, drinking deep and trying to imagine making it through two more days without the pills. Or even two more hours. "Everything?"

UNLESS A CHARACTER *is engaged in fighting a force of nature*, Darren had preached in college, *never leave him alone in a scene*. He wouldn't know what to do with himself. He'd get lost in his head. And no, Darren had added when Marguerite had asked, neither mental nor physical masturbation counted as *fighting*.

"That you're calling from home bodes badly," Darren said.

"Can't come," Justin told him. "Character solo-mio, action heading nowhere. Author's cutting the scene."

"People are up on the roof taking cocktails in the middle of the storm. Umbrellas and high heels and lightning, all very dramatic. Marguerite will be crushed you won't hear her read."

"She can *read* now?"

"Bree's rubbing off on you. How very uncharming."

"I can see it now, Marguerite presenting her opus in the open air just for the drama of it, hangers-on holding umbrellas over her while she reads in an über-dialected accent: '*Aw Bubba Puppy,*' Annie sobbed, *as she dug the mutt a grave in the pumpkin patch against Paw-Paw's wishes. 'I knowed you wadn't nipped Paw-Paw Cree 'cept you reckoned he was set to done whoop me.'*

She verticates her shoulders, jactitates her hair, and repossesses her I-work-at-Sotheby's-voice as she makes eye contact with the front row. *Aubergine clouds gathered overhead, an amuse bouche of the hurricane to come."*

"If you're well enough for sarcasm—"

"Put on Bree." She was the last person in existence without a cell phone.

"She hasn't shown yet. Hurry, and you could still make it here before she starts racking up the faux pas."

"I can't," he said, "just can't."

The calls began soon thereafter, every fifteen minutes. Marguerite, he figured, or Darren, or both. He let it ring as he huddled on the couch.

THE DUMPSTER SQUEALED as Bree pushed it beneath the fire escape in the alley where she'd crouched until she saw the lights extinguish in her former cokelord's windows. Hopefully he was out getting dinner or a fix. The not-quite-disowned youngest son of a small-time mobster whose father had him managing the art-gallery-cum-money-laundry on the building's ground floor, he'd been renting Bree the storage room across the hall from his loft ever since she'd finished college. Until today it had been symbiotic: he was unbalanced even when he wasn't high, paranoid about the FBI, DEA, and UFOs infiltrating his residence, yet desperate for extra cash; friendless, she never brought home people to pique his paranoia. Though the "apartment" was illegal, he'd installed a fire escape at her request, and though this part of Alphabet City was still more sketchy than gentrified, her landlord's reputation for insanity and proclivity for handguns reassured Bree of the unlikelihood of anyone targeting the building for a break-in.

"They were recording me," her landlord had said at the front door. "You let in rats."

"The girl was just feeding my fish."

"Not *she*, you buggy bitch. *He*." Drumming his fingers against the heel of the gun, he'd stared her to the curb.

Calling the police would be at best ineffective, at worst dangerous. Technically the apartment didn't even exist, and he wasn't someone anyone would want as an enemy. But there were things she couldn't leave behind—

her fish, some mementos, and three years of handwritten notes for *Geppetto in Florence*.

She climbed up onto the Dumpster and pulled herself up onto the fire escape ladder. Her black leather maxi-skirt, vintage seventies and now hiked up around her waist like a tire, forced her to climb the rungs hunched. Shaking, she lay down on the landing outside her locked apartment window.

The heaviest object in her purse was Marguerite's book, which she'd borrowed from the Fox Glen library earlier in the week and had tried to force herself to read on the train so she could have something positive to say. *The theme song from* Cops *emanating from every trailer simultaneously,* Bree had rehearsed saying to Marguerite, *is an interesting twist on the Greek chorus.*

On the third try, it shattered the glass. She reached in, unlatched the window, and gagged. Her home smelled like death.

CARLEY RUBBED HUNTER'S temples as he lay with his head in her lap looking up at the glass ceiling of the tennis court into the darkness. Her back was against the ivied wall, her legs stretched out straight so that beyond Hunter's head she could see the faces on her pants mocking them, their yellow smiles remembering the conversation she and Hunter had let fade away the way so many conversations about his hurting her got forgotten halfway through. His feelings *about* hurting her always ended up being somehow bigger than her hurt.

"Never," she told Hunter. "I've never wanted to . . ." She couldn't even say the word *die*, though everyone from Sinkman to her Social Issues teachers acted like every teenager in existence had thought about it sometime.

Every year at Montclair they had a Feelings unit in Social Issues, the name given to Health class so it would qualify as a transcript-worthy grade for college applications. Last year she and her classmates had sat in a circle and each picked from a bowl a rock that was supposed to represent their lives or parents or something else they hated. Like, *This stone is flat and pale, just like the chest my parents won't let me fix until I'm eighteen.*

Or, *No matter how you many ways you try to balance this rock, it always rolls onto the same side—just like my father who's always saying he wants to balance work and family and all that shit* (they were allowed to curse during Feelings), *but then he operates on the heart of some stranger on the opening night of my school play and I don't care if he came the next night, how did he think it looked for the lead's father not to show up while Bunny's father was waiting at the edge of the stage with four dozen roses as if she was anything except a no-name in the chorus? Sorry Bunny, but it's true your parents went overboard, everyone thinks so.*

Or, *This stone has shiny flecks all over it, but if you dropped it, it would still hurt because being shiny isn't everything and maybe the rock has to work really hard at being shiny and maybe people gossiping about it after last week's party—like anyone hasn't ever done what the rock did when it was trashed—is exactly like being dropped.*

Eventually someone always brought up When Things Are Too Much. *I want to fill my pockets with these rocks and walk into the Sound.* (*The Hours* had been on that year's summer reading list.) People got quiet and then everyone starting talking all at once. Nearly everyone. No one ever questioned Carley's quiet.

Maybe it was all those *ifs* and *could haves*, all the do-overs she imagined every night, all the trips she took to Aftermemory, that made her cling to the idea that something amazing could always happen next that she wouldn't want to miss. Or maybe—as she suspected her Social Issues teachers thought—she just wasn't deep enough to understand wanting to die.

"You don't have to go to Princeton, H. You don't have to go to college at all. You don't have to do any of this shit you don't care about—applications and student council and precalculus. You could just read books and write."

"In what world?"

"We'll go away. Somewhere no one will find us. Live on the cash you have left in your safe and the money I'll get at my Sweet Sixteen. We'll make it last. Cook stuff. Eat cheap."

Hunter wiped his eyes and sat up. He refolded his shirt cuffs. "You only know how to make pancakes."

He said it like a reason to die.

"I'D BEEN SO looking forward to meeting your son," Suzanne heard for the twentieth time that evening. She still couldn't fathom both the coach and headmaster backing up Hunter's decision to stay in Fox Glen. Championship or not, it only was a *game*, for godsake. And these were the *Talbrights* celebrating her in their ballroom with a hundred-piece orchestra.

Hunter didn't want her to be happy—something Suzanne had suspected ever since he'd ruined her marriage to Griffin. As surely as Hunter had kept their affairs from each other for years, he'd one day engineered their discovery. A phone call to one parent to leave the spa and pick him up from school because he was ill and the au pair—where *could* she be?—wasn't answering her cell. A suggestion to the other parent that the pediatrician had been making house calls when the patient wasn't home.

She imagined, as always, the child she would have had with Francis, the one she'd aborted without telling him at the end of a summer long, long ago. In her dreams, it was always a daughter. Gentle, kind, disinclined to smash things open to see how they work. She would have understood Suzanne. She would have been here.

SHE'D BEEN MAD at Hunter and then she wasn't and now she was again, and he felt like he was going to sleep and waking up over and over in front of a TV set, like when he had a fever and she was staying with him and as soon as he grasped a snippet of plot or a line of dialogue he'd be drifting off again.

"You can't walk away from a serious conversation to play drinking games," Carley said, and though he didn't remember deciding to do so, he was already on his feet and it *did* sound better than serious conversation if serious conversation is what had her yelling at him.

"Talk to him in the morning," Amber was telling her. "He's halfway into her pants."

"My pants are *on*," said the girl who was tugging at his hand.

"That's what you think," said Amber. She turned to Carley. "We're gonna go to Jake's soon, some of us. Not so crowded and not so much . . . weirdness. Colin and those guys, they're looking for a fight."

"Partners?" said the girl, leading him through his own house back to the atrium, where someone had set up for Lap Pong.

It was like being a guest at his own party, which he must have said out loud because Carley said, "Send yourself home" before Amber pulled her away.

"HELP ME," SAID Bree when Justin finally answered. "Please." Ten times she'd called from the Laundromat, where she could keep getting change and didn't look completely out of place holding two Hefty bags—boxes of note cards in one, mementos in the other—all she'd been able to make it out of her apartment with before she'd heard noises coming from her landlord's apartment across the hall.

Her fish were decomposing when she'd gotten to them. There was a sleeping bag knifed to ribbons among all of the brokenness of her apartment. *He*, her landlord had said. She supposed the fish-sitter had had a friend she'd given the key and let squat there. She supposed the friend had set off her landlord's paranoia. She supposed that's why he'd smashed everything electronic in her apartment, including the aquarium's filter and heater. *Buggy bitch.*

His story, not hers—she'd never know for sure.

The bags were disintegrating from her dragging them down the alley and over sidewalks. They wouldn't make it another block, let alone down the steps to the subway and through two transfers on the Long Island Rail Road, but even before she'd begun feeding the little money she had left into a pay phone slot, she hadn't had enough money to replace them. She'd come to the city with just enough for round-trip train fare. It was every cent she had until the book was done.

"Look, I can't come to Darren's. Things are . . . falling apart . . . and . . . I need a ride." She burst into tears. She'd been so ashamed for him to see where she lived, and now she was calling him with garbage bags.

"Hold tight and keep talking. It'll take a little while. I'm not at Darren's. I'm home."

"My home's gone. My fish are gone." The operator came on to ask for money.

"Call back collect," he said. "Keep talking until I'm there."

THE FRESHGIRL'S GIGGLE was a hiccup, her pink dress a baby-doll. Carley saw Hunter press her hand onto his crotch before he missed the target badly.

"Drink!" people yelled, and the girl hopped out of Hunter's lap to dip a shot glass into the bowl of Grey Goose, vermouth, olives, and ice.

She was a Spirit Supporter—girls who bounced around with pom-poms at games but hadn't been called *cheerleaders* since the Montclair board had renamed them to make the activity viable for the Community Service section of college applications. Until the girl had decided to upgrade to Hunter, she'd been soccer co-captain Colin Bradley's sort-of-date.

Colin, who was playing but only drinking water, glared at both her and Hunter. Like Amber said, he was looking for a fight—and Hunter was giving him reasons.

He wasn't a bad guy, Colin. They'd messed around at a bunch of parties before summer vacation, and she'd liked him enough at the time to try a couple of things with him she never had before. For a while, she'd even thought he might like her enough to ask her out. Though after the summer he'd never tried to hook up again, he'd been nice while it had lasted.

"We don't have to watch this," Amber said, as Freshgirl bounced the ball so hard it skipped over the table into the pool. It was like she *wanted* Hunter more wasted.

Hunter filled his shot glass and raised it for a toast. "To Montclair's soccer team. One game down, another to go."

"Asshole," Colin said under his breath. His lap partner, Bunny, giggled nervously.

Hunter pointed. "The door's that way."

"Brandon," Colin called toward the pool. The final member of what Hunter used to call *The Triumvirate*—co-captains of the soccer team with Hunter until today—came over. "Cay's *proud* of this afternoon," Colin said. Brandon stood over Hunter, dripping water on Hunter's shoulders.

"Did I say that?" With a flick of his wrist, Hunter hit Colin in the forehead with the ping-pong ball. "Don't be a cretin."

Even at the beginning of the season Brandon and Colin had resented his being appointed with them—they were serious athletes, whereas Hunter had been chosen because he played smart and hard and because people respected him. Plus Colin and Hunter had had a weird incident last June—a fistfight in the Montclair parking lot for which both of them had been suspended and which neither of them would explain to the headmaster or anyone. It was the only time Carley had heard of Hunter raising a hand to anyone, and he'd come out of the fight with his face one huge bruise. She was pretty sure he had no idea *how* to punch someone. It wasn't something you could learn from books.

Brandon pulled Hunter's chair back from the table. Freshgirl jumped out of Hunter's lap. Bryant Gabel came over and grabbed Colin's arm before his fist could connect with Hunter's cheek.

Bryant, an ice hockey player, had developed an abiding loyalty to Hunter last year when Hunter had called Nagel *an intellectual bully* for responding to Bryant's question about what differentiated similes from metaphors with *You're as smart as a puck.*

"Not cool to beat up the host," Bryant said, stepping between the co-captains and Hunter. Colin and Brandon backed up. Hunter didn't move, his fists still clenched.

"H," Carley said, "let's take a walk. *H.*"

"I heard you," he said. "And *no.*"

"Come on. It's down to a drizzle outside. Fresh air."

"Leave me *alone.*"

"You don't even know how to fight!" A second later she knew it was the exact wrong thing to say.

"Thank you," he said. She followed him as he stalked out of the atrium to the front hall. "*Don't,*" he said before he slammed the front door. She figured he was going to walk off his anger down at the beach.

"Jake's calling a cab," Amber said and took Carley with her to the women's poolside dressing room. The mirror was crowded with girls reapplying makeup that wasn't supposed to look like makeup because they didn't want to seem like girls who thought they needed to wear it in the pool.

A cell phone lying on the vanity chimed "Party Puker," the same Whiplash Bouffant song that Amber's phone always did.

"Not mine," Amber said, seeing Carley turn. Freshgirl grabbed it.

Amber wrapped her wet suit into one of the guest towels and put it into her bag. "What? He has, like, a *thousand* towels. I'll bring it *back*," she said, misinterpreting Carley's silence. Hunter's cell number had been displayed on Freshgirl's phone.

She walked out of the dressing room at the same time as Carley did, taking off toward the Great Room, where the staircase rose to the second floor.

Later, Carley would think of it as the coldest thing she'd ever done, texting Colin to tell him exactly where his girlfriend was. At the time, all she could think about was Hunter doing it with a ninety-pound girl in the bed where he and Carley had shared their secrets. He'd probably slept with a hundred girls, but never with Carley right there. Until now, she and they had inhabited different spheres; like characters in *Gatsby* and *Godot*, they were never supposed to be in the same place.

It was Freshgirl's screaming that brought people upstairs in time to pull Colin off Hunter before he did him serious damage.

Hunter was still washing blood from his split lip when Carley and Amber found him in his bathroom. "He wanted me to know who told him." Hunter stared into the pink-tinged water in the sink. "He said, 'No one's really your friend here. Not even her.'"

"H—"

He staggered past them, his face still wet.

"Get out."

"H."

"Let's just go," Amber said.

"I can't," Carley said.

They followed him downstairs, where people drank his booze and ate his food and treated the Palace like the set of *Bouncy House*, where it was okay for contestants to trash things because even though they slept and ate and shat and fought and kissed and played in there for fifty days, the set wasn't anyone's home, just a giant inflatable ride.

Hunter walked into the men's poolside dressing room, passing Freshgirl and two of her friends without acknowledgment. Freshgirl started to cry. Colin, who'd changed out of his bathing suit into street clothes, eyed both the girl and the door Hunter had just walked through, looking unsure of which, if either, he wanted to take on.

Amber walked over to Freshgirl, who still wore a towel around her chest and carried her bathing suit top, like she wanted to remind people it was *she* who'd caused all this. "Someone called the cops," Amber lied. "Someone's mother could tell they were trashed on the phone and ..." She shrugged and left Freshgirl and her friends to imagine the cops arriving and calling their parents. It took four Freshgirls five minutes to spread the word to two hundred people.

"Ready?" Amber said when they and Jake and Olivia were the only ones left. They walked into the great room, where Hunter had relocated himself during the chaos of departures. The shirt he'd put back on was misbuttoned. His lip was swollen. An empty scotch bottle sat in front of him on the hearth. It was the kind he kept in his safe that he only used to take out when it was just him and Carley.

"I can't leave him like this."

"You just don't *want* to." Amber shook her head. "When he's like *this* he's all yours. At least tell yourself the truth: you'd take *this* over nothing."

GRETCHEN WELLS RAN her finger over an antique gilded-brass wall sconce in the Talbrights' home and wondered how on earth it could be taking Francis so long to change into a fresh shirt upstairs after having dripped red wine on himself. Their guest room was the smallest room in the mansion, Gretchen suspected, feeling sure that everyone in attendance *knew* this. She wondered if Larry Talbright had told his family about Francis's behavior last week at Suzanne's party. Anyone but Suzanne, the only woman she trusted in the world, would have balked at their coming to Newport at all.

Nodding at Suzanne's and Plum's discussion about Hunter's joining Ian at Princeton and Suzanne's redecorating and Larry Talbright's governor-of-Connecticut brother's bid for the U.S. presidency, she felt anxious with envy, and bitter about being Mrs. Marvel-Bra, and choking on *almost*.

A husband whose license plate read BRST MAN. A daughter who outgrew clothing before wearing it. A house with a tit at its center. It wasn't the life Gretchen had imagined at age twenty, when Weston Graham, an associate at her father's firm, had promised her a tailored marriage. He'd had pinpoint taste and always smelled wonderful, and on the rare occasions he'd wanted sex, the act had been straightforward and efficient. They could have had marvelous draperies and gorgeous parties and mutual privacy. She would have been useful, he would have been grateful. No one had ever been grateful to her, despite her efforts at coercing such sentiments with compliments and charity.

But two days prior to their wedding, on the night of Wes's bachelor party, Gretchen's brother had discovered the would-be groom in bed with another stag. When she'd told her mother she would have married Wes anyway (suspecting such a predilection, she'd hoped it meant infrequent sex and no children), she'd been called *pathetic* and *craven*.

After the wedding-that-did-not happen, she'd spent six months changing everything in the house on which her parents had put a down payment as a wedding gift, replacing brand-new fixtures and furniture with antiques. Old things to give her life weight. She filled her days combing shops for the new-old until one rainy evening driving back to Westchester from Long Island, where she'd been visiting an antique dealer in Port Calaban to discuss an elaborately carved Louis XV walnut settee, she failed to notice the brake lights in front of her and rear-ended a ten-year-old Toyota Tercel.

A giant wearing a shiny-at-the-elbows suit emerged. Seeing him appraise her own car, she was sure he would sue. When she got out to assess the damage she'd caused, she noticed the entire backseat of his car was filled with giant panties.

She looked away from the underwear. He laughed so hard she figured the joke was beyond her.

"Are you a performer? A . . . transvestite?" she ventured. She had seen them on television. Often they were tall.

"Salesman," he laughed. He kicked his dented bumper. "No harm, no foul," he said, an expression she'd never heard before and which seemed to her creative in a working-class way. He admired the marble-topped French side table tucked into the backseat of her BMW, examining its legs for soundness like a veterinarian. Determining one suffered from a slight wobble, he offered to come over sometime and *make it good as new.* He was the kind of man who knew how to fix things, take care of them. When he held her car door open for her, it seemed to *mean* something—true thoughtfulness instead of just good breeding. By the time they went out to dinner that night she was imagining him in a different suit, redecorated. By the time her parents disowned her, taking back the house and furnishings and car for eloping with him, she believed they would customize a life.

"H, HOW MUCH was in there?" Carley asked when Amber, Jake, and Olivia had left. The empty bottle gave her a bad feeling after their conversation about making things *all go away,* but she hadn't wanted to strip him of his last bit of dignity by telling them all what she was worried about. "I need to know if you drank like a shot or a *quart.*"

"Enough. I drank enough."

Larry would go apeshit if Suzanne got a call from the hospital saying her underage son was having his stomach pumped. And Hunter would kill her if it turned out he was just normal-wasted and there'd been little left in the bottle. There was no way of telling for sure.

"You need to make yourself throw it up." She tried to get him to his feet.

"Watch the fire," he said, shaking his head.

"*Please.*" She thought about calling Bree to ask what to do, but she didn't have a cell. Justin must, of course, but she didn't know his number.

Hunter's head lolled. There was only one other person she could imagine who wouldn't freak out. After all, it wasn't like he didn't *know* Hunter drank. She blocked Caller ID in case Francis's phone was somewhere Gretchen could see it.

THERE WAS DIRT on one of the tulips, a graininess trapped between its swordlike leaf and stem. Francis lifted it from the arrangement, coaxing the petals to his cheek. His phone buzzed in his pocket. Gretchen, he was sure, nagging him to hurry back. The petals caressed him. Bringing the flower to his tongue in Suzanne's fiancé's parents' guestroom, he tasted the past.

Francis had been twenty-two on the fourth of July weekend when he and Bernie had found themselves out of place in East Hampton among young people who'd pre-tanned in the Caribbean; and uniformed women their mothers' age being summoned for more lobster, more quickly, no excuses; and Tanqueray that overflowed into the pool and out onto the sand. They'd lost track of Merle Stewart, the wealthy college friend who'd brought them, and didn't know whose party it was.

"At Jones Beach," Bernie had said, "we'd at least be getting action." They'd been mistaken twice for Help already, and for all Francis and Bernie knew, Merle was passed out for the day or the weekend at a different party. He'd been celebrating graduation for two months straight while Francis and Bernie had been sweating away their days selling plus-sized women's underwear wholesale for Bernie's uncle Lew.

"Let's go," Francis said, hoping between them they had enough for a cab back to the Long Island Rail Road station.

"You *can't* leave," demanded a voice behind them. "It's my party, and I say so."

She was a tall girl, nearly six feet. She wore a white bikini over a deep tan. Her hair hung in loose, white-blond curls down to her beautiful ass. He knew just where that hair would graze him.

Suzanne took both men by the hands, lifted their fingers to her lips and kissed them, a gesture that made Francis think she was having fun with them.

"Merle's spoils," she said, introducing them poolside to her friends, "our treats." Bernie settled into a pitcher of martinis. Suzanne didn't release

Francis's hand until they were upstairs in a bedroom girlish with lace curtains and canopy, underneath which she let him unhook her top with clumsy fingers and pull down her bottom with his teeth.

Since the day he'd gone off to college, leaving behind his police officer father's rules and hopelessness, Francis had believed in nothing but himself. But with Suzanne's hair smelling like a flower he couldn't recall with a fragrance that brought to mind *white*, and her kisses coming in patterns he was born to recognize and her vagina holding him tight, he suddenly believed in *home*.

Yellow stamens and bits of pollen scattered onto the carpet as Francis bit and bit into the flower. The phone stopped buzzing, finally. He went to the bathroom to drink water from his cupped hands and dislodge the grit between in his teeth. Until now Francis had given no thought to where flowers grew—not in crystal vases or vermeil bowls, but in earth.

"I'M SORRY," CARLEY told Hunter, shaking him by the shoulders. Francis hadn't answered. Hunter was nearly passed out. "There's no other way."

She brought over a bucket from the laundry room and wished it were as easy as washing a shirt or mopping a floor, things you could tell yourself were *useful*, things you ought to know how to do.

His tongue was soft against her finger like things that aren't supposed to be touched: underbellies of animals, wings of butterflies, baby birds whose mothers reject them no matter how quickly you put them back in the nest.

She pressed down. She pushed. The first wave of vomit was liquid.

"What the fuck?" he said, pushing her away. She fought back and thrust deep until he gagged again, missing the bucket this time. She wiped his face with a wet towel. "What the *fuck* is wrong with you? Stay out of my *body*."

"You think I *want* to do this? You need help."

He smiled, dead-eyed, and pushed himself back from the vomit. "You really want to help, C?" He unzipped his pants. "Colin told the lacrosse team last spring that what you lacked in technique you made up for with brio." He winked. "I'm a mouthful. But we both know you can put away a lot."

CHAPTER 37

Twine webbed Justin's cottage, notecards clothespinned like flies.

Rousseau, Henri: was so naïve that "friends" played tricks on him, e.g., telling him he'd won awards he hadn't won. Have Geppetto retrofit him, à la Wizard of Oz Tin Man, with canniness? Rousseau could sing, "If I only was urbane!"

Epstein, Jacob: sculpted Night and Day for London underground. Forced to shorten sculpture's penis after passengers wrote outraged letters. Have Geppetto render board members castrati? (Note: possibly renders protagonist unlikable.)

Manet, Edouard: ▮▮▮▮▮▮▮ in the Grass. Taken by many critics as porn . .

Justin held the next sodden card by the top corners. "Caravaggio? Carpaccio? Possibly . . . Cézanne. *Yes.* Friend of Emile . . . ah Bree, do you *really* want to inflict *that* on Zola?"

She got up and grabbed it.

"You're supposed to be taking notes on the unsalvageable." He pointed to his laptop, on which she'd been transcribing what he read aloud from the disintegrating cards. The intact ones he hung. "Type this: Cézanne, Paul. Interesting yet macabre vengeance exacted upon his behalf to include—"

"It doesn't matter." She squeezed the card to pulp and kissed him. He pulled back.

"You're shock-a-fied, Love. Head-fucked. Fish-grieving." He put an arm around her waist. He liked to think he'd become *better* over the years. Not *good*, but at least not a man who'd take advantage of need. "Pray remember I disgust you."

"You don't."

"I think I'd know." He walked her back to the couch, flopped down beside her, and poured her another glass of Armagnac.

"You look terrible," she said.

"That was a pity-kiss, then?"

"Your hand's shaking." She took the bottle from him. "If you're having issues . . . with drugs. Your injuries and everything that happened, Justinian . . . *Justin* . . . it's understandable . . ."

"Will you invite me to sleep on your hide-a-bed and fix me up? Are we reduxing?"

"You remember that." She blushed. "It's awful, how you can't kill your past."

"Always there is someone to cryogenicize you. As in, once upon a time, there was—and is, and ever shall be—this sweet girl named Bridget Theresa."

Wearing one of his T-shirts and a pair of sweatpants three inches too short for her, she looked fresh-scrubbed, still.

She put her hand on his knee. He got up and dug deep into the bag of cards. His hand came out ink-stained, black and blue.

> *Kokoschka, Oskar: escaped his female patron's advances by climbing out a window. (Hardly requires vengeance, but perhaps in a footnote Geppetto could pay her a booty call?)*

"Didn't imagine *booty-call* to be in your vocabulary," he said.

> *Orozco, José: alums moaned about the college being destroyed by brutality when he began the frescoes at Dartmouth. Orozco responded, "Perhaps they may save the students from drowning in a sea of sugar. Everything there is so <u>sweet</u>!" Have Geppetto candy the entire campus. People frozen in place? Overrun by ants? Both?*

"I'd think years of devising vengeance schemes," Justin said, "might warp one."

She got up again and settled her hands on his waist from behind him. "That was a comprehensible sentence you just uttered. The drugs are dulling your edge."

"Tad fatigued," he told her, "momentarily lapsidized." *Not drugs,* he wanted to say, but the thought of truth was too tiring. "Not myself," he said instead.

"Do you take them to sleep?" Her hands drifted to his buttocks.

"Take whom?" He laughed, though it hurt his head. After an attack, everything felt like he'd been running for his life. He faced her and stepped back again. "I'm afraid I've poured you too much."

"You did it again." Her hands went to his erection. "Sounded like a *person.*"

> *Monet, Claude: "impressionist" was a term invented by critic*
> *Louis Leroy to make fun of one of Monet's paintings, "Impression,*
> *Sunrise," in a review. Have Geppetto mummify Leroy in a thousand*
> *poster-prints of Water Lilies stolen from college dorm rooms?*

"Did it ever occur to you these guys *needed* hardship to become interesting?" He took her hands away. "You and Geppetto could very well turn the entire history of art into Cheez Whiz."

"Like you know from Cheez Whiz. Have you even *tasted* ... wait, don't answer. I know: Starr Spindle squirts it into her mouth in *Clinging* before her boyfriend uses the can for a whippet. Thus, you must have tried it once for the purpose of *research*. You'll try anything *once* to get the feel." She shrugged. "Might as well try *me*. Might jumpstart book number three in the Starr Spindle tril—"

"What you just said ... that *look*, is why I won't ... I refuse to wake up next to someone who hates me."

She dug into the bag. Her fingers came out covered with pulp. "Now why would I hate you?"

EIGHTEEN-YEAR-OLD JUSTINIAN VIRGIL Leighton had never been much of a student—only the massive endowment left to Blaine by his deceased grandfather had shoehorned his application into acceptance—but he liked making up stories well enough to stumble into a major. He wasn't much of a boyfriend, either, but because he was attractive and famously wealthy and Marguerite was shallow, they'd fallen into an easy couplehood a few weeks into his freshman year.

Since coming into his inheritance that August, Justin had had little to do with either his father, James—who had been cut out of the will by Justin's grandfather after years of unremitting prodigality and who had communicated with Justin throughout his childhood with boozy breath and fists and lit cigarettes—or his mother—who'd always just stood by—except to pay her credit card bills and send salaries directly to the servants to keep her from the worst shame there was: moneyed descent into shabbiness. But he sent no cash, even when James sent a series of letters begging for a loan to extricate him from what James termed "an unexpected financial predicament" and signed them *Love*.

That December, three days after James's embezzlement from the company of which he was CFO was made public, he drank a bottle of vodka and hung himself in the dining room of the Leighton estate.

Justin had gone back to school as if nothing had happened, though the news had made the front page of *The New York Times*. Two hours after the funeral he was catching dinner at Stinson Hall, consuming coq au vin followed by apple cobbler and discussing the Knicks, actions that scandalized both his peers at Blaine and his mother's in Fox Glen far more than had his father's having hung himself from the family's Waterford chandelier by his Ferragamo tie.

None of his classmates, least of all Marguerite, who regarded the entire topic of death to be vulgar, had any idea how to deal with him. They spoke quickly, without pauses they feared he'd fill, delivering their variations of *sorry, don't know what to say.*

Justin's professors urged him to close out the semester with the C's he'd earned so far, skip his finals, and go home, but when he stayed on campus, popping into classes that weren't necessarily his own, unshaven and unfocused and only vaguely disruptive like a not unfriendly poltergeist, Professor Darren Connelly decided it would be good for Justin to do something constructive. And so Justin began Connelly's final assignment for that semester: *Demonstrate in fifteen or more pages the unexpected.*

He awoke every afternoon hating and deleting what he'd written the night before. At dusk, he stole little white pills from the top drawer of his roommate, who was too intimidated by Justin to mention it. By three a.m. on the last night before the last day of finals, Justin found himself alone and craving, his roommate having left behind a single pill in the bag with a Post-it saying GET HELP when he'd left for vacation. Justin wheezed from the combination of chain-smoking and a chest cold that Marguerite had complained made him sound *like a phlegmy old man.*

Sweating, he trudged through new-fallen snow to wake her—though she'd been making excuses to avoid him since he'd stopped bathing—and ask if she might know where to procure drugs at such an hour. Perhaps by accident she'd say something, anything, to make him feel part of the world.

Instead to the door came Bree, the roommate who when Justin and Marguerite would decide to, say, waltz through the dining hall in ballroom apparel because it was something different to do, led their classmates in the dactylic *one*-two-three claps.

That fall, the semester before she'd become Bree-of-the-footnotes, Bree-the-simulacraescent, Bree-the-anti-story, seventeen-year-old Bree had allowed him and Marguerite to treat her like a toy. Like an exchange student, she turned everything familiar to them new. At restaurants she asked the waiters to translate menus already in English. She stuck her head out of limo sunroofs like a dog. Once they got her drunk on some hideous, herb-derived liqueur that Marguerite kept calling a *digestive*, then took her shopping and laughed when she got sick on the blond floor of Versace.

"She's out," Bree said, holding a Western Civilization textbook and with a yellow highlighter tucked behind her ear.

"Come debauch virgin snow?" He coughed. "You'd make the sweetest angel."

She touched the back of her hand to his cheek, tentatively—she wasn't demonstrative like he and Marguerite were, both believing the world ached to be touched *by* them. "You're sick, Justinian"—after reading his full name on his driver's license, she'd never been able to resist its every syllable—"come lie down, I'll call her."

"She claims I reek."

"It's okay, really."

"Do I?"

"You want me to run a bath for you?"

"Perchance I enjoy my fetidability. It's a superheroic quality, you know—untouchableness." A sob escaped. He had not cried at the funeral. He ran down the fire stairs before tears could take him over.

She caught up to him on the quad, where he was coughing and panting, hands on his knees. She'd taken the time to put on a coat, hat, and gloves—

she was sensible even at three a.m. She draped her scarf around his neck, slipping the two ends through the loop of the fold and pulling them carefully. In the fall she'd knotted her poly-blend neckgear that Marguerite said looked *knitted from lint* bulkily at her throat. *Bank-robber-cum-tracheotomy,* he and Marguerite had called the look before they'd taught her better.

They walked in circles around the fountain in the quad and around every dorm and classroom, so he could leave footprints for the sake of leaving something. He pulled up his shirt and showed her the cigarette burn marks on the base of his spine. He told her he'd as good as killed a man and wasn't sorry. He told her he might die from lack of remorse and he couldn't go home. She said he was good inside, she could feel it—and that she was pretty sure he had pneumonia and really just needed to rest somewhere.

Her house in Vernal was small, her mother slept in one bedroom and Bree and two sisters in the other, but they had a foldout couch in the living room, she told him. He could come home with her tomorrow after her last exam, she said, and she'd look after him. She said *foldout couch* like *presidential suite.*

"Angel," he said, and threw himself into the snow. He moved his arms like flying. As Bree fell back next to him and took his hand, he imagined being with her. He imagined her kindness warming him like those last rays of sun back in September. He imagined saying to each other the sorts of things her characters said, exclamations of baby-bald feelings like, *I'll love you forever* and *I want to live in you* and *I'd die for you.* He imagined becoming the person he sensed she thought he was—a maverick—instead of just a jerk too lazy to follow rules and too rich to have to.

And then, as they reentered the dorm, he began to imagine her family, and Vernal, and the porta-bed. And having to act like he cared about the things he supposed people in Vernal cared about: holidays and church services, sobriety and rules. When Marguerite had asked, *Why is the twenty-year-old protagonist worried about a curfew?* during the workshop for Bree's last story, Bree had frowned, puzzled. *She lives at home,* she said, as if the answer were obvious. *Quaint,* Justin had written in the margin.

He imagined her family conversing about plumbing and doctor appointments, God and flag. He imagined vegetables from cans. (Marguerite had nearly choked laughing when Bree had squinted at the mushrooms in the dining hall salad bar and asked what had happened to their *juice*.)

Alone beneath pounding hot water, taking his first shower in two weeks, he felt Bree's sincerity grow as cloying as the cling peaches she plucked from the salad bar with plastic tongs instead of taking fresh berries.

"*Qu'est-ce que c'est?*" Marguerite said when she got home to find Justin half-asleep on the couch, wrapped in Bree's robe. Marguerite ran a finger over his collarbone.

"He's sick," Bree said, sitting next to him. "He's got a temperature."

Marguerite laughed. "It's *fever*. If he didn't have a *temperature* he'd be dead."

Justin's laughter knotted together with hers. Because it made him feel a part of something. Because it was easy. Because not laughing would have *meant* something he wasn't sure he was willing to mean.

Bree's eyes teared. "Take care of him," she told Marguerite, and walked into the study lounge without looking back, as if she'd never expected him to be better.

CHAPTER 38

"I need ...," Hunter said, as he'd been saying all morning. He shoved aside Carley's bedcovers and rushed to her bathroom. Through the door he slammed closed she could hear his choked, substanceless vomiting.

She'd woken up to him falling onto her bed at dawn, half-drunk and half-hungover, saying, "Everyone was gone. Why was I alone?"

For the first time, she'd wished they didn't have keys to each other's houses. She'd wanted to tell him to leave, but she hadn't wanted to tell him why. To explain what he'd done last night, to say aloud, *You asked for a blowjob like I was a receptacle* would be more humiliating than his having done it.

When he came back to her bed, he squeezed his eyes closed way past what you'd need to shut out the light. She got up and soaked a washcloth in cold water and laid it over his eyes and forehead, the way she did when he was sick, then got some chipped ice from the zero-calorie closet.

She put a sliver on his tongue. "Let it melt." He hadn't even been able to drink water without puking it back up.

"Please talk to me," he said.

"I just did."

"Please, just tell me what I did to make you leave. I shouldn't have to call everyone we know in front of you to find out something *you* could tell me. C, I *need* ..."

"You need to keep down water. You need medicine for your stomach.

That's all you *need*. Learning about your black hole of a night? That's just something you *want*."

"Jake said on the phone you'd told them you were staying to make sure I didn't fall into the pool or choke to death or anything. So what did I do to make you go? You'd *never* leave me like that. I *know* you."

"I don't know *you* anymore."

He grimaced and rolled onto his side. He ran to the bathroom holding his stomach. She put on a Whiplash Bouffant CD, turning the volume high to give him privacy. When he didn't come out after five tracks, she turned down the music.

"H? You okay?"

"I want to die."

"I'm gonna come in."

"*No!* Please. I—I didn't make it—I had to go . . . my stomach. I couldn't . . ."

"*Oh.* But you haven't . . . you're not thinking of hurting yourself?"

"I'm *thinking* of burning my pants." He laughed in a harsh, choking way.

She'd never heard of a hangover being this bad, like something determined to leave Hunter inside out and naked and soiled. Hunter really *would* rather die than say *diarrhea*, than say *I shat myself*. Until today, she'd never understood how putting something into words could be worse than it happening.

"My car keys are in my jacket, C. Could you get me some things from the Palace? Clothes. Medicine."

"I'll get something of Francis's for you to wear."

"Won't fit."

"I could just drive you there. In a robe."

"But I won't make it without having to. . . . Please, C. I know you want me gone. But my stomach hurts so badly I wouldn't be able to walk down the stairs. As soon as I can go ten minutes without . . . going . . . or vomiting, I promise I'll leave."

"I'll put a guest robe out for you on the bed." She thought for a moment. "And a bag, so you can put . . . for anything you want to burn."

"There should be something for the . . . in my bathroom." She'd already searched Francis's cabinet, but he seemed to have taken anything stomach-related to Newport, as if anticipating indigestion. In Gretchen's bathroom she'd discovered a lock on the cabinet that never used to be there.

She could hear him starting to sob. She wanted to hate him, but all she could think about was that field trip when she'd gotten food poisoning and how Hunter had held her in the cab to the Plaza, his hand pressed against the hollow pain in her stomach. She remembered inhaling his cedar cologne as she lay her head against his chest and feeling his cool hand stroke her cheek and hearing him whisper that she was safe. She remembered looking into his eyes and seeing that he really, truly, wasn't disgusted by her at her most disgusting and thinking *this* was what love was. The story of that afternoon that she'd told herself so many times felt more real than *now* could ever be.

"I'll find it," she said. "We'll fix you up. You'll be good as new."

"New. That would be something." His voice cracked. "C, there's something else. And . . . if I didn't hurt so much, if I didn't feel so *fucked*, I swear I wouldn't ask. You're not going to like it. I've been wanting to tell you and just couldn't. But . . . I need one more thing from the Palace. Or I really *will* die."

Hearing what he said next was like reading his journal last night, a single truth turning history into lies. She cried because for months he hadn't trusted her enough to tell her. She cried because the truth should have been as obvious as Buck talking Medieval—the times Hunter had seemed too quickly drunk, the afternoons there wasn't alcohol on his breath but he wasn't himself. Only much later, alone, would she realize she'd cried with the door closed between them because she'd never gotten the chance to cry in *front* of him about everything he'd done to her and because part of her knew this was as close as she'd get.

CHAPTER 39

> *Rodin, Auguste: sculpted <u>The Age of Bronze,</u> a life-sized male nude that caused an outcry at the Salon of 1877 because it seemed <u>too</u> real, as if he'd cast a living model. Have Geppetto mummify critics in plaster.*

"You do realize, I hope, that you've resorted to mummification no fewer than three times." Justin wrapped his arms around Bree's waist from behind. After she'd given up trying to seduce him, he'd tucked her in on the couch and sat by her until she fell asleep. Clearly she hadn't slept long, though—the webbing in his living room had tripled since last night.

She turned. "Could you drive me home?"

"A little coffee first? Breakfast? Aspirin?"

"Please." She shook her head. "This isn't where I want to . . . be."

He sighed. "Imagine your resentment this morning if I *had* slept with you."

"I don't resent you." She stared at something over his shoulder—probably one of her damned cards.

"You never used to lie, Bridget."

AFTER JUSTIN HAD recovered from pneumonia over Christmas in
St. Bart's with Marguerite and her family, he returned to his dormitory
to find in his mailbox a thick envelope of pages, tri-folded and ragged-
margined.

> *Justinian,*
>
> *I know you were high and sick, and I'm not sure what you remember
> saying. When I wrote it down it was just for me. But then I decided
> what you told me was too personal for me to hold on to. I didn't want
> to tear it up because maybe you'd want to remember you got this all out.
> Maybe it would help. The other parts of the entries—my thoughts and
> feelings—I'd appreciate if you don't sit around making fun of with
> Marguerite. Looking back on it, it was stupid for me to worry about
> what my mother would think of you when you never said you were
> coming home with me.*
>
> *Your friend,*
>
> *Bree*
>
> *P.S. Tell Marguerite my moving out isn't personal.*

She didn't glamorize him in those pages, or even demonize Marguerite.
She saw them from all angles, recognizing even her own loneliness and
need.

> *Mom is going to hate Justin's hair and ask me if he's a "hippy" even though
> I keep telling her no one ever says that anymore. And Lara's going to make a big
> deal out of the way he talks, since when I came home for Thanksgiving she
> and Sheila kept saying I talked "fakey" just because I'm trying not to say mall
> like mawl, and that's nothing compared to someone who makes up his own
> words.*
>
> *I don't know how to explain there are rich people who are so rich and afraid*

of money being the thing about them people notice that they expend a lot of effort trying to look and act bigger than their money. I can't explain it doesn't make them fake more than uncle Sean is fake for having a prosthetic leg. He's just using what he needs.

The night before the next semester began, Justin wrote fifteen pages in the voice and viewpoint of a woman who looked forward to things, and got crushed, and possessed what Bree described at the end of the torn-out journal pages as "big feelings," about which she'd written, *I wish I could love them, they're so unnuanced. Naïve. Like Marguerite says about my characters, they "don't know irony from cumin."*

It was a new voice for Justin. It *had something*, Connelly said, converting his incomplete to an A. Over the next semester that voice became Starr Spindle.

That second semester also marked a sea change in Bree's writing. She'd been taking a postmodernism class taught by a green-and-pink-haired visiting professor whose fiction was published under the name JuJuBee and was addressed in the classroom as J.B.

Marguerite, who was also taking the class, would lie in bed with Justin with socks on her hands, puppeting the verbal sparring that went on between Bree—who since break had become what Darren Connelly referred to as "chippy"—and J.B., who thought Bree was a rube. Their first unit, metafiction, Bree kept claiming made "no sense." She understood what she read, she kept insisting, but she didn't understand what it *meant*—a response J.B. viewed as "missing the point."

Bree Sock: So it doesn't mean *anything*?

J.B. Sock: To put into question the *idea* of meaning is not *meaningless*.

For weeks Justin laughed at these skits, encouraging Marguerite, pretending she was funny just to hear every detail about a girl he couldn't get out of his head.

Though he no longer crossed paths with Bree much outside of Connelly's class, several weeks into the sock skits, she approached him in the dining hall. J.B. had assigned a short story from *The Anthology Meta* called "Shrimp," which did not at all concern crustaceans, but rather an ever-diminishing penis whose decline was represented by ever-decreasing sentences, words, and font.

"I've read it ten times and I just don't get the *point*," Bree told him.

Perhaps the point was the lack of a period at the end of the story, Justin proposed after barely skimming it. It was just the first thing that came into his head, as he cared little enough about stories assigned for his *own* classes. But making a case for his ridiculous theory gave him an excuse to keep talking to Bree, to study her, to break down the way she spoke and thought and grinned and ate.

Bree Sock: Because it takes the point of a pencil to make a period, the period-less ending is pointless. Thus the period-less pointlessness is the point.

J.B. Sock: *(To class)* How many of you buy into the presupposition that the author of "Shrimp" is a Luddite who writes in *pencil?*

Marguerite squealed with laughter. Justin, who after talking to Bree had found himself finally able to complete a Starr scene that Connelly said embodied poignancy, felt sick to his stomach. He blamed Marguerite's puppet-hands for his inability to get it up that night, snapping, *Socks are not foreplay.*

A week later, Marguerite crowed that J.B.'s ten-page assignment to "delineate the essence of metafiction" was going to drive Bree *back to Vernal.* (Marguerite had taken Bree's moving out as personally as she had Justin's increasing fascination with Bree.)

"I'm giving up," Bree told him in the library as she typed on one of the public computers the night before the paper was due. "I'm gonna write J.B. a ten-page Fuck You and let her fail me."

And fail Bree she indeed tried to do. "Hungry," about self-cannibalizing, therio-anthropomorphic short stories who progress from nibbling at their own tails ("The End tasted minty") to swallowing their own heads, ended up striking J.B. as too *good* to be Bree's. For weeks she threatened to have her expelled for plagiarism, until finally, begrudgingly convinced of the story's originality, she submitted it on Bree's behalf to the *Simulacra Review,* where it was accepted for immediate publication. No one but Justin recognized it as parody.

By sophomore year Bree had placed two more pieces in literary magazines. She dyed her hair blue and dressed like a cross between androgyne and Cyprian in neckties and the tightest pants on campus. In creative writing classes she responded to other people's work with careful responses devoid of Marguerite's sarcasm or Justin's glibness but imbued with something more threatening—a shrug in her voice that implied a lack of *import* to what she'd read. Such comments were personalized with paper-cut slights about the authors, for whom their protagonists were usually stand-ins.

"I get the *pathos* here, I *really* do," she said to Marguerite, "but might the protagonist be just a tad too preoccupied with the thinness of her own lips?"

"That's just *one* line."

Bree smiled. "Perhaps it was something about the word choice that made it *feel* like preoccupation."

She spoke with newly crisp vowels. She wrote one-word sentences and un-sentences and page-long sentences that knotted around themselves vinelike and opened up into huge blooms that sucked down all the carbon dioxide in the air and all the minerals from the earth. She brought into class stories in which characters thought so much and said so little that every page was choked with print. Stories where characters knew they were characters. Hopeless stories that everyone hated to read and found impossible to criticize without sounding ignorant. Stories that made you want to crawl into bed and stay there.

She was the pet of the English department and the idol of every classmate who hated her.

When a year after they graduated, Justin—whose writing his classmates had always deemed *fine* but not spectacular—hit the top of the bestseller list with *Crawling*, the only negative review appeared in the back pages of the *Simulacra Review*, where Bree McEnroy called Justin's writing "Splenda-esque," accusing the novel of "theme-parking the experiences of the lower-middle-class" and "possess[ing] the verisimilitude of Vegas-casino-versions of Paris or New York."

> *Blake, William: antimaterialistic painter and poet, a genius mostly unrecognized while he was alive. "The Imagination is not a State," he wrote, "it is Human Existence itself." William Hayley, a minor poet, became Blake's patron, arranging jobs such as painting portraits of poets for Hayley's library. "O God, protect me from my friends, that they have not power over me." Revenge: Geppetto shows Hayley the future two hundred years hence, when Blake's art hangs in the Tate and his poetry fills library shelves and Hayley is unknown.*

Justin handed her the cards that had dried out overnight. "You're going to heap vengeance upon him for *helping* Blake?"

"Helping? Those jobs were beneath him. Their relationship was about power."

"You don't change." Justin leaned on his cane.

"You don't know me well enough to know. You've always had this *idea* of me. At first you thought it trashily glamorous to know an actual poor person. Later, I *informed* your writing. I was your *research*. And here's the irony, Justin: you didn't even get me right."

"You're like a bad review, still," Justin said, holding the front door open for her, "high-handed and bitter."

CHAPTER 40

It was because she was crying that Carley nearly hit Justin head-on. She knew to stay to the right. She just hadn't expected anyone to be coming into the driveway. Also, she was searching her purse for a tissue.

Justin swerved, clipping his fender on one of the red maples lining the driveway.

"I'm sorry," she said again and again when he yanked open the driver's side door. She cried into her arms on the steering wheel. "I *know* how to drive, I was just—"

"Might we fast-forward to an explanation of why Minor Wells was bat-out-of-helling Alchy-Cay's vehicle?"

"Hunter's, um, *indisposed*," she said, a word that sounded appropriately uncomfortable. Almost *onomatopoetic* (List Thirty-six: "More Words About Literature)—except with feelings.

"And why might Hunter's indisposition," said Justin, "be causing you such sorrowfication?"

She looked at Bree, who'd come over and sat next to her in the passenger seat. "Is that a word?" Bree shook her head and tugged at the sleeve of what was obviously Justin's shirt. She looked embarrassed about being in his clothes.

"Write it down, I'll get it," Justin told Carley when she explained that Hunter needed clothing and medicine.

"I'll come with you." While he was upstairs she could duck into the changing room to get the Vicodin that Hunter had begged her for. *Just three . . . no, four,* he'd had said, wanting to make sure she wouldn't get caught with a whole vial if she were stopped by a cop while driving a hundred-and-fifty-thousand-dollar car without a license.

"I don't desire a Cry-Brat sidekick. Write down what and where."

Carley gave him the key and drew a map to Hunter's room on the back of Justin's hand.

"What's going on?" Bree asked. Carley followed her to the guest room. She didn't know how to tell Hunter that his pills weren't coming, at least not until Justin was out of his house, and not until Carley's tutor—who was due in less than an hour—had come and gone, else Grace would come looking for her and discover Hunter in a state of "indisposition."

"Hunter's sick," Carley said, "nothing new."

"You don't know what it's like," he'd told her through the bathroom door. "The grind of getting sick, and being sick, and recovering from it. It's not an excuse, but I just want you to understand why, pathetic as it is, I sometimes need something to help me bear with the indignity of . . . snot. And, right now, to buffer me from pain and from the humiliation of . . . what happened in here. I'll stop tomorrow. I swear it's only once in a while. I'm not hooked. I *swear,* C. But just do me this one favor now? Please."

She imagined people shaking their heads at the absurdity of taking pain pills to deal with a head cold. Not even Bree, who created characters like Internet Odysseus who masturbated himself raw while stuck inside a Pay-for-Porn site, would understand. (Unable to sleep before four a.m. or summon an Aftermemory, Carley had been trying to bore herself unconscious by reading Bree's published doorstop, of which she was currently on page three-seventy-nine.) Everyone else's absurdity was always more absurd.

"You look cool in Justin's Lamborghini," Carley said to keep Bree from pressing her about Hunter.

Bree shook her head.

"What? He's cool. You're cool together. So did you guys get trashed at that party last night, talking about onomatopoeia and stuff with your writer friends? And in the limo back was he like, *You're the personification of assonance, Bree,* and you were like, *Well if you think* that's *assonant, wait till I—*"

"My fish died," Bree said, and for a minute Carley thought it was an expression she didn't understand. Something about sex, like in those books Hunter kept under his bed. There were five hundred expressions for oral, she'd learned last spring when she'd begged him to tell her what guys liked when a girl went down on them because she was so into Colin Bradley. Hunter had taken out the books and shown her pictures, blushing as he explained, and smoked two joints down to his fingertips.

"My apartment's gone, there's no home. And before you say anything else about Justin, or imply that we slept together—which we didn't—and tell me how *lucky* I am for his liking me, you should know something about him. Our . . . backstory."

"He told me—"

"Whatever he said, whatever *his* story is . . ." Bree shook her head. "I'm sure he prettied it, like he does every tale he's ever told. Here's the truth: Once upon a time I was a stupid girl a year older than you are, starstruck by Justin before he was a star . . ." she began. Some people, when they cried, looked so naked you'd rather feel their pain *for* them than watch. Hunter was like that. And so, it turned out, was Bree.

CHAPTER 41

Hunter's boxers caught him in the face. His jeans hit Carley's nightstand, crashing an antique rose-painted Limoges bowl full of sand dollars and mermaid purses to the floor. He ducked as Justin threw a bottle of sports drink—purple, and not the sort of thing Hunter ever drank. It bounced off the headboard. Imodium grazed his cheek.

"In books," Hunter whispered, as Justin dropped a bottle of Pepto-Bismol onto the bed, "illness is either elided—*after getting over the flu that kept him from the festivities*—or horribly indulged—*alone and fever-wracked, Oliver rued having jilted Lady*—"

"You don't have the flu."

"My point," Hunter said, fixated on the packaging, which trumpeted *stomach upset!* in front of the man whom Hunter, as a ninth grader, had daydreamed about engaging in conversation about Proust on the deck of the Glen Club while staring out at the Sound, "was that novels spare characters the fussiness of nose drops and sodden tissues and"—his stomach cramped horribly—"that fuzzy-throat sensation that makes drinking milk dreadful when one is ill, and the take-every-four-to-six-hours-ness of OTCs and"—he held up the Imodium—"contraindication of use in the presence of *black or bloody stool.*" He stood, pulling tight the belt of the bathrobe before he shuffled to the bathroom. As if nakedness could ever shame him as much as Justin's two-word note had.

"Get help for your drinking," Justin said when Hunter returned. "Or lose her."

"Carley and I aren't—"

"You belong to each other, Alchy-Cay." Justin shook his head. "You think you *decide* who your love is?"

Hunter sat on Carley's bed, bending his knees against the cramps. "*Belong* doesn't strike you as stalker-ish? I'd think after that woman, the one who did *this*"—he pointed to the cane—"you'd be chary of obsession. I'd think you wouldn't be a guy who engineers bringing his college crush to his hometown to have someone to play with. Were you sitting in your cottage running your fingers over your knotty scars, Pinocchio turning back to wood, when you heard from Darren Connelly about the gauche man from Fox Glen who'd been trolling the O'Neil Foundation for Adult Literacy dinner with the most *laughable* offer?" He put his head to his knees. "With that 'grant,' you'd already made the leap from puppeteering your own pretend life—*Where should I be rumored to be next week?*—to puppeteering Bree's. And now you took the next step. You asked Connelly to recommend her to Francis."

"You've gotten to love the booze more than the people you love," Justin said. "Even the girl at the center of every one of your stories."

"I liked you better when you didn't sound like everyone else," Hunter said, the words sticking to his mouth. He took a sip of the sports drink and gagged. Justin grabbed the wastepaper basket from Carley's desk as it came back up.

"Tell Jackie-O you need a time-out at a clinic," Justin said when Hunter had finished, "or I ring up Larry and put an insect in his auricle. *What big ears you have, Stepdaddy! Why the better to* . . . I'll toss out a few tree-name places: Shady Pines, Oak Ranch. Wait lists, all, but I know folks who'll cat's cradle you to the head of the class. E-pass to twenty-five mile hikes, talking sticks, faux-camouflage-wearing counselors tough-loving kids like you into term-coming with your shit-spoilage."

Justin lowered himself to the floor. "Forty-five days and you come back sober," he said, collecting pieces of china and beach treasures into the largest intact piece of the bowl. It seesawed.

"Why do you care?"

"She deserves better. A shiny new you." He swept the residue of sand dollars into a talc-y pile he scooped up with a piece of paper from Carley's printer tray.

"Is that what *you're* doing, bettering yourself? Looks from here like you're trying to change *her*."

"It's complicated. A long story. Call it a morality tale, if you will." He wiped the sand dollar residue off his hands onto his jeans. "One Friday afternoon, not two weeks into Bridget Theresa McEnroy's freshman year..." he began, as if he knew the thing Hunter wanted most in the world was for him to leave and was determined not to oblige.

CHAPTER 42

Later, the producers would contend that if neither Buck's real family nor gameworld girlfriend suspected he was delusional, why should <u>they</u> have? Though his introversion hadn't made him an ideal contestant, the rest of his family—his brother Dale, the bonehead athlete; his recovering meth-addict father; his former-beauty-queen-turned-abused-wife mother—made for good TV. They were the first family in reality history to have been plucked from a homeless shelter.

It was not, in fact, the first time Buck had lost grasp on reality, a fact his family had concealed from the psychologists who vetted the contestants. Some years earlier, after immersing himself in old Jacques Cousteau videos every afternoon in the AV room of his school library, where he'd stay until the custodians went home rather than go back to the shelter or the car in which they'd been living prior to that, he'd had episodes of believing he was a beluga whale. In school he answered questions only in squeaks, though because he was a quiet, shy child, it had taken two weeks for his teachers to stop attributing it to the onset of puberty and realize it was not merely his voice changing.

A knock at the door interrupted Bree's typing. She looked up from her laptop as Hunter stepped in, his eyes passing over the things Bree had salvaged from her apartment and settling on the water-stained gray beaded gown hanging over a chair. Threads dangled where beads had been lost through a tear in the plastic bag as she'd dragged it.

It had belonged to Bree's mother—*my fancy dress,* she used to say, letting her girls run their fingers over it in the closet only after they'd washed their hands. When she was out, they'd dance with it on the hanger, pretending they were at the sort of party their mother had been to only once in her life, the wedding of a girl from the neighborhood who'd gone away to college on scholarship and come home with a two-carat ring. (For too long, she'd held out hope that college would bestow a similar prize upon Bree.) Black Tie, the invitation had demanded; her mother had made the dress herself, hand-beading for months. To hear her speak of that evening spent among the girl's new husband's family and their fancy shoes and manners, you'd think *it*—rather than her own wedding—had been the best night of her life.

"I was looking for Carley."

"She's downstairs with her SAT tutor."

He looked at his watch. "Right. She must have come in and grabbed her books while I was in the ... shower."

She broke off a piece of an apricot muffin from the basket Carley had ordered from the kitchen for Bree and had had to promise the staff she wouldn't touch before they'd agree to leave the basket in proximity to her.

"The secret to those?" Hunter wrapped his arms around himself. "Nectar. The cook has to hide it, though—Gretchen has this thing about *cans*."

"I could say *Really*? And then you'd share more backstage secrets about Swann's Way, both of us pretending this information was being imparted to me for reasons other than your characterizing yourself as someone who pals around with the servants or cares about baking, so as to dilute my impression of you as an indulgent, incontinent asshole."

"Your boyfriend called me *shit-spoiled*—or I think that's what he said, his parsage can be difficult to follow. But I prefer your characterization." He pressed his hands to his stomach. "And not just because you aren't throwing things or threatening to tell Larry to ship me off to rehab." He took a deep breath. "Excuse me," he said, heading for her bathroom.

Jules's family had entered the competition because they loved games, Bree typed. Scrabble, chess, Risk. What else did she know about Jules? She struggled to come up with the backstory Carley had asked for in the bra museum.

When Jules deduces that the reason neither her family nor Buck's has been voted off by the viewers is that the audience loves their secret romance, she wonders if she's in love with Buck or with the idea of people *loving* her in love. But why *does* she doubt her own motivations? NOTE TO SELF, Bree typed. Opportunity for backstory dump: to explain Jules's self-doubt, have someone in her past have broken her heart?

"I have a tailor who can fix anything." Hunter closed the bathroom door and walked a circle around the gray dress, nodding to himself. His eyes were swollen.

"I'm not going to ask if you're okay."

"Thank you." He lowered himself slowly onto the window seat. "I wish . . . I wish we could be introduced again for the first time. He buried his head in his arms.

"I won't lie, Hunter. I thought you were—"

"Better. I know. People expect of me so many qualities I don't possess: joie de vivre, savoir faire, sangfroid." He lifted his head. "Continence."

"Listen, I can't guess what you did this morning to make Carley drive out of here in tears. But she told me what you did last night." It had come out after she'd told Carley about Justin, about how it felt to have someone who had everything take the little that was *you*. "She doesn't want you to know. But you need to."

Fifteen minutes later, his hand shook as he left a folded note on Carley's pillow. "Thank you for the truth," he said, handing Bree two hundred-dollar bills and his car keys. "I can't imagine what you think of me. Well, I *can*. I just don't want to."

"You don't need to pay me to drive you home. I don't want you doubling over behind the wheel or fainting. Just have a cab waiting at your house to get me back here."

"You're giving me your time despite hating me. That's the definition of a *job*."

"I don't hate—"

"Justin told me what happened to you last night. About not even having enough money for the train. I suspect he just needed to tell someone and I was handy, so he slipped it into his you-don't-know-how-lucky-you-are-you-rich-spoiled-brat speech. It really shook him up, the idea of you running around the city with five dollars to your name. Kind of unfathomable to a billionaire."

"And *you*, of course, fathom it."

"Look, you just *can't* go around with no money until Carley's birthday. If you feel that strongly about it, just pay it back when you get paid for the book. Oh, and let me have that dress repaired for you." He wiped his eyes. "Please. It would make me feel useful."

CHAPTER 43

Justin pulled out Carley's dressing table chair, looking at her through the square foot of mirror not covered with paper. He untied the ribbon from his ponytail, brushed his hair, and retied it. He sniffed her perfumes, moisturizer, and makeup. There was a smudge of metallic green eye shadow on his nose when he turned.

"Do you ever think about what it's like for everyone else in the room when you do stuff like that?" she said. "When you try to be weird, I mean, and then pretend you weren't trying?"

"What *what's* like?"

"Most of us have to try so hard to be normal just to make people like us, and then *you* get all this attention for acting *ab*normal. Could you wipe that off your nose already? You *know* it's there."

He complied, then uncapped her black eye pencil without asking.

"I don't know where Bree's gone to, so you can stop pretending you're here to talk to me."

"What's with the bitters, Minor Wells? Thought we had a rapport last weekend."

"Thought you were cool last weekend. You tell cool stories. Too bad they're not the *whole* story. And you were wrong, by the way, about how Bree talks about herself. She doesn't do any weird point of view stuff when she *talks*. She just says 'I.' Like, 'I loved my roommate's boyfriend and he—'"

"The reason I came back?" he said. "To apologize. I broke something you care about." He pointed toward her night table. "Alchy . . . Hunter called it *the only thing in the room that's her.*" He stretched the skin beneath his left eye taut with his right thumb and drew the pencil beneath his lower lashes. The line was dark and shaky. He smudged it to smoke with his thumb. "It was an accident, and I'm sorry. I know an antique dealer who can—"

She'd been so preoccupied by Hunter's absence and the note he'd left that she hadn't noticed the breakage. "It wasn't the bowl," she said. "It was what was in it."

He turned to face her directly. She wanted to think he looked ridiculous. For Bree, she wanted to hate him. But he looked too sad to hate, and anyway, eyeliner looked right on him. "Well, Minor—"

"Bree told me about how in college she had a crappy desk that you saw her trying to keep from falling apart when she was moving. You helped her. And afterward, off-hand-like, you asked her what it was made of."

"Particle board."

"Right. And then you bought a whole set of furniture made of it and gave a party just to have people sit on it and throw stuff at it. You were writing about poor people, and you wanted to know how easily their stuff broke. It was *research.*"

"You drop more on your Libertine jeans than I did on that furniture."

"It's not *about* . . ." She tried to wrap her lips around the thought, then snapped her mouth closed, and shrugged. "Forget it." Words always failed her.

"Take your time," Justin said. "You know what you *think.*"

"It's not *about* money," she said finally, the words there as soon as she stopped looking for them. "It's about someone's *less* being her *everything.*"

He nodded slowly, like he was really listening. "In the collected works of Hunter Cay, you know, there's a character fitting your description who is outrageously sage."

"Like *with* Hunter's stories," she said. "See, I *don't* know what's in them because he doesn't show them to me. But I know your opinion was *everything.* Everyone loves your books. You have way more love than you need. So couldn't you have said just one nice thing about someone else's writing? Even if it sucked, it was the best he had."

Justin smiled. She wanted to hate him—for Hunter's sake, for Bree's—but she felt light-headed. For once everything she meant had just come pouring out. For just a moment she could understand why you'd get hooked on words if they did what you wanted. It was a head rush better than getting drunk or high. It was like driving.

"He could turn out to be good, actually," Justin said, "if he doesn't get corrupted by people telling him how good he is."

"But all you wrote was Live—"

"Didn't think he'd do it so badly."

"And you're living *well?*"

He sighed. "I drove my own car last night for the first time since the shooting. Turns out the right hand can still shift."

"I didn't mean *Is your life good?* I meant, *Are you doing good?* Hunter helps people. He helps, like, everyone. What do you do?"

"Offered to get Bree a lawyer—"

"A *lawyer* can't fix what happened to her. The important stuff's gone. Her fish."

"Considered buying her an aquarium, but didn't think your mother would appreciate my setting up a hundred-gallon tank in her guest room."

"Not any old fish. *Her* shitty little fish named after people in *The Odyssey.* They *meant* something to her and they're gone forever. You're supposed to do something emotional when something unfixable happens. Like, um"—she'd heard Hunter use the phrase—"a *grand gesture.*"

"I don't know what you expect from me, Minor Wells," he said as he stood. He extended his hand to her to shake—his bad hand. "I can't bring back the dead."

"*Bring back the dead,*" she repeated when he'd gone, the words opening a doorway to Aftermemory that all week had been closed. For the first time there was a story she wanted to tell herself that wasn't about getting Hunter or keeping him.

IN AFTERMEMORY, SHE tells Justin, "We're bringing back the dead." He holds a Tupperware of dead tropical fish in his good hand and a net in the bad. A broken crystal mobile hangs above him by the window, severing sunlight onto his clothes and skin. He stares out past the shattered glass, a breeze coming in and sequins dancing on his face. He looks green.

Teary and light-jeweled, he turns away from the window and forces himself back to the tank where she nets plants out of the death soup to clear a view to the bottom. They cross nets as he goes to scoop something up. The head falls off the used-to-be-orange fish he's going for.

He covers his mouth. "I'll do it," she says, taking the net. "What we save should be whole." She whispers, hoping Bree's landlord stays asleep across the hall, as he has through her climbing up the fire escape and going down the front stairs to let Justin in. It's been her plan, the whole thing, and she doesn't want to get Justin killed over it.

It's slow going, the recovery of fish corpses. But she wants Bree to have something to bury, so she can say good-bye. A symbol.

Justin holds open the plastic bag as she dumps the torso into a plastic bag with the brown mush of plants. He strokes half-fish through the bag like anything that was once Bree's is precious to him, and she thinks, *What a beautiful mess love makes of us.*

She digs deep and comes up with another intact body. The thing that used to be a fish is curled and browning at the edges like a fallen leaf. Precious or not, Justin looks five seconds from puking or letting loose the tears that have been welling since the moment he stepped inside. She's pretty sure the tears are about Bree's apartment—the fact that the toilet is right there in the room with everything else and there's a hot plate instead of a stove. Like people can't be *poor*-poor outside of books.

She places the fish into the Tupperware and scoops deeper, coming up with gravel, plastic tubing, and an eye. As she turns the net inside out, she sees movement in the gravel. She blinks, unable to believe it.

"Justin!" She scoops and scoops at the bottom of the tank and comes up finally with something the color of a newborn baby, thumb-sized, with the whiskers of something ancient. It wriggles in her net.

She tells Justin to fill a Wonder Bread bag full of clean water. The albino catfish burrows into the net, twisting and thrashing as she tries to transfer it. She can feel in her chest how desperate it is to breathe whatever fish breathe, the opposite of air.

When she reaches in to free it with her hand, it's like something between her brain and body has disconnected. She expected the fish to be scaly and slimy, but instead it feels exactly the way mercury looks, like warm glass.

"Odysseus," she says, and sighs when he has no idea what she's talking about. She points to the crescent-shaped scar on its side. "She didn't name them randomly. You know, if you want to be with her, you should learn what she likes."

The fish snouts the bag fiercely, attacking the Wonder Bread polka dots and then she and Justin are cracking up, slap-happy, teary-insane with that feeling that comes from getting exactly what you need when you don't know what to ask for.

CHAPTER 44

"I know why you did it," Carley said that evening as they sat on the silk-cushioned viewing bench in front of Francis's dioramas. "You think truth's what Hunter needs. But it wasn't your truth to tell." She wrote something in the margin of one of the pages Bree had given her. Bree couldn't read it upside down. "Until you *told* him, it was like a bad dream that would have faded. He's too ashamed to even look at me now. He said so in his note." Writing something else, she sighed. "Look, I know you were trying to help—"

"You deserve—"

"Respect. You said. But you didn't respect me enough to. . . . Forget it. It's done. I'm tired of talking about it." She waved the pages at Bree. "Listen, I don't know anything about writing, but I don't think you have to work so hard to fit in the backstory. You don't need to say, 'The sight of Buck failing to free his sword from the stone in the Ever-Stick Glue-All Wresting Challenge reminded Jules of how her parents had never let her win at Candy Land. It all started when she was three, in the Gumdrop Woods—' "

"That's how you think I write?"

"Well, more sophisticatedly. But still it sounds like you're saying to the reader, *There's a reason I'm telling you what I'm about to tell you, it's a really good reason, sort of, and.* . . . Like you're apologizing for the most important thing in the whole book—letting them understand the people. Aren't *people* the point of stories?"

"*Characters.*"

"Same difference. Anyway, what you wrote here makes it sound like you're more interested in the backstory of *things*. As if how a reality show works—how host Cliff Daniels manages to hide his lavalier microphone on his doublet, and what kind of snacks are on a craft service table, and how the stunt coordinator makes sure challenges are safe—is more important than the *characters*. Those books you have on your desk downstairs—*Caveman Land: Behind the Scenes in Prehistoria*, *Moonwalking: A Month in the Bouncy House*, and *The 'Real'-ity Reader: Critical Readings on the Commodification of Banality*, all of which are, to you, far more interesting than the shows themselves—aren't gonna make the story feel more *true*. It's like putting on a million accessories with no dress."

Bree sighed. The review in *Kirkus* of *Scylla* had accused her of *masticating the wrappers of uneaten candy*. "So, two weeks before I'm supposed to have something to give to the printer you still hate everything I've done." In the nearest glass case, the fascia-wearing mannequin, exponentially bigger than the world outside her pretend window, stared out at the coliseum in which she'd never fit.

"Not everything. Just, can't you let your people . . . characters . . . think about their pasts because they're *feeling* something? Grateful or sorry or . . . missing something. Like how you told me about you and Justin this morning because you were pissed off at him and sad. Or like how in *Crawling* when Starr spends her first night ever in a city, away from home, and it's summer but what's keeping her awake isn't the heat or the sirens but instead what's *not* there—the rumbling of her refrigerator, whose fan is always breaking when it's hot—she thinks back to when she and her husband bought the refrigerator and how it was the first *new* thing they ever had together and how they imagined a whole life of new things before he was in the accident at the factory and started putting away a twelve-pack every night and—"

"That wasn't in the movie."

"What?"

"The refrigerator."

"Oh. Yeah. I, um, read it. Justin's book. Part of it. This afternoon. My parents have it in our library?" She shrugged and looked at her feet. "I know you're not Starr, but I wanted to read his *idea* of you. Does it bother you? I mean—"

"Why would it?" She didn't intend sarcasm, yet there it was in her voice.

Carley put the pages facedown between them on the cushioned bench. Bree looked out to the coliseum, where on the other side of the toothpick-high arches, gladiators were being torn apart by lions.

"So what's *your* backstory?" Bree finally said.

THE HAND-ADDRESSED INVITATION to Hunter Theodore Cay's clambake, a linen card bearing his monogram, had arrived by messenger two weeks into September of Carley's seventh-grade year.

As soon as she'd called Amber and Olivia to discover *they* hadn't received one, she understood how important this piece of paper was. She knew she'd only been invited because Francis and Hunter's mother had known each other a million years ago and became reacquainted when they recognized each other at a Montclair parent tea the prior week. But even if the invitation was unearned, even if she'd never had the nerve to say one word to the host in the month since he'd moved to Fox Glen and attained instant popularity, even if the host's mother had had to force him to put a seventh-grader onto the guest list, she held it out to Gretchen like a prize.

She knew that every day until the party Gretchen would bask in the possibilities of what could happen for Carley there—the groups that might include her, the friends she might make, the people she might end up *better* than afterward—every night tucking Carley into bed with hope. The last time Carley had presented Gretchen with *possibility* had been at the beginning of the summer, when Violet Burroughs had talked about her upcoming sleepover so openly by the snack bar at the Club pool that Carley had assumed everyone was invited. For weeks Gretchen had talked about how proud she was of Carley's finally "working her way into a good group" as she sat at the edge of the bed each night, brushing Carley's hair with her own silver-handled brush. "Like silk," she'd say, and Carley felt beautiful.

Three days before Violet's birthday, when still no invitation had arrived,

Gretchen sat down at the foot of Carley's bed holding a pamphlet for Camp Metamorphosis instead of a hairbrush. It was important, she said, that Carley understand the difference between truth and wishes. She didn't *have to* be so unhappy that she made things up. There was a place that could fix her.

And now, a few weeks after Carley's return from what was to be her first of many trips to Fat Camp, she had a chance to redeem herself. She imagined coming home from Hunter's party with phone numbers of popular girls programmed into her cell, which she and Gretchen would pore over while eating reduced-fat, reduced-calorie ice cream. She imagined gossiping with her about the children of people who'd denied Gretchen's application to the Glen Club. But most of all, she imagined the boar bristles of Gretchen's brush against her scalp, a hundred strokes of love.

Though only last month, Gretchen had been discussing with Cissy Gardner the impropriety of co-ed sleepover parties—that Bunny hadn't been invited to Violet's either had dulled the edge of the Burroughs's slight a bit—Gretchen's sole concern about Carley's sleeping at the Play Palace was finding her adequately minimizing swimwear and sleepwear. The fabled Cay estate, after all, would be like heaven—a place where beer and eighth-grade boys' horniness weren't allowed through the gates.

Francis, knowing better, took her aside before she left for the party to mumble warnings about boys and beer and to make sure she had cab fare in case she wanted to come home. Gretchen, on the drive over, reminded her to take small bites and keep hips and thighs covered with a sarong and look out for opportunities to make people grateful to her. "The more powerful a person is," she said, "the more determined he or she is not to *owe*." To discharge debt, people would go so far as to make friends of those they hated. It was a lesson Gretchen had been drilling into Carley with renewed vigor ever since Amber had been last-minute invited to the sixth-grade spring dance by a boy too attractive for her whom she'd let copy from her on math tests without his having to ask.

A servant stood waiting to take Carley's overnight bag at the front door of the Play Palace, a building Carley had been hearing about ever since Hunter Cay had arrived. She tilted back her head and squinted at the muraled ceiling of the entranceway. From the way the people were dressed—half-naked, half-robed—she thought they were maybe biblical, though there wasn't an ark or apple in sight.

When she looked in front of her again, Hunter was there, arm extended but with an empty look, like he was peeved that his mother had made him invite a fat baby to his cool party, when everyone else was twelve or thirteen or fourteen. She was the youngest person in her grade—almost a year younger than Amber. Not until later would she discover that he was also the youngest in his. Or that his expression wasn't annoyance, but light-headedness from the antihistamines he'd taken to quell the beginning of a head cold.

"Welcome," he said with a one-armed hug. He showed her upstairs to the guest rooms, the servant following with her bag. "Girls are sleeping up here; guys will be downstairs in the great room or the atrium or wherever they pass out."

Each room had a theme, the walls covered with art deco murals: a circus, a bullfight, Coney Island, a safari, a rainforest, a lakeside picnic—she counted at least fifteen. The hallway seemed endless with worlds.

She didn't know if people were doubling up in the queen-sized beds or how many people had been invited in the first place. Near the end of the hall, she chose one of the few rooms that didn't have bags in it.

"Beach. A favorite," he said, and showed her back downstairs and out to the shore, where a uniformed staff grilled meat and corn and supervised a pit for clams and kept the coolers full of water, soda, and juice. "If you want to doctor anything, the means are inside for now," he said softly. "Don't want the caterer put into an uncomfortable position." His voice was breathy but warm; she had to stand close to hear him but didn't at all mind. She'd heard the word *golden* used to describe people, but never before had it made sense. With the light of the setting sun on his wavy hair and suntanned face, Hunter seemed to glow.

"Enjoy," he said, taking a step back but looking at her quizzically, as if he didn't feel like he could walk away. He shifted his weight from foot to foot and then, seeming to catch himself, pressed his hands into his pockets as if to plant his legs. "Do you feel okay here?" he said so softly that she had to ask him to repeat it. She realized he expected her to wave hi to someone or get herself a soda to free him from his obligation. "If you're uncomfortable—"

She was the little kid at a party for grown-ups—one you stuck in front of the TV with a bowl of ice cream. She worried Hunter would tell his mother she felt out of place, and Suzanne would mention it to Gretchen at Club brunch on Sunday—*I'm sorry little Carley was so overwhelmed*—and then whatever accomplishments she might smuggle home—a compliment on her sweater, a camera phone photo of her with cool kids, even an invitation to go to someone's house—would turn to dust.

"I'm fine. You don't have to ... you can go."

He frowned. "Okay. Going."

"I didn't mean I wanted you to ... I just—"

Ian and Violet, both ninth graders, led over a group of people who'd clearly been "doctoring." Hoisting Hunter into a litter of their arms, they carried him down to the Sound.

Hours later, after Suzanne Cay had come down to the beach several times and implied she wouldn't see them again until morning, the party still hadn't moved up to the indoor pool. Despite it having been an Indian summer, the night was cool, but the rum and vodka were being passed freely now, and darkness nurtured freedom. Mainly, to touch each other beneath their suits in what poolside would have been in plain sight.

Carley sat near the bonfire, away from the couples groping each other in darkness that despite the moonlessness wasn't as complete as they wanted to think (she'd seen Ian Buchanan's *thing* in Violet Burroughs's hand). She wanted to cry with how alone she was on a beach with fifty people—top-rung eighth and ninth graders who'd gotten there the only way *anyone* got popular: intimidation.

When Ian staggered off to puke in the dunes, Violet announced a game. A making-out game. A swimming-in-the-Sound making-out game. Like spin the bottle. Except the bottle was a person.

Carley had never kissed anyone on the lips and knew no one wanted to kiss her, but didn't want to be the girl everyone talked about on Monday who was afraid to play. There were fifty people. All she had to do was stay behind a clump in the circle of swimmers.

Five rounds into blindfolding "bottles" with Violet's sarong, spinning them, and waiting for them to touch someone in the circle, it happened. The girls in front of Carley floated away just as blindfolded Ian reached out a pruny hand. The Sound echoed with laughter—the ninth grader who was already a starter on the varsity soccer team was about to lock lips with the girl in the purple swimsuit who Violet Burroughs had been calling, in an unwhispery-whisper, *The Teletubby*.

When it was done, Carley dove under the water where she could spit, and wondered if playing a make-out game was something Gretchen would be upset or proud about. After all, Carley didn't need to mention Ian's puke breath. Or that she'd heard him tell Violet, "It was like kissing bacon."

And then it was her turn. She was being spun much longer, it seemed, than the people before her, though she attributed it to the way time slowed down when you wanted to disappear into the whirlpool of yourself because you didn't know what "like bacon" meant or how not to kiss like it. She kept hearing whispers and splashes and giggles, and she knew people were trying to guess where she'd stop, treading from side to side to keep away from breakfast-meat tongue. *No*, she thought she heard, *No*. Finally, she was let go to drift. She heard the spinners swimming away from her as she counted to fifty. And then it was quiet, *too* quiet.

She sidestroked, the fingers of her right hand expecting to connect with a person every time she extended it. The ends of the blindfold dragged against her opposite shoulder. She swept her arm again and again, until her fingers brought up sand. She stood and pulled the blindfold off. She was alone.

She imagined them all sitting in the Palace, laughing, waiting for the Teletubby to walk in so they could tell her *no hard feelings, just a joke*.

At the shore she sobbed, not knowing how she'd ever explain to Gretchen why she was coming home. How would she even *get* home without going into the Palace for her things or at least her phone? She was sitting at the water's edge with her towel wrapped around her, imagining walking the whole way home barefoot in a swimsuit rather than face the laughter that awaited her inside, when she first heard the splashing. A small sound, like a bird taking off from the water's surface, or like a fish coming up from below to snatch a bug.

She squinted out into the water, but she could only see a few yards in front of her. She turned back to the beach littered with footprints and bottles. By the dying bonfire she saw a pile of clothes and a cell phone someone left behind. Stepping closer, she recognized the moss-colored sweater Hunter had been wearing once the sun had gone down.

"Hunter?" she called out to the Sound.

There came a splash in return.

Francis had taught her everything he knew about the water—about moving through it, about respecting it, about surviving it. People who were drowning, he'd once told her, used so much energy staying afloat that they usually couldn't shout for help.

She swam toward the sound and called his name again. "I hear you! Keep splashing, I'm coming."

His eyes were closed when she reached him, as if he were resigned to drowning but unable to watch as it happened. One of his legs was bent to his stomach—a cramp—and he was treading feebly. "You're okay," she told him. "Just don't grab me. Fight the urge." It's what people did, pulled their rescuers under.

He nodded and gasped as she massaged the leg, pressing as hard as she could until she felt the muscles start to relax.

"Okay, now just let yourself float. I'll pull you."

He tried to lean back and panicked, thrashing at the water.

She treaded back away. "I won't *let* you drown. Trust me. Close your eyes again, lean back, and say the alphabet slowly in your head. By Z it'll be over."

She put her hand on the small of his back. He closed his eyes. His lips mouthed letters.

"We're there," she said when she'd pulled him to where she could walk. "It's okay."

His knees buckled when he tried to stand.

His weight pulled her underwater when she grabbed him under his arms. She felt his hands against her head as he struggled to get his face above the surface. She fought to get loose of him, the water resisting the feeble blows of her fists, her lungs ready to burst.

"Let go, stop panicking," a voice said, hands pulling her up.

"She could have killed you," said someone else.

"Should we do CPR?"

"Everyone's *breathing*," gasped Hunter. "Is *anyone* here not imbecilic?"

He staggered to his towel and brought it over to Carley, who sat shaking at the edge of the water where the hands had dumped her. He wrapped it around her shoulders, holding her tightly, like he was afraid she'd shiver apart. She'd swam in serious tides, been yanked around by rip currents in Hawaii, and was once stung by multiple jellyfish in the Caribbean and had to swim to shore with her skin on fire. But she'd never before felt like she could die, the way she had right here at the edge of the Sound, only a couple of miles from where she lived, in four feet of water.

Ian sat on the other side of Hunter and held out a bottle of vodka. "It's over. Cool down with the insults. We should have thought to leave people behind to make sure she could swim. It's good *you* thought of it."

Carley could see the disbelief on Hunter's face. It had taken him that long to understand everyone thought *he'd* saved *her.* "What? Ian, that's not what—" He shoved the bottle away and looked around them.

She saw him realize he was about to lose everything. Once he admitted he'd been rescued by the Teletubby, girls wouldn't think the breathiness of his voice was *sexy* as much as *effeminate.* Guys wouldn't call his manners *classy*, but *soft*. Everything about him people thought *independent* they'd call *weird.*

"I was lucky he stayed," Carley said. "I got a cramp and got scared. He was amazing. Like someone in a movie."

I did something huge for Hunter Cay, she imagined telling Gretchen. *Huger even than saving his life.* She could almost feel Gretchen brushing her hair as she retold the story again and again, a secret they'd share.

Hunter stared and shook his head.

"Trust me," she whispered and squeezed his hand.

"Oh my God," said one of Violet's friends, "she's crushing on him. *Cuuuute.*"

It was the way everyone but Hunter laughed, like she was a joke instead of a real live person, that made her realize that even the prospect of Hunter's gratitude—the parties to which he might invite her, and the dresses Gretchen might buy her for those parties, and the shopping trips they could take together for those dresses with Gretchen putting her arm around Carley as they walked into the fitting room—didn't make up for being bacon. Or being the kind of girl you make the butt of a joke because you know she'll never be someone you'll be sorry you insulted. The kind of girl you might have let drown.

It was only ten, and nobody else would go to sleep for hours, but nearly dying gave her an excuse to just go to bed. No one else had put luggage in Beach, so she could cry alone.

She pretended to be asleep when a knock came at the door a little while later. Eventually, the pretending turned real.

It was three a.m. when she woke up without knowing why. She listened hard for the giggles of girls next door or the guys laughing downstairs, but all she heard was faint music, adult music—jazz. It spooked her, made her think she was imagining things, and the more she thought about it, the less she could tune it out.

Finally, she stepped into the hallway. The music was coming from the room next door at the very end. She knocked softly. When no one answered, she eased the door open.

On the far wall of the room, a painted tuxedoed man wearing a bright orange lion's mask shimmied with a painted fringed-dress lioness. A painted angel wearing a cloche and plumed half-mask to match her ivory wings pointed out the real window to the real sculpture garden below. A painted angular cobalt cat warmed itself by a real fireplace ablaze with real flames below a painted brick mantle. And in front of it, Hunter slept in a chair with a book in his lap and tea and tissues on a small table.

He opened his eyes and shook off a startled look.

"Sorry," she said. "I didn't . . . I heard the music, and—"

"No, *I'm* sorry." He got up and came to the doorway. "I'm not supposed to be up here. Guys downstairs and everything. But I couldn't sleep, and . . . even with them all asleep, it's a lot of people, and . . . I just wanted to be alone."

"Okay, well, cool. I just . . . wanted to make sure you weren't a, um, ghost. Like a ghost with music. Just . . . forget it."

He coughed and stepped back from her, bracing one hand against the ruffled collar of a clown pouring martinis for a couple dressed as Native Americans, feathered headdresses to their heels. In the other arm was his book, pressed to his chest. "I don't want you to catch this."

"I don't—"

"But could we talk if I promise not to get too close?" He sneezed. "Excuse me," he said and walked into what she assumed was his bathroom, sniffling.

"You don't need to leave to blow your nose," she called out. Gretchen claimed it was a vulgar thing to do in public, but Carley figured if you were the one lucky enough not to have the cold, the least you could do is just look away a little and let the other person take care of what he needed to do.

"I'm repressed," he called back. She didn't know what the word meant— she knew only that it wasn't the same as *de*pressed. Probably. She heard him wash his hands and then he was standing in front of her again, his arms crossed. "I like things that are supposed to be inside to stay there," he said. "And I hate being disgusting."

"Are you serious? Have you ever *looked* at you? You're like a hot guy on TV who sneezes a couple of times and everyone watching is supposed to think *Uh-oh* because no one sneezes on TV unless it means something like he's gonna have to miss the big test or big date or big dance, and then he's home in bed for like sixty seconds in cool pajamas with a matching robe— unless he's secretly a superhero, in which case he ditches the PJs and saves the world even though his powers are weakened, which you can only tell by how he's a little sweaty"—why did she say *sweaty*? She didn't want him to think he looked sweaty—"and the next scene he's back at school without flaky nostrils or cold sores or—"

"Superheroes don't almost kill people who are trying to save them. Superheroes don't take credit for someone else's—"

"You didn't take it. I gave."

"What *you* did was heroic. Not just saving me, but then afterward, well . . . *saving* me. I don't even like those people, but to be the guy who almost drowns at his own party—a guy with his own pool who, you probably figured out, can barely fucking swim."

She laughed. *Fucking* sounded so wrong out of his mouth, nearly diplomatic. His accent was what Gretchen would later tell her was called *patrician*.

"You stayed behind," she said. "You didn't want to be like them. You didn't care what they thought. You said *no*, I heard you. You knew you were a shitty swimmer but you stayed out there anyway. That's the definition of brave." She wanted to tell him she didn't deserve his thinking she was noble. She was just a girl who wanted to bring home a story of someone *owing* her.

He stood there, quiet, then finally walked her to the divan by the fireplace. He put another log on and tucked a blanket over her knees as if she was the one who was sick. It felt so good to be touched, even through something woven and thick.

"I need to—" he said, grabbing some tissues from the box and wiping his nose as he headed toward the bathroom.

"It sucks to be sick," she said when he returned. "You probably want to be alone, like you were saying."

"You probably want to go back to sleep."

They shook their heads at the same time.

"Want to take a walk?" he said. "I'm restless. And"—he winked—"sweaty."

Gretchen had packed Carley for fashion and streamlining, so her warmest layer was a thin knit sweater coat. He tried to get her to wear his navy pea coat over it, but it was inches away from being able to button. In the end, he gave her a heavy wool sweater from his closet, new with the tags still on it. He pocketed them quickly, but still Carley caught the two-thousand-dollar price tag. As much as Gretchen liked to spend money, Suzanne outdid her.

"I can't," Carley said. "I'll stretch it out."

He didn't say, "No you won't," wedging a lie between them. He said instead, "I don't care." He pulled it over her head and over the swell of her hips. It came down to her knees. "Perfect," he said and turned her away from the mirror, an arm around her shoulders the whole walk through the Palace.

They walked down to the beach, where he pulled two lounges next to each other to face the water. They sat back and stared at the water, silent until he was overtaken by a fit of sneezing. "God, I'm selfish," he said, his voice cracking. "I almost drown you and take credit for *your* heroics, and I'm going to send you home with a cold as a souvenir."

She peered at him in the moonlight and saw his tears. "I almost never get sick," she said, and then, "You know when you come back from a whole day at Six Flags and try to lie down and it feels like you're still on a roller coaster? Every time I closed my eyes upstairs it felt like that, except with being underwater instead of with going upside down. The feeling of drowning didn't go away until I cried. What I mean is, I think you *need* to cry after something like that."

"I made out with this girl tonight by my pool," he blurted out.

"Um . . . good for you?"

He shook his head. "What I mean is, I knew I was sick, even if I seemed well because of this shitload of pills my mother made me swallow this afternoon." He sneezed again. "I'm not taking them right now because I hate the way they make me feel."

"Like, floaty."

He nodded. "Separate from myself. Anyway, I wouldn't have done something so selfish—messed around with someone knowing she'll catch this—except that Ian and some other guys were racing in the pool. I didn't want to swim in front of them, and she was an . . . excuse . . . to do something else."

"Was it that friend of Violet Burroughs's with the white suit and the huge—"

"Yeah."

"If it helps, I don't think telling her you had leprosy would have mattered."

He smiled through his tears. "Still, I *used* her. I just . . . that's not who I want to be."

"You're different," she said, as much as to herself as to him.

"*Different.* That's one way of putting it."

"I just meant, I don't know anyone who *thinks* about who they want to be. I think thinking about that makes you brave."

He wrapped her in his arms before she knew what was happening. What was most amazing was how *soft* he felt, though his leanness and his cheekbones suggested all angles. "Thank you," he whispered, and then, "Could we be friends?"

No one ever just came out and said things like that. People felt each other out and acted mutually cool, and for the first time she realized how cowardly that all was when all you had to do was say, I *like you.*

"I like you," she said, the words scary.

"I like you, too."

Only many years later, when she learned the phrase "sea change," would she know words even existed to describe your whole world shifting. At that moment, Hunter became a *person* to her instead of a hot guy, a popular guy, a superhero, a character. *Everyone* who'd ever seemed so different from her, beyond her, above her, all at once became just people. And even though it would be long time until she could fully imagine the world through anyone's eyes but her own, the seed of it was planted that night when she realized that every person in it—Hunter and Ian and even Gretchen—just wanted to be liked.

"I'll teach you to swim," she said, and he hugged her tighter against his blue cashmere pea coat.

For another half hour they said nothing, just moving the lounges right up against each other so they could stay warm. "One thing," he said, just when she thought from his breathing that he was falling asleep. "About us being friends."

She'd been expecting a caveat. It was too good to be true. "I know. We can't be friends *in front of* people. It's okay. I can't see, like, Ian Buchanan inviting me to—"

"No. *No.* God, no. That's not it. What I wanted to tell you . . . warn you . . . about is *me* . . . I'm sick, like this, a lot. Someone ten rows away on an airplane coughs, I catch it. It gets old. And it's disgusting. And I'll be a . . . drippy . . . friend."

It seemed like such a strange thing to worry about. You couldn't *help* if you got sick. "Did your friends in the city used to give you shit about it or something?"

"Didn't have friends."

"Any?"

"People weren't cruel. Not like what I saw tonight. *I* just didn't . . ." He shrugged. "When I'd go to people's houses because our parents knew each other, I'd try to figure out what you were supposed to do. How to hang out. I'd be thinking about how I was supposed to be being, which would get me to thinking about how people in books acted, and the next thing I knew I was so caught up in being in the book I wanted to live in that when someone called my name, I didn't remember where I was or what we were doing. All of which is to say, when it comes to being a friend, I don't quite know how."

She couldn't imagine wanting to *live in* a book. "You're supposed to do whatever you want. We could do, like, *anything*."

"Anything."

"Yeah. We can make it all up. I mean, if you want."

"I want."

They held each other, whispering secrets about who they were, Carley resting her head on his chest and her hand on his forehead, the coolness of which he said felt "delicious." It had never occurred to her that she could make someone feel good. She lied about having to go in to pee, then came back with blankets and more tissues and a washcloth soaked with water, like she'd seen Glory lay over Liam's forehead after he got an infection from a knife wound inflicted by the Order of Lethe.

Hunter's eyes were closed. When she smoothed the cloth over his forehead, water dripped into his hair and down his face.

"What the . . . ?" He laughed. Glory had known to wring it out first. "My God, you're the sweetest thing ever."

She fell asleep snuggled into his side, resolved to coming home to

Gretchen empty-handed. She wouldn't drag home Hunter's *gratitude* to present to Gretchen like a dead mouse.

They awoke surrounded by a foot of water, high tide. They huddled on their island of chaises, laughing. The Sound had taken on an unreal blue. Everything as far as Carley could see was that color, a reflection of the cloudless sky.

"You could get lost in it," he said.

"Like heaven," she said. "Not church-heaven, but the one in movies or on TV. Pretend heaven."

"May I . . ." Shyness flickered across his face. He took a book from his coat pocket. She'd never met anyone who carried around a journal, but for Hunter it seemed right. "May I write that down?"

For a moment she thought he was making fun of her. Nobody had ever in her life wanted what she had to say.

"It's beautiful." He wrote it down, pressing the words flat between the pages like a flower he was saving.

"It isn't babyish?" They were such *small* words.

He repeated it two, three, ten times, *Pretend Heaven*, making her listen to what she'd said, *the assonance*, he whispered, vowels echoing each other and turning her baby words deep, deep, deeper, a well of sound.

"I want to be you," he said. "Selfless. Honest. Brave."

She wished she'd been a girl who hadn't wanted his gratitude. She wished she'd been noble. She wished she'd been the person she'd let him think she was. But all she could do now was *become* that girl. Maybe a lie could become truth if you wanted it enough.

PART V

Theme

*All life is just a progression toward, and then a recession from,
one phrase—I love you.*

—F. Scott Fitzgerald, "The Offshore Pirate"

The Officers and Board of Directors of
The Glen Club
Cordially invite you to

"GIVING THANKS"
A GALA AUCTION

To benefit the following foundations:
Save the South American Pupsnail
Fox Glen Historical Preservation Society
Parents Against Ecstasy
The O'Neil Foundation for Literacy
Teach a Man to Fish

Saturday, the Twenty-first of November
The Glen Club
Fox Glen

6:30   Cocktails and Silent Auction
8:00   Dinner
9:00   Live Auction Commences

$500 per person   Black Tie

CHAPTER 45

Once upon a time, the invitations to the Glen Club's charity auction had urged its members to *Bid Against Hunger!* Even when the South Shore Soup Fund and Milk for All had been edged out as beneficiaries by organizations like the O'Neil Foundation for Adult Literacy and the Fox Glen Historical Preservation Society, *Bid Against Hunger!* had remained. But this year, given Emily Leighton Logan's insistence upon Save the South American Pupsnail being the headline cause, the event begged renaming.

A species so recently discovered in the rain forest that only last month did it receive a Latin name, the pupsnail faced extinction due to the rituals of indigenous tribes that worshiped the snails' anima and thus ceremonially devoured them during rites of healing, matrimony, and death. Despite the efforts of the American-based Save the South American Pupsnail Society, tribal leaders were proving intransigent about breeding some nice plump cattle in the snails' stead.

And so, with Emily Leighton Logan, vice-president of the Fox Glen branch of the Save the South American Pupsnail Society *and* vice-chair of the Glen Club Gala Auction Committee, threatening to deny her continued support to the latter unless the former was made a headline cause, the Auction Committee had settled on a new title that would exclude no organization, offend nobody, and match the gala's seasonal theme: *Giving Thanks.*

"And the point of this story," Bree said, from the chair she'd pulled beside the bed where Carley was propped up with pillows, pretending to be sick as she had all week, "besides convincing me that I really don't want to attend this event tomorrow, is—"

"If you get too hung up on forcing things to fit a theme—like *hunger*—it gets stupid. Like, last year the committee shoehorned in Parents Against Ecstasy as a beneficiary by saying it *quelled the hunger for drugs*." She held up the newest stack of pages Bree had given her. "Your 'hunger,' the theme you like way too much, is the blurring of what's real and what's not. Buck's delusions alone are enough to drive it home. So really you don't need these pages about how what the contestants say is going to be used out of context to make up a completely different story the producers want to tell, or this stuff about them reshooting the contestants' entrance to a challenge over and over so that they spend a whole morning walking through the same door again and again. You take up so much space over-obviousing the theme that you lose what the book's *about*. A girl and boy, remember? How she helps him hide his going Medieval so he won't be taken off the show and his parents won't want to kill him or send him to the loony bin for ruining their chance at a million dollars. It's about her saving him."

"Like I keep telling you, people don't *save*."

Gretchen's voice bounced into the room. "They offer weekend ski trips," she said from her threshold sweet spot.

Inaudible reply from Francis.

"Well, she can *help* the other girls, *teach* them. It'll be good for her self-esteem."

Taped to Carley's mirror was a brochure for Cypress Hill Academy. "Fat School," Carley had called it. *Where the new you awaits*, it promised. Below a photo of five smiling zaftig girls arm-and-arm were before-and-after shots. Befores were stripped to swimsuits on a stark white background, their eyes avoiding the camera. Afters posed in flowing dresses, leaning against trees, inviting the photographer to come listen to a secret.

It was hard to know if Carley's week of faking illness had been a response to Gretchen's pushing the issue of Carley spending next semester at Cypress Hill "to get her ready for a *beautiful* senior year at Montclair" or just a way to avoid seeing Hunter. Gretchen had summoned doctors to test for Epstein-Barr, Lyme, mono, and other potentially Sweet-Sixteen-ruinous diseases, every one of them deeming Carley healthy.

As far as Bree was concerned, Carley was doing more staying home from school, anyway. She was reading. And asking questions. And who could blame her for not wanting to subject herself to an English class where the teacher proclaimed: *In a well-executed story, theme is umbilicus; in badly executed one, it is menses.*

No, Bree had told Carley, she had no idea what that was supposed to mean. Was her teacher perhaps on medication?

"They teach young women *lifelong healthy habits,*" Gretchen's voice touted. "And look at this graph: scientific evidence of an inverse relationship between weight and self-esteem."

After a thirty-second respite, Gretchen appeared in the flesh, opening Carley's door without knocking and clad in a nautical-style double-breasted jacket that made Bree want to walk her off the plank.

"Just for a semester," Gretchen said, without prelude, as if forgetting that the conversations she had with her husband on the threshold were not supposed to exist. She took the pamphlet off the mirror and brought it to the bed. "Just *look* at this list of activities. They offer *ice skating.*"

"Nothing prettier than fat girls in skating costume," Carley mumbled.

Gretchen read statistics aloud. Three hours of fitness daily. Five miles. Three pounds a week. Sixty pounds a year. Absently, she added, "I doubt they have costumes." She tore herself away from the pamphlet. "Tell her how much easier it is to be *normal,*" she said to Bree.

"I'm no authority on that."

She looked at Carley. "I'll buy you *anything* you want to wear when you return. You can be *anyone.* Just *happy.*"

"The artist John Singer Sargent," Bree said, "was once commissioned to paint a portrait of a woman who didn't know when to be quiet. She was constantly moving her lips, asking which smile looked better. Finally, he suggested painting over her mouth."

"There's a reason most artists are starving," Gretchen said, slitting her eyes.

"Stop insulting her," Carley told Bree after Gretchen had slammed the door.

"I told her an anecdote. I can't control what she reads into it."

"You called her dinner two nights ago *chicken simulacra*." Skinless, poached, and odorless.

"It wasn't like she *cooked* it."

"She *ordered* it made. Which for her is even *more* personal. Nagel's always saying that everyone is the hero of his or her own story. The bad guys don't know they're bad guys at all; what seems evil might just be good, inside-out. Listen, at least go to the stupid auction, like she keeps asking you? She paid for the ticket. Paid equals personal, get it? And anyway, showing you off is in your contract."

"Since when do you know what's in my contract?"

"Did some reading. I've been bored. You want to get paid after all this, right? And anyway, Justin needs you there. He let his mother add him as an auction item—Brunch with Author Justin Leighton. I know because Gretchen was bitching about it holding up the program being printed. I know he's a jerk. Or was. Or whatever. But you still can't make him go alone. I can't believe you haven't figured it out, but he gets these attacks where he's afraid he's dying. He gets so lost in the fear that he's as good as dead. Kind of like what happens in your book."

"*Dark Ages?*"

"*Scylla.*"

"You mean, the way *Odysseus* gets lost." Carley was reading *Scylla*?

"I mean the way the whole *book* gets lost. I'm sure there's a lot in it that's too smart for me to understand, but I got this feeling it wasn't Odysseus being lost or stuck or whatever as much as *you* were. I figure writing is probably like one of those Choose Your Own Adventures. The writer picks from *ifs*. Little *ifs* like, *If you, Odysseus, try to escape from the sea of pop-up ads by force quitting, turn to page five hundred and ninety-two. If you try to escape by attempting to click on the little X's faster than the ads appear, turn to page five hundred and ninety-seven.* And also big *ifs*, like, *If sounding smart is more important to you than telling a story, keep putting your characters into hopeless situations so you can make your point about the meaninglessness of life or plot or whatever. If telling a story is more important, let your characters get saved.*

"I think you couldn't make yourself choose. You redid a famous story that's supposed to be about finding home, but then you wanted to be too cool for the happy ending that came with it. So you just sat down and refused to move, like that time in the maze. No adventure at all."

" 'Obesity is a choice,' " Gretchen's voice opined from her sweet spot. "The pamphlet says so. You can *choose* to be thin."

"She's trying to do what she thinks is right," Carley said softly.

"It's a mistake," Bree said, trying to control the tremble in her voice, "to conflate the author and her work."

"Nagel always says, *You are what you do.*" Carley handed Bree the pages, marked up mercilessly with comments.

Just tell me a story, it said at the top.

CHAPTER 46

Hunter sat at the foot of Carley's bed. All week she'd refused to see him, insisting she was contagious and couldn't deal with getting him sick, no matter how many times he'd left her voice mails saying he'd catch his death for her. If it weren't for Gretchen walking him upstairs this afternoon and insisting Carley receive him on his birthday, he would have been driving home crying as he had all week.

"*Listen*, C, please: this morning when I woke up, I thought about what I really need. I'm done with the pills—they're over, gone. Flushed. They were circumstantial, not routine. And I honestly think I could drink like a *person*—I don't have to go into treatment to be in control. It's my birthday, and I want to start fresh, and Carley Wells is the only thing that ever makes me feel new."

"Wow," she said. "Is this where I clap?" Wearing Bree's burgundy corduroy smoking jacket with black satin lapels unbuttoned over candy-cane flannel pajamas, she looked like the kind of girl who didn't care what people thought and didn't care for people who *did*. People like him.

"What do you want from me?" he whispered.

"Nothing."

He tried to take her hand; she pulled it away. Every action felt so stilted, like reading stage directions aloud.

"It's not the pills I'm pissed about," she said. "It's not even so much what you said the night before. It's that you ran when Bree told you the truth.

You left me a *note* instead of apologizing face-to-face for treating me like a condom you would have used and thrown away if I had let you."

"*Used.* C . . ." He wanted to say that hadn't been *him*. He wanted to tell her how it had felt to be so out of his mind with shame that he'd had to numb himself as soon as he possibly could. He wanted to tell her that even now he was, in fact, being swaddled by five Vicodins, and that he wished he could stop lying to her and that he couldn't remember the last time he'd told a whole truth.

"Can I just lie down with you for a few minutes? Before I go? Once . . . before you leave . . . me—Rock Star *said* I'd lose you—I want to be able to say to myself, *That was the last time we lay in bed together.*"

He considered the vial in his jacket pocket. Were there enough pills left to close it all out? He wouldn't be afraid to die like this, inhaling the smell of her neck. Soft, like talcum. Like the smell of good. He used to be good.

"H? H, don't cry." She sat up. "Even if I wanted to leave you, you're, like, part of me. No matter how you change, no matter who you become."

You belong to each other, Rock Star had said. *Belong.* Like a toy with scratched-up paint or matted fur that could still be loved. Like in a story.

"I could be better," he whispered in her arms, grateful to be held. He hated his body for never having been able to summon attraction for hers. It would make her so happy to be wanted. He so wanted to *want* her. "Maybe not good, but *better.* There's just so *much.*" He woke up every day to the certainty that someone—Larry, Griffin, Suzanne, his teachers, his friends, the Princeton admissions board, Rock Star, Bree, Carley—would discover something else about him. This morning Ian had texted him Bad luck, with a link to You Tube.

What had been a tiny item in last week's local paper—"Against All Odds, Montclair Triumphant in Tournament"—had turned into online entertainment—"Soccer Freakout"—when somebody realized the rampaging player tossed from the game was the stepson of none other than Camilla Campden Cay, *Wake Up America!*'s resident dermatologist, whose perky medical segments and perfect skin made her—according to this year's *People* magazine poll—America's favorite TV doctor.

The footage had no doubt been shot by one of Hunter's friends' parents. He'd clicked the arrow on the screen and watched himself fuck up again and again.

"If everyone else would just go away . . . ," he sobbed.

She whispered words over and over like waves, until they lulled him into listening. "H, we don't have to be here."

She told him about running away, a plan she said he'd been too drunk to remember hearing last weekend. And for the first time in months he felt something like hope.

"Let's go right now," he said, imagining being someplace open and new, taking care of each other. Even if he couldn't love her the way she wanted, he'd love her every other way. It could be enough.

"We just have to hang on a couple of weeks, H. Until my birthday."

"We don't need your Sweet Sixteen money. I have almost thirty thousand left in the safe. And I can *work*. Get a job in a restaurant or a store. Let's just go before something gets in our way. Come to the auction with me tonight, tell Gretchen you're staying over at the Palace afterward. She'll be so thrilled you're leaving the house that she won't try to bother you about coming home until late tomorrow. No one will realize we're gone until then." With tomorrow being Suzanne's birthday, which always eclipsed his own, his own mother might not notice until next week.

"But *Bree*," she said. If they left now, Carley reminded him, before the book was complete, Bree wouldn't be paid. "We can't do that to her," she said, stroking the back of his hand. "We'll have time to plan this way. Buy stuff, sell stuff. It'll make it more exciting. Like packing for a trip or picking out clothes before you go out. Or, um"—she dropped her eyes—"foreplay."

"Yes," he said as they got out of bed holding hands and he watched her pack into an overnight bag what she'd need for the auction tonight—makeup and shoes and a dress and a lacey pink bra and panties set that made him feel like crying again for their being so large and sweet and brave.

"Yes," he repeated as he carried her bag down the stairs and out to his car. On they'd go to the Play Palace, where he'd make himself go cold turkey, distracting himself from the cravings by planning what they'd need to take with them and what they'd leave behind. On they'd go to his room to map out a future while he ignored what his body yearned for. On they'd go to the rest of their lives, where in only a few weeks he could be clean and *be* somebody—a busboy or a waiter or a dishwasher—instead of wading through years of school and rules and judgments just to end up stuck as Griffin Cay's son, Suzanne Cay's ornament, Larry Talbright's blot.

I am a busboy, he practiced in his head as he turned the key in the ignition. He imagined coming home to Carley's arms tired and dirty, knowing he'd *done* something for real. "Yes."

CHAPTER 47

Hunter's bed was nested in lists. To Bring. To Buy. To Sell. To Learn. All around them painted masqueraders danced and drank, the party on his walls growing louder and hotter, while in the middle of it all they lay together speaking almost in whispers. They'd stopped at a bookstore on the way to the Palace to buy guidebooks and maps, which they'd divided up once they'd gone up to his room, searching them for places they might reinvent themselves.

He pulled back from where he was running his finger down Idaho and looked at her with brimming eyes.

"What's wrong, H?"

He shrugged and wiped the tears with the back of his hand. She could see it tremble. "Sore throat. Headache. Same old. A million germs colonizing me."

She'd never seen him so upset about coming down with something.

He wiped his eyes again. "I look good, right?" It wasn't a question he'd ever asked her—not one she'd ever heard him ask anyone—though she realized for the first time that he wanted to ask it all the time.

"You look amazing, H." It was the truth. It was always the truth. "Even when you're sick you look better than anyone. You'll look gorgeous in the new tux." It hung on the back of his door—a severely fitted suit with narrow-cut lapels, it was a more dramatic look than he usually went for, as if Justin was rubbing off on him.

"It's when someone's most contagious, you know. Right before the symptoms. Right before you can tell." His voice broke.

She put her arms around him. All week she'd thought about what he said last weekend—about feeling eroded by repeated illnesses, about his being so self-conscious and ashamed about it that he'd been drugging himself to escape it. "Are you worried about our field trip? About getting sick once we're gone? Because it'll be okay. I mean, you *will* get sick, but we'll put aside money for doctors and antibiotics and sick days, and I'll always take care of you and I'll never, ever mind. We'll laugh all the time and you won't have to worry about going to school the next day. We'll hang out in bed and I'll bring you library books and soup, and you know what? I bet you won't get sick so much after a while. I think you just need rest. You've been tired for, like, *years*."

He pulled back and smiled through his tears. "What if I'm too selfish to be a good field trip buddy? You want to be happy and I don't really know *how* to be happy anymore and you'll *catch* my unhappiness and—"

"You don't need to be *fun*, H. You're not a toy. You don't have to worry about making me unhappy, or making me happy, or about . . . what we talked about that time at the Sound. I know we'll never. . . . You don't have to worry about me wanting . . . you."

He shook his head for a long time, wiping at tears that kept returning. "You have me," he said at last, cupping her chin. "I love you." He brought his lips to hers like it was the most natural thing. He kissed her eyelids and then her cheekbones and the hollow of her neck. It felt like being tasted.

They lay down together, the maps rustling like leaves, a whole country trapped beneath them. He unbuttoned her blouse and teased her nipples through her bra. She stroked the bulge of his erection beneath his zipper. He groaned deep in his throat.

They ran their hands everywhere. It was nothing at all like the groping with Colin or the few other guys she'd messed around with at parties. She remembered thinking about those guys' body parts as something separate from *them*: there was Colin, and then there was also Colin's mouth, and Colin's hands, and Colin's penis. But Hunter was all one canvas that she finger painted with strokes he kept returning and doubling with colors playful and serious and sweet and even sad, forming something beautiful and complicated and new. No one had ever told her that sex could be a whole bunch of feelings at once, all layered and swirled.

"Could we do this all the time?" she whispered.

"Constantly," he laughed. "Though I think it'll get us thrown off that Greyhound bus you're intent on taking."

"Okay, not on the bus." She giggled.

"We could *just* do this for now, C. There's no rush. We don't have to do anything you don't—"

"I want everything."

He smiled and stroked her cheek. "There are things that I want to do for you, things you'd like more than intercourse." That he used a book-word for it didn't seem cold. He'd learned to make love by reading books, by seeing the word *intercourse* again and again until the word itself made him hum. Hunter *thought* in book words—and now, together, they were bringing the book to life. "Oh, that's gorgeous . . ." He squeezed his eyes closed tight as she stroked him, like someone fighting not to wake up from a dream. "What I meant before, C? We could save your first time . . ."

She waited until he opened his eyes again. "I don't want to be saved."

CHAPTER 48

Item #3—Trio of Brassieres (see trophy case display)

Three one-of-a-kind collectables—with Marvel-Bra lift built right in!

a. Gaultier reproduction—relive the eighties in this Madonna-esque cone bra!

b. Adam+Eve—get natural in these silk fig "leaf" cups supported by fabric "twig" straps!

c. Ho Ho Ho—make it a very merry Xmas in this red leather and velvet bustier trimmed with white fur and bells. *Santa!* embroidered on one cup, *Baby!* on the other!

Donated by the Wells Family

Francis stood in the hallway outside the Club ballroom, smiling at the case where his creations had for two weeks supplanted the usual tennis loving cups and silver statuettes of golfers frozen at the apex of swings. He knew for a fact that Cissy and Greer Gardner had complained to the Auction Committee about their once-owned-by-F.-Scott-Fitzgerald-and-authenticated-by-Sotheby's croquet mallets being in proximity to his torsos. The decorative cornucopia spilling faux food between the two donations had been inserted as appeasement.

The live auction began in five minutes; the Trio was up in twenty. Five minutes an item, give or take, with applause. Last year Francis and Gretchen hadn't gotten out until three a.m. Hunter and Carley had fallen asleep hours earlier on a sofa in the Club's parlor, snuggled like puppies. The catalogue of items seemed especially endless this year with emperor's-new-clothes items like the right to bestow upon the pupsnail an official common name. Most likely, it would be Carson Logan and Emily Leighton Logan who would trump everyone else's bids and dub it *Logans' Mollusk*. Francis himself had no desire to be the savior of *Wells' Slug*. The proceeds of his own donations were specifically earmarked for Teach a Man to Fish, a charity that helped actual poor people acquire training for actual jobs. He *believed* in Teach a Man to Fish, and thus, in addition to his donations, had underwritten such a large portion of the event that he could have had the Gardners' pretentious mallets relegated to the ignominy of the *silent* auction on his demand. When a man believed in something he did it big.

Big, as in telling Suzanne, whom he saw coming toward him in the reflection of the glass case, that she had to call off her engagement. He'd file divorce papers tomorrow if he had to, never mind waiting. He'd be the husband who treats her like a flower, the stepfather who loves her son like his own child. It was time, he'd realized this afternoon as he'd ripped the stamens out of a lily before taking it.

"We need to talk," he said, turning.

She nodded. "Someplace discreet."

In a coat closet at the other side of the building, he took from inside his jacket a single red tulip plucked from one of the silent auction table arrangements. With a bar of empty hangers as witnesses, he asked for her hand.

Item #4—Political Brunch for Eight on the <u>Dawn Bright</u>

Ahoy! Lawrence Talbright IV invites you and seven guests for an afternoon aboard his yacht in the company of his father, Senator Lawrence Talbright III (RI). Perfect birthday gift for child with keen interest in government. Mutually agreed upon date.

Donated by the Talbright Family

Marry him? Francis? Suzanne hadn't suspected he was delusional.

"Leave Larry," he repeated. "Leave Fox Glen. I'll build us a house far away. A place the kids would like. The *beach*, Carley loves the beach." He held her face in his hands, stroked her cheek with his right thumb, callused from years of holding sewing needles. "Fox Glen's a coffin," he said, "and I won't be buried."

He smelled to her like he had twenty years ago, a hot strong scent she'd loved the way she did the horses at her parents' stable. Something to be ridden, then washed off her hands. She'd buried her head in those animals' necks and run her hands over their withers. They'd loved her with their eyes, the way Francis had in the Hamptons the summer they met, fucking with his eyes open. But she'd had people to groom them. Train them. Sell them. She hadn't been raised to be a caretaker of beasts.

The kids, he'd called Hunter and his daughter, like they were a pair. The exact issue she'd come in here to discuss. She and Larry needed Carley to spend time away from her son, who hadn't let go of Carley's hand since they'd arrived. The girl was so immature, so ill-at-ease. Her tent of a dress was made of a thready ecru material, like silk that had been attacked by a hairbrush, the hem and cuffs unfinished. It might be cute on a smaller girl who could wear insouciance—but in Carley's size it brought to mind a cocoon. Her just standing near Hunter diminished his crispness.

He'd insisted on taking his own car to the Club so he and Carley might leave early, despite Suzanne's reminding him that Ian had engaged a limo to take Hunter out for his birthday after the auction. He'd been rude to her fiancé when Larry had mentioned that driving entailed not drinking. And then he'd criticized Suzanne's dress.

"As I've mentioned, chartreuse isn't your color."

It was a beaded silk faille gown, nearly identical to the one Jackie had worn—according to Suzanne's dressmaker—when Pablo Casals had played at the White House.

"Do you even know who Pablo Casals *is*, Mother?"

"Why, Pablo *Casals*."

"Do you know what he *played*? Where he was from? Why it's important?"

Do I hear one thousand for brunch with a four-term senator and his charming son? she heard the auctioneer say as she closed the closet door, leaving Francis alone inside, rubbing his eyes.

Item #16—Name the South American Pupsnail

Save a Species, Win Immortality. In a once-in-a-lifetime opportunity, the winning bidder earns the right to bestow upon the newly discovered and greatly endangered pupsnail (Latin name *Cepaea canis*) a common name. A species eternally named for you would be a legacy; a species named for someone you love would be a priceless gift. Name plaque and pair of pupsnails in hundred-gallon aquarium home will be presented to winning bidder at a tribute lunch for twenty at the Leighton-Logan estate on a mutually agreed-upon date in December. One hundred percent of the winning bid earmarked for efforts to protect the pupsnails from their aggressors.

Donated by the Leighton-Logan Family

Fifteen thousand once, fifteen twice, called the auctioneer. *Fifteen-five to save a species.*

"Sixteen!" shouted Cissy Gardner from her table.

Do I hear seventeen to christen this hitherto undiscovered creature?

"Seventeen," said Suzanne, who had her groundskeepers salt snails to death.

"Eighteen!" shouted Cissy.

Hunter sneezed. The illness he'd all but forgotten about in the warm rush of this afternoon was starting to drain him.

"Are you never not sick?" Ian said. Smirks bloomed at the table and were swallowed. He'd put into words what no one ever did.

"Perhaps not." He took a shallow breath that caught. Eight hours now without a Vicodin. Not a drink all night.

He plunged his trembling hands into his jacket pockets. His pants pockets had been sewn shut by Antoine to keep their line crisp.

Carley squeezed his leg.

He could *do* this. For her.

Ian whispered something into Amber's ear that was probably about Hunter, something Hunter could tell from the look on her face was cruel. Much of what came out of Ian's mouth was mean. He'd always said Amber was well liquor—good for a buzz, but why settle for it? But with the date he was supposed to be bringing home from Princeton having dumped him last night, he was paying Amber attention he never had before.

A server placed in front of Hunter a lavender-scented crème brûlée topped with cage of hardened sugar syrup filled with a drift of sugared rose petals.

At a table across the room, Suzanne would be picking up her spoon, putting it down, tilting her head at the cage like a bird while wondering how Jackie might approach such a dessert. Carley's father would pry his apart, snapping bars like wishbones. Justin would wonder what Bree would do if he tried to pass her a petal on his tongue, while next to him, Bree would deconstruct the dessert as a symbol. Amber's mother would tap a silk-wrapped fingernail against the cage to examine its soundness and imagine commissioning for a summer party a sugar ornament twenty times the size, which she would hang from the center of a tent and fill with blue and green hummingbirds that would buzz around the vitreous cage until they pecked themselves free in candied bursts.

Hunter begged them to quiet their thoughts. His head was full, and he no longer wanted what Nick Carraway called *riotous excursions with privileged glimpses into the human heart*. He just wanted to be with one person. He just wanted two weeks to fly by. He just wanted to be *home*, somewhere else.

He looked at Carley and relished the way she dug into the custard, the way she made food look worth eating. He took a petal in his mouth and felt its velvet caress.

For her, he told himself, even if he ended up throwing up for days. It would be all out of him, then—the cravings, the lies. But how to conceal from her the withdrawal?

The auctioneer's patter amplified, quickened, beating like an anxious heart: *Do I hear, do I hear, do I hear . . .*

Twenty-seven thousand, twenty-eight. Thirty! Thirty thousand dollars going . . .

The shouting grew frenzied, everyone bidding on the last unnamed thing on earth.

Item #24—Lift Yourself to the Stars!

Be the first woman in the universe to wear THE GALAXY—the only bra with ELEVEN POINTS OF SUPPORT. Own a MARVEL-ous prototype six months before its public release. Private, custom fitting in your home.

Donated by the Wells Family

Do I hear five hundred for eleven points of support? Eleven points, an historical bra...

Every friend Gretchen had—and *didn't*—was tittering at the idea of anyone paying Francis to paw her. The torso was midnight blue with constellations that looked like eczema. The white cotton prototype was naked and raw. Gretchen could taste scorn in the air, like when people had raved at the Club's end-of-summer dance about how wonderful Carley looked while whispering to each other that Gretchen should have sued that diet camp for a refund.

"What are you trying to *do* to her?" Francis had yelled when the Cypress Hill application had arrived. "Why are you always wanting to change our *kid*? Can't you make a hobby of redecorating, like Suzanne?"

Seven hundred going once, going twice...

"Cheap fucks," her husband said now, and not in a whisper.

"What is *wrong* with you?" she hissed. Earlier, leaning down to get a pill from her purse, she'd seen him *touching himself* under the tablecloth as he ate the rose petal dessert. She stared now at his hands—huge, yet able to hand sew a hundred tiny stitches as neat as a machine. She had loved those hands when she'd met him. She'd imagined them protecting her.

Larry Talbright diverted attention from Francis's outburst with a story about taking flying lessons in Newport.

Francis looked up from his drink and gave Suzanne Cay a long look that told a story Gretchen wished she hadn't read and that for months afterward would wish she could forget. "Sounds like courting death."

Item #31—South African Dream Safari

The ultimate hunting experience awaits you at Wildebeest Game
Ranch. You and a guest to enjoy seven days of hunting, airfare,
two days of massage (couples or individual), private cottage, meals
and beverages, and reserve wines. Package includes four trophies:
black or blue wildebeest, impala, eland, and zebra.

Donated by the Logan-Leighton Family

"Good for what ails you," Ian said, doctoring Hunter's soda with his
flask. Hunter drank half of it without coming up for air.

"What are you *doing*?" Carley whispered.

"It's barely a drink, C." Hunter flushed and passed her his glass. "Taste.
It's practically medicinal."

"You're tons of fun tonight, Wellsie," Ian said. He refreshed Amber's
drink and squeezed her ass.

"Don't," Amber said.

"Carley's right, I'm driving," Hunter said.

"Limo," Ian said, shaking his head. "The City. Underground party. Your
birthday, cousin."

"No," Hunter told him for the tenth time. He leaned in to her. "I'm sorry,
C. I won't finish it. I thought you understood what I meant by *drink like a
person*. But if it makes you nervous I'll turn into an asshole, I'll stop
altogether."

He was so calm that she felt bad about making so much of it. "I don't
know, H. You don't have to . . . I . . . I don't want to tell you what to do."

"Stop being a pig," she heard Amber said to Ian. "My *parents* are at the
next table. Would you do that to Violet in front of the Burroughses?"

"Heads," she heard over her shoulder. "In Vernal we collected snow
globes. Rich people keep *heads* for souvenirs?"

She turned. Bree looked classy-hot in the dress Hunter had had his tailor repair for her. Like someone who belonged with a wounded billion-aire who twenty minutes earlier had bid an obscene amount on a Cartier women's diamond fountain pen.

Bree knelt next to Carley's chair on the side away from Hunter. "Justin wanted me to check on you. He thought you looked . . . serious. His exact words being *Minor Wells is vexing*."

"We're fine."

"I didn't ask after Hunter, who, if you ask me, looks like an endless night. I'm checking on *you*."

"I'm great. Hunter just has a cold. And tell Justin I'll try to look unserious. So how's the last challenge going?" Having made it to the finals in the pages Bree had given her last night, Buck's and Jules's families now had to battle for a million dollars by trying to kill a mechanical, fire-breathing dragon that kept backing them toward the edge of a cliff. Bree had sounded way more interested in the safety mechanisms involved—particularly the harnesses and bungee-type cords the contestants wore that attached them to out-of-camera-sight cranes for when people stepped off the cliff—than in whether Buck and Jules would end up together at the end of the show.

Bree shook her head. "I'd planned to talk to you about the end, but when I looked for you this afternoon, you'd left the house. Finally."

Carley had a feeling she was going to have to read paragraphs upon paragraphs about the history of stunt safety.

"*Do I hear forty-five thousand?*" cried the auctioneer. License to kill was going over even bigger than snail rescue.

Carley looked around at all the paddles, then noticed Justin rubbing his face and looking pale. "Bree, he's having an attack, I think. Go *be* with him. And remember he's too scared to be told not to be scared."

She turned back to the table just as Hunter took something from the small mahogany oval from which he was always dispensing remedies to people with headaches. "Can he say *eland* any louder?" he whispered, and then, smiling, "And are you *certain* you want to run away from life with a dandy who owns a pillbox?"

"Totally sure. Sorry you're sick on your birthday, H."

He shook his head. "It's been the perfect day. Some aspirin and I'll be good as new."

She rubbed her temples and stuck out her hand. "Spare a couple? The auctioneer is giving me a headache. H, did you hear me?" she asked when he didn't answer. "You sure you're okay?"

He nodded slowly, looked about to say something, and didn't.

Later, she'd remember that long pause before he put the pills in her hand.

Item #37—Tea with Bestselling Author Justin Leighton

Four guests to join Mr. Leighton for a private midday repast and a stimulating salon at the Rose Room at the Fox Glen Inn. Includes signed copies of *Crawling* and *Clinging*, plus a sneak peek at the first page of the final installment in the Spindles Trilogy, *Climbing*.

Donated by the Leighton-Logan Family

At item number thirty-three, twenty minutes before he was due to stand at the podium, the numbness began. He rubbed at his chin as if he could revive it like a leg that's fallen asleep, as if all his face needed was blood. His own breathing sounded like someone else's, a person waiting over his shoulder with something piercing.

Until Tori, he'd never given thought to the fragility of skin, not even when people had thrown things to him onstage—teddy bears and underwear and once, at an O'Neil Foundation dinner, an antique pocket watch whose monogram revealed it to belong to a drunk, closeted heir to an oil fortune. When the watch had bruised his cheekbone, he'd only laughed. Later, people would remember Justin ignoring how gifts could hurt.

The day of the shooting, he'd been reading a chapter from *Clinging* in which Jenny Spindle kneels in the snow at her grandmother's grave and sings her solo for the Christmas concert. He couldn't remember the sound of the gunshots now. Only the pain.

The numbness rushed over his face, no creeping tonight, and plunged downward to his lungs to steal his breath.

"Justin?" Bree said from miles away. "Justin, hey—"

And then he was running.

Outside on the empty deck he gasped for air, but there wasn't enough. He grabbed the railing, leaned over, and gagged. Bree's hand was on his back. He felt her holding back his hair.

"You get sick like someone fictional," she said, an arm around his waist. "Quick and neat."

She walked him out of sight of the windows. They sat at the top of the flight of steps that led down to the beach.

"How long till it passes?" When he didn't answer, she added, "They'll just think you were trashed. At worst, people near the door might have seen the *idea* of you vomiting. Not like when I barfed all over Armani."

"It was Versace. I was an ass and Marguerite was mean and you were ashamed, nothing changes." He shook his head. "Anyone else would have just hated us. Why didn't you hate us?"

"Didn't know any better."

His hands shook as he tried to light a cigarette and gave up. "Tried to burn this whole place down when I was twelve," he said, gesturing at the Club, "thus guaranteeing my being sent away to school." He'd started with petty vandalism a few months earlier—he'd hated it for its pretensions of being like a home, one where people who didn't know each other could afford to be nice. After the tulips he pulled up from its gardens replanted themselves, and the curse words he'd scrawled on the walls of the ecru bathrooms were scrubbed away, and the severed fringes of rugs magically regrew, he'd set fire to the couch in the parlor just to see if he could turn the Club into *real* home, a place where things could be broken for good.

"If you want to talk, Justinian. About what happened, about that day . . ."

"You think I need to *get it out*, as they say?" He shook his head. "Like it's something removable. A tumor. A bullet. Did you see the TV movie? RealLife Channel: *Lit Star: The Rise and Fall of Justin Leighton*? I couldn't miss it myself. Needed to see how I turned out."

The actor who'd played him was taller. And Character-Justin had sex with a fan in the History section of a chain bookstore, then signed her ass, *Best*. But otherwise it was accurate enough. Billionaire playboy, clad in costume-y clothing and an idiolect only sometimes comprehensible, writes a book. America crushes on him. The highbrow and lowbrow both claim him, saying each other can't really *understand* his work. He writes a second book. When he reads, it's performance.

He saw taller-him being shot five times. He watched the deaths of the woman in the front row and her three-year-old boy. The boy wears a green shirt with a turtle on it, and though he is not the real boy and it's not the real shirt—though he's a tiny actor whose eyes would pop right back open after the director yells *cut!* and who'd get chocolate ice cream afterward or a puppy—all Justin could think about was that shirt that stood in for a shirt that probably didn't have a turtle on it that his mother had picked out special that morning to go see Rock Star Leighton.

Screaming, then sirens. Fade to black. *Dear Justin*, said a voice-over. Tori's fan letter—the last of seventy she'd saved to her computer—appeared on the screen:

> When you read, I hear God. <u>Crawling</u> is my Old Testament,
> <u>Clinging</u> my New. Your words I consume, body and blood.
> Soon we will be we, cleaved together in heaven. Ascended.

A single cello began an elegy. A blurb reported Justin Leighton had never again made a public appearance.

"Know what the movie left out?" Justin said to Bree. "The *form letter* she received seventy times. The letter they all received."

Dear Tory:

Thanks for reading my books! I hope to have <u>Climbing</u> finished
soon. In the meantime, check out my Web site,
www.justinleighton.com, for behind-the-scenes info on the
Spindles, my blog, and my updated schedule of readings.

Better get back to writing!

Best,

Justin

His fan mail came in sacks. The college kids from Blaine who interned
for him were told to send form responses care of the return addresses on the
envelopes, whenever possible not even wasting the time to open them.
People's love and respect were tossed in the recycling bin unread, little pieces
of heart.

"All those people—the letter-writers, the reading-goers, that woman
with her child—thought I was someone to trust. They didn't know me.
Words I put on paper, *things I made up*, made them think I was real."

Bree shrugged. "You asked people to believe while they turned the
pages. That they still believed afterward—that they thought you were who
they wished you were—was their choice."

A door opened from the back of the ballroom, the auctioneer's voice
pouring out as Emily Leighton Logan peered out, looking for her son. *Lot
thirty-seven*, the auctioneer announced, saying Justin's name like a
commandment.

He ran his hand over the back of Bree's beaded dress as she helped him
to his feet. It felt alive, like water.

CHAPTER 49

"Wake up."

Carley swatted at the hand shaking her shoulder. If she squeezed her eyes tighter, it would go away.

"We have to go!"

She was having a dream about shiny, swimmy things that—

"Carley! *Please*, wake up!"

She opened her eyes and saw legs. Denimed and neoned and stockinged and bare, they stomped and glided and hopped. In pairs. Every leg had a partner, a match, someone to go with on the ark. Was there an ark? She looked up. There were people attached to the legs, head-bobbing and smiling and dancing themselves to liquid. An ocean of people lapping at her corner of the floor.

"Stay awake, stay awake, stay awake," Amber said beside her. She brought a bottle of water to Carley's lips. "You're scaring me."

She drank it because she didn't want Amber to be scared. "Where's the ark?" she said when it was empty. "Where's Hunter?" All those legs, and none in narrow-cut tux pants.

"I don't get you," Amber said. "You spend half the night telling Hunter not to drink and then you decide out of nowhere to get *wasted*?"

She didn't remember deciding to drink. She didn't remember coming here. She didn't even know where *here* was.

It was impossible to tell where one glow-sticking water-guzzler began and another ended. Hundreds of people sucked and chewed pacifiers like babies, none of them paying her any attention, as if there was nothing strange about someone having gone to sleep in a corner of a massive dance floor. The air smelled of VapoRub.

"It's late," Amber said, "*really* late. We need to go. You've been passed out forever. How much of Ian's booze did you *have?*"

She tried to remember back to the auction: Hunter measuring out in sips the first drink Ian had doctored for him, telling her with his eyes *I can drink slowly, see, I can drink just a little.* Her parents leaving all of a sudden wearing the tight smiles of a fight they wanted to have at home. Justin going, going, gone for fifty grand to Suzanne, who won him for Hunter like a carnival prize he didn't want. Hunter on his fourth doctored drink. Ian saying the limo was waiting and saying the night was waiting and saying Larry keeps looking over at Hunter so wouldn't this be a good time to leave.

She remembered feeling the way you did right before you fell asleep, there but not there, kind of floaty, and watching. And yes, now that she thought about it, she'd let Ian doctor one of her drinks, too, but she didn't remember why. "Maybe you shouldn't," she remembered Hunter saying, and remembered thinking he was teasing her, imitating her.

Flashes of being in the limo. The bottle she and Hunter and Amber and Ian were passing around. *We're like winos,* she'd giggled. *Except with brandy. Like, brandos.* Hunter, thumping Ian's gut from the facing seat: *Marlons.* She'd spilled on herself. *Fish?* And then the touches, touches, touches that Hunter had kept giving her as the two of them had curled up on the seat, a treasure hunt of touches, Hunter hiding clues in clever places and Carley finding them and needing the game to end, finally, and wanting it to go on and on. *Hold back as long as you can,* Hunter had whispered. *I'll bring you over, trust me.*

"It's three a.m.," Amber said. "I'm supposed to be home by now. My parents are going to freak if they wake up before I get there. I only came because I didn't want you going alone with them. Ian's a pervert. Hunter's wasted. I was afraid of . . . well, *this.*"

"Where's Hunter?"

"They said they were coming right back. Hours ago. The place is huge. I didn't want to leave you to look for them. And my phone's fucking dead."

Carley looked around her. "Where's my purse?"

"In the limo."

Standing was like getting up on a wire. Carley walked with one hand around Amber's waist and the other on the wall. The strobes slowed time. "Right hand rule," Carley kept saying as they worked around the edges of the space, a series of rooms, like in Francis's museum.

They found Hunter three rooms in, sitting with his arms stretched straight over his knees. A girl with layered, wispy platinum hair rolled a wooden device that looked like a spider over his back. It had painted eyes and a smile. Carley had an urge to pat its head and pull its owner's hair.

"Hi?" she told Hunter.

"Hey, C." She knelt next to him and he stroked her hair. "Feels good to touch."

"Where's the limo?" said Amber, standing over them.

Hunter shrugged. "Ian went for a ride."

"Call him. My parents are going to kill me if we don't get home."

He handed Amber his phone. "Mmm," he told the spider and stretched his neck. Carley glared at the girl, who smiled back and kept up the arachnidan massage.

Hunter ran two fingers up and down Carley's arm. "Perfect," he said.

If she was perfect, why was he still letting Spider Girl touch him?

"Tickly," he added, and she realized he meant the material of her dress.

"I keep getting his voice mail," said Amber after a couple of minutes. "Let's just call a car service. Put it on one of your credit cards, Hunter? We'll pay you back or whatever."

"Cancelled," he said, eyes closed. "Doesn't make sense, Griffin blaming *cards* for my poor sportsmanship. They're just plastic. I've got what's called an *allowance* now. Not that it matters. Just a couple of weeks now, right C?" The girl rubbed harder, putting her weight into it. He handed Carley his wallet. "What's mine is yours."

Amber took the wallet from her. A second later she was holding it open in front of him, empty. "Someone ripped you off, Hunter."

"Ian, he needed to borrow some for . . . stuff . . . and then maybe he needed to borrow more. He'll be back."

"It couldn't have cost *that* much for ecstasy."

"He wanted . . . company."

A flash from the limo of Ian trying to get Amber to let him do something she wouldn't. Knowing Ian, he was paying a hooker to do whatever it was right now during a drive through the city.

The problem with using one of Amber's credit cards to get home was that Edie and Bernie were the only parents in Fox Glen to pay attention to charges. A hit from a car service for a four-thirty a.m. car trip from Manhattan to Fox Glen would have Edie freaking out faster than she could say PAP, PAX, and PAO. Amber got a cash allowance—which she'd spent already this week on jeans—and didn't have an ATM card because Edie took seriously the PAP, PAX, and PAO precepts like *Teenagers who are stressed, bored, or have excessive spending money at their disposal are more likely to get high.*

If Amber's mother figured out Fox Glen's golden boys had taken her kid to a rave, the whole world would hear about it. Amber would be grounded forever, Gretchen would think every weekend Carley slept at the Palace was an excuse to go take ecstasy or something, and Larry Talbright would make good on his threats to curtail Hunter's freedom. Disappearing would be so much harder with everyone *watching.*

Amber counted her money: forty-two dollars and seventy-five cents. Normally she complained that change stretched out what she called *the tummy* of her Prada wallet, but tonight she looked like she wanted to kiss each quarter.

"Think this is enough if we take the train?" she asked Hunter.

He shrugged. The spider scurried up his shoulder.

"Do you *mind?*" Carley asked the girl. She gave Carley a different smile this time, squinty-eyed, as if maybe she knew her.

"How much do you think it costs to get to Penn?" Amber said to him.

"Are we close? We're *in* Manhattan, right? Are we in Greenwich Village or—"

"Lower."

Carley tried to remember what was south of the Village, then realized he was talking to spider girl. He reached behind him and stroked the girl's arm. She mewed like he'd reached under her silver miniskirt.

Carley yanked his hand away from the girl. "What are you *doing*?"

"It's just *touch*, C. A tingle on my fingertips."

"We *have to* go and we don't know what we're doing," Amber told him. "Come with us, *please*."

"Please, H," said Carley. "Stop touching her. Pleasepleasepleaseplease. *Please*." She said the word again and again until it unworded itself into consonants all flattened together.

She said it as he unbuttoned his shirt for spider-girl to run her fingers over his chest. She said it as he told her not to cry and tried to tickle her and then tried to get her to tickle the girl, too. She said it as Amber told her they had to go *now*—the bouncer had found them a cab. She said it over her shoulder as she watched Hunter through the strobe lights, spider girl moving in slow motion, a finger in his fly and her pacifier in his mouth.

At Penn the escalators were steep and fast, the cracks moving past her upheld foot before she could put it down. She stumbled when Amber shoved her forward, riding with her hands two steps below her knees until the escalator spat her out at the bottom.

Amber pulled her to a bank of schedules and checked one. "Run!" she said.

She yanked Carley by the arm like she was one of those prizes you won at Six Flags and had to drag with you everywhere the rest of the day. "Hold the railing," she said at the top of a concrete staircase. Hissing rose from the platform below. A snakepit, Carley thought, as Amber kept an arm around her and kept begging her to hurry.

The doors to the train started to close as they reached the bottom of the steps. "Wait!" yelled Amber to the empty platform. She let go of Carley to run toward the nearest car. "Hold the doors!"

A man in a suit stepped forward from the car into the doorway. The doors bounced open.

"Come on!" Amber said, coming back for her.

Carley caught the toe of her shoe in the gap between the train and the platform as Amber pushed her ahead. She stumbled into the car, her hands hitting the ground.

"Thanks," Amber told the man and pulled Carley to her feet.

"You girls have been having fun." He said it like a statement. Like he knew something they didn't about fun-having.

"Do we know him?" Carley said. He looked like he could be one of their parents' friends. Graying at the temples and a little bleary but respectable, like Francis at the end of a party.

"I like your tie," she told him before Amber shook her head and walked her to the other end of the car. The tie was red with tiny elephants being ridden by tinier men.

She sunk into a green vinyl seat and watched the electronic message board flash a list of destinations, stations the train would go on to without them after they changed at Jamaica. Kingsville, Fisherton, Jackson Square, Vernal—the names in red lights.

"She's fine," she heard Amber say, and she opened her eyes. She didn't remember closing them. She didn't remember so much. The man had moved to a seat on the other side of the aisle from them. She heard Amber tell him they were in college, home for Thanksgiving break. They were with friends, Amber told him, friends who'd run ahead and gotten on before them. She took out her dead cell phone and tapped it like proof. "Just talked to them, they're at the front of the train."

"They should come to *you*," the man said as Amber took Carley's arm. They walked up car after car, Amber turning and looking behind them until they reached one with a twenty-something couple who stopped making out long enough for the girl to glare at Amber for seating herself and Carley right across the aisle from them.

The conductor came by, his hole puncher making scissor sounds as he marked the slips of paper Amber paid for with everything she had left but a few coins in her wallet's tummy.

They would need to take a cab from Fox Glen station when they finally got there, Amber told Carley when the conductor had moved on. Could Carley get the fare without waking her parents while the cab waited? "Do you have *any* money in your room?"

Carley shook her head.

"Me neither. Guess we could give him a fake address and get out and run at a stop sign?"

Carley shrugged. Even if she hadn't felt like throwing up it would have been hard to imagine her and Amber running from a car and hiding in someone's bushes, waiting for a cabbie's headlights to leave. It was something Glory and Tern might do—though only if it was necessary to, say, save someone's life. And even then, they'd send the fare later, having written down the cabbie's name and operator number on one of their hands.

"We got lucky, you know," said Amber, holding out to Carley a schedule she'd grabbed at Penn. "The next one wasn't until seven."

Carley nodded at the undulating columns of orange numbers. "Lucky," she said, looking away from them because they were hurting her head and making her dizzy. To distract herself from wanting to throw up, she tried to focus on things farther away, the way Bunny Gardner's father had told everyone to do during one of Bunny's birthdays in elementary school when they'd had her party on the yacht and a storm had kicked up. Watch the horizon, Greer had said as girls puked over the side into the Long Island Sound, but there was no horizon in a tunnel.

There was only darkness on the other side of the windows. She looked down the length of the railcar, where everything seemed a rectangle: the electronic message board, the fluorescent lights on the ceiling, the Lucite-covered transit maps, and the posters clustered near the entrances—ads for Libertine jeans, a movie about an ice-skating elephant, cheap one-way airline seats to California, and a radio show where the host talked in Pig Latin to callers when he disagreed with their politics. In the photo, he wore a snout.

She leaned back. Above her the chrome luggage rack was runged, like a ladder lying down, going nowhere. She counted its rectangles over and over, breathing deep and trying not to think about throwing up or about Hunter or anything.

"We have to change," Amber said, shaking her awake.

Carley nodded. She was trying.

"Come on, or I swear I'll leave you to wake up in the rail yard or Vernal."

"It's dark," Carley said as they stepped onto the platform. Upside down, a yellow warning on the concrete told her WATCH THE GAP. A sign above them said Jamaica. A rat ran across the train track, its tail an untied shoelace. So much concrete, the platforms endless.

"It's fine," Amber said unconvincingly. "Less than ten minutes till the connection." She pointed to the electric sign across the platform, where a ticker tape of destinations flashed that included Meridian. At the end of the list it said, *If You See Something, Say Something*, followed by a phone number to call if you had a phone.

They went into the nearest waiting room. A vent pumped out heat and the smell of piss. Carley told her stomach, *be strong* and studied graffiti to distract herself from the smell. MOTHERFUCKER was scratched deep into the orange plastic seats across from them and traced over in marker.

She doubled over, everything coming out. How had she gotten so messed up?

A gust of fresh air came in the door on the far side of the narrow structure. The man with the tie raised his head at them with the wordless greeting of someone you know by sight but not name. Carley moved one seat down from the puke and tried to wipe her dress and shoes with a tissue from her jacket pocket, as if this would make him think the puke wasn't hers. She'd filled her pockets with tissues before leaving the Club, just in case Hunter needed them. She wondered if Spider Girl would want to take care of him, if she'd understand you didn't just love someone *despite* their weaknesses. You loved all of him.

She gagged again, an orange stream stretching from her mouth to the ground. She saw the man watching her as she wiped her face and wanted to tell him she didn't usually do this, get drunk and take trains.

"Where do your parents think you are?" he asked. His wingtips approached.

"They're coming," Amber said, putting an arm around Carley. "They're meeting us."

The man laughed. "I'm sure."

He grabbed her by the hair. "We're just girls," Amber said as she tried to pry his fingers off. "Please. We're just . . ." She broke free and tried to pull Carley to her feet, but the man grabbed Carley's hair and arm instead.

"Run!" Carley screamed.

"Think *you're* too good for me?" he said when the shelter door had swung closed. His breath stunk of heat and liquor. His tie hung twisted to reveal a horse-drawn carriage and driver on the label. He tore at her dress, shoving his hand into her bra, twisting her nipple like he meant to unscrew it. *He's wearing an Hermès tie,* she kept thinking, *he can't be doing this.*

"Think everything's free? Paid in full. On the house. Want to stay a little girl? Little girl with big tits." He squeezed her breast so hard she screamed. "Like fairy tales, little girl? Waiting for your prince? Pretty boy in tights and a crown." She kicked. Scratched. He spat hot phlegm on her cheek. "I used to be a pretty boy."

She felt coolness as the door swung open again. Seconds later he was howling, releasing Carley as Amber clawed at the back of his neck.

When he turned, Amber jabbed at his eyes with keys she held spread between her fingers, the way they'd learned in Social Issues during the one-day self-defense unit that had degraded into everyone comparing car key fobs instead of using the keys as weapons on the practice dummy.

The platform rumbled. Amber grabbed Carley's arm, pulling her away from the man and his bloody face. Outside the shelter, their connection was arriving with a sound like knives being sharpened and a rushing like you heard when you put your ear to a seashell. It was a sound that had never sounded to Carley like the ocean, the way people always said it was supposed to, but like static, like nothing, like the white noise and snowy screen she'd seen on TV sets within TV programs set in the past, where at sometime a.m. an American flag appeared and a patriotic song played and all programming went away to be replaced by fuzz. She'd never seen fuzz like that in real life outside of TV *about* old-time TV. Now they just played reruns until dawn.

"That was so Glory," Carley said, the two of them holding each other in the train as it pulled away from the station. Through the train window they'd seen the man run for the stairs to the street, probably thinking they were reporting him to a conductor.

"On *Arion*, Glory wouldn't have run."

"On *Arion* she carries a knife strapped to the small of her back."

"Only after Season Two."

"You're, like, a superhero."

"I just want to be home."

"Home," Carley said, and realized all at once what they should have done all along. At Meridian, instead of connecting to Fox Glen she called a taxi from a pay phone.

"We're good for it," she told the cabbie for a third time as she directed him. At the Play Palace Amber waited like collateral while Carley went in.

The dressing room next to the pool glowed cerulean and gold. Lights shone from beneath the blue glass floor. The walls were covered with blue glazed tiles painted with gold dolphins. A gold sunburst shone above the mirror. She had to stand on a chair to press the latch, a gold tile at its apex. All these years she'd known his safe was there, but she'd never looked in it. He'd always trusted she wouldn't.

It swung open. In front of the cash were two vials of pills. She remembered the look on Hunter's face when she'd asked him for aspirin, his slight hesitation, and his almost saying words he'd swallowed. It was like holding Gretchen's blouse up to the mirror, the story of a whole night suddenly making sense.

At Swann's Way, after Amber had been dropped off, Carley took the servants' staircase up to the second floor, opening her bedroom door slowly, as if afraid to wake someone inside—another Carley, a *before* Carley. She stripped off her dress, then tore the papers off her mirror, staring at all of herself while she shredded them. Holding her breast, black and blue with

342   TANYA EGAN GIBSON

perfect prints of four fingers and thumb, she wondered if a bruise counted as something new, or just old blood misplaced.

IN AFTERMEMORY, SHE asks Hunter . . .
    In Aftermemory she tells him . . .
    In Aftermemory she says . . .
    There are no magic words.

CHAPTER 50

He awoke to what sounded like a thousand people roaring and a girl who looked different with her clothes off. Sand burrowed into his nostrils and ears and under his nails. He didn't remember how they'd gotten from the city to the South Shore. He didn't remember deciding to go to Jones Beach, though he must have thought it would be sexy or ironic, because it wasn't a place to arrive at by accident. His watch was gone. He stared at his bare wrist and called up a vague memory of selling it for nothing near its worth. Ian hadn't returned with the limo, and the girl had wanted to go somewhere.

She tugged on her silver skirt and shoved her panties into her purse. The waistband was broken, she said like an accusation. She rubbed her eyes with sandy knuckles.

"I'm sorry," Hunter said, though he wasn't sure what for. She didn't answer. "I didn't hurt ..."

"No," she said flatly. When the wind caught her hair and blew it around her face, she looked like a dandelion. "I'm not *like* this," she said, starting to cry.

"It's okay," he said, holding her. "Neither is anyone."

Finding cash left from the watch sale in his jacket pocket with his phone, he said he'd call a cab. When the dispatcher said he couldn't send anyone until Hunter could give him a parking lot number—did he *know* how big Jones Beach was, was this a joke?—he said he'd call back.

She said she needed to pee and looked over toward the other side of the dune. That she was a modest girl made him sad. He needed to take a walk anyway to find out where they were, he told her. She'd have privacy, he promised.

He called back the dispatcher with the words Field Two, then took another path back over the dunes, west of where the girl was, where he could blow his nose and cry. All around him beach grass bent in the wind, drawing circles on the sand.

Dry-swallowing four Vicodins, he wished more than anything that he were dreaming and about to jolt awake to find Carley next to him, stirring at his movement and whispering, "It's okay, H. Just a nightmare." She'd kiss his forehead and diagnose a fever-dream, whispering to him about something fun they could do later. It didn't have to be complicated, just something he could fill his head with so there wasn't room for the nightmare to return. *Let's rent sea monster movies,* or *I haven't finger painted since kindergarten,* or *can I try the hot stone massage kit on you again if I promise this time to read the instructions?*

He strode toward the ocean, the wind stinging his face.

He dialed Carley's cell. When it went straight to voice mail, he tried her landline.

"Hey," he said when she picked up on the fourth ring. "*Hey. C.*" His voice cracked. "Oh, God. I'm so—"

"You drugged me," she said. "I don't know you."

He called her again and again, whispering apologies into her voice mail. Finally, he threw the phone into the ocean. He stared at the horizon until it wavered. The cold stole his breath.

He heard the girl calling out to him, but he was already running, diving into the crash of the waves and swimming past the breaking point. People said he made a fine figure diving off a sailboat or racing at the Club—*a natural* they called him—but the truth was he'd learned every stroke from Carley, who'd taught him patiently in his pool. She was slower, and when she freestyled her butt bobbed like a cork, but her instincts for the water were perfect. She never panicked in currents. Always, she knew how to save herself. He closed his eyes and waited for something to come for him that never would. A riptide or an off-course shark. Or a mermaid in purple, he thought, as he shivered back toward shore, who'd hold him up and promise him that at the end of the alphabet it would all be over.

CHAPTER 51

On the cover of the book, a kohl-eyed, red-lipped face shed a tear on the carnival below. She wasn't reading it for school—she'd decided to let Nagel fail her and had a feeling make-up English at Fat School wasn't going to be what anyone would call *challenging*. She wasn't reading it for Hunter, though it was his copy of *Gatsby* with his notes, the one he'd brought over that time to help with essays he'd never asked her about again. She read it to *understand* Nagel and Hunter, and also Bree. Because Nagel loved it and Hunter lived it and Bree said she hated it—which meant it scared her. Stuck between its pages should be clues to who they were. Clues bigger than what you might learn from watching someone try to brush his teeth or cut his toenails in a bouncy house.

Her door opened without a knock. Hunter stepped in. He sat on the floor next to her bed, knees to his chest, soaked. Her parents were at Club Brunch like always on Sundays, and Grace was off, so he'd known he'd be safe coming up to her bedroom looking like death. "I came right here from picking up my car. I—"

"I don't want to know where you've been. Don't want to take care of you."

"I fucked up, C. I wanted to be stronger. I wanted to be fresh. I—"

"I'm tired of hearing you. All the words. You think they make things better. But you know what words are? Just noises."

Yesterday afternoon in the warmth of Hunter's room, it had been words that most of all had gotten Hunter off. *Areola*, she'd whispered to him after they'd been touching so long that the pleasure nearly hurt. She said the word because she liked the way the vowels tumbled over each other, and because she happened to remember it from her Social Issues "Your Body and You" unit, and because that was where Hunter's tongue happened to be at the time.

It was a funny word, the pronunciation of which they debated until they laughed and the word broke down and Carley realized how Hunter's breathing had changed, how turned on he was getting.

Scrotum, she whispered, cupping his, and he bit his lip and groaned. She tickled him with words for parts and sensations and acts until he couldn't bear it. He fumbled so badly with the condom wrapper that she'd sheathed him herself. "Just let go," she whispered as he tried to ease into her gently and fight his urge to thrust, "it's just me."

He'd been having sex since he was twelve, he'd said later as they lay wrapped in each other's arms. But that had been the first time he'd felt entirely *there*. She'd kept him out of his head, anchored him in his body. The words had made it real for him. She'd kept him in the world.

He lay on her floor now, wet and balled.

"I *believed* you about getting rid of the pills, Hunter. That you were going to try for a night at least. That you *meant* to try—even if I figured you might not last long without them. I was just proud of you for wanting to, even though I was pretty sure you were hooked on them like you're hooked on drinking. I knew you'd probably mess up a hundred times, and that going away together would mean a lot of holding your head over the toilet in hotel rooms and your asking me what you did in the morning, and crying, and mood swings, and apologies before any of that fun stuff we'd talked about— all the cuddling and cooking together. I didn't say anything because if you thought I didn't believe in you, you wouldn't try at all. And I *did* believe. I thought after enough fuck-ups with me still loving you more than everything, watching you barf yourself inside-out and never leaving, you'd realize you *deserve* to be loved. And then you'd be ready to stop for real.

"All you had to do when I held out my hand for those pills, H, was shake your head. You didn't have to explain why. Or apologize for lying. Or say *I convinced myself wanting to flush them was the same as flushing them. I* would have gotten it. I would have known the only reason you'd refuse me anything would be to protect me."

He rubbed his face like he wanted to wipe it off. "It should have just made you relaxed, sleepy. We were supposed to be leaving early, and I didn't count on Ian being so persistent about going to the city. Or about Suzanne coming over to whisper that she couldn't bear to see me so 'antisocial' on my birthday and saying Larry wanted to lock me out of the Play Palace if I kept 'holing up' there with you. And I didn't count on you being so relaxed from the pills that you'd accept Ian's flask when he offered and end up wasted from mixing. All I thought was going to happen was I'd hold you all night in bed and stay up to make sure you were breathing right. You would have woken a little groggy, feeling a little off, like you were coming down with something. I'd have taken care of you just like you were sick, and it would have passed, and it would have been like nothing happened."

"*Nothing* like passing out at a rave, throwing up on myself, and nearly getting raped."

She unbuttoned her pajama top so Hunter could see the man's hand.

He closed his eyes.

"*Look*," she said.

He placed his cold fingers on the bruises. They fit.

"You need help," she said. "If you can't tell Suzanne, tell Francis. He'll go explain it to her. He loves you, H."

"But our escape—"

"No escape." For the first time since last night, she let the tears come. "It was a really good dream. Sturdy. Or like Gretchen says, *well made*. Had it for a long time, and it never wore out. Talk to Francis. If you don't tell someone, I will."

"I can't let you." He shook his head slowly. "I really can't."

He got up off the floor and sat next to her on the bed as if he didn't care that he would leave water and sand behind on her quilt. He took her hand, kissed the back of it, and met her eyes with the coldest look. "No one will believe you. I'll tell Suzanne about a weird thing the guard at the gate recorded right before sunrise: you came by, in a cab. And when I got home from celebrating my birthday with my cousin, I discovered some things were missing. My watch. Some of the money I'd been putting away for a wedding present for my mother. Pills left over from when I had mono, still in a prescription vial with my name on it. I'll show Suzanne the safe—I wasn't *hiding* anything, it doesn't even have a lock. Just a place to keep my watches and cufflinks so the Help doesn't get tempted.

" 'Oh the *things* Carley has been doing,' I'll tell her. 'Oh the strain it's been! Making scenes. Getting drunk . . . God, the drunkenness. Taking *drugs*. Slapping me in front of Ian. Teasing some guy in a train station and putting poor Amber at risk. Behavior that gets a girl in trouble. She's seeing a therapist, you know, for *issues*. Problems with control.' "

"Amber knows that's not true. She'd—"

"You think Gretchen would believe you *or* Amber over me? And Francis? He'd stare into his wife's pill cabinet and know the apple hasn't fallen far from its mother. *Therapeutic school* instead of *fat school*, and before you're shipped off I make sure everyone knows you tried to smear me. You'll be the girl willing to ruin everything for everyone—the parties at the Palace, the nights at the Station, the flasks people carry just to be able to *breathe* in this goddamn town—just to have me to herself."

There was this parallel universe, a glass-blown place in which everyone's parents believed, where kids drank two rum-and-Cokes apiece out on the golf course at night and giggled themselves to sleep; where they *went out on dates* in which euphemisms happened; where only adults bought pharmaceuticals from the tailor on the edge of town. It was *this*, he meant, that she'd be taking from everyone.

"Is that who you want to be, Carley? The girl everyone will hate? Someone who smashes open a world?"

CHAPTER 52

Bree McEnroy <btmcenroy@yahoo.com>   November 22 8:55 AM
to: Carley Wells <seawells@gmail.com>
cc:
re: Ending (attached)

After you get to reading the pages I mentioned to you at the auction last night (they're on your desk), could you take a look at this? The ending came to me all at once, and I'm hoping you'll agree that even if it wasn't what you wanted for Buck and Jules, it's what's inevitable.

CHAPTER 15

The Knightsport Credit Repair Dragon Slaying Challenge

They were supposed to turn their swords on the dragons in front of them, but the real demons were lurking behind. They were tied to these demons by restraints they were commanded to ignore—no touching the safety equipment, host Cliff Daniels and the stunt coordinator kept reminding Buck. The demons were long-necked, like the unholy spawn of a giant bird and a giraffe.

They fought side by side, Buck and his lady Jules, each lunging at a dragon as it backed them closer to the cliff, each waiting for it to cry "Beep," to let them know they touched its heart.

"Five touches to Buck, three touches to Jules," the host announced. The demon behind them readied itself to snatch them from the fall to heaven when the land beneath their feet ran out.

His lady gasped. He looked over to see her heel right at the edge.

"Back to your side of the line," the host yelled at Buck as he dashed to Jules, "or you'll forfeit."

"Do you trust me?" Buck asked her. Before she could answer, he unbuckled their harnesses. He put his arms around her and together they stepped back, free of the demon, into pure air. Avalon awaited.

Carley Wells <seawells@gmail.com>   November 22 10:12 AM
to: Bree McEnroy <btmcenroy@yahoo.com>
cc:
re: re: ending

i tried knocking on your door but ur not home so I figure ur at j's and wrote this there? u have a messed up idea of romance.

when u get home I really need to talk to u about something that is not the book.

about the ending, r u serious? did u really just make them jump off a cliff or did I not understand something. no. seriously no.

i get ur point about how people cant save each other for real.

but I still think we need stories that tell us we can.

just so we wont stop trying.

CHAPTER 53

A piece of paper with Larry's handwriting was taped to the Palace door. Hunter ignored it, thrusting his key at the lock. It wouldn't fit. He squinted at his key ring to make sure he hadn't picked the wrong piece of metal. Only then did he read the note.

Hunter,

We have much to discuss, but you have been unreachable. Suffice it to say that Justin Leighton came by this morning with the Wellses' Author to share concerns about you. Apparently your behavior has been even more egregious than we had been privy to.

While you are acclimating yourself to your new bedroom in the main house (third floor, first door on the left) where you can be supervised, we'd like you to contemplate your choices. Though it will be impossible to hide from colleges your admission into a "program," I agree with Mr. Leighton that this is the best course of action. (In the interest of honesty, I must disclose Griffin is not in favor of this.) If you and Griffin insist on taking care of this locally, I have left a pamphlet with a list of organizations suggested by Parents Against Alcohol on the desk next to your laptop and schoolbooks, which I took the liberty of bringing over so you can make good use of your day.

We will have professionals pack your belongings and vet them for
contraband before they are transferred to the main house. We look
forward to a mature conversation with you about this upon our return
from the Club, where we will be celebrating your mother's birthday
over brunch. It is unnecessary for you to join us.

The paper shook in his hand. He sat in front of the locked door and sobbed. He hadn't wanted to threaten Carley. All he'd wanted was her forgiveness, a chance to go back to yesterday. If only he'd taken more pills to smooth him over. He'd so needed that solace, he'd *stared* at them in his safe when he'd come back to the Palace to get his car, but then he'd turned away from them, telling himself he would go to Carley as *himself*—wet and ragged, sober-ish and shaking. In truth, he admitted to himself now, he'd just hoped the worse off he seemed, the more sorry she might feel for him.

And now, still, the pills were out of his reach. He stood and turned the knob over and over, kicking the door. They were right *there*, on the other side.

He heard the crunching of leaves. With the trees nearly denuded, he could see Bree on a path in the woods halfway between the cottage and the Palace, sipping from a mug and dressed in Rock Star's too-short clothing. She was looking at something in the distance—a bird or the clouds. He considered just going up to the cell Larry had assigned him, the Lincoln Bedroom, but he was too angry to walk away.

"Spending the night deciding how *other people* should live their lives," he called out. "Is that two writers' idea of making love?"

"Justin felt negligent doing nothing," she said when she joined him on his front stairs. She shook her head at his drenched clothing but offered no comment on it. "He thinks you're talented. And that you're wasting yourself. And that at this rate, you'll outdo Fitzgerald for self-destruction before you're eighteen."

"He sure likes saving people, that Rock Star," Hunter said. "Without their permission."

"One day you'll thank him," she said, seeming unaware of having uttered a horrible, condescending cliché. This, from the writer of *Scylla*. It was as if her edges had been dulled by love.

"I liked you when you were angry," he said. "Happiness washes you out."

"You sound like a brat right now, you know. Spoiled. Pissed off that Justin and I won't make believe you don't have a problem like everyone else."

"*Make believe*," he said, shaking his head. "Wow. Well, Bree, to tell you the truth, Rock Star's the *king* of that land." He felt hot despite his wet clothing and the breeze and the November weather. "I never thought I'd tell you this. . . . Or maybe, maybe I *did* know I would." Had he really believed he'd never betray the man he idolized? After all, it *was* what Hunter did, betray people.

"The single honest thing about the E.T. Wahlrod Fellowship," he began, "was the mission statement on its Web site: *To support the creative work of an artist in the process of reinvention . . .*"

He told her about Justin's living in that cottage all those years, about how when he couldn't fix himself he'd turned to trying to fix Bree from afar the way everyone in Fox Glen fixed everything—with money. About how when the "fellowship" ran out and he heard from Darren Connelly that she was just perseverating with research for a novel bound to be even less likeable than *Scylla*, he was determined to *make* her change. But how? And then, about how a few months later, Darren had mentioned to Justin a conversation with Francis Wells at the O'Neil Foundation for Adult Literacy dinner about a ridiculous commission beneath everyone else's dignity.

"I suppose Rock Star imagined you cut off from the world the same way *he* was. I suppose he imagined that if you came to Fox Glen, you could be alone *together*. He could have you right here, take care of you like an exotic pet that catches cold at the slightest draft. The kind of creature you're not supposed to keep, but enough money will buy."

Rock Star came out of the cottage, cane in hand and a smile on his face like he owned the world.

"Call me a cab?" Bree said, tears rolling down her face.

"I'm sorry," Hunter said.

"Bree!" Rock Star called out.

"You're not sorry," she said. "Call me a fucking cab."

Hunter pointed toward the main house, his hand trembling. "I'll have to do it from there," he said. "My phone's lost, and it seems I've locked myself out."

THEY SAT ON the marble wall of the reflecting pool facing each other, Justin chain-smoking and Bree crying. "I thought it was real," she said. "I believed."

"It was. It *is*. I love—"

"Don't. There's no 'you' in that sentence except the 'you' that you created. That you *fabricated*. You love the person you *made*, not me. I could deal with finding out you lied about *yourself*—for as long as I've known you, you've confused *persona* with person. But you made *me* think I was someone I wasn't. For that, I'll never forgive you."

He flicked cigarette ash into the water. It floated across the marble-bottomed pool toward an invisible boundary on the other side, what she'd learned during her stay in Fox Glen was called an "infinity edge," and then disappeared.

"I thought I'd earned something," she said as the taxi Hunter had called for her finally came up the driveway of the Cay estate. "*Done* something." She stood. "Even when *Scylla* bombed, even when I was answering phones as a temp so I could pay the rent in a place that would scare the shit out of you, I didn't feel like I had nothing. I had *me*. And now? I don't even have that."

FROM THE LINCOLN Bedroom, Hunter watched Bree's cab pull away. Rock Star looked up at the window, meeting Hunter's eyes before he began his way back to the woods. It was as if he'd known the whole time that Hunter had been watching, *listening*, his window wide open. Perhaps it was something a performer learned to sense.

He closed the window and sat on the massive replica of the Lincoln Bed with his laptop, deleting stories. He came to the one he'd wanted to submit with his college application. After the college counselor had told him fiction was an unacceptable response, she'd added, *You're supposed to show yourself in the best light, you know.*

He scrolled through it slowly now, though he knew it by heart.

PRETEND HEAVEN
(OR COOL THINGS I WISH I'D DONE)

"You always look so cool," [Daisy] repeated.

—F. Scott Fitzgerald, The Great Gatsby

Under the weight of summer's end, the sand rippled and bowed. Amory tried to stare past it to the coolness of the Sound, but the setting sun kept catching on the iridescent fragments of mussel shells washed up on shore, drawing back his gaze. He squeezed closed his eyes, but the beach was still there behind his eyelids, the grit of a billion broken things.

Named for the protagonist of Fitzgerald's *This Side of Paradise,* Amory cannot shake the burden of his heavily symbolic moniker any more than the Sound from which the fat girl saves him can rid itself of reflections. *Love,* his name means, but until that girl—gentle and funny and too pure for the world—he'd never felt it.

She'd stayed with him all weekend, until finally, as the sun began setting on Sunday, he had to release her to her parents and homework and a world with which he didn't want to share her. He wanted to float away with her on their chaises to a place without mirrors, a deserted island where they would make everything they needed themselves. Where they could make themselves up.

Where he could be brave. Where he could be honest. Where he could be a boy who hadn't tried so hard to tread away from a fat girl's reach, whispering "No, no!" as his cousin tried to push him into her path and she'd revolved endlessly in the water, that he'd given himself a cramp from the exertion.

Surrounded by Victorian furnishings, Hunter sat at his laptop wishing the story were something deleting would erase. He could trash files, set on fire every paper copy of every one of his memories, but still they would exist in his brain. Maybe *that* was the point of *Scylla*—it was easy to get lost in a world like the Net, where nothing ever went away.

He kissed the computer screen. Dragged the file into the trash icon. **Empty,** he told it, though it meant nothing.

CHAPTER 54

While her tutor drilled her on Words of Emotion, Words of Economy, and Words of Language, Carley kept imagining Suzanne Cay calling her parents to inform them that their daughter was a drunken thieving slut. But it never happened.

Upstairs, later, in her bedroom, she kept imagining Bree coming home to argue about the end of *Dark Ages*, but every noise she heard ended up being only the Help cleaning and straightening. Her knocks at Bree's door went unanswered.

She kept imagining telling Francis everything about Hunter and everything about *everything*—about how life really was for her and Amber and everyone their age. But then she'd remember how he'd reacted after the PSAT class public humping episode, and she'd envision him sending her directly to Sinkman or sitting her down in the Bra Museum and telling her she didn't have to make up "stories" just because she was jealous of Hunter's "spending time with girls." She could hear him saying *girls* like she wasn't one herself, like she was a teddy bear Hunter had outgrown.

At six, when Bree still didn't answer her door, Carley swung it open.

The room felt empty with her first breath in it. In the closet, bare hangers swung softly on the breeze created by her opening the door.

Instead of going downstairs to announce to her parents that her present was *gone*, instead of opening the sealed envelope with her name on it sitting on top of the *Arion Annals* collection and the stack of microcassettes in the middle of Bree's desk (the desk she had come to think of as *Bree's*, as if this room ever *was* Bree's), Carley searched the room for clues Bree had ever been there. In the closet, among the hangers padded with the same fabric as the pillows on the window seat, was one stark wire one that must have come from Bree's apartment. In a desk drawer, there was a penny and a button. In the bathroom, a clot of toothpaste in the sink.

She brought the envelope back to her own room. Inside was the pen Justin had won for Bree at the auction and a sheet of paper.

Dear Carley,

I don't usually skip to the last page of a story, but I couldn't resist watching the last episode of The Arion Annals. *It's a long series, and I couldn't imagine finding the time to see the whole thing through, but after hearing you say so many times that you loved it* until *the last season, I did want to see how it turned out.*

I can understand why the end pissed you off. Nine years is a lot of time to invest to find out that Glory's life isn't her life at all, and that the island of Arion is a government-built observatory where every ten years people's memories are erased and life repeats itself so that scientists can study what factors (the insertion of certain people like Liam, or the deletion of others like Glory's parents) can most change the course of a life. To be honest, though, when I think back to the couple of seasons-worth of episodes I did watch, I think I can see the clues to this being planted. One of these days, if I ever do watch the whole thing, I'll let you know if I think the writers played fair.

I could attempt a smooth transition here about my motivation for leaving without finishing the book I promised you—I was thinking about riffing on the word "fair"—but I won't. I could make excuses for my sneaking out while you're downstairs with your tutor, but in truth I have no excuse. I can't face disappointing you, but I can't make myself stay. Best I can say is that I found out something today that was like discovering one's life is just an Arion experiment.

I know I'm leaving with <u>Dark Ages</u> still completely unreadable. Each section is written differently: the meta-part; the part without meta- but without enough backstory; the meta-less, backstoried, but overly heavy-handed-on-theme part—every section not quite like the others, yet not quite what you wanted, all of which culminates in an ending you hate. (I just looked back at my notes and reread your Manifesto. "No One Dies," you asked, and I couldn't even give you that.)

I'm sorry I couldn't give you the book of your dreams. Even if I'd stayed, I doubt I could have done it. In any case, tell Francis one of these days I'll send him back that stipend, though it might take a while.

I hope one day our paths will cross again. You never know with these Choose Your Own Adventures.

Bree

She lay in bed, more alone than she ever thought she could be. She couldn't feel the sheets on her skin or her tongue in her mouth, and yet she knew she must have eyes, *blinking* eyes, because the ceiling kept being there and not there.

She was emptier than when the man was attacking her. Emptier than before she met Hunter, when all she wanted was Gretchen's love. The emptiness turned back time, and then she was zooming backward past before she and Hunter kissed, to before Bree's arrival at Swann's Way, to before the endless beautiful weekends of Hunter and her building their own world in the Play Palace, to before the first time they lay together holding hands in two lounge chairs pushed together at the edge of the Sound.

She recognized him there—her Aftermemory Hunter, twelve-year-old Hunter with his whispery voice and blue pea coat, who was everything good and every dream she'd ever had. And realized how long he'd been gone.

PART VI
Time and Tense

In a real dark night of the soul it is always three o'clock in the morning, day after day.

—F. Scott Fitzgerald, "The Crack-Up"

MOUNT YOUR STEEDS
AND DON YOUR ARMOR!

Please join us for

A (K)NIGHT OF MEDIEVAL MERRIMENT

In celebration of
Carley's Sixteenth Birthday
Friday, December 4th
7:00 until 11:00 p.m.
The Glen Club
Fox Glen
Francis and Gretchen Wells

Coat and tie

CHAPTER 55

In the driver's seat of his Mercedes, Hunter pondered his non-future in the past subjunctive:

If he hadn't been so ill and panicked on that morning a month ago, he never would have sent the application.

If he hadn't been so afraid of Griffin's and Suzanne's and the college counselor's criticism of his time-management skills, he'd have insisted he was better off skipping Princeton's early decision deadline in favor of applying a month later among the pool of regular applicants.

If he hadn't been so tired and lonely and caught up in a deus-ex-machina dream where Carley forgave him and the door to the Play Palace miraculously sprung open for him to retrieve his cash and pills and the two of them ran away together to live happily ever after, he might have completed all the rest of his applications by their December first deadlines. Or any of them.

The world was full of past subjunctive *ifs* that promised revisionist choices. But like Nagel had said about *The Great Gatsby* last year in one of his few coherent lectures, Jay Gatsby doesn't control his own destiny by the time the reader is introduced to him. The causes for what the reader witnesses playing out are embedded deep in the past, and Gatsby can no more direct his future than he can change his history. "*And so we beat on,*" Nagel had said, thumping his fist rhythmically against the whiteboard, "*boats against the current, borne ceaselessly into the past.*"

"Get clean," Antoine had said when Hunter had come by his shop this morning before school. "No more. You're a great kid. I can't save my own from dying, but I've got choice in this."

Ten pills left. Barely enough to get him through the next couple of AA meetings. Nowhere near enough to deal with Griffin's wrath. He hadn't expected to get into Princeton after My father, Griffin Cay, could buy you, but neither had he thought his application would ever be shared with Griffin—as the personal note included in his rejection letter suggested it would be next week over a private lunch. The development office felt it necessary to provide such a devoted donor with an explanation. A *not our fault*.

The word *wrath* wouldn't even begin to cover Griffin's reaction to learning about what the note called *the most arrogant response the admissions committee has read in ten years*. With Princeton no longer at stake, he'd probably accede to Larry's plea to send Hunter to a facility to relieve Suzanne of the burden of a son. A place where they searched you for real. Where they watched you get sick over and over and no one comforted you. Where he would have too much time to think about what he'd become.

He drove around Fox Glen aimlessly. His throat burned. His chest hurt when he breathed. He'd given up on ever staying well.

He pulled into the drive of Swann's Way just to have somewhere to stop. No one would be home. Carley and Grace would be with Gretchen at the Club preparing for tonight's party. Francis, at work. He could walk down to the pond and pretend everything was what it used to be, that Carley still wanted his friendship instead of treating him coolly in school and refusing his phone calls at home, that any minute he might trot up the stairway to where she would promise him tomorrow he'd feel new.

When he reached the house and saw Francis's car, he nearly turned around. He parked and sat staring at it until, finally, he willed the courage to get out. Letting himself into the house with the key he'd had since he was twelve, he took the stairs to the third floor. He'd force himself to tell Francis how badly he'd messed up college before even getting there. Francis would shake his head but laugh and promise to convince Suzanne that there were decent schools with January deadlines. Hunter didn't need to go to a place like Princeton or Blaine—Francis hadn't, after all. Perhaps the two of them

would indulge in cigars in lieu of the scotch Hunter couldn't have made a
secret of giving up even if he'd wanted to—Bunny Gardner had been
walking past the Fox Glen Presbyterian Church as he'd emerged from a
seven o'clock AA meeting in the basement. Every student at Montclair and
every friend of her mother's had known by the next morning.

Francis could convince Suzanne to let Hunter continue to "recover" at
home. He might even convince Suzanne to *like* having her son around.
People said he was good company. He could be funny, he could entertain
her. He could be of use if she let him.

He imagined her having coffee with him after meetings. Imagined
bringing her those little pins she could be proud of. Imagined finding
another source for the drugs. Imagined tapering off. This time, for real.

The lighting in the Bra Museum was low, the torsos casting shadows.
He walked through the sweetish smell of rubber and elastic, past the series
of Maidenform bra posters from the sixties, and finally toward Francis's
workspace in the back. In the half-dark it took him a moment to understand
what he was looking at below the print of Tintoretto's *The Origin of the
Milky Way*.

Atop Francis's desk, amid dozens of lilies, were Francis and Suzanne.

"DO YOU LOVE him?" Hunter asked so calmly that Suzanne at first thought
it to be one of his trick questions, the ones he engineered to make her feel
stupid. When he'd refused to answer his phone, she expected that he'd gone
on what she'd heard people call a "bender." But when she'd returned home
from Swann's Way, she'd found her son sober, standing in the front entranceway, like a sentry.

"*Do* you?" he repeated with what she realized all at once was *hope*.

She thought of Francis dressing her this afternoon in panties he'd made
himself for her by hand, French lace and velvet sewn into rose petals that
parted at the crotch. She thought of the look on his face when he penetrat-
ed his handiwork.

"No."

"But you love *Larry*?"

"That's not the point."

"What *is* the point, then? What's been the *point* of all those bastards you've fucked?"

She slapped her son across the face. "If you'd only been a girl," she said, "I wouldn't have needed all those men."

INTO ROSE VELVET bags with satin drawstring ribbons, Carley and Grace placed maroon leather-bound copies of *Le Morte d'Arthur* bookmarked with fourteen-carat castles. The leather matched the tablecloths. The bags matched the napkins. At the bottom of the last box of books Carley found the two volumes bound in brown that Francis had let her add to the order despite the extra setup cost.

She opened one and nodded at it. It was all wrong, but also perfect. She walked to the lobby of the Club to get a FedEx pouch from the concierge and wrote on the mailing label the emergency address she'd copied from Bree's contract.

JACKIE KENNEDY WAS nearly finished explaining to America the history of the White House and Suzanne was lying in her water-green, silk-canopied bed practicing the word *floor*, trying to get her voice low enough and breathy, when Hunter walked in without knocking. The white and green floral curtains in Suzanne's bedroom were drawn tight against the daylight. Suzanne gasped, apparently more ashamed of being caught practicing to be Jackie than of having been caught in flagrante delicto with her best friend's husband.

"I'm having that suit made," she said, sitting up. Jackie began leading America through *A Tour of the White House with Mrs. John F. Kennedy*. She clasped her hands in front of her like a schoolgirl ready to answer a question from her interviewer. "You can't tell in black and white," Suzanne said, her hands clasped identically, "but it's a beautiful red wool boucle."

"I need the key to the Play Palace."

Jackie led America into the Diplomatic Reception Room. "There's a system," said Suzanne. "Remember the chart Larry made? You need one hundred stickers before privileges."

"I have a cold. A few minutes in the steam room would help immeasurably."

She waved her hand at him. He was speaking over Jackie.

"My head hurts, Mother. My sinuses. My face. *Please.* Come supervise, if you'd like, to make sure I'm not *drinking* the steam."

Suzanne picked up the remote and restarted the scene. "*What is the Diplomatic Reception Room used for aside from receiving diplomats?*" asked the interviewer.

Jackie beamed. "*This is the room people see first when they come to the White House.*" Suzanne's lips moved silently. "*Everyone who comes to State Dinner comes through it and leaves by it, so I think it should be a pretty room.*"

Hunter stepped between Suzanne and Jackie. His mother pointed the remote at him. "Larry will never know," he said. She pressed Pause. "I promise, Suzanne ... Mother ... he'll never know *anything.*"

Floating in the pool, looking up through the glass ceiling at the sky while waiting for the five Vicodin from his safe to take effect, he tried to remember being good, but all he could remember was promising Carley as they'd drifted to sleep the afternoon they'd made love that it was the beginning of everything, that it would always feel that good, that they would always laugh and play when they did it, that it would always be like candy. Drunk on wanting to be good, he'd believed it.

He remembered his hand between Amber's legs and the way he couldn't look her in the face. He remembered his tongue in a hundred girls' mouths. He remembered Glenlivet and Glenmorangie and Laphroaig burning his throat and healing it. Lying about credit card charges. Stealing from medicine cabinets. Cooler lies, cold lies, cruelty. Making fun of a poem Carley wrote about the ocean that he'd always known was about him.

He dressed, then went upstairs to the room he used to live in and made a fire. Suzanne lost time when she was with Jackie. Ten minutes or two hours were the same.

He opened his laptop, leaving the bottle of fifty-year-old scotch he'd

taken from the safe standing at attention unopened for now. He wanted
what he wrote to be clear and letter-true.

Friday, December 4th
    Dear Bree,

    Please forgive my intrusion into your life. Francis gave me
your sister's address from the emergency contact section of your
contract. I hope this package finds you there.

    Please accept the enclosed as a gift, if you will. An apology if
you won't. I shouldn't have told you about Justin. It was not my
truth to share.

    If you won't accept a gift from someone you despise, take it as
a loan to be paid back, say, thirty years hence. No interest. No one
else knows about the money, no one will miss it. I was saving it for
something I no longer need, and it's best right now that I don't
have cash at my disposal. (Haven't had a drink in twelve days, by
the way. But who's counting?)

    Use the money to buy you time to write your Geppetto book. Or
something else. And though I know you're furious at Rock Star for
deceiving you, perhaps when you have that book in your hand—
something yours and yours only—you'll be ready to forgive him.
What he did was weird, yes. Maybe crazy. But he loves you, and
anyway there's a literary precedent for such obsessive behavior.
Gatsby, after all, bought a mansion from which every night he
could stare at the green light at the end of Daisy's dock.

    " 'Can't repeat the past?' [Gatsby] cried incredulously. 'Why of
course you can!... I'm going to fix everything just the way it was
before.' "

    Sincerely,
    Dionysus

He opened the scotch and drank deep for the courage to write just one
more letter.

CHAPTER 56

The horse swung its head from side to side, then stopped halfway through the arch of gladiolus. Carley sat sidesaddle, reigns in one hand, a fistful of mane in the other. The horse lifted its tail.

"This," Edie whispered to her husband, "is what happens with *stunts.*"

Gretchen clutched the party planner's arm as dung overwhelmed the fragrance of lilies. "Couldn't it have been given an enema?" she said, her voice breaking. "Couldn't have it been starved?"

Carley petted the horse's neck.

Francis stared across the room at the woman his wife knew he was sleeping with but would rather keep as a friend than confront. A woman more important to his wife than *he* was. A woman whose son had called Francis after the debacle this afternoon to say into his voice mail, "You're better than her."

Guests sat down to plates of field greens arranged into dragons with artichoke scales and asparagus tails and breath of minced yellow and red peppers. The dragons' eyes glowed juicy with pomegranate seeds.

Two men fenced in full armor in the center of the room, a performance choreographed to the soundtrack of *Lancelot*. People nodded absently at the fight while whispering speculations about Hunter Cay's falling-out with the birthday girl. The most popular rumor was that she hadn't supported his brave decision to stop drinking. She was *that* kind of girl, a hanger-on, in it just for the fun.

Two hours into the party, as the Camelot Canard entrée was being served, he still hadn't made an appearance, though his mother and stepfather kept insisting he was on his way. To support him in his noble sobriety—to be *there* for a young man like Hunter Cay—would be an honor, thought his classmates and their parents both. They looked forward to his arrival far more than they did the fire-breathing dragon their programs promised would entertain them with dessert.

A MILE AWAY in his car, Hunter thought about how short the list was of what you wanted when you only had minutes. How simple your needs: to be missed, to be held, to leave the world unbroken. He marveled at the idea that every minute, everywhere, people were about to die. He drank deep. He wouldn't be alone.

He was thankful for the ice coating the road, and for the snow beginning to fall. An accident was the best way. Just one of those things that happens when a kid in a tux speeds to a Sweet Sixteen with a bottle at his side. The sort of thing you read about in the paper. Tragic, but beyond anyone's control.

"HEY," CARLEY SAID into Hunter's voice mail. Hearing his outgoing message felt weird, foreign after not dialing his number for two weeks. "Just wanted you to know people are missing you." She tugged at her dress, which kept slipping because she hadn't been hungry for so long. She was held together by safety pins and basting stitches. "And that I'm proud of you for what people have been saying you're doing. I know it has to be really hard. And that even if we can't be friends right now because of what you said . . . because what you threatened was. . . . Well, I don't want to get into that. But maybe one day, again, we'll. . . . Look, I'll always . . ."

His voice mail beeped its time limit. A tinny voice asked if she wanted to send the message or start again.

CROUCHED BEHIND A lounge on the deck, having walked around the back from the parking lot, Hunter watched through the glass as Carley danced with Amber and Olivia, wiggling her hips in the dress chosen by her mother—off-white, with a capelet to cover her upper arms and an empire waist to conceal her waistlessness. The capelet impeded her lifting her arms over her head, so she danced with her hands at shoulder height, like a bank teller during a stick-up.

He hadn't been able to keep himself from listening to her message. And once he did, he had to see her one more time.

He wanted to stroke her hair. To catch her when spinning made her lose her balance. He wanted to kiss every bit of her skin, which always smelled so new. He pressed his hand to his mouth and loved and loved and *loved* her.

Since he was a child he'd read about the feeling attached to that word. Animals got to feel it, and orphans, and soldiers and mothers, and even badly behaved boys. He grew older and read about men feeling it deeply, and ironically, and desperately. By the time he was twelve, he'd read it in Lawrence and Joyce, in Carver and Chabon, and the better it was rendered, the less he'd believed. Until Carley, who'd turned book-love real.

CHAPTER 57

"H?" she shouted. "H!"

While she'd been dancing, she'd kept just *feeling* like he was there, and then, as she spun around, she'd glimpsed him through the window as he headed for the stairs that led down to the beach. Now, slipping out the side door of the Club and catching him coming off the path that led from the beach to the parking lot, she understood why he hadn't come in. She could tell he was trashed from how carefully he walked.

"Sorry I'm like . . . this." He studied his feet.

"It's okay," she said, putting an arm around his back. "I've got you."

"I'm over there," he said, pointing to where his car was parked at the back of the lot.

"You can't drive."

For a moment he looked about to argue. "Shouldn't have. You're right. Could we just sit? It's so cold." He wiped his nose with the back of his leather glove like a little kid. It made her want to cry.

A Whiplash Bouffant CD blasted when he put the key in the ignition to get the heat going. He muted it, held her hand across the gearshift, and closed his eyes. "Just let's do this? Just for a minute? It's like sleeping next to you again."

She let him sleep for ten minutes, tracing every bit of his face with her eyes, then leaned across for his keys. She'd get Francis. He'd help.

"Don't go," Hunter said, his eyes snapping open. "It's cold." He smothered a sob into his coat sleeve.

"Come inside with me, okay?"

"Do you miss me?"

"All the time."

"Suzanne says Gretchen's shipping you to fat school after Christmas."

"I'll go and come back and then it'll be over."

"We still could disappear. I swear I won't slip again if I'm with you. I'll go to meetings, they have them everywhere. I'll work so much I won't have time to get drunk or high; I'll wash dishes in a restaurant while dreaming of what I'll cook for you when I get home. We'll eat in bed and watch TV and make love, and I'll always think you're beautiful. I'll never make you feel bad for eating. I'll *feed* you, C. It'll be our adventure. Just us, forever. Home."

He stroked her cheek with two fingers, as if she were something fragile. She squeezed closed her eyes and tried to become that thing—a baby chick, or egg. She longed to be cradled in his hand, tucked into his pocket, carried away.

"We can *do* this," he said. "The field trip of our lives."

For once she knew what she was supposed to say. One word: *Yes.* She saw them feeding each other the very best parts of things, asparagus tips and filets. Decorating a little Christmas tree with shells she'd gathered. Pooling their money and having to choose what to buy. Hugging each other when they had to give up things. Comforting each other and loving each other and knowing one person in the world would think you were perfect even when you were sick or sad or mean.

And then she saw her future-self summoning Aftermemory, lying in bed next to Hunter and still trying to fantasize real life away. Rewinding past Hunter's lips forming *sorry*, the syllables all reversed and meaningless. His meals reducing themselves to their ingredients; her shells returning to the sand as waves uncrested and the tides flowed in reverse. When you rewound past the ugly parts, you lost the lovely ones, too.

She opened her eyes. Every bit of light in the car and outside of it—the streetlamps, the mini-moat, the glow of the Club—had settled onto him. The waves that fell over his face were the color of childhood. The eyes behind them were translucent with tears. He would never be more beautiful.

She stared at him, his face already becoming a memory. She thought of how sea glass couldn't keep from clouding once it dried off on shore.

"No," she said. "I love you more than everything, but no."

Through her tears, she could see people coming out the front entrance, walking into the bluish glow of the mini-moat and peering out into the lot. One of them was Francis.

"They're looking for me," she told Hunter. "We have to go in."

"I can't," he said, sobbing.

"Let's just talk to Francis," she said, her hand on the door handle. "It's okay you slipped. No one will judge you. He'll tell Suzanne to take *care* of—"

The car squealed as Hunter backed out.

"What are you *doing*, H!"

The car skidded as he threw it into drive and squealed past the mini-moat. "Please stop," she begged, though she knew he was past listening. "You're scaring me, H."

He turned toward the exit, accelerating.

"No," she said as she flung open the door. The car skidded. "No," she screamed as she covered her face with her arms and rolled out onto asphalt laced with snow.

CHAPTER 58

When the packages arrived for Bree by FedEx on Saturday, she let them sit unopened for hours on top of one of her suitcases. She should have refused to sign for them. She wanted everything from that *place* left behind. But that night, after she'd opened the hide-a-bed in her sister's living room and settled onto its pokey springs to read, she found herself so distracted by their presence that finally she gave in to curiosity.

Friday, December 4th

Dear Bree,

I wanted you to know I understand why you left. Because of stuff that happened that I didn't get to tell you about before you left, Hunter and I aren't really talking, but he did send me an e-mail the day after you left explaining everything about Justin and you, and how Hunter messed things up for you guys by not just keeping his mouth shut. Mostly, the e-mail apologized while saying it wasn't really his fault. Which, I'm starting to understand, is how he usually apologizes.

Anyway, I wanted you to have something to remember your time here. I thought maybe some of those memories weren't bad. I liked talking to you and I thought sometimes you were having fun, too. I know nothing "matches" in what I bound together here, but I wanted you to have it anyway. I just put the pieces in the order you wrote them. I hope you don't mind I made a copy for myself, too.

Also, there are two endings. I know you thought yours was the right one. But after you left I wrote one, too. Mostly because I couldn't figure out what else to do with myself. It's not good because I don't know anything about writing, but I couldn't leave Buck and Jules jumping off a cliff. I know they're not real or anything, but I liked them, and I didn't want them to die.

Sorry that the tense doesn't match how you wrote it—"was" sounded wrong when I tried to use it to describe the movie in my head that was going on in the present. Also, it's written in first person. You were always saying how you hated Justin using that point of view in his book, so I know you're not a fan of it.

One of these days you'll have to explain to me how writers can use past tense and still make it seem like everything's happening right now, or how you can write stuff you believe in without saying "I."

Anyway, hope you don't hold it against me that I put in both endings—like a Choose Your Own Adventure.

Your friend,

Carley

THE END

(by me)

I disarmor him behind the castle as host Cliff Daniels gets our mothers ready for their turns at the dragons after a stop at the makeup station. "Plan is changed," I tell Buck. "The challenge is cancelled. We're going on a quest. For the <u>Grail</u>. Which is a big cup, with powers."

We sneak out through the back lot. I'd worried about electrified fences and alarms and guards, but it turns out there aren't even any locks on the gates to keep us in Medieval world. We could have walked away anytime we wanted—we were volunteers, after all, not prisoners. But if you're a serf long enough, you forget things like that.

At the road, Buck covers his ears to block out the sounds of cars, which he calls <u>the screams of demons.</u> He squeezes his eyes closed and asks, "Is this hell?"

I take his hand. "It's just the world," I say. "You'll recognize it eventually." And then we disappear into it.

Bree sat with the volume a long time, and then, finally, turned to the second package, the one with Hunter's return address.

"You still up, Bree?" She heard the murmur of the eleven o'clock news escaping from Lara and Joe's bedroom.

"Yeah."

"That place you worked, Fox Glen? It's on the news. Some kid got himself fucked up at a Sweet Sixteen last night, went head over fender into a tree."

Bree came in and stared at the screen of the thirteen-inch TV her sister and brother-in-law watched from their bed. The colored lights of police cars reflected off the new snow around the mangled Mercedes, the accident site flashing brightness, like a carnival.

CHAPTER 59

The letter arrived on Monday by regular mail.

> Friday, December 4th
>
> Dear C,
>
> I've broken everything there is to break. I am so sorry. I always loved you, even before I knew "love" was the word for it.
>
> Whoever you end up with will have the adventure of his life. Choose someone awake enough to appreciate the wonder of a dream.
>
> You've kept so many secrets for me, yet I'm selfish enough to ask you to do it just once more. Keep this letter to yourself. An accident will cause Suzanne much less pain, but I knew you'd want the truth. You always have.
>
> Je t'aime. Pour toujours.
>
> H

For months she would reread it, running her fingers across his initial, the only part of the letter than wasn't typed. She'd cry on that ink and smudge it with tears.

If she'd stayed in the car, she wondered every night, would he have pulled over and let her take the wheel? Had he changed his mind about dying? Had he come to her hoping to be saved?

On dark days, she would feel like she'd killed him, no matter what Amber and her parents and Sinkman said.

On the darkest, she'd think he'd meant to take her with him.

But then she'd remember the way he'd been the only person, ever, to treat her like something delicate. He'd fed her beautiful meals, and tried to make her feel glamorous on her ugliest days and during the most ignomini-ous illnesses, and wrapped her body in clothing he bought her in New York and in Europe, silky robes and pajamas that she wore in the Palace like a princess.

He'd looked past the *much* of her and pretended to lift her down from the rocks and pedestals she'd climbed onto, holding her waist as she jumped. He'd rubbed suntan lotion on her at the beach, massaging not just her back but every part of her, girls around them staring as he attended to her shoulders and neck and arms and legs. He'd covered her stomach with kisses when they'd made love, whispering into its skin words too soft to hear.

It was impossible to believe he'd ever hurt this body he alone knew was fragile, that he alone had ever loved.

EPILOGUE

Point of View

"I've been drunk for about a week now, and I thought it might sober me up to sit in a library."

—F. Scott Fitzgerald, *The Great Gatsby*

Justin Leighton <justin@aquaria.com>   November 23 7:30 PM
to: Carley Wells <seawells@gmail.com>
cc:
re: Unpublished Writers Sunday Reading Series

Dear Ms. Wells,

I am delighted to offer you ten minutes at Aquaria on the evening of
Sunday, December 20th. Please arrive by 7 p.m. Reading order to be
determined.

Your host,
Justin Leighton

Sitting on the floor of a bedroom I haven't lived in for years, I determine what's worth keeping—the bound copy of *Dark Ages*, notes Amber and I passed in classes, Hunter's copy of *Gatsby*, shells from long ago. I leave everything else for the Help to pack up and give away. The divorce is final, the house sold. Gretchen bought a place in Connecticut, where nobody will know her as Mrs. Ex-Marvel-Bra. Francis long ago moved to California, where he lives in a house on the beach a half hour from where I go to school. His newest enterprise, West Coast–based Marvel-Swimwear, recently received national exposure on *Wake Up, America!* for producing designs up through size twenty-four. Host Gia Pepper called him *the woman-friendly designer of the decade.* When I stand, I catch a flash of my younger self in the mirror, trying to claw through layers of papers that have been gone now five years.

From the taxi I look over my shoulder for the last time at Swann's Way, hoping the new owners learn to avoid the echo spots. And then I turn away.

I tinker on my laptop on the Long Island Rail Road, decide a line sucks, and sigh. Goth Sinclair, my advisor for the creative writing half of my double major, is making me do this before I leave for field work required for the marine biology half: a semester in Costa Rica, where Gretchen swears I'll catch a worm.

You need someone to hear you, Goth had insisted. *Your words need to breathe.*

I wait for a transfer to Jamaica at Meridian, Moreland Galleria glowing holiday green and red behind it. Down the platform, high school girls stand in a group glossing their lips and passing a cigarette and crackling with the charge of not knowing what will happen next. Next to me, people from Meridian Community College laugh at each other's jokes, the hot fruity smell of happy hour liquor on their breath.

At Jamaica I wait outside for my Manhattan connection, avoiding the shelters and braving the wind.

Right before Penn, the lights go out for a moment, but my laptop keeps on glowing.

EVERY SURFACE IS a fish tank. The front window of Aquaria is a coral reef where angelfish and clownfish and sea stars can be seen from the street. The ceiling is living mercury, a school of anchovies catching the light as they swim in circles. Blue jellyfish glow and pulse and drift through a flattened cylinder embedded in the wall next to my table. And at the center of the whole place is the man-made swamp featured in magazine articles, mangroves twisting their roots into sand in a tank half-water, half-land—an engineered estuary. The photos couldn't capture what it feels like to be in the middle of so much water and movement.

People sip drinks clownfish bright and glassfish transparent, common names above their prices, Latin names below. I order an *Amphiprion ephippium*, which comes in a martini glass, tastes like mango, and looks like fire. A paper fin swims through it on a toothpick anchored to a pineapple slice. I feel a hand on my shoulder and turn.

"Minor Wells."

"I'm twenty-one. Major." I stand and hug him. People at nearby tables gawk because Justin doesn't make many public appearances, and when he does, he's low-key. He stays behind the scenes at his bar-cum-literary venue, choosing which famous authors read here and giving unpublished writers a chance to be heard one Sunday a month. Reserve has ended up working for him, people finding it as sexy as they once had his flamboyance. His only appearances to promote *Climbing* last year were charity events where attendees had to submit to airport-type screening. He travels with bodyguards. At the door to Aquaria, the bouncers frisk.

I haven't seen him since Hunter's funeral, where he gave me the copies he'd kept of Hunter's stories. He left Fox Glen the next day, making a tour around the world for real this time before settling in Manhattan. He still wears leather and velvet. His hair, though receding, is still long. He limps, but walks without a cane.

"Major-Minor Wells," he says, shaking his head, "well, look at you." On television, his words would signal an important moment. What is called *a reveal*, the pulling back of a metaphorical curtain. Which, on TV, is often also a *literal* curtain. Like the white hospital curtain on a squeaky pulley that the scientists draw back in the last episode of *The Arion Annals* to reveal Glory made young again and restripped of her memory so she can live through another cycle in the Arion experiment. Or the red velvet drape on the finale of *The Frog Princess*, under which a girl has been sitting on a stool all episode while her friends and the television audience all guess aloud what her "After" will look like. What color is her hair? What's her new style? And the question everyone hangs on: What does she weigh? Before the drape is pulled off, there's a drum roll.

You won't catch a glimpse of me in the glass here, in case you're wondering: the tanks are lit from within to minimize reflection. That's my kind of story. That's the kind of story this is. And this isn't TV.

ACCORDING TO WORD List Thirty-six: More Words About Literature, an *epilogue* is a final chapter that lets the reader know characters' outcomes and fates. It stands apart from the rest of the book in time or setting or style, a big The End that reframes the story, past-tenses it, says *nothing else will happen, but here's how things turned out (or didn't)*.

Here's how I turned out (or didn't):

A month after Hunter died, I surprised my mother by saying I wanted to go off to Fat School after all, an issue she'd stopped pushing after Sinkman told her it wasn't "the right time." To keep living in Fox Glen would have been like holding hands with a ghost. I transferred after a semester to a regular boarding school where I spent my senior year plus a "post-graduate year." [If you didn't happen to go to private school, by the way, a P-G is pretty much a euphemism for *do-over*—an extra year of high school to offset your worst prior grades (think English 11: The Archetypal Journal and Its Insubvertibility).] Despite frustrating my college counselor and Gretchen by refusing to write my college application essays about someone close to me dying, I was accepted at a small college on the West Coast.

I didn't start writing about Hunter—or about Bree, or for that matter about *me*—until a year ago. That I'd been the only person in my creative writing classes who wasn't desperate to write about her dysfunctional family or getting trashed at parties or losing her virginity had misled Goth Sinclair, author of *Backwater Hamlet*, into believing I was less insipid and more mature than my classmates. Among Goth's favorite sayings in class was *Regurgitation of debauched weekends does not good fiction make.*

I wrote about the water. I wrote about shells. I wrote about the beach. I wrote about strangers. Anything but the past. Anything but Hunter. Anything not to have to be who I'd been. It seems strange to me now that I'd thought you could just decide to be someone new. But, as Goth also says quite frequently in class, *You cannot force upon characters' epiphanies.*

On the other hand, sometimes they just arrive by e-mail.

A year ago Amber sent me a link to a real estate site Edie had told her about. Suzanne was finally putting the estate on the market, though she hadn't lived there for years, having made Newport her home since Larry had been elected to office. I don't know if you want to see it, but I thought I'd let you know.

It was a photo tour of the estate that included the Play Palace. The Web site provided a 360-degree view of points of interest. Hunter's bedroom— the Masquerade Guest Room, the site called it—was one of them.

I stood in the center of his virtual room and turned in circles, the costumed people on his walls partying as hard as they ever had and the bed as crisply made as it had ever been and the fireplace burning ever hot. The room had been staged to look like whoever had lit the fire had just stepped away and would be back any minute. A blanket too thin to be warm was folded over the arm of the divan. A book with a leather cover lay facedown and open on the table next to it. I zoomed in, desperate to read the title, but couldn't get close enough. Later I'd realize it was probably just a prop, blank inside. I spent weeks in the middle of that room, searching for traces of Hunter that were long gone, and skipping all my classes, and writing and writing. Only when Goth threatened to fail me did I emerge holding the first draft of the story I'd been desperate not to tell.

"You have *material*," Goth said when he read it. "Thing is, you only know part of it. A quarter, or eighth. The first person part. Which is a good start—you need to *be* in your life before trying to understand it. You need to *live* in the 'I.' That's probably what Justin Leighton meant in that note to your friend. But now that time has passed, you need to look at it from different angles. See it from other perspectives, different points of view. Then you'll see what you missed, whole other stories."

WHEN JUSTIN MOVES on to greet the other readers, I go back to watching the mangrove tank where catfish snout the bottom and archerfish display their stripes. Here, water meets land and mudskippers and fiddler crabs lead their lives. I can imagine Justin planning the bar, researching it like Bree's art book she never wrote. Saltwater tanks, freshwater tanks—which should go where? And then, the literarily graceful symbolic centerpiece: a place where fresh and salt water meet. An estuary.

The problem with symbolism? It can make a bad idea sound good. Mangrove swamps are estuaries like the Long Island Sound, places where tides change everything. Land turns to water and back, creatures constantly unearthing themselves from sediment, then reburrowing. They are transition, estuaries—to put one under glass is to miss its point.

Through the tank I see Justin freeze, mid-greeting, and stare back toward the door. I wasn't sure Bree would come. And not just because she's so busy making appearances.

A *complexly simple act of revelation*, Lex Pritchett called Bree's novel, *Unwritten*, when it was released. It's about this writer who's betrayed by another writer, a guy she really loves. He also happens to be a vampire, which is where the whole betrayal thing comes in—he once bit her and even though he neither killed her nor turned her into a vampire, she just can't trust him anymore. Plus, now she has writer's block. The book starts off sounding like everything Bree used to write, all meta- and footnote-y. But with each successive section, it sheds a layer of writerly-ness. By the end, in the last section, it's this honest, real, emotional thing about a writer who learns to be honest, real, and emotional. Or, to be more accurate, by the *ends*. There are two endings: In one, the protagonist writes a bestseller. In the other, she forgives the guy. You choose, it says on the last page.

From the wonder on her face as she looks around the bar, it's obvious she's never been to Aquaria before. From the look on Justin's, it's obvious that even after her grand gesture of a novel, he hadn't been able to hope until now that she'd forgive him.

"Thanks for coming," I tell her when she comes over. And then, "Good choice."

I STEP UP to the podium. Behind me a wall swims with sharks and rays. I wonder if Justin thinks it's funny to put writers in front of them like bait. Through the dimmed lights I look out at hundreds of people wearing black clothing and shiny, feverish expressions. I see Francis, whom I asked to stay back at the Plaza because it would make me too nervous for him to be here but who's snuck in anyway, holding flowers in his lap like it's a high school play. I see Justin standing in back with Bree, pointing to all his tanks and whispering and wondering if she knows the whole place is a temple to her. I see Amber walk through the door waving just before I begin, having come straight from taking the train in from Princeton, where she's a senior. I stare into their quicksilver faces and read my first lines.

"There are people who understand life the first time through. They grasp what someone's saying when it's said. Read stories into glances and expressions."

In the reef tanks, anemone fingers flutter and wave, pumped into motion by machines. On the ceiling the silver school moves in formation against the man-made current. In the still water of the mangrove tank, a single estuarine moment is frozen, the time between tides.

"Draw out moments, slow down time."

In my peripheral vision I see him, late but expected, a ghost standing on the sidewalk looking in through the reef. On the other side of that water Hunter is twelve years old in a blue pea coat, shifting his weight from foot to foot because he doesn't know yet what to do with his body, and hugging a book to his chest as if there's safety inside it. I tell him in my head that I love him more than anything, still, and that I'll miss him always, but that he just can't come in.

"Shape what happens as it happens, sculptors of their lives."

When my eyes come back up from the page, he's gone like a promise, returning to the place I've carved out for him in Aftermemory, where he is safe and I still visit, but where he needs to stay.

There, in Aftermemory, we're forever Hunter at twelve and me at eleven, sitting at the edge of the Sound on the clearest morning ever, high on our brand-new-nothing-ever-like-it friendship, looking out at the water and the sky and about to speak, about to say *It doesn't seem real* and *Pretend Heaven*, about to begin an adventure that will take years and change us into people we'll maybe like and maybe won't—people about to feel at home in each other, people about to have for the first time a home you would miss if you lost it.

I bite my lip to keep back tears and taste the salt in my blood. I read my next line and look up, my eyes settling on the estuary that Justin got so wrong. See, even in protected places there are currents, forces stronger when the tide ebbs than when it flows. Then, in the ebbing, water races through the narrowest of inlets in search of ocean, rushing back to that place where everything began.

ACKNOWLEDGMENTS

There are so many people to whom I owe thanks.

My agent, Susan Golomb, first of all—for her patience, warmth, and wisdom. And for making real my dream.

Trena Keating, my editor at Dutton, for helping me bridge the gap between what I'd put on paper and what was in my head, and for recognizing the heart of this book.

Lily Kosner, at Dutton, for being so smart and hardworking, and for treating this book—and its author—with such care.

My early teachers: Rona Kalin Moss, the late Paul Marino, Warren Steele, Lorraine Nagel (whose wonderful teaching bore no resemblance to that of my loopy character who shares her surname), and the truly inspirational Lois Lenett. The amazing writing professors at Cornell whose workshops, twenty years later, still resonate with me: Molly Hite, Stephanie Vaughn, and Lamar Herrin. And, finally and most recently: the late Stephanie Moore, who every Tuesday would cast enchantment over ten of us in her cottage, where for a few hours we could feel beautiful and brave, and eat cat cookies and drink sock tea, and believe we could make the impossible possible.

The Tuesday Night People that Stephanie once-upon-a-time brought together, writers I love and trust with whom I now band together semimonthly in Amanda's kitchen to wage the war against "suckage": Cyndi Cady, Chris Cole, Tom Joyce, John Philipp, Jill Rosenblum Tidman, Maya Lis Tussing, David Winton, Jon Wells, and of course the prodigiously

392 TANYA EGAN GIBSON

talented Amanda Conran, whose spot-on comments always force me to rethink and rewrite.

The wonderful, kind caregivers who have kept my children so happy while Mommy does that boring typing-stuff on her laptop: Katy Gilbert, Katie Raphael, Leah Doyle, and Raquel Zacarias.

The directors and staff of Squaw Valley Community of Writers, especially Brett Hall Jones, Louis B. Jones, and Lisa Alvarez, for running a conference that deepened my excitement about writing each of the four summers I attended; and Glen David Gold, for his encouragement, generosity of spirit, and willingness to mention my manuscript to The Best Agent in the World (see above: Golomb, Susan).

My family, and my friends-that-are-like-family, for their love and support: Joan Egan (I love you, Mom!), Bonnie Egan, Jonathan Egan and Danielle Insalaco-Egan, Linda and Jeff Forsman, Matt Forsman, Judy and Gregg Gibson, Eliza Gibson and Virginia Alber-Glanstaetten, Katie Gibson, Joe Gibson, Laura Stravino, Sherrie Doyle, and Kim Culbertson.

And most of all, my husband, Josh Gibson: for his immeasurable encouragement, advice, and support; for his reading and commenting on so many drafts over so many years; for reminding me that stories are made up of people, not words. And for being the love of my life.